Praise for *The Sixth*

"An adventure involving political assassination, revolution and a disturbing painting that bears a secret code. Hays' ambitious effort offers a vibrant portrait of the Paris art scene of the early 20th century [and] captures the heady bohemian glamour of Florbela's world."

-Kirkus Reviews

"A well-written, energetically paced storyline that both history and art buffs will find highly enjoyable."

-NY Books Examiner

"Hays shines in her portrayal of the artists who frequent Gertrude Stein's salon—Picasso, Modigliani, Rivera and Chagall—prior to their fame: an unusual approach. Hays effectively reveals Florbela's insecurities as an artist searching for her own particular style [and] shows Florbela as a revolutionary-by-proxy into whose hands falls a painting that becomes the key to the overthrow of Portugal's Manuel II."

-IndieReader

The
Sixth

Avery Hays

διαδεμα

www.avery-hays.com

DIADEMA PRESS

First published in the USA
in 2013 by Diadema Press LLC

www.diademapress.com

Copyright © Avery Hays 2013

ISBN 978-0-9854182-4-3

Second Edition

Jacket design by *the*BookDesigners

FOR M

Chapter One

O n the fifth of April in the spring of my twenty-first year, all the world was turning nervous eyes toward my native Portugal, gazing aghast as she teetered giddily between the abyss of anarchy on the one hand, and that of totalitarianism on the other. But I, exiled since the age of fourteen, had my eyes turned elsewhere, for I was just arriving in Paris—that perennial crucible of youthful experiment. This is not to say that Portugal's affairs weighed only lightly upon me. Far from it; I could feel the plight of my nation like a diseased organ of my own body, threatening to explode inside me at any moment. But at the time of my arrival on that pretty spring day, Paris had my complete attention.

I was standing there panting on the cobbles outside the building known as La Ruche, "the Beehive," clutching the grip of my single valise. Having half lugged, half dragged that bulging leather bag all the way from the Montparnasse train station, I was now all but certain I must have made a wrong turn. I began rummaging through my handbag to find the slip of paper upon which Monsieur Castell, back at the academy, had written the address. I stood with my back pressed firmly to the stone wall of a building that was situated across the Dantzig Passage from a rather large and unusual but utterly unprepossessing wooden edifice. I was keeping well out of the way of the vigorous flow of cabriolets and carriages, peppered here and there with remarkably aggressive automobiles. Until that day, I had never seen a road that contained more than one automobile at a time, and it looked to my eye like a certain recipe for mayhem.

To my crushing disappointment, the address proved to be the correct one, and there was nothing to do but cross the street and approach the ugly building. I knew no one in Paris, and La Ruche was widely reputed to be the one place that an aspiring young painter as nearly penniless as myself could find acceptable lodgings. I should add that I did have the names of a few sympathists of the populist cause in Portugal—friends of my father, a well-known writer. Father had been enduring the unspeakable sufferings of political imprisonment in a Lisbon jail for nearly two years now. His Paris friends would, of course, know me by name, and I intended to approach them in good time. But I could hardly knock on their doors and beg for food and lodging.

La Ruche was built of wood and in the round, three stories tall, and though its style proved it to be a Modern building, it was already showing signs of sore neglect. After negotiating my way across the narrow but dangerously crowded street, I approached it diffidently, even suspiciously. It really didn't appear to be the sort of place a respectable young lady might seek lodging. The verge along the front was utterly unkempt, with tall weeds growing among assorted bric-à-brac that the tenants had apparently thrown from their windows: paint cans, several half-completed sculptural assemblages, a broken guitar, an old easel, and quite a number of empty wine bottles. Through the dozens of open windows, one could hear a number of conversations, several of them loud and animated, plus the sound of someone practicing on an oboe.

I noticed a Gypsy girl approaching me along the row of shadows under the chestnuts that separated the squalid building from its neighbor. My heart sank a little at the sight of her. She was a scrawny thing in a white shawl, perhaps fourteen or fifteen years old, no doubt approaching me to ask for alms, which I could not afford to give. To avoid the awkwardness of conversation with her, I began dragging my valise toward what appeared to be the front door.

Just then, I was stopped in my tracks by a horrific sight. An absolutely immense fat man suddenly lurched into view at a second-story window at the side of the building, with his big hands wrapped around the throat of a slender man with brown hair. Now, my life up to that point had been somewhat sheltered, and the sight of that homicidal fat man was the most bone-chilling thing I'd ever seen. He had long and greasy black hair, beady, bloodshot eyes and a preposterous little black beard, and he was glistening in a patina of unwholesome sweat. Extending his two thick arms straight out until the elbows locked, he bent the slender man backward over the windowsill until his victim's head was completely upside down, with cheeks flaming red. The slender man was holding a bottle of red wine that sloshed about as he waved his arm around helplessly, but oddly enough he neither used the bottle as a weapon to save himself, nor did he let it go. The fat man, in the throes of a murderous ecstasy, threw his head back and gave out a long, vulpine howl at the cloudless blue April sky. Then the slender man apparently gathered his forces, threw up his knees, and pried the center of gravity of the fat man completely out the window. I let out a shriek and watched in horror as the two men plummeted straight down to land upon a large and very sad-looking shrub.

I realized at this point that something had become locked to my arm, and I looked sideways to find the Gypsy girl standing right there beside me, with both of her skinny little hands wrapped tightly around my forearm. She was staring at the two fallen men with such a fixation of shock and terror that I doubt she even realized she was touching me. Given the circumstances, I didn't pay her much mind, but I did notice that she wasn't actually a Gypsy after all: her hair was fair, her eyes silvery-gray, and though her shawl might have looked more at home in Krakow or Budapest than in Paris, it was in fact a fine and quite expensive-looking lace.

A great amount of animal hooting and snorting was coming from the crushed shrubbery, and it took me several long moments to ascertain that it was laughter. To my astonishment, the fat man and his victim both pried themselves slowly to their feet, leaning on each other's shoulders as they brushed twigs from their clothing and hair. Both of them were trying to speak at once, but neither was able to emit a complete sentence, because they were laughing too hard.

The head of a young woman emerged from the open window they had fallen from. She wore her black hair quite short and I could tell at a glance she must be a head taller than I was, and her face had a frank and classical beauty. She was looking quite concerned, and she called down in passable French with a thick Russian accent: "Amedeo! That was last bottle of wine. You be good and place it on table before you go jump out of windows."

The two men were still laughing too hard to form words, but the brown-haired one responded by lifting the wine bottle, proudly showing that he had carried it through the ordeal without breaking it. He was tall and fashionably dressed, though his shirttail was out and his collar askew. In fact, he was a very handsome man, with a face that was filled with both sensitivity and arrogance in equal measure. He and his companion were both in their mid-twenties, and despite the early hour of the day, they were drunker than I would ever have guessed a man could be, and still be on his feet.

The fat man no longer looked dangerous at all—in fact he rather resembled a jolly country friar. He had an Iberian look about him that made me wonder briefly if he might not be one of my countrymen. He waved at the Russian woman and puffed out, "Go inside, Angelina. You're making a scene!" Then he doubled over in mirth and could say no more. I took his accent for Spanish.

All these events had taken place in a few seconds. I became aware once again of the oddly dressed girl beside me when she came to her senses and abruptly withdrew her hands from my arm. I turned my face to her and smiled, intending to reassure her that I perfectly understood her reaction.

She was still visibly agitated and suddenly blurted out, "Oh, this is a frightening place! I didn't think it would be like this."

I examined the girl with some curiosity now. Though she was taller than I, her wide and frightened eyes and trembling

~ 4 ~

shoulders gave her the look of a child. Perhaps if she hadn't looked so helpless and childlike at that moment, we never would have become friends.

"You have business at La Ruche?" I asked her gently.

Almost immediately, she began to contain her fear and compose her features. "Yes, I do," she articulated carefully in a high, clear voice. "I shall take residence here, while I am earning my fame as a sculptor."

I almost laughed at this absurd bit of conceit, coming as it did from the mouth of one so young. "Then we'll be neighbors," I replied. "I myself intend to become a painter, if the world will have me. My name is Florbela Sarmentos. And you are?"

" Irène," she answered and then hesitated.

"May I ask whether you have attended some academy Irène?"

She frowned a little and turned her gaze rather coldly back toward the front of the building, where the two erstwhile combatants were still staggering their painful way around to the front door, pausing now and then to pour down mouthfuls of wine. She said, "I have received elementary training from some of the finest sculptors in France. I am now sixteen, and I shall pursue academy training in good time."

Now I began to regard this strange creature with real interest. She spoke with such poise and confidence for a girl of sixteen! And indeed, from the look of her, I might not have guessed her age to be even so advanced as that. I believe that right there, before we had ever set foot in La Ruche, I already perceived that Irène would prove to be unlike any person I had ever met. And to think that, only minutes before, I had taken her for a beggar girl.

I let my eyes wander back to the building, where the two disheveled young drunks had made it as far as the stoop outside the front door, and there had paused to rest. Sitting on the peeled paint of the warped wooden stairs, they had finally noticed that two young women were standing just beyond the weeds of the verge, watching them.

The fat one called over to us, "Don't be shy, girls! Come and have some wine. The springtime only lasts a little while, you know!"

I said to Irène, "Well, I don't like this very much. Allow me to confess that I have come all the way from Cherbourg since yesterday, and furthermore that I know of nowhere else to lodge in this city. And yet, I do not believe that a young lady can stay in a place such as this."

Irène turned to face me fully and crossed her arms across her skinny chest, lowering her rather prominent eyebrows over her strange, mirrorlike eyes. "If I may say so, that doesn't necessarily seem a reasonable conclusion to me. It is widely stated that La Ruche is a residence intended for young people who are pursuing a career in the fine arts. I cannot see that serious aspirants such as you or I should be turned away by a pair of drunken boors."

Before I had opened my mouth to reply we were nearly bowled off the path by a pair of thick-shouldered men striding purposefully toward the front door with their heads down, apparently lost in deep conversation.

I must have gasped a little with surprise as they shoved past us, because the smaller of the two men looked up at the sound, as if coming out of a trance. He seemed very old to me, perhaps sixty, and he was nearly a dwarf. He was a full head shorter than I, with a wild mane of gray hair and a bushy, forked beard. His face had solid, rustic features, and his head was as broad as it was long. He looked at Irène and me as we stood there immobile, I with my valise in hand.

"Volodya," he called out, pronouncing the Russian nickname in a husky French accent.

His companion stopped on the path and turned around. The taller man's eyes immediately became sharp and watchful, and whatever thoughts he had been brooding upon were apparently banished instantly from his mind. He had dark features and a broad mustache, and though he did not look far into middle age, his hairline had already receded halfway back his head. There was something very familiar about his face, though I couldn't place it at a glance.

"I may have some business here," the short man told him, in a voice that was deep and gravelly, with a rich provincial accent. "We'll speak again tomorrow, yes?"

"Yes," said the other man, turning away already to walk toward the building. Even from that one word his Russian accent was easily discernible.

The shaggy little dwarf approached us with an eager smile. "I am Alfred Boucher," he said, and politely bowed a few degrees before us. "If you are seeking a studio, you are truly in luck. I have one for you on the third floor, with morning light."

I glanced at Irène, formulating a polite way to explain that we were in need of two studios, not one. But Irène was way ahead of me.

"That will do perfectly," she said, generating an amazing amount of formal gravitas with her thin little piping voice. "I should assume that the rent of a single studio shall not be raised due to double occupancy?"

Boucher shrugged. "For the two of you? I wouldn't think of it. Indeed, I imagine that your residence here will increase my property value. And . . . you are, perhaps, intending to work as artists' models?"

Irène and I must have both bristled in the same way at the same time, because Boucher smiled as if he were seeing a familiar pantomime. He immediately amended, "No, no! Artists, then! Very fine, that is very fine indeed. Yes, you may pay single occupancy rate, and I believe I shall lower the rent five francs a week for you as well, provided that you will please not tell the other tenants that I have done so."

And with that, he grabbed my valise. Despite his short stature and advanced age, he swept it up as easily as if it had been empty, and he began leading us to the front door.

That was how I met Boucher. I have never known any person who was more like an angel upon this earth than Alfred Boucher. The moment I was bestowed residency at La Ruche, Paris was mine to do with what I would. For those in Paris who did not have Boucher, the predominant factor that forever threatened to exclude them from the twentieth century's emerging creative elite was simply lack of funds to pay their rent. Rent was not an issue at La Ruche. Not only were the weekly rates inexplicably low, but if the day came that you could not pay up even the pittance that you owed Boucher, it wouldn't matter. No one was ever kicked out of La Ruche for nonpayment of rent. The result of this situation was that practically every artist of note in my generation (with the conspicuous exception of Pablo Picasso) emerged from La Ruche.

"Watch your step," the bustling little gnome told us, darting up the steps with my sixty-pound valise. The two pseudo-belligerent drunks had vanished off the stairs, so there was plenty of room for Irène and me to march up and cross the threshold into La Ruche without incident.

Alas, I was in for another shock. If La Ruche looked a bit disreputable from the outside, from the inside one would have to say it was truly offensive. When I caught the smell that emerged from the first-floor kitchen and noted two mouse-sized cockroaches taking a leisurely promenade across the common room floor, I nearly fainted dead away. Irène was more stoic. Once that girl made up her mind, she had a will like iron.

It wasn't much past noon, but the third floor was already as sticky-hot as melted cheese. It didn't take a lot of imagination to see that, come August, we would be wishing we had a ground floor room. On the other hand, in a building crammed with loud and festive tenants who no doubt did a lot of stomping about on the thin plank floors, we would at least have the luxury of a ceiling that no one lived above. There was quite a lot of noise and activity going on throughout the building, and by now I was sure that my young acquaintance had been exactly correct in assessing that she and I would do better to live together than separately in the midst of such turmoil.

"This building was designed by Gustave Eiffel," Boucher told us proudly, as he shoved open the door of our new studio with the toe of his boot and slid my valise into the room. "Ten years ago, the whole building was created as a wine-tasting parlor for the World Exposition. They were going to tear it down afterward, and I thought, 'What a waste! A hundred young artists could live in such a building, and at no cost to anyone, really.'"

I passed through the doorway and strode slowly up the length of my very first atelier in Paris—my dream come true, and the dream of a million young artists around the world. I tried not to show how ecstatic I was. The place was perfect. Putting aside all issues of basic sanitation and fire safety at La Ruche, the studio I found myself in was more than adequate for any artist's needs. Each floor of the circular building was composed of thin, wedge-shaped studios facing outward, each with a large window at one end to admit plenty of natural light, and a door at the other end opening onto the common space in the center of the building.

"Ah, wait! This unit has only one bed," Boucher said. "I'll go find Gaston and have him bring you in a second, from one of the other studios. People always come and go."

As soon as we were left alone, Irène and I happened to look into each other's faces, and each saw the reflection of our own smoldering joy at finding, so suddenly, a proper place to live in this vast and hazardous city. We fell into each other's arms and embraced, and I, for one, was near to tears.

Chapter Two

As soon as we pulled apart, Irène hastily wiped one cheek with the back of her hand, arranged her expression, and said, "Let us be introduced, now. My name is Irène Langevin, and I am from Lille."

"It's a great pleasure. I am Florbela Sarmentos of Lisbon. More recently, I have just graduated from the painting academy at Cherbourg."

"Did you say Lisbon?" Irène asked hesitantly. "I had noticed a slight accent, but I didn't think . . ."

"You are correct, my accent is not Portuguese, but English. Before the academy, my education was at a girls' boarding school outside London. Alas, I speak my native tongue more poorly than either French or English."

Irène accepted all this information without asking for the name of my school in England, which I thought a little odd. I certainly noticed that she didn't say where *she* had been educated, though it was perfectly obvious that she had been very well educated indeed. I was also burning with curiosity to know where her luggage might be, though I assumed it would be arriving shortly. Very gradually, over the next few hours I would realize that there was no luggage.

She pointed at the left side of the broad window. "I would prefer to set up my worktable on this side, if you please," she piped, in that crisp tone of hers that brooked no argument. "I shall sculpt in the evening light."

Very well, I thought; evening, morning, I was happy to let her have her way. As soon as I could acquire an easel, I would set it up on the right side of the room, and I was content to adjust myself to a morning schedule, when the light would be at its best.

Boucher returned with a rather dull-looking man carrying a narrow cot upon his back to complete our furnishings. Our new landlord looked like he was about to wander off at that point without even mentioning the rent, strange little angel that he was, but naturally that would not do. Irène and I both had a fair month's rent handy in our pocketbooks, and we made a quick verbal agreement with Boucher and handed over his due.

While I was unpacking my things, Irène simply sat down on the edge of her little cot and watched me. I don't remember much of our conversation, as I was too excited at my new arrangements to be paying much attention to her. I do remember asking her for the names of the sculptors she had trained under but she was reticent to speak of it. Naturally, I concluded that she had exaggerated her training out there on the street when we met, and I marveled at her youthful and unabashed self-confidence.

It didn't take me long to unpack. Although my valise was massive to carry, it was hardly spacious enough to contain a versatile wardrobe.

"Do you ride?" Irène asked me, seeing me unfold and hang my split skirt.

"A bit. I rode often when I lived in England and when I first moved to France, but only a few times in the last year. Of course, in England I rode sidesaddle." I could tell she was curious, so I took down the split skirt and showed it to her before putting it away. Sidesaddle riding was still the norm in England, and in fact was mandated by law in many places, but France had all but abandoned the practice. This had come about, as far as I could see, due to the mass production of the bicycle. A woman could hardly pedal one of these contraptions sidesaddle, and so the ladies of France had risen up in mute revolt, donning culottes so they could join the fun. Within a few years, sidesaddle equestrianism just seemed silly and split skirts had become the fashion for ladies to ride.

As I finished distributing my meager wardrobe into the various pieces of beaten but serviceable furniture scattered along the wall nearest my cot, I became aware of distant drums. Their pounding grew alarmingly louder and then transformed into the noise of a great stampede of hoofed and heavy-bodied beasts, coming quickly our way.

"I believe someone is outside the door," Irène said nervously, folding her hands tightly in her lap.

The door, which was ajar, sprang open without so much warning as the rap of a knuckle. There, in the gaping doorframe, stood the jolly, drunken fat man with his oily black hair and beard, and behind his shoulders were the beautiful brown-haired man and the beautiful black-haired woman. I recalled the names of these latter two from their conversation through the window: Amedeo and Angelina.

After that bold entrance, which had brought Irène and me to our feet in alarm, the fat man became tongue-tied and stood wobbling in the doorway for what seemed a very long time without saying a word.

The one called Amedeo came to his rescue. "We found another bottle," he explained from the dimness of the hallway. He had a suave voice with a beautiful Italian accent, hampered by no more than a trace of drunken slur. He added, "Not yet uncorked! And most appropriate for a welcoming party, or so we feel." He gave the fat man an irritated poke from behind his shoulder.

The fat man seemed to come to his senses and remember where he was. He held up his left hand and indeed was carrying an unopened bottle of cheap Medoc. "Inexpensive," he said apologetically in his broad Spanish accent, "but surprisingly rich in character."

"Yes," Amedeo agreed, shoving the fat man into our room and making way for Angelina. "A delicious vintage—and also most effective, when taken in sufficient dosage. Do you mind if I close your door? There are some very low characters in this building. The sound of a popping cork has been known to cause a feeding frenzy."

"It's true," the fat man agreed, plopping down on the floor with a great release of breath, then leaning his full weight back against the door to seal us all in. "Some of them here . . . some of them . . . behave like drunken lunatics." He produced a corkscrew from under his shirt, where he apparently kept it permanently on a leather cord around his neck, and deftly opened the bottle with three economical and highly practiced movements.

I glanced at Irène, but she looked no more alarmed at this clownish and rather charming invasion than I was myself. For one thing, the tall and elegant Russian, Angelina, didn't appear drunken at all, and she provided a civilizing counterweight to her two rambunctious companions. She was carrying a canvas sack, from which she began producing a number of small blue glasses and a board of bread and cheese. The sight of the food settled matters once and for all, as far as I was concerned: I hadn't eaten at all that day, and suddenly I could think of little else.

"We are very rude," Angelina said matter-of-factly, struggling a bit with the French idiom. "But you'll become used to this rudeness very quickly, I think. I do not live here long time, but I am with this one. With him, I am become used to coarse manners such as we do not often see at my homeland of Russia. And also some craziness of the brain."

As she made this declaration, she clearly indicated the fat man, but I nonetheless assumed that there must be some misunderstanding attributable to her poor command of French. Surely this lovely woman was with the debonair Italian, Amedeo, and not with the great sweating hulk who was sprawled against our door! But there was no misunderstanding.

"If you will permit me the introductions," Amedeo proposed, reaching over to snatch the bottle from where it dangled forgotten in his friend's hand. He began pouring glasses all around. "I am Amedeo Modigliani, second floor, northwest corner. I am"—and at this point his voice deepened into an exaggerated sententiousness—"a *professional artist.*"

His two companions apparently found this very funny, and the fat man began rolling around so violently on the floor in his mirth that it seemed likely he would knock over furniture. Angelina explained. "Amedeo sold his first painting this morning. We laugh, but we are very proud. It was great triumph, I think, but money is all gone now. All gone to buy wine for the celebration."

"Wine *and cheese*," Amedeo corrected her. He waved a hand to offer me the liberty of the cheese board, and I did not hesitate to accept his hospitality. He added gravely, "And I still have three francs left over." He carefully handed a glass of wine to me and another to Irène, and I noticed that despite his drunkenness, the gesture was perfectly controlled and graceful. Those hands . . . what beautiful hands Modigliani had!

He continued with his introductions: "These two fine people are my . . . long-term houseguests. Angelina Beloff of Russia, and Diego Rivera of Mexico." He leaned a little closer to Irène and me, and added, *sotto voce,* "They are *not* professional artists. They are professional houseguests."

This comment occasioned another outburst of hilarity and a rapid consumption of Medoc, followed by a deft refilling of the glasses by the vigilant Amedeo.

To my surprise, Irène, whom I might have expected to be cowed by such loud and forward company, piped up, "Are there any *famous* artists living here?"

I would have thought that this question might elicit another wave of laughter from our drunken guests, but it did not. I suspect that all three of them understood that this was a question made by a young person with sincere aspirations. They may have been buffoons in many ways, but Amedeo and Diego never made light of that sort of thing.

"No famous person *would* live here," Diego explained to her, suddenly sounding surprisingly sober. "They become famous, you see, and then they leave."

I wandered over to cut myself another slice of bread and cheese. It was a perfect accompaniment to the wine.

"There is Vladimir," Angelina objected. "He's famous, and not only in Russia neither."

"But he's not an artist," Amedeo replied. He turned his placid brown eyes on Irène and clarified, "You have heard of the Russian rebel, Vladimir Lenin?"

"They saw him outside," Diego reminded him. "He came in with Boucher."

I glanced over at Diego. Then there really *was* someone living in this shabby old building of whom I had heard! The balding man with the wide mustache was a political exile like myself—and someone who had actually been in the newspapers just a few years earlier. Mr. Lenin had been one of the fomenters of the ill-fated Russian revolution, or at any rate I was sure he had been involved in it somehow. The whole thing had happened when I was quite young, but I certainly remembered the name.

For Portuguese people such as my father and me, who hoped to throw off our nation's yoke of tyranny, the failure of the Russian revolution was one of the most salient and sobering facts of recent history. The Russian revolt, of course, had achieved nothing, and at the cost of tens of thousands of lives. Now here it was 1910, and for better or worse the Tsar again reigned supreme over his empire. The instigators of Russia's rebellion were all dead, or (as in the case of Mr. Lenin) were living in disgraced exile in tenement apartments in Paris and New York and Buenos Aires.

Reflecting on such things always made me melancholy, because I longed to see Portugal rise up and throw off her loathsome King Manuel II, and not only for my dear father's sake. But there hadn't been a successful revolution or even a coup d'état anywhere in Europe since long before any of us in that room had been born, and there would probably never be another in Europe. *I may never see Father again*, I reflected sadly, staring into my wine glass. I had begun thinking of how I might machinate to bring about his release when I became a famous artist, but Diego interrupted my thoughts.

"You should talk with old Volodya some time," Diego slurred to Irène. "Give him . . . give him some vodka, and he'll talk your ear off."

"I do not care for vodka," Irène replied. I looked over at her and suspected that she was too young even to know who Mr. Lenin was, since his fame had come and gone five years before. She turned toward Amedeo and Angelina, and went back to the pursuit of her earlier question. "But famous artists *have* lived here in the past?"

They hesitated, presumably weighing an answer that would do justice, and yet not be too discouraging. "Well, there's Boucher," Amedeo offered. "He's won the Grand Prize of the Salon."

Diego snorted. "Right, but thirty years ago! And he *doesn't* live here," he added smugly. "He's the landlord."

"Robert Delaunay," Amedeo continued, counting on his fingers and looking upward thoughtfully. "Constantin Brancusi. Fernand Léger. Guillaume Apollinaire."

"Those," Diego objected, "are not all famous. Selling one or two pieces to the Steins doesn't make you famous."

"Who are the Steins?" I asked, suddenly taking an interest in the conversation again. If that was the name of someone who made speculative purchases from young artists, I was eager to make a note of it. I wandered over to my cot and sat down.

Angelina replied, "Leo and Gertrude Stein are Americans. They discovered Pablo Picasso."

Amedeo made an exasperated hissing sound between his lips. "Nobody *discovered* Pablo! He was just there."

Angelina rolled her eyes and spread her hands, suggesting that the distinction didn't mean very much to her. "They have a lot of American money, these Steins, and they have good eyes. They live over in Montparnasse."

Diego raised an insistent finger in the air. "Ah, not merely Montparnasse, my wildflower! They live in the *Sixth*."

I glanced at Irène to see if all this information was as interesting to her as it was to me, but she either was not paying attention, or perhaps was already better informed than I. My knowledge of the geography of the Left Bank of Paris was incomplete, but I knew that there was a small wedge of bohemian Montparnasse that extended a little way north into the Sixth District, *la Sixième Arrondissement*, in the neighborhood that was just west of the Luxembourg Gardens. I deduced that this small triangle of a few city blocks was the place that aspiring artists like ourselves would choose to live, if we could afford it.

Just then, there was a rapping at the door, followed by a futile effort to open it against the considerable bulk of the recumbent Diego Rivera. We all heard Boucher's distinctive voice mumbling through the panels, and Diego made haste to roll out of the way and let him in.

"I'm sorry to interrupt," Boucher said, sticking his hairy head into the room. "Ah! I see you have met some of your neighbors. Good, that is very good! And these two have great talent, if I am any judge." He waved his stubby index finger at Amedeo and Angelina. They smiled with pleasure, beaming like schoolchildren. Then the old gnome turned his lively eyes to Diego, with obvious affection. "But be careful of this one! This one is a *Cubist*. That would be scandal enough, even if he were a Frenchman. But a *Mexican* Cubist? Impossible!"

Everyone but Irène and I laughed raucously at this gibe. I had heard vague stories in recent months, while I was at the Cherbourg academy, of Paris's newest young firebrand talents, Pablo Picasso and Georges Braque, and the strange form of African primitivism that these brash young men were advocating under the name of "Cubism." I hadn't been in Paris long enough to see any example of the style, so I knew only that, whatever it was, it infuriated my teachers and apparently disgusted them to the brink of nausea. I was inclined to agree with Boucher that it was a bit scandalous for a painter to travel all the way from Mexico to France, only to adopt such modish habits.

Then, to my surprise, Boucher turned to me and said, "Pardon me, mademoiselle. You *did* say your name was Sarmentos?"

Surprised, I rose to my feet and set down my glass and confirmed that it was.

"In that case, young mademoiselle, there are two men to see you, sitting out in the back courtyard. I must add that I don't like the look of them. If you are in some sort of trouble, it is no business of mine, but . . . do you wish to see them, or shall I summon the *gendarmes*?"

Chapter Three

O nce I caught sight of the two men, I found they were every bit as alarming as Boucher had suggested. They were sitting on the broken wall that bordered the small courtyard behind La Ruche, staying well back from the street. I approached them cautiously. I couldn't imagine who would be looking for me in this city of strangers. And *here* of all places! I myself hadn't been sure that I would be lodging at La Ruche, as recently as an hour ago.

I glanced up nervously while I crossed the yard, and was somewhat relieved to see the great, round head of Diego Rivera appear in my third-floor window. He eyed the two men in the yard with dull curiosity as I approached them. Then Amedeo abruptly leaned out over his shoulder, gave the two men an openly hostile stare, turned to me, cupped his hands and called out, "If you have any trouble with those ruffians, little neighbor, just shout! I will shove Diego out of the window onto them!" Then they both withdrew, and a fair amount of whooping and laughing emerged through the empty window frame.

I was somewhat embarrassed by this outburst, but fortunately the two men in the courtyard ignored the baiting with equanimity. They pushed themselves slowly to their feet and dusted their pants as I walked up to them.

It was the large one who was most alarming to the eye. The man's arms, shoulders, and thighs were almost grotesquely muscular, and he had the thick neck and head of a wrestler. His nose appeared to have been broken a number of times and sat almost flat in the middle of a broad, heavy-browed face. One could not imagine that dark countenance smiling. As I came closer, I saw to my shock that he had a crude image of a scantily clad woman inked into the skin of his forearm. I had heard of tattoos, of course, but even in a port town like Cherbourg I had never actually *seen* one, and the sight created in me a reaction of visceral horror. It was rather like meeting a cannibal. Now that I was standing close enough, I saw that he might have been less than forty years old. They had evidently been hard years.

"You are the daughter of Tiago," the other one said to me. I hadn't yet paid him much attention, but it wasn't surprising that he should be the one to do the talking. The big one didn't look like much of a conversationalist.

I nodded meekly, glancing toward the slighter man. I should have known this business would prove to have something to do with my father. I opened my mouth, thinking of a dozen questions at once, but then I prudently closed it and waited to hear what the young man had to say.

"Your father sends you this," he told me, and handed me a letter on heavy paper, folded tightly and sealed with wax. I accepted it dumbly from his hand and glanced at it. There was nothing on the surface except my name, but the penmanship was indisputably my father's.

"But . . . how . . . ?"

"Will you sit down, mademoiselle?" The young man was much less fearsome than his companion. Though dressed similarly in rough clothing of burlap and coarse wool with wooden shoes, there was something noble, even elegant in his bearing. He was only a few years older than me, and he was quite tall and slender, with a handsome face and kind, dark eyes. He said, "You're looking rather pale, and I know you have been traveling, so you must be very tired. Here, this large stone seems to be quite clean."

I accepted a hand from the young stranger and set myself in the shade, feeling rather dazed. His grip was firm and gentle as he helped me to my seat.

"My name is Armand," he told me. "And this is my comrade,

Paulo Quieroz."

I looked up sharply at the heavy man. "You're from Portugal!"

"*Sou*," he told me with a nod.

"You are perhaps wondering how we found you here?" the young man called Armand suggested. He gestured at the broken wall. "Do you mind if we sit?"

Only then did I realize that both of them had remained standing in polite deference to me. Their gracious manners were at such clashing odds with their brutish garb that I immediately felt embarrassed to have left them standing, and hastily invited them to sit.

"We belong to a group that sympathizes with your father's cause," Armand explained. "Our official name is Bande Liberté du Monde. Around the city, you may hear us referred to as Les Souris Trempés."

A laugh escaped me, and I tried to disguise it with a brief fit of coughing. The *Soggy Mice!* How perfectly outrageous. "The other name doesn't sound very flattering," I opined carefully.

Armand grinned. He had one of those wide, pleasant smiles that one only sees on the faces of people who have not yet tasted too much of the world's bitterness: all full of hope and easy good cheer.

But it was Paulo who answered, in his deep, brusque voice. His heavy accent soon began making me homesick for the coast of Portugal, though his fine command of simple French told me he had been living here many years. "It is because our headquarters is found in the abandoned public works, right beside the Seine, over in the Thirteenth District. During the Great Flood, it was completely under the water for nearly a week. In fact, some of the rooms still have not drained completely."

"We don't mind the name," Armand quickly inserted. "We're not so stiff that we can't laugh at ourselves a little."

The flood that Paulo referred to had inundated most of Paris about three months before, when the river overflowed both banks. There had never been a flood to match it in all the centuries of the city's history. Thousands had fled their homes, and the damage to property had been beyond calculation.

I had no idea how to reply. My eyes fell on the letter in my hands. "But . . . do you know my father, then?"

"*I* do," Paulo told me. I was amazed. Though my father had been in prison for nearly two years, I still could not imagine him in such rough company. Then again, if he had seen me at that moment, he might have made the same comment.

"Your father is a very great man," Armand said fervently. "He is an example to free people everywhere. Though he may be held behind iron bars, we of the Souris Trempés feel that he knows more of freedom than most of the dullards who are walking the boulevards today."

I found this impassioned praise of my father rather stirring, to tell the truth. But at the same time, I realized that for some time my eyes had kept coming back to a small yellow object adhering to Armand's lapel. Leaning a little closer, I identified it as a mustard seed.

"If I may," I said, and without further ado reached out and quickly flicked it from his shirt with the tip of my nail. I had already deduced that Armand had not grown up wearing shabby clothes, and I found it somehow irksome to see him settling into slovenly habits. He was clearly lacking a woman's care. If all his companions were like Paulo, it was no wonder that he was slipping into disrepair.

"Thank you," he said, with only the quickest glance downward to see what I was doing. He continued smoothly, "Your father must have been aware that you would soon graduate from your academy and that you were likely to come to Paris afterward. Is that right?"

"I think he would have guessed as much," I confirmed. I hated speaking of my father with strangers, because the subject always brought me close to tears. So I explained very shortly, "If this letter is truly from him, it will be our first communication in nineteen months." I heard my voice break a little near the end of this disclosure, and I kicked myself mentally for it.

Armand graciously pretended not to notice my emotion. "Now,

as to the letter. There is no *easy* way to get a message out from the sort of place where your father is held, but evidently it can be done. This letter came to us six weeks ago, through channels of which I can only guess. It may have taken a month or more to get from Lisbon to our headquarters. The man who brought it also gave us a very garbled message of explanation, which had probably passed through the faulty memories of several others before it was told to him. The only part we really understood was that the woman whose name was on the letter's face was none other than the daughter of that great writer and hero of the people, Hermes Tiago. Alas, none of us had any guess as to your whereabouts, so we placed the letter into a cabinet, and there it has remained until today."

I turned the folded sheet over in my hands thoughtfully. "Thank you for all you've done. Thank you especially for keeping it dry."

Paulo spoke up and added: "Unfortunately, that one corner is missing." He pointed with a blunt finger that was as thick as a plantain. "A rat ate it."

"I see that," I replied gently. "Thank you anyway. I don't think it ate very many of the words."

"You are familiar with Professor Bierhoff?" Armand asked abruptly.

I started with surprise. "Yes! He is the history professor in Cherbourg. At the Academy of Fine Arts."

Armand nodded. "Let us say that the professor is aware, like ourselves, of the great struggle that is happening in Portugal, and of your father's heroic place in that struggle."

This was no news to me, though I couldn't guess how this charming young Parisian in his costume of rags should have found it out. Within the halls of the Academy, Professor Bierhoff never made any secret of his radical leanings. He had twice caught me up in zealous conversations about my father's persecution and imprisonment.

"When Bierhoff heard that another instructor had recommended that you to seek a studio in La Ruche upon your upcoming graduation, he alerted us by post, just a few days ago. And so here we are, discharging our duty to your father's cause by delivering his letter into your hands." And again Armand gave me that marvelous smile, like a personification of the Parisian springtime.

I couldn't help but smile back, and then for some reason I blushed and dropped my eyes.

"But why?" I demanded. "Why should Professor Bierhoff contact *you*? Did he know that you had a letter from Father, addressed to me?"

"I suppose that's possible . . . but not likely, I should guess. It doesn't matter, though. He would have sent word to us that you were coming to Paris anyway."

"But *why*?"

Armand paused and seemed not to know how to respond.

It was Paulo who explained the matter. He pronounced in a flat tone, like the tumbling of heavy rocks, "Because you are the daughter of Hermes Tiago and you may be in danger."

His words made me very nervous, and I immediately tore open the letter.

*　*　*

Dearest daughter,

If this letter has found its way miraculously into your hands, then I give praise to whatever sort of Providence may have placed it there. Or, if there is no Providence above this world at all, as claim the intelligentsia of the northern countries, then I thank blind fate—I thank it on my knees! Better, you will agree, to kneel before lifeless but beneficent forces, than to kneel before a cruel power that bears a human face.

I know you are impatient to hear of my condition. Suffice it to say that I am being treated very well by my captors, who rightly fear that if they make of me a martyr then I will be more useful to the will of the people than ever I was alive. But they are also keeping me rigorously (even obsessively) *confined, so that although my cell here is clean and dry and is also comfortably furnished, it is provided with but a single paltry window, and that so high and deep-set in the stones that I cannot see the sky. But I am certainly not complaining at such mild hardships! Not in times like these.*

As for you, my darling, I know in my heart that this letter finds you well and in good cheer under that lovely sun that I have not seen in some time now. I pray this is so. You and I are the last of the line of Tiago, my dear, and look at how we span an entire universe between us! I am evidently Pluto, patient and brooding lord of this underworld, ever fretting in the darkness with my hidden hope to someday send forth a new springtime into the world above me. And you, who have grown now to womanhood, must play the role of Juno and cast your glow widely from a high place, over all the lighted world.

At this point, I had to put my father's letter down for a moment to wipe my eyes so I could continue reading. I regularly had nightmares about his condition and circumstances; so my relief at hearing that he was not being maltreated by his captors was overwhelming. I glanced hastily over at Armand and Paulo, who had moved discreetly to the other side of the courtyard to allow me privacy in which to read. They were now pretending to ignore me, for which I was grateful. I stole a quick glance up at the window of my studio. There was no one leaning out of it now, though I could still hear raucous voices pouring from inside. I certainly hoped that Angelina was looking after poor Irène, as I felt a bit concerned to be abandoning my young roommate to a roomful of drunken bohemians.

I sighed and read the third paragraph of my father's letter again. Despite myself, I felt a twinge of protest, even as new tears welled up behind my eyes. He had always been habituated to purple prose, my poetic father, and I was beginning to perceive that he was also a relentless and subtle rhetorician. I was scarcely in a position to go casting a glow over all the world!

At any rate, the letter continued:

I instruct you, no, I beseech you as my budding peer, to exercise what talents you find within you and achieve your artistic ambitions. I would not have you seek a political career, even if it were your disposition to do so. Like myself, you will find that your power to move the hearts of the people comes as a natural outgrowth of your creative spirit, and the world will hear you speak through the voice of your brush, better than if you spoke from the orator's pulpit.

Someday we will be reunited, you and I, in a free Portugal, a republic under the rule of neither king nor pope. There you will find—perhaps to your amazement—that you have grown into an exemplary modern woman who is rightly admired by the maidens of a new nation. As they gaze at you, an accomplished woman of the world, the girls of Portugal will harvest from you the strength to stand and seek their own education and the empowerment that is their birthright. So you see, the most revolutionary act you can perform is to fulfill your own dreams, to paint your pictures as they come from your heart.

Now that that has been said, I only wish I could express my love and best wishes and let this letter come to an end. But circumstances force me to add one or two matters of grave urgency. It is my sad duty to warn you that, though I pray you will not seek the dangerous path of revolutionary activity, its dangers may soon find you. If so, then of course the fault is mine. Though I have been jailed and my books burned, nonetheless many copies of my "dangerous" writings still exist in Portugal and elsewhere, so my voice has not been truly silenced. Also, our mutual friend Teófilo Braga is still a free man, and he lives not in exile but as a public thorn in the side of the monarchy, openly walking the streets of Lisbon every day. That clever man has such a monk's life; he is so immaculately innocent that it would be impossible to bring charges against him without inflaming the wrath of the common folk. Under such circumstances, the king and his apparatus grow understandably wary and impatient, and they have begun hunting aggressively for any hidden dens of opposition. They would like to nip the coming troubles in the bud.

It is thus my painful duty to warn you that agents of the monarchy are probably seeking your whereabouts. By the time this letter reaches you, they may already know where you are. The monarchy has its supporters, even there in Paris, and it is my greatest nightmare that they may do you mischief in order to weaken me. At the risk of alarming you, I must speak plainly: these are evil men, daughter, and they are possessed of deep resources. A plot may be in movement already to have you kidnapped, or even assassinated. Try to forgive me for the role I have unwittingly played in creating these troublesome straits through which your life must now pass!

Read carefully my next words, and inscribe them deeply in your heart. Beware the Ordo Crucis Incendio. If only I could elaborate upon those grim words, to forearm you against the mischief that that fearful cult might be planning for you! But I only know they are moving against us— that they are likely moving against you. If I were to try and guess at their tangled schemes, it would merely do you a disservice, and perhaps increase your danger through misinformation. You must seek to uncover their intentions on your own.

Oh, child, I have taken a great risk with both your life and mine to write out that warning so boldly! If this letter's seal has been broken by any party other than yourself, your life and mine may already be forfeit. Show this letter to no one, and when you have read it through, burn it so that no ash remains.

Now, although it is my firmest wish that you should pursue for as long as possible a course in life that is free of politics and strife, devoted to the muse of your art, I nonetheless must commend you to the protection of the men who bore you this letter. Although I doubt that I should know them personally, they are surely representatives of our cause, in some way or another. If it should chance that they look to your eye like ruffians, never fear! They will lead you to better men, who share our ideals and commitment. You must not face the coming times alone, so you will have to trust yourself to their allegiance.

There are but two brief matters more. The first is this: Regardless of the dangers, you shall send me a message consisting of a single word. I will speak no more of this. Whoever has borne this message to you will aid you in the matter.

And second: I give you the following commendation. Present yourself to 'the carver of stones.' I apologize for the obtuseness of this instruction, but once again the bearers of this message can either unravel the sense of my advice or else lead you to someone who can.

We will meet in better times, beloved daughter: under the sun, and in the company of the freed people of Portugal. From now until that time, I wish you the best of fortune as you enter upon your career. Be bold, and the world will smile upon you.

Your loving father,

H. U. Q. F. de P. Tiago

Chapter Four

I folded the letter and sat holding it on my lap. At moments like this I felt very alone and missed my father dreadfully. I sat for a time with my thoughts, weeping at first, and then later simply holding my chin in my hands and gazing at the ground.

At length, Armand and Paulo made their way cautiously over to me and stood nearby until I acknowledged them. I asked if either of them had a sulfur match. Paulo did, and without a word he helped me to light the corner of that precious letter and consign it to flames.

The first thing I told them about the communication I had received was that my father had instructed me to send, through them, a "single word" of reply to him in his confinement.

"*Caramba!*" Paulo muttered, but then quickly mastered himself and restored his face to its habitual stony front.

"That will be quite difficult," Armand explained. "And it will also be very dangerous. But if Hermes Tiago requires this, then we will see that it is done."

"But I don't even know what sort of word I might send!" I told him. I certainly couldn't unburden my heart to my poor father in a single word.

"He wants to know your partisan name," Armand explained. "All of us have them. We speak them only among ourselves and are sworn to keep them secret, even under torture. If your father is ever freed, then no matter where you may be, even in deepest hiding, he may find you if he knows that name." He gave me an ostentatious bow and said, "They call me Sabot."

I did my best to keep a little smirk from creeping across my face. *Sabot* struck me as a very silly name, being the name of an ugly wooden shoe, and also a rather trite symbol of political resistance from the old days of the Paris Commune. I believe he noticed my reaction, and perhaps one of his eyebrows rose a little, so I said frankly, "I feel that Armand is a *much* finer name."

"Thank you," he replied, in his disarmingly gracious way. I was immediately ashamed of myself.

Paulo, who seemed not to have noticed much in this exchange, said, "And I am called Pirata."

The word was Portuguese. My eyes dropped for a moment, against my will, to glance again at that scandalous tattoo on his forearm. I asked hesitantly, "And have you, in fact, been a pirate?"

Paulo frowned, but not so much with displeasure, I think, as with simple gravity. He said, "I was a merchant seaman. We sailed out of Porto. Sometimes we ran cargo for the king's men, sometimes for merchants, sometimes for the rebels. Whoever would pay. One day we were boarded by troops and accused of piracy. All lies. They hung the officers from the yardarm, on the spot. The rest of us were taken for slave labor. I worked in the stone quarry at Estremoz for eight years. That was where I joined the resistance and where I took my name. One night, one of my friends killed a guard, and there were three of us who escaped. But the only one who lived was me."

This story was shocking to me not only for its grisly content but also for its sheer length, coming as it did from the mouth of a man who appeared to live by very few words indeed. Then again, I reflected, he had just condensed ten years of suffering into a few brief statements.

I glanced at Armand and saw that his gaze was on the ground and that he was nodding thoughtfully, as if meditating upon this story, though I am sure he had heard it before. I could see that he was deeply moved by this familiar tale of injustice, and I began to surmise how he might have made the transition from some comfortable upbringing to his strange life among the Souris Trempés.

With sudden inspiration, I said, "I should like for my name to be Leaozinha." For Armand's sake, I translated. "It means the cub of a lion, in Brazilian Portuguese. My mother was born there and she used this sobriquet when I was a child." I was especially pleased with the name because my father was a great and brave man in my eyes. In some ways it was my simple way to honor him and I knew it would mean a lot to him to hear it.

The two men looked at each other and frowned thoughtfully, then nodded. "I don't believe I have heard of anyone taking this name before," Armand told me. "It is yours."

"We will see that your father learns of it," Paulo said simply. And that was the last I heard of the matter.

Just then, a window opened on the first floor, and three dour Slavic faces looked out, almost simultaneously. I imagine they might have been checking for spies outside their window, but when they spotted the three of us, their eyes immediately locked upon us. They watched us gravely from across the yard for a long time, wordless and unmoving. I recognized the one in the middle as Mr. Lenin.

"Bolsheviks," Armand noted. "And look, that one is Lenin. I didn't know he lived here."

Paulo gave a single nod. Apparently, this was no news to him.

"Are the Souris Trempés members of the International Communist Party?" I inquired, hoping to sound knowledgeable. In fact, I knew next to nothing about communism, Russian or otherwise. Though I had grown up in the company of republicans and other rebels, I had never met an actual communist and had only the vaguest idea of what their beliefs might be.

"No." Armand laughed, though I hadn't intended my question to be amusing.

"Thierry is," Paulo noted.

"Well . . . he *thinks* he is," Armand replied. He and Paulo were still making unbroken eye contact with the three Russians in the window. I kept expecting the two groups of men to hail each other and perhaps come together for some sort of conversation, but they seemed content to simply stare at each other across the yard. At last Armand turned to me and clarified: "We Souris Trempés are of all sorts. We have a few anarchists. One nihilist, I think. Three utopianists. Some anti-monarchists, like Paulo here."

"And you?" I asked.

"My belief? I'm not sure what you would call it. I just feel that all men should be free."

"An idealist," I suggested.

He gave me that wonderful smile again. I suddenly felt silly for labeling him, when the view he had stated was so natural, and nearly universal among the young. "As you say," he demurred politely. "At any rate, I think we of the Souris Trempés are all *interested* in the Bolsheviks—at least in principle."

"Portugal shall rebel, as the Russians did," Paulo said. "But not the same way. We would like to *win*."

I changed the subject. "There was more to my father's letter," I said. "He also advises me to present myself to a man whom he calls 'the carver of stones.'"

Both of them groaned aloud.

"What is it?" I asked, alarmed.

"By that phrase, he means to say a Freemason," Armand said, rolling his eyes. I was becoming amazed at how this young man could go from a look of natural nobility to one of boyish petulance in the space of seconds.

"It's probably Grimm," Paulo muttered, looking very displeased.

"Of course it is," Armand agreed. To me, he said, "The damned Freemasons always want to take control of everyone's revolution. Especially if it is happening in a country that has been so sorely burdened by the Church of Rome as yours has."

I knew nothing about Freemasons. "But if they feel that way, shouldn't you all join forces?"

Again they both groaned and rolled their heads around in a way that I could only find comical. Armand said, "But you surely don't want to end up with *Freemasons* running your country!"

"I've never given it much thought."

"And this man Grimm to whom your father sends you, he's not

merely a Freemason but an Englishman!"

I stiffened a little. "And what is wrong with the English, if I might ask?" I had spent the latter years of my childhood near London, so I didn't have the slightest sympathy for the nearly ubiquitous French loathing of all things English. In fact, the attitude struck me as boorish and small-minded.

Armand threw out both hands, as if my question was too preposterous to be worth his consideration. "Ah, but once again, anything for your illustrious father! If he wants us to toss his only daughter into the clutches of English Freemasons, I suppose we must obey."

Paulo merely grimaced, apparently sharing this sarcastic sentiment.

I was beginning to become annoyed and said with a certain cold superiority, "Why don't you just tell me who this Grimm gentleman is, and I shall find my way to him myself."

"That's fine," Armand agreed immediately. "In fact, you're likely to do better on your own than in the company of common dogs of the street like us. The man your father sends you to is named Brian Torrence Grimm. You'll find him at the British Embassy, where he works as an aide."

"We must go," Paulo said to Armand abruptly.

Armand glanced up at the sky, checking the angle of the sun. "Yes," he agreed. His fit of pique was passing as quickly as it had arrived, and he turned a look upon me that was civil, indeed almost sweet. He asked blandly, "Did your father have any other instructions for us?"

"Well, yes," I admitted. "He suggested that I might be in immediate danger of kidnapping or assassination, and that I should turn to your organization for protection."

They both stared at me with their mouths open, utterly nonplussed. After a long pause, Armand said, "Well . . . I don't know that you will care for it. Our rooms are all underground, and . . . they are a little wet."

A little laugh escaped me. "I certainly hope he didn't mean that I should come to *live* with you! In fact, he advises me to pursue my career as a painter, and I've only just found a very suitable studio in this building. I believe what he meant was that you might advise me and help me to be alert to danger."

"Did he say who might be the source of that danger?"

I wasn't sure if Father meant for me to say the name of the Ordo Crucis Incendio aloud to these people or not, but if I was going to seek protection from them, I didn't see how I could long avoid doing so. So I repeated the dire warning.

Their eyes widened. They lowered their voices at once. I soon noticed that they were careful never actually to say the name of the order aloud, as I had done.

"You cannot live in such an open and public building as this, if *they* are after you," Armand whispered at me. "Don't you know? They can send assassins who might slip through your window and leave you dead upon your bed, without even waking your neighbors."

Paulo frowned. "Or, if they cannot be bothered, then they will simply burn the building down in the night."

I was starting to feel very nervous and glanced up at the open window of my new studio, wondering whether someone really could slip in while I was asleep. I had naively believed that the Ordo Crucis Incendio, the Order of the Burning Cross, had passed the zenith of its power many decades before, and that today it consisted of nothing more than a few crazy old men who liked to dress up in strange costumes on feast days. But as a child, of course, I had heard strange and terrible tales of this shadowy cult: the order that was sworn to restore the Inquisition. They were supposedly found throughout the Catholic countries of Europe, but they were said to be most powerful in Portugal.

I will never forget one evening, when I was eight years old, sitting at the feet of my spry great-grandmother Sancha during a visit to her country estate, listening raptly as she spun macabre stories (undoubtedly softened for my childish ears) of the horrors of the Inquisition, which her mother had seen firsthand as a young woman. If Portugal seemed a dangerous place for off-beat families like mine during the monarchy of 1910, how much more so under the reign of the Inquisition just over a century before!

Armand was astounded when I admitted to him my bland assumption that the project of restoring the Inquisition to Portugal was just a fantasy in the heads of a few sickly old men.

"Are you joking?" he demanded heatedly. "In the past century, since losing the Inquisition, the Catholic Church has only grown stronger in Portugal. The Jewish population there may have recovered somewhat, but anti-Semitism has become unbelievably strong—not only in your country but throughout Europe. The Inquisition could return at any time!"

"You exaggerate," I corrected him. "We are living in the twentieth century. These are not the Dark Ages, when people might round up Jews by the thousands and simply put them to death."

The point was so self-evident that he had to accept it, and now he looked a little sheepish at his rash and excited words. Nonetheless, he went on: "You mustn't take such a threat lightly. If *the order of which you speak* has marked you for death, then your life is in grave danger."

"But they don't know where I am, since I have been in exile for many years. My parents also changed my last name when I was sent to Britain—to protect me. That is why my father is Hermes Tiago and my last name is Sarmentos, my mother's maiden name."

"We found you," he countered.

I had lived much of my life under the shadow of such threats, though the rumored dangers were usually a little less close at hand. But both my parents had taught me that living a life according to one's own lights is often cause for others to persecute and, in some cases, to kill or imprison. I was proud of my parents' courage and was inspired to be courageous myself. Long custom had also made me stubborn, and I preferred not to leap wildly out of the way of onrushing troubles when a small sidestep might suffice.

"I thank you for your concern," I told Armand politely. "And I will further thank you to keep me abreast of any news that you might acquire regarding my father. You see, he has specifically forbidden me to try and contact him for fear that his enemies might discover my whereabouts and use me as a means to shut him down. I receive very little news of him and so I am particularly grateful for the care you haven take to deliver his letter. He instructs me, as he has many times before, to begin my life as a painter and to remain safe until Portugal is free. And so in keeping with his request, I believe I will simply return to my room and finish seeing to my arrangements."

Was it my imagination, or did Armand seem a bit dismayed to find me so unruffled in the face of his dire warnings? But he only frowned and shrugged ostentatiously, then turned half away from me as if making a show of abandoning me to the consequences of my own rash decisions. That was just fine with me, though admittedly I hoped he would tell me when and where we might meet again, before he went wandering back to his flooded basement. If nothing else, Father had made it clear that he wished for me to stay in contact with Armand and his comrades, so I intended to do so.

The three Russians had by now withdrawn from their window, and Paulo turned back to face us. He said again: "We must go."

Armand glanced at me, and I had the touching impression that he was truly loath to leave me there unprotected. But he only said, "I shall see what news I can find. In the meanwhile, please be cautious. Look for me to return here tomorrow."

And with a curt nod of their heads, the two Souris Trempés took their leave.

Chapter Five

I awakened at dawn the next morning to a clattering coming
through the wall. I pried open my eyes and looked around me,
and with a rush of joy remembered where I was.

Across the narrow room, I could see Irène curled up under a
pile of blankets, fast asleep. How tiny and fragile she looked! Like
a little pile of bones tangled among the bedclothes. I had fallen
asleep late in the evening, but she had still been wide awake when
I dozed off, gazing out the window at the night sky as if deep in
thought. I guessed that she was a late riser by habit.

I arose and made my simple toilet using the basin and pitcher
of water by the mirror, then dressed myself in gay clothes in
anticipation of another fine April day. Then I went out into the
hallway, to see what was causing the disturbance next door.

A young man was moving into the adjacent studio. He
appeared to have only a few things with him, but among them was
a small easel, and the noise was caused by his arranging and
rearranging it with fastidious obsession. I glanced around his
room through the open door and saw no paintings that he might
place upon that easel, no canvas, no stretcher bars, not so much as
a slab of cardboard to paint on. But he would sit and stare at the
empty easel for thirty seconds at a time, oblivious of my presence
in his doorway, gazing at nothingness as if judging the precise
angle of light falling upon some imaginary masterpiece, making
sure all was just so before he might dare to place his next
brushstroke. And then, still dissatisfied, he would move his easel
again.

Since I was being ignored, I took the liberty of examining the stranger carefully. He was a short, soft-bodied man with disheveled tufts of soft brown hair curling out from the top of his head in all directions. He was my age, which made me guess that he was, like myself, a new graduate from some academy. At length I cleared my throat to alert him of my presence, and he looked over with gentle brown eyes that were as bright and alert as those of a bird. Rather unnervingly, he simply gazed at me without saying a word and then began to move his head very slightly from side to side, as if examining me for a portrait.

"Good morning, monsieur. I am your neighbor from next door," I informed him, rather formally. "I gather that you are just moving in?"

Apparently remembering himself, he leapt suddenly to his feet and gave a small bow from the waist. He spoke up then, with a strong Russian accent but in carefully correct academic French— the sort of French that has been learned in a schoolroom and seldom put to test in conversation. "My name is Moishe Shagalov of Vitebsk," he told me. Then he added, quite unnecessarily, "I have just arrived from Russia."

I gave him my name and then added, "I believe you shall feel right at home here, Moishe. Though I have only just moved into the building myself, you're the third Russian I've met here." He smiled politely, but I could tell that he hadn't understood much of what I said. I repeated it very slowly, using simpler phrases.

Now his eyes lit up with delight, perhaps simply at the joy of having understood something that had been said to him in French, by a real person in real life. Indeed, I wonder now if I was the first person who ever spoke a comprehensible sentence of French to poor Moishe. He had clearly arrived in Paris just within the past few hours, and he would have been lucky indeed to have encountered anyone at the train station or on the street who was willing to take the time to repeat themselves slowly for the benefit of such an unassuming foreigner.

"I shall go out and look for breakfast," I told him carefully. "Would you join me?"

I watched him repeating my words inside his head. I could almost read them on his lips. Then he smiled and nodded vigorously. But he said, incongruously, "I would like to paint!"

Since I couldn't understand what he meant, I gave him my most understanding smile as consolation. "But you have no materials," I pointed out. I believe I attempted, somehow, to make the meaning of my objection plain to him with gestures of my hands. "You cannot paint without materials. And since you cannot paint yet, you might just as well join me for breakfast."

In truth, since I was still a stranger to the neighborhood myself, I preferred to go out in force of numbers if at all possible. With Irène still asleep, it seemed most efficient to take the opportunity to become acquainted with our new neighbor. He certainly seemed like he would make pleasant company.

He laughed apologetically and made several weak attempts at refusal. I guessed his reason even before he turned out his pockets to show me the sum of his wealth: three rubles in coin. How this meek little person had managed to come all the way from Vitebsk to La Ruche in such a manner as to arrive safely, and yet in possession of only three rubles, well, that is anyone's guess. But naturally it's a great pleasure, when you are as poor as I was, to find that you are sufficiently well off to extend magnanimity to someone even poorer. So I dragged Moishe out onto the street, and we followed our noses to the neighborhood café, up at the corner of the Rue de la Convention, and there we had milk and coffee and shared a heavenly croissant.

Moishe wasn't much of a talker, but he was crazy for the city. You could see it in his eyes. Under my interrogations, he told me that he had studied in Saint Petersburg, so I knew it wasn't the sheer size of this city or even its grandeur that was capturing his imagination. It was simply that he had come to Paris, Paris, Paris! All of us were that way when we first arrived, to varying degrees, but Moishe more than any of us. And this was odd, because he would prove to be the least willing of us all to go out into the city and enjoy it.

The two of us sat on wooden stools outside the café with our little bowls of coffee in our hands, watching the heavy drayage horses draw the milk wagons and vegetable carts clattering along the otherwise empty street, readying the city for another day of life. I recall very little of that first conversation, but there was one moment that I remember quite clearly. Moishe exclaimed in pure joy, "We are in Paris! Now, we will become great French painters."

I corrected him gently. "I shall be a *Portuguese* painter, though I live in France. And you shall be a Russian painter."

He shook his head firmly. "A French painter! I need a French name. So please help me."

I asked him to repeat this odd request, and to confirm that he intended to sign his canvases under a French name rather than his real one. I had never heard of such a thing. But he was quite adamant, so I gave the matter several seconds of careful thought, then frankified his name to Marc Chagall. He was delighted, and borrowed a fountain pen from the waiter so he could write it down on the palm of his hand.

The other thing I remember was the sadness that came into his eyes when he told me about his lady love, apparently still languishing back there in Russia while he prepared to make his fortune here in France. Her name was Bella, and I gathered that he had only known her for a very short while. All of us who knew Moishe were going to hear quite a lot about Bella as time went by. He worshiped her the way Dante had worshiped Beatrice, which is to say as an angel of God. I didn't know men sometimes worshiped women that way in real life, but Moishe did. Other than his painting, I don't think he gave much thought to anything besides Bella, ever.

At any rate, when our coffee was done, he thanked me profusely, and we walked the short distance back to our building. As we approached, there was no evidence that anyone in the entire structure had awakened yet, other than ourselves. This impression wasn't entirely fair: not everyone in La Ruche drank and socialized every night till dawn, and awakened every day at noon. But the few residents who felt the need to work by morning light tended to cherish the silence of the building at that hour.

As we approached the front door, Moishe give a little gasp and dashed off into the weeds that grew almost to the sills of the first floor windows. Bending over, he vanished momentarily into a great tuft of grass, then emerged triumphant with a discarded canvas in his hand. The thing was small and unevenly stretched, but its wooden bars were unbroken and the canvas itself had not been torn. It was heavily layered in brown shades of paint. I congratulated him on this fortunate acquisition, then waited patiently while he began a thorough search through the scattered rubbish that lay among the weeds of our yard. To my amazement, at the end of ten minutes or so, he had added three more discarded canvases to his collection, all with broken stretchers but one of them quite large, and he had also acquired several small, dried-out husks of leaden tubes of oil paint, presumably still good for a few last squeezes. I helped him carry this sad little treasure trove of free materials up to his studio, and he immediately got to work scraping the old paint off the smallest canvas. I poked around among his meager possessions just enough to make sure he had brought a few brushes along with him from Russia, and then I went back to my studio and rummaged until I found a small jar of turpentine that I could lend him. I left him there scraping away at the canvas with the edge of a broken board, as happy as I have ever seen any man in my life.

*　*　*

My comings and goings had awakened Irène, and I found her sitting up in bed. She gave me a look of real alarm when she saw me barge in again, almost as if I were some sort of marauder rather than her roommate. She pulled the sheets close around her.

"Good morning," I said, a bit uncertainly.

"Good morning," she replied with her usual formal tone. She blinked at me, and her big gray eyes were as alarmed as those of a forest animal surprised in its den. She said, "May I trouble you to give me a few moments of privacy, while I dress?"

I'm sure I smiled at this unusual modesty, but I humored her and retreated from the room.

Ten minutes later, when we were reunited, I told her: "We have a new neighbor."

"Does he paint, draw or sculpt?" she immediately wanted to know. She was gazing into a mirror and applying makeup to her face, which I found a bit silly in one so young. But she didn't wear it in any garish fashion, and it seemed to add maturity to her childlike features, which I suppose was the idea.

I told her that he painted, and she accepted the news blandly. Presumably she had been hoping for a fellow sculptor.

She began gathering up her things, giving every appearance that she intended to go out soon.

"I have found a pleasant café nearby. If you are planning to go out for breakfast, I'd be happy to accompany you," I proposed.

"No, thank you," she replied. "I never eat anything before noon. I am going out shopping for sculpting supplies. Would you care to join me?"

Since I, too, needed supplies, it was agreed that we would spend the morning shopping together.

During the thirty minutes since Irène had raised herself from bed, she had been becoming steadily more animated, and was by this point darting around the room so energetically that it seemed the small space couldn't contain her much longer. Her face was composed and didn't betray even a hint of excitement, but her feet and hands wouldn't let her be still. At one point, she leaned out the window to check the weather, and it looked as if she were actually going to take wing and fly away. Watching her, I found the performance both very charming and very odd. It was like being in a room with a grave and thoughtful adult brain that had somehow become transplanted into the body of an excited schoolgirl.

I made her sit down and listen to me, before I was willing to go anywhere. With visible effort, she placed herself on a chair facing me, sat up very straight and still, and folded her hands on her lap. Occasionally, as we spoke, the hands would unfold themselves of their own accord and begin fidgeting with something, or fussing with her clothing. Then she would notice them, and her eyes would turn downward to give them a single accusatory glance, at which they would meekly fold themselves back into position.

"I'm obliged to tell you," I said, "that I have recently been given reason to believe that I may be in some physical danger. I don't believe that there is any immediate cause for alarm, but I also don't wish to risk your safety by continuing to share this studio. I intend to move out as soon as I can find another room."

Irène thought for a moment, then inquired, "May I assume that you received worrisome news from those two men in the yard yesterday?"

"Yes, that's correct."

"I know that we are only recently acquainted, Florbela. But may I ask you the nature of your troubles?"

So I told her, briefly, about my father's political difficulties, and his worry that I might become a target for royalist agents or religious fanatics. As I was explaining the situation to her, I have to admit that it made me rather nervous just to talk about it. She heard me out patiently and without the slightest emotional reaction.

"And so you see, that is why I use my mother's maiden name, Sarmentos, instead of my father's last name, Tiago. My parents changed my name when I was sent into exile, so that I became invisible to his enemies, " I concluded.

Then she said, "I understand your father's worries, but I believe it would be unwise for you to seek separate lodging. For one thing, I'm sure you will agree that the social environment of this building is too chaotic for any sensible young woman to inhabit it alone."

Of course I felt exactly that way. Most particularly, I had qualms at the thought of leaving so frail a creature as Irène alone in this bohemian bedlam. But still, I felt I had an ethical obligation to press my point, and so I said, "But, Irène, wouldn't you prefer to find another roommate who is *not* a target for assassins?"

She frowned, just slightly. "Misfortune may befall anyone," she told me, "not only the daughters of political prisoners. Personally, I do not believe a young woman can go far in this world if she backs away from every rumor of hazard that she hears. I believe you will make a perfectly suitable roommate, and I do not wish you to leave."

"Well, I think I will at least speak with the local gendarmes— to ask their advice," I said thinking aloud.

"No!" Irène exclaimed. I stared at her, surprised at the outburst. "That is to say, I really don't think it's necessary at this stage. Let's just be sure to lock our door and you should never go out alone. You will be very safe here at La Ruche, with all these people around."

I made her sit still for a few moments longer, carrying on the conversation until I was sure that her mind was made up. Then I released her, and she fairly sprang from her chair and led me downstairs and straight out into the beautiful spring morning.

I followed Irène at a good pace to the corner of the street, where she approached a Hansom cab that was waiting at the large intersection at the Rue de Dantzig.

"Oh, Irène," I said. "I'm afraid I don't have the money for cabs at the moment. I just assumed that we would walk."

"In that case, please allow me to pay. I intended to take a cab anyway and it's no more expensive for two," she offered graciously.

I thanked her and off we went, clattering quickly up the cobbled boulevard behind a strong bay mare.

Anyone who has ever been twenty-one and dashing along the broad streets of the Left Bank in a horse and carriage on an April day will know how I was feeling as I gazed out the window at the city rushing by. As soon as we were out of our drab neighborhood and across the large and somber train yard of Gare de Montparnasse the signs of the city's opulence began to multiply quickly. We made our way around the walls of the old cemetery, through the parks and the rows of little houses belonging to the professors and doctors north of Place Denfert-Rochereau, then straight up Boulevard Saint-Michel, past the observatory, and then up the entire length of the Luxembourg Gardens. I had never seen the gardens before, and their glittering fountains and tree-lined promenades sparkled so invitingly in the morning sunlight that it took all my willpower not to beg Irène for an hour's respite from her day's agenda, just to wander aimlessly among those radiant flowerbeds.

But as we came down the slope toward Boulevard Saint-Germain, such flippant thoughts quickly lost their grip on me, for now we were coming into one of Paris's warm and beating hearts. And yes, like a few other great cities, Paris has more than one heart. For the rich, there is the Rue de Rivoli. For the intellectuals, there is the Latin Quarter, from the Sorbonne to Odéon. We artists have the Sixth, of course, and I suppose a bit of Montmartre as well. And for everyone else, there is this strip along Saint-Germain in the vicinity of Notre Dame, lined with gorgeous townhouses and with shops where you can buy anything from the rarest manuscript to the finest silk top hat to the most obscure of cheeses, and with brasseries and cafés with red velvet chairs spreading out along the sidewalks so that customers can ponder the intricate spectacle that they are a part of, and with a labyrinth of tiny side streets that meander up the steep hills or else down between the medieval stone buildings to the edge of the Seine.

We alighted at Place Maubert and set to work. There are a few excellent art supply shops in that neighborhood, and although I eventually would have found them on my own, Irène knew precisely where each of them was hidden. It took me very little time to gather together the few supplies that I was able to afford: a nice big jar of white paint to replace the nearly empty one in my paint satchel, a tiny tube of rich cadmium red (so expensive! and always so quick to disappear from my palette), a sable detailing brush to replace the one that I had worn to a nub, and a bundle of small wooden stretcher bars. I already had a fair length of canvas back at the studio, still folded inside my valise. I examined the easels longingly, but I wouldn't be able to afford one for another three weeks, when my solicitor would be depositing some modest dividends into my account. In the meanwhile, I would have to prop my work on a chair.

Once my few items were wrapped in a parcel of butcher paper and folded under my arm, I had done all the shopping that I could afford, so I followed Irène around and watched her make her selections. She seemed to be quite liberal with her money. I saw that she had already told the clerk to box up a small but very fancy-looking kerosene stove, about the size of a small hat, to be used for melting wax. She had also selected a kit of dozens of brass and rosewood tools for carving and pouring wax at various temperatures and states of fluidity. Back at my academy, I had experimented with elementary bronze sculpting, so I understood the basic "lost wax" process by which a sculpture is made in wax and then transported to a foundry for conversion to bronze. But I had done the work with simple, student-grade tools, and had never seen a professional toolkit like the one Irène was assembling.

After all that, she spent over an hour selecting her wax. Wax, it appears, is not one material but hundreds, and Irène proved to have an unfathomable depth of knowledge of the range of chemical and physical properties of these various substances. She needed several different types, apparently, and kept the clerk in constant motion, bringing samples to her so that she could thoughtfully crumble or melt them, or rub them against sandpaper, only to complain that the stuff would never do for one reason or another. The reasons she gave meant nothing to me, but the clerk understood, or pretended to, and he would rush once more to the back of the shop and return with new chunks of wax in white, or honey yellow, or chocolate brown, or tar black.

At long last, Irène had selected three huge sheets of black wax that was tacky to the touch, and two large blocks of brown wax, one of them hard and one soft, both very expensive. Though her manner and voice had remained aloof and phlegmatic throughout this process, her body was jumpy in a way that I was coming to understand meant that she was very excited with these purchases. I was wondering how we were going to carry so many heavy things back to the studio, when to my surprise, Irène told the clerk that all of these materials should be delivered in the early evening. This request added considerably to the cost, since delivery was not a standard service that the store offered. But Irène didn't seem to mind that. She paid in cash, collected her receipt, and led me back out into the sunshine.

It was lunchtime by now, and Irène pointed out a restaurant with sidewalk seating, not far away. I wasn't hungry, but I was happy to sit with her and rest my feet, enjoying a cold *citron pressé* while basking in the mild sunshine. But Irène, who seemed to provide no end of surprises for me, ordered a great plate of sausages and sautéed vegetables together with a large baguette, and proceeded to devour the entire mass as rapidly as decency would allow.

"You *amaze* me," I confessed, watching her consume her meal with such fervor. "You must have been nearly starved, you poor thing!"

She paused in her labors just long enough to tell me, "I always eat like this. Though dinner, of course, is my main meal." Then she returned her full attention to the task at hand.

I suspected, wrongly, that she must be exaggerating. It seemed quite certain to me that no woman could eat that much food and fail to attain a full figure. Irène was possessed of many assets, including admirable poise and intelligence and also, apparently, abundant funds, but one thing she sadly lacked was a womanly figure. Prior to watching her eat, I had briefly considered the possibility that her frail shape could be the result of some wasting disease, but I would not have dwelt on that thought very long. She certainly didn't *eat* like a sickly person.

No sooner had she finished this meal, which would surely have laid me low for several hours, than she began to look restless again. "I have some more shopping to do," she said abruptly, pushing back her chair. "Will you join me? I will buy some things for the studio, and perhaps you can help me in making some of the decisions."

I hesitated to agree with this, because I was eager to get back to the studio and begin planning my first canvas. I intended to collect wildflowers from the yard, and a few wine bottles, and to sketch a still life that I could begin painting in the mornings, during the hour or two after dawn when the light through the window would be at its very best. But there was really no hurry, and I was curious, so I decided to tag along. We left sufficient money at our table to cover our bill and headed for the boulevard.

It was fortunate that I agreed to her suggestion, both because I would have missed out on the fun and also because Irène was a very impulsive shopper and really needed the ballast of a companion to slow down her rate of purchases a little. We spent the whole afternoon shopping, entering literally every store that had anything interesting in the window. Irène bought furniture, rugs, comfortable bedding, lamps, and two or three times as much clothing as I had in my meager collection. I don't think I had seen anyone shop that way since my childhood, in Lisbon.

She paid cash for everything, and gave all the clerks the same instruction: to deliver the goods to La Ruche in the early evening. There was one store where the clerk flatly refused to send any delivery into our neighborhood, saying it was against the store policy—and when he heard the name of our building he apparently recognized it and had the temerity to wrinkle his nose! Irène came as close to losing her temper as she ever would, blinking her eyes rapidly but still maintaining the same piping, carefully articulated voice that she used for all occasions. She gave the man to understand, mainly through nuance, that he *would* have the delivery made, unless he intended to reduce his store to a commercial pariah in the eyes of the public at large. He began to lose his nerve almost at once, and after a few minutes he backed down entirely and promised to do everything she asked. When she was done with him, I actually saw him discreetly take out his handkerchief and mop his brow.

The whole adventure made for a very recreational afternoon for me, but it certainly got me wondering how Irène had come into possession of so much cash. Or, to state the question from another view: Why on earth she would choose to live at a place like La Ruche when she could evidently afford anything she wanted?

Chapter Six

We shopped our way to the end of the main stretch of the boulevard. When we ran out of shops, late in the afternoon, we were close to the Pont Neuf—the main bridge into the First District. I remembered my father's instruction that I should seek out Mr. Grimm at the British Embassy, which was not so far away on the other side of the Seine. Although I was tired, I felt that I should obey his wishes, so I resolved to take advantage of the opportunity.

When I explained my intentions to Irène, she insisted on coming along. Although I made a polite effort to dissuade her from bothering, I was secretly relieved when she hailed us a cab. I would have had to walk about a mile to get to the embassy, and my feet were already tired.

The cab took us across the river, around the Louvre and halfway up the Champs Elyseés. The boulevard was lined on both sides with fashionable Parisians promenading in groups of two or three among the great rows of carefully trimmed chestnut trees that extended all the way up the hill to the Arc de Triomphe. The sun was already low in the sky, and it was an exquisite afternoon.

The British Embassy was located at the ambassador's residence on Rue de Faubourg. Hidden behind a blocky, imposing exterior and guarded by English soldiers in garish scarlet dress uniforms, the residence of the ambassador is one of the truly beautiful old homes of Paris. Irène and I climbed to the ornate lobby, where we approached a row of busy-looking clerks, all sitting stiffly behind desks. They looked like bank tellers. Something about the sight was so terribly English that I felt a pang of nostalgia for the four years I had spent in that quiet and gloomy country. Mingled with my nostalgia there was, as always, the memory that during my first year away from Portugal I had never felt warm and dry even for a moment. One gets used to it.

"Would you be so kind as to announce us to Mr. Brian Torrence Grimm?" I asked at one of the desks. The young man lifted his head and leaned it well back to regard me, aiming both barrels of his nose right between my eyes. I imagine that what he was seeing across his desk was a very Portuguese-looking young woman, sufficiently well dressed but nothing fancy, who was performing the strange trick of uttering the King's English with carefully cultivated and (I believe) flawless cadences. I always enjoyed springing this surprise on Englishmen.

"I take it you have no appointment?" The young man was overdoing his Etonian drawl just a bit. This was no doubt a bad linguistic habit that he had acquired for intimidating Frenchmen.

"We do not," I confirmed. "You may tell him that Florbela Sarmentos begs a moment of his time."

The exoticism of my name really seemed to flummox the poor man. He slowly lifted his upper lip, revealing his four top incisors right up to the gum, and slowly pushed a slip of paper, a pen and an inkwell toward me. "If you would *please* write that down."

I did so and added, "You may also announce my companion, Mademoiselle Irène Langevin. We shall be seated, thank you."

Ten minutes later a plump young man in a cheap three-piece suit emerged from a door at the end of the foyer and herded us into the building's surprisingly cramped interior. The halls were narrow and they branched this way and that in a most confusing fashion, giving the whole place the feel of some sort of maze. The young man stopped abruptly before a tall door on the second floor, rapped once, and hearing the word "Come" uttered from within, gave us a quick bow and bustled way.

I hesitantly opened the door and leaned inside for a look around. It was a high-ceilinged room paneled in smoke-stained wood. Bureaucratic, but somewhere near the top of its bureaucracy. Brian Torrence Grimm was sitting behind a wide desk of polished ebony, no doubt very expensive, and he was writing furiously. Who can guess if he was really so very busy, or if he was just in the habit of pretending to be so, whenever unknown visitors appeared.

After thirty seconds, he looked up slowly from the desktop and regarded my head, which was still inclined through his doorway. "Do come in," he encouraged me, and at last put his work aside.

As Irène and I crossed his plush Afghan carpet, he came around the desk to greet us, eyeing us warily. Mr. Grimm was one of the tallest men I have ever met, too tall certainly for the average doorway. His impeccable Savile Row suit was remarkably imposing, draped as it was over such a long person. Such a great amount of fine linen, all in one place! He was thirty, or perhaps a little less, and he had a pleasant face with very blue eyes that might have been quite beautiful if the man bearing them had seemed a little less careworn.

He arranged us in our seats with cautious formality, then retreated behind his huge desk, folded his hands (which were the size of badminton racquets), and examined us thoroughly, one by one. While his gaze was upon Irène, his left eyebrow came down slightly, as if he were puzzled by something just outside his grasp.

"Mr. Grimm," I said in English and without preamble, "I'm here because my father, the Portuguese writer Hermes Tiago, recommended that I make your acquaintance. I am embarrassed to add that he failed to give me any specific itinerary to justify my imposition upon your time." I was, of course, not really embarrassed at all, and was careful that my tone made that clear.

"How terribly awkward," Grimm replied in a tone that made it clear, in turn, that he didn't find it awkward at all. "But yes, I know of your father by reputation. Allow me to offer my condolences for his outrageous treatment at the hands of the Portuguese government. I believe I speak not only for myself, but for all England in expressing my fervent hope for his immediate release and the restoration of his good fortunes." He added, with a tired smile, "I'm speaking outside my official capacity, naturally."

"Naturally."

"Permit me to say that your command of English is quite impressive." He turned to Irène. "And may I ask, mademoiselle, if you also speak English?"

"Yes, I am speaking the English not bad," Irène told him slowly, and with great aplomb. "I study this, already it is long time."

"I see," Grimm said, nodding politely and moving smoothly into fluent French with a strong English accent. "But as we are in France, I would consider it more appropriate that we should converse in the national tongue. If you will please indulge me." I watched his face very closely, but he gave not so much as the ghost of a smile at Irène's expense. That was when I began to warm to Mr. Grimm.

"Before we go further," he said, still regarding Irène as he spoke, "may I ask, mademoiselle, if we have met somewhere before?"

Surprised, I turned toward Irène to observe her reaction, and was amazed to see that rather than blushing, she had turned deathly white. Her skinny little fingers were clutching the arms of her chair so hard that they seemed to be trying to punch holes in the leather upholstery. But her voice betrayed no hint of her tension as she replied, "Why no, Mr. Grimm. I feel quite certain that we have not met before."

"I see that I was in error," Grimm murmured apologetically, leaning his head forward and dropping his eyes for a moment. He turned back to me and seemed to forget Irène completely. "As for your father's business, please be assured that you have done the right thing by coming here. I might almost say that I have been *awaiting* a visit from you, or from some other emissary of your father's." He gave me a sly look. Blue eyes, I think, have a greater capacity to look sly than those of any other color. "More precisely, I should say that *we* have been eagerly awaiting such a visit."

I smiled innocently. "We? You are perhaps referring to your government, Mr. Grimm?"

"I think you know that I am not." He arched one of his eyebrows very high. "Has Adah come to fulfill Jephthah's vow?"

It took me a moment's reflection to realize that he was

prodding me with some sort of Masonic password or code. I let out an uneasy breath, and told him frankly, "I am not acquainted with the phrases of Freemasonry, Mr. Grimm. Furthermore, to the best of my knowledge, my father is not an initiate. I hope you're not disappointed at that news."

It was clear from the look on his face that he *was* disappointed, but he nodded gamely and rolled his fingertips in the air, as if to encourage us to move swiftly past the uncomfortable moment. "Nonetheless, I'm sure you are aware that our interests are very much in line with your father's. You wouldn't be sitting here if it were not so."

I was beginning to feel a little awkward. For one thing, I hadn't seen my father in four years and it occurred to me that it was entirely possible that he had become an initiate. I wondered whether I really knew my father's will at all. "To be honest," I told him, "I know almost nothing about your organization and its interests. As I have mentioned, I came here solely at my father's request. Perhaps he wished me to ask for your assistance to petition for his freedom. Is that something you can arrange?"

"I am not in a position of such authority myself," he began, and I had the distinct impression he was about to launch into a long explanation of why he couldn't help. Despite my father's express wish that I remain detached from his political machinations, I had tried on numerous occasions over the past two years to obtain assistance for my father through what I considered to be trusted sources, and always received some excuse or another. I was not about to listen to yet one more.

"Then, it is not at all clear to me what assistance you can be to me, nor I to you," I interrupted.

Mr. Grimm's eyes were registering alarm, and his hands patted the air a little, inviting me to settle down and relax. He took a deep breath and said, "I see! Or, that is, I *think* I see how things are. You are young and you have never served as your father's agent before now. No, no, I see that you don't like the word 'agent,' and I shall endeavor to avoid it. Senhorita Sarmentos, I am a diplomat by vocation. I am accustomed to participating in meetings that may be of the gravest international import, but in which neither party actually knows what he hopes to achieve. Oh, both sides in such discussions know precisely what their *ultimate* goals are . . . but their *immediate* intention is usually too opportunistic to be given a definite form. So, you see, senhorita, when one of the most important organizers of Portugal's populist movement sends someone—anyone—to meet me, then there is no need for any sort of itinerary. We both know, your father and I, what the ultimate goals of our respective organizations are. You have walked into my office, and with that, a diplomatic event has occurred. You and I are meeting, and that means that *your* people are meeting *my* people."

I had to laugh at this tidy formulation of a matter that was still far too vague for me to comprehend.

"Mr. Grimm, if I am supposed to be a representative of the people of Portugal, or even the representative of my poor father who cannot currently speak for himself, then I have been very poorly chosen for the role. Please understand that I moved to Paris to become an artist and that my father has given my intentions his blessing."

He nodded while I was making this reply, but his eyes had wandered up to the ceiling and he hardly seemed to be paying any attention to me at all.

"You'll be in some danger," he said reflectively, and though he was looking me in the eye now, he seemed to be mainly wrapped up in his own thoughts.

"So my father tells me."

"Really? Did he say from what quarter?" His eyes darted to Irène for a moment, then back to mine. "No! Don't say any names aloud, not here. But did he mention a certain . . . dangerous . . . *order* or *brotherhood*?"

"He did."

By now, Mr. Grimm was sitting very upright in his chair and holding me riveted with his clear blue eyes. He asked, enunciating precisely, "He communicated this to you in writing? Without the use of any enciphering system?"

"Yes, that's correct."

"But the message was at least sealed? You're sure the seal on the letter was unbroken at the time you opened it?"

"Absolutely."

"And this letter has now been destroyed? You didn't merely throw it away, or, heaven forfend, place it in a drawer? It is well and truly destroyed?"

"It is." This line of interrogation was starting to make me nervous.

He leaned forward over his desk. "Senhorita Sarmentos, please consider my next question very carefully. Your personal safety may depend upon providing me with a complete and correct answer. Whom have you informed of the contents of that letter?"

The question required no thought at all, naturally. "Only the two men who placed the letter in my hand."

"These two men, they had come from Portugal?"

"No. They said they were local partisans."

He looked confused for a moment. "*Local* partisans? You mean French? Parisians? But there are no . . ." Suddenly one of his big hands flew up and slapped him on the forehead. "Oh my God! It's those damned Souris Trempés, isn't it?" Then, remembering himself, he looked apologetically back and forth between Irène and me. "Ladies! Please pardon my language."

My eyes narrowed a bit. "Yes, these men did say that they were representatives of the Bande Liberté du Monde," I said using their correct name. "Also that they had taken substantial pains to convey my father's letter to me. Do you have something of a negative nature that you would like to impart to me about their organization?"

He gave an exasperated half laugh. "Only the obvious."

"And what is that?"

"Oh, well just look at them! Do you really think that such people should involve themselves in politics? Honestly, what if they happened to actually *win* some cause or another? There's no one among that lot who's fit to govern a boardinghouse, much less a nation."

Since the blood in my veins is Portuguese, I'm afraid it did not take much to make me really angry. But my years of education among the people of colder nations had taught me to express my anger within the confines of civil rhetoric. I said, "I'm not sure you understand the principles of a populist political movement, Mr. Grimm. If we were to grant that the only people fit to rule a nation are those who have already proved themselves worthy of the task, then I believe we would have to conclude that whoever is the *current* ruler is the only acceptable candidate for the job. Isn't that true?"

He was sitting up very straight in his chair, watching my anger unfold with the wide eyes of a chastened schoolboy. "Oh, yes, of course I agree with you! I didn't mean to suggest . . ."

"Don't you imagine that the royalists in my country frequently level these same judgments of yours upon my father and Mr. Braga and their colleagues? I assure you that they do. They even express these narrow-minded and self-serving opinions with the same highhanded phrases that you have chosen." I gave this observation a moment to sink in, and meanwhile checked my breath to make sure I wasn't hyperventilating.

"Oh dear." The poor man looked awfully crestfallen. "Please accept my *sincere* apology for any offense that I have given you, Senhorita Sarmentos. I see now that I have allowed my personal distastes to displace my better judgment. But please! Do calm yourself and consider. It was your father who sent you to contact me, not the other way around."

That was true, and it made me bite back a further snappish comment that I was preparing.

Perceiving my hesitation, Grimm took the initiative and said, "I don't know exactly *what* common ground your father has in mind for us to meet upon. But quite a few things come to mind as possibilities. We share a lot of the same enemies."

This was also true, so after a moment's hesitation I nodded. I averted my eyes for a moment. As always after I have let my temper take control of my mouth, I needed to run through the script of the things I had said, so that I could assess the damage. I couldn't see that I had done too much harm on this occasion, so I turned my face back to his, smiled distantly but politely, and said, "I suppose you're correct. And I'm sure you are aware, now that you've considered the matter, that our circumstances have led my father and me to accept the friendship of any number of people whom we might not encounter in our usual social sphere."

"I take your point. Indeed, perhaps I myself am one of those people." Mr. Grimm was eyeing me very strangely now. Though his expression was cautious, even contrite, there was something about his gaze that was so personal that I dropped my eyes and could feel my cheeks blush a little. I may have smiled, just a bit, under that gaze. As a young woman, I was fairly accustomed to getting such looks from men, but I was not used to them from men who were either as important or as imposing as Mr. Grimm.

He said gently, "You are very eloquent and clearly have a talent for oration, senhorita. Perhaps an inheritance from your father? The fruit does not fall far from the tree, they say."

I thanked him for this compliment, and also for making time for our meeting. But I had noticed that the sky was turning golden outside the windows behind him, so I said that it was time for us to leave.

"I'd be very grateful if you could use all channels at your disposal to make inquiries into the condition of my father," I added.

As we all stood, he said, "I should very much like to meet again, and quite soon, if you please. We must discuss matters of your personal security, in the light of your father's remarks."

"Thank you for your concern. But I'm likely to be very busy with work, as I'm sure you are also."

"But you must pause to *eat*, at least, Senhorita Sarmentos. Perhaps we could have our next discussion over dinner? Shall we say, Friday?"

Surprised at his forwardness, I craned my head up to give him my most confrontational stare. I wondered what he would think if he knew the squalid circumstances of my daily life. "Why, certainly, Mr. Grimm," I said, a touch dryly. "You may find me in the Dantzig Passage. At the building called La Ruche."

I should have known better than to try and fluster a diplomat. He didn't bat an eyelid, but said graciously, "I shall bring my carriage around at eight. Goodbye, then. I do hope that upon our next meeting, you will call me by my Christian name. I'm sure your father had some particular intent in arranging our meeting today, and so I suspect that we will be seeing a lot of each other."

When Irène and I stepped outside and descended the ornate stairs of the embassy, the western sky was a rich tapestry of reds and golds. We stepped directly into a cab at the curb out front and made it home just in time to begin accepting deliveries.

Chapter Seven

The fuss generated by all the deliveries ended up providing early evening entertainment for the entire La Ruche community, which after all was an easily excitable group. The first wagon came clopping up just before sunset, bearing our new sofa. The loud voices of the workmen as they struggled to bring this heavy and ornate piece of furniture down from the wagon bed and up the steps to the third floor naturally brought dozens of our new neighbors to their windows. Within an hour, the yard was crowded with wagons. There was even a motorized drayage vehicle with three wheels and a large box built onto its frame behind the driver's seat, delivering our new floral draperies and a Chinese dressing screen. The whole thing turned into quite a circus, with workmen lining to carry their goods up the narrow stairs, reminiscent of porters in a safari.

"Congratulations," said Amedeo. "You now have the best-furnished studio in all La Ruche." He and Diego had come outside, along with practically everyone else in the building, and the two of them were poking around in Irène's boxes and generally getting in the way.

Something seemed to be wrong with Amedeo's voice. He spoke very slowly and laboriously, as if an unusually complex thought process were required to generate even simple sentences. His meditations seemed to overwhelm him at times, and he would leave off a sentence half finished, then close his eyes and seem almost as if he had fallen asleep standing up. These spells might last for a minute or so, after which, as likely as not, he would start speaking again in the middle of some other sentence.

Diego added to Amedeo's comment, "Indeed, I believe your studio will now contain more furniture than the rest of the building, combined."

Angelina appeared with a small basket and began unpacking it. She slapped Diego's thick upper arm with her pale, fine-boned hand. "Stop this teasing! You girls, you ignore all this what he says. Is beautiful, all of these things, is wonderful good taste. Green fairy?"

Angelina was pouring glasses of absinthe. I decided to accept one, though Irène refused. As Angelina poured drinks for Diego and for me and herself, she had to simultaneously elbow away quite a number of thirsty neighbors who were hovering around the tree stump where she had set up her makeshift bar. She prepared the drinks in the usual way, as you might see at a café, pouring the strong wormwood liquor into a half glass of water, trickling it over a sugar cube, which she balanced on the tines of a fork. I was not partial to absinthe as a rule, since it inevitably gave me a terrible headache the following day, but this was a special occasion.

I sipped cautiously, while taking my first good look at the resident population of La Ruche. They looked more like an assembly of beggars than a new generation of fine artists. Almost all of them were unkempt (except a few fops like Amedeo), many were unshod, and the only sign that they had anything better to do than mill about in the weeds and chatter idly was the occasional paint-spattered smock among the crowd. Anyone listening closely to their conversations would discover that most of them were very interesting people, and a lot of them were wonderfully witty, and a few had simply brilliant minds.

My attention fell again on Amedeo. "He isn't drinking?" I asked Angelina. Amedeo had discovered Irène's Art Nouveau lamp with its colorful shade of stained glass, and he was examining it with such fixation that he seemed to be deep in conversation with it.

"Amedeo is pursuing other recreations tonight," Diego told me, slapping his friend on the back. Amedeo didn't even seem to notice the big, meaty hand pounding him between the shoulder blades. "Which is good, because it means this bottle should carry the rest of us quite far indeed."

I chose not to inquire further about Amedeo's recreations. Instead, I asked, "But I thought you spent all of his money on wine, yesterday. Does this mean that one of you has sold another piece?"

Diego wagged a finger at me. "Ah, you still have much to learn about the creative process, little academy graduate. We never have money, but we *always* have wine. You'll soon find that people who are rich but uninteresting are often happy to extend endless credit to those who are interesting but poor."

Irène, who had been chasing the workmen around, piping commands at them and scolding them whenever they became careless, now trotted breathlessly up to our studio to arrange her new domain. I remained out under the stars, chatting with Angelina, sipping at my green and cloudy drink with its seductive flavor of licorice, and watching the last of the wagons trundle off the weeds and back out into the street.

The absinthe was so good that I had a second glass. Several of our neighbors came over to introduce themselves, and to join Diego and Angelina in ribald chat. The scandalous quality of their conversation, which might have bothered me at another time, seemed very funny and sophisticated with a head full of wormwood. Only Amedeo remained aloof from the hilarity, lying among the weeds not far away, looking up at the glittering sky.

At some point later, Irène came back outside, carrying a small brass telescope on a slender tripod. She had bought this telescope from an import store in the afternoon, along with many other attractive and interesting little objects, and I had assumed that it was solely for ornamental purposes. But as we all watched her, she selected a position in the yard that afforded a clear view of the eastern sky, carefully set the legs of the tripod on the rocky ground, aimed the telescope a bit above the horizon, and began adjusting its little knobs with one-minded concentration.

The three of us wandered over, and eventually Amedeo got up

from the ground and followed. "You're a stargazer?" I asked Irène.

"I intend to observe the comet," she replied.

Halley's Comet rose above the skyline to the east about ten minutes later. All of us stared at this extraordinary manifestation in a state of rapt awe, and Amedeo even more than the rest of us. I'm embarrassed to admit that, among the myriad practical concerns of my move to Paris, I hadn't read the newspaper for days and had completely forgotten that the comet was scheduled to arrive that night. Furthermore, the public sense of anticipation had been somewhat limited, since science was apparently unable to predict whether the comet's appearance would be humble or grand.

Of course, as it turned out, the 1910 visit of Halley's Comet proved to be one of the most extraordinary in history. Over the next week or two, it would grow brighter and brighter each night, soon outshining the brightest stars in the sky.

Irène proved to be remarkably erudite on the subject of comets. She explained to us with great confidence the current status of theories regarding the composition of the head and tail, and why the tail always faces away from the sun, and the amount of time that would elapse before it arrived at its perihelion, followed by an explanation of what on earth a "perihelion" might be, *et cetera*. Through the little telescope it was possible to make out in some detail the great tail, spread out like a diaphanous gown from the explosive pinprick of the head. Irène was polite and gracious as she gave us turns staring through the eyepiece, and her face remained impassive, but her poor little feet and hands were so impatient to get back to the telescope that she practically danced a jig.

Boucher was with us. I hadn't seen him walk up. He said quietly, "Enjoy the sight, *mes enfants*. We will none of us be here to see it when it comes again."

*   *   *

Nine o'clock is dinnertime in Paris, but it must have been ten or later before Irène and I were at last ready to lock our studio door and to go up the street in search of food. It was hard to pry myself away from the studio, after its miraculous transformation. It was now a den of creature comforts and sumptuous colors, with an emphasis on rich reds and browns. It looked rather like a place where servants ought to bring you food. But there were no servants and there was no food, so out we went.

We stopped on the second floor on our way down, to invite Amedeo's group out with us, but only Angelina came along. The two men were sitting out in the public hallway with their backs against the wall, engrossed in a discussion of theosophy (which I had heard of) and the *Upanishads* (which I had not). I was beginning to wonder when these two did their painting—and indeed whether they were really painters at all or just liked to describe themselves as such.

Angelina led us up to the Rue de la Convention to a *trattoria* called Le Troubadour Gros. "This is best place for dinner," she told us with great confidence in her thick-tongued Russian accent. "Everyone is go there, all the time."

And it was true: every table in the place was filled with festive bohemians from La Ruche, and they all appeared to be an hour into a lingering meal. I imagine that nearly everyone in the building who was able to afford dinner was there. We were lucky to find a table for two near the kitchen door, where we managed to squeeze in a third chair. Angelina and I shared a small carafe of the house red wine and spent two hours nibbling our way through a fixed price meal consisting of five tiny courses.

Irène ordered a la carte every time one of our courses arrived, and then apologized when her plate of food would turn out to be larger than both of ours put together. Then she would rapidly devour every morsel. Angelina and I watched her incredulously. Irène was very polite over her dinner, or as polite as a woman can be while gobbling up enough food for a two-hundred-pound workman. Whenever a new platter of food arrived, she offered to share with us. Both of us refused these offers. I, for one, was eating my customary sort of dinner and feeling no desire for more. But I believe Irène only made these offers for form's sake, because the moment she heard our refusals, she would set to work one-mindedly and eat until everything had disappeared.

At the end of the last course, she had the waiter wheel out the dessert cart. She made a great show of being unable to decide, and in the end ordered two.

While Irène was enthusiastically devouring her desserts, Angelina gave up trying to be polite and simply stared at her with frank amazement. "There is some law of science, of the what-do-you-call-this, the physics. This law says that what we are seeing here, this is not possible."

Irène hesitated for a moment, clearly disinclined to give up precious momentum for idle chitchat. "I hope my table manners aren't giving any offense," she said carefully. "It was a full day, and I seem to have worked up quite an appetite."

"No, you eat, you amazing girl," Angelina told her, and nodded her approval as Irène immediately obeyed. "I'm only thinking, I am pondering, upon the physics. Which is not possible. Anyone can see the truth of this."

I nodded, agreeing that something rather unnatural-looking was happening over there on Irène's side of the table. I don't think it was mere envy that made Angelina and me feel this way, though admittedly two weeks on Irène's diet would have left me unable to fit into any of my clothes and also unwilling to show myself in public in the new clothes that I would be forced to buy. But although I'm sure that all of us sometimes long to order a second dessert, I don't think anybody *wants* to eat as much food as Irène was eating. Even she herself made it look like serious labor getting it all down.

Somewhere close to midnight, we each had a *demitasse* of coffee, paid the waiter, then headed out onto the cobbled street. As after lunch, Irène didn't require the shovel and crowbar that would have been required to get me out of that chair, but rather bounced lightly to her feet, gave a discreet little yawn behind her hand, and commented upon the lateness of the hour. But she didn't look at all sleepy, and I half expected that she was actually eager to get back to her telescope.

Upon our return to La Ruche, it turned out that the evening had yet one more amazing spectacle in store for us. On the second floor landing, as we were saying good night to Angelina, we heard the loud voices of Diego and Amedeo wafting down the stairwell from the third floor. All three of us went upstairs, and followed the noise to the studio door of Moishe, our new neighbor.

Now, I should say that Moishe's door had been closed throughout the evening, despite all of the hubbub of our deliveries—not to mention the arrival of Halley's Comet, which had turned the entire city of Paris out of doors for a few hours. I had assumed that he was out visiting someone or attending to some kind of business. But he was not. From the time I had last seen him in the morning, Moishe had been at work, painting his first little Parisian canvas. He hadn't opened his door until the work was done and signed, and that had happened sometime during our long dinner outing.

Amedeo and Diego had come up to the third floor, wondering what was keeping Angelina for so long, and they had noticed the open door next to ours. As was their custom, they promptly barged in to meet the newcomer, and since then they had apparently been making futile efforts to ply Moishe with absinthe. When they saw the three of us peeping in at the door, both of them began howling at us: "Light, light! Bring some light!"

I was a little embarrassed, because Moishe was sitting there looking so imperturbable, or perhaps merely abstracted, while these two drunken louts whom I was already coming to regard as friends were rolling about on the floor and yelling incoherently. They looked like cats that had eaten bad fish. But to be fair, there was only one chair in the room, so they could hardly have been anywhere except on the floor, and they were also right that the studio was nearly pitch black, lit only by a tiny stub of candle.

I unlocked our studio door, and when Irène and I returned to Moishe's studio a few moments later, we were bearing two glowing spirit lamps. Moishe leapt to his feet, as he had in the morning when I first met him, and he gave each of us a small bow of welcome.

Diego held up the bottle of absinthe and waved it about, apparently trying to offer it to all three of us at once. He seemed to have given up on the water and sugar, and was sipping it straight from the bottle. "Drink!" he demanded. "We're celebrating my retirement."

"Not a retirement," Amedeo said insistently. He was lying flat on his back with his eyes wide open, staring at the ceiling. "Some sort of . . . beginning."

"I will leave Paris by the morning train," Diego insisted. "First it was Pablo, and now this. Look!" He grabbed Angelina by the hem of her skirt and pulled hard enough to nearly tip her over. He said again, with an intensity that seemed almost angry: "Look!"

Moishe, with an air of embarrassment, made way to let us through. Irène and Angelina and I filed around him, holding the lamps, to see what was on the easel.

It was a little hard to understand what the fuss was about, I confess. At first glance the little painting struck me merely as a crudely rendered portrait of a woman with black hair and over-large eyes, done from memory and with no great effort made to utilize the stylistic advances of the past five hundred years. It wasn't a particularly competent rendering—in fact, rather childish, in a purely technical sense. But one was certainly getting used to *that* as the twentieth century unfolded, and the days of the old masters were clearly long past.

Still, since I had the impression that Moishe was a very sensitive person, I took a moment to give him a pleasant expression and a supportive nod. "Well!" I exclaimed. "That's very nice."

He returned my smile with great gentleness and said, "This is Bella."

"Of course!" Bella was his lady love, back in Vitebsk.

"Perhaps if I copy it carefully," Diego proposed, to no one in particular, "I can adopt the style. I will use it for my own ends."

"That's what you said about Pablo," Amedeo reminded him. "And look at you now! Ruined."

"I am not ruined. I'm a Cubist. There's a difference."

Angelina and Irène were leaning in close to examine the little canvas in the lamplight. I noticed with a bit of pride that Moishe had signed it with the name I had recommended: Marc Chagall. I leaned in closer and gave it a further examination.

The colors were certainly sumptuous. Somewhere he had attained a good quantity of phthalocyanine blue, probably the new shade that was being called "ultramarine." Also the usual bright patches of Indian lake yellow, and some marvelously discreet rose madder highlights. If you liked high-saturation colors, this thing was a real feast. I also noticed that there were some extremely confusing liberties being taken with form and perspective. There was an upside-down man, presumably the artist, who appeared to be kissing Bella on the cheek. There were also a few chickens and donkeys that were either supposed to be somewhere off in the distance or perhaps flying helter-skelter through the air, as if launched from a catapult. I found it all very confusing.

"You can't paint that way," Amedeo told Diego. I looked over at him with some concern. I don't think Modigliani had blinked an eye since we walked in.

Diego lifted the bottle to his lips and took a rather deep draft, considering that the stuff was about 150 proof. "I *could*," he insisted petulantly. "*Anyone* could! Look at it, it's easy! Surely it's easier than Cubism. We just didn't *know*."

"You can't paint that way," Amedeo repeated. "It's impossible. Try it, you'll see that I'm right."

"*He* did it!"

"No, he didn't. Oh, all right, maybe he did. But he probably can't do it again. What about it, Marc? Could you paint it again?"

"His name is Moishe," I inserted.

Moishe smiled blandly, probably not understanding very much of what was being said. Seeing that something was expected of him, he said carefully, "I will paint again tomorrow."

Angelina caught the Russian accent. Her face lit up, and she seemed delighted. She began speaking to him rapidly in Russian.

He looked into her face with his beatific smile and said something briefly back to her. She beamed and looked around the room, apparently forgetting that none of us could follow their conversation.

"I think I'll just go home to Mexico," Diego said, ignoring them. "Perhaps I will begin some sort of honest labor. Do you suppose there's a train to the coast that leaves tonight?"

I cleared my throat. "I'm not sure that I see what the fuss is about. Perhaps tomorrow, Diego, when you're sober, you'll feel differently about things."

Diego gave me a brief glance. "A depressing thought," he replied. "If that is so, then I will be wrong tomorrow." He lifted the bottle over his mouth again.

"Your mistake," Amedeo said to the ceiling, and then repeated, louder, "*your* mistake is that you copied Pablo. *Anyone* can copy Pablo. There is a whole army of Cubists, marching along in ranks and files. I told you not to join them, but you had to go and join, and now of course you're weeping."

"I'm not weeping! I'm packing up my things and going home."

"I told you not to join the Cubist army. Just paint, I said. Look at me, I don't join the army. I just paint."

"Maybe so, but what you paint is not so interesting as Cubism."

Amedeo paused, composing his words in his head. Since he was still staring fixedly at the ceiling, when he spoke again it seemed as if he was addressing his statement of self-justification directly to the heavens above. He said, "I am more interesting than any *twelve* Cubists."

Angelina, who had apparently been trying to get a word in, finally interrupted to say, "Moishe is from Russia! And he wants that he should paint me!"

"Nude?" Diego asked immediately, though he didn't sound like he cared much one way or the other.

Angelina and Moishe spoke back and forth rapidly in Russian for a few moments, then she said, "He thinks no. But he says, is no matter, I don't need to stay in room while he paints it."

I would have suspected as much, but nonetheless the reply seemed to blacken Diego's depression even further. There was a prolonged silence. Irène took advantage of it to lean close to Moishe's ear and say, "I think it's pretty."

Moishe looked very pleased with this comment. "Bella is pretty," he told her.

Irène smiled. "For the next one," she proposed, "I think you might use a lot of red. I like red."

Moishe sat up a little, as if at last hearing something sensible being said about his artwork. "Me too! Help me to find some red paint."

"You can't copy it. Not *this* style," Amedeo repeated, beginning to sound like he was falling into a sort of trance. "You can't copy this style, Diego, can't copy it. Don't even try to copy the style, no, don't try, don't even try." He hesitated, and finally his eyes blinked. "Say! Do you know who could copy this style?"

Diego, slouched against the wall with the bottle cradled against his chest, made a sad snoring sound through his nose without opening his eyes. "I must warn you, Amedeo, that if you say that *Pablo* could copy this style, I am going to throw you out the window. And remember, we are on the third floor."

Everyone in the room was silent for several seconds after this pronouncement. Knowing Diego, it was perfectly plausible that he might have been serious. But Amedeo just said, "No no no. Just forget it. It can't be done."

Things went on in this fashion for quite some time, long enough that I began to think about going over to my own studio to see if I could get some sleep. I was finding the conversation a bit hard to follow, but it hinged primarily upon a disagreement between Amedeo and Diego over whom they should introduce Moishe to first. Amedeo wanted to get him up to Montmartre to meet Picasso and the other painters of Bateau-Lavoir, and he also felt that they should drag him over to the Sixth to meet a man called Apollinaire—a name that was vaguely familiar to me. Diego, on the other hand, wanted to take him along to some party at the home of the Delaunays', a name I was not familiar with. Diego apparently believed that this party would be a place where Moishe could be introduced to "everyone that matters," and also that the supply of wine would be more abundant than at a Montmartre party.

About half an hour into this conversation, Moishe apparently began to understand the topic of discussion, and he began shaking his head adamantly. He evidently had no interest in being dragged all over town on a prolonged drinking binge. Neither Amedeo nor Diego seemed able to comprehend this attitude at all, and began regarding him as some sort of freak.

Moishe explained to them, in his slow, cautious French, "I don't have money. I will stay here. I want to paint."

"You don't need *money* in Paris, my friend!" Diego had somehow coaxed Moishe to sit on the floor beside him and now clapped a fat hand around the little man's shoulders. "This city is bursting with abundance! Come with us! We shall show you how to harvest it."

Moishe turned his melancholy smile on each of his two new bosom buddies in turn. He thanked them for all of this camaraderie that he was so determined to refuse. He waved away the bottle of absinthe, for at least the twentieth time. Amedeo and Diego soon gave up on trying to communicate with him directly and went back to planning his future for him.

The only place they were both certain that they *must* take Moishe was to the salon run by Leo and Gertrude Stein, but neither of them could come up with a plan for getting him there. Apparently, they had managed to wear out their welcome at the Steins', and they hadn't been invited back for months.

"It's your fault," Diego said bitterly. "Gertrude was very nice to us, before you vomited on her Braque painting."

"I'll bet it washed right off," Amedeo said dismissively, flicking the air with his hand. "But she should have let it dry on. It looked much better that way."

After a while, a wave of energy seemed to sweep up both of them at once, and they staggered to their feet and became quite animated. They went out on an extensive tour of the building, pounding on doors and barging into studios on all three floors, demanding contributions of art supplies for the impoverished Moishe. The inhabitants of La Ruche, though poor, were apparently very generous. To poor Moishe's distress, Amedeo came dashing back up the stairs at one point, darted into the studio, and despite our chorus of objections, grabbed the little canvas with its wet paint right off the easel and went running back into the hall with it. I suppose he wanted to wave it under the noses of recalcitrant contributors, to show that the charity was for a worthy cause. Whatever the case, after an hour they came clumping up the stairs with the wet painting still in pristine condition, and lugging an impressive pile of contributions.

When Moishe saw what they had done, he began to weep silently and embraced them each in turn. They laughed and accepted his embraces, carefully returned his painting to the easel, and then went back to ignoring him while they spent half an hour sorting through their haul. They made separate piles of canvas and glue and sizing and gesso and old jars of paint and linseed oil and turpentine and chunks of damar varnish and of various dry pigments.

"He wants red," Amedeo remembered, looking over the neat rows they had made out of dozens of squashed and half-exhausted tubes of paint. "There's not enough red."

"He shall begin a blue period," Diego proposed in a pontific tone. He was wobbling pretty badly by this point, and seemed to be having trouble focusing his eyes.

"No, he must have red," Amedeo insisted. "Come along, we shall give him some of yours. Come! All of you! This is important." He moved to the door and waved insistently for us all to follow.

"Well then," Diego amended, "I suppose that *I* shall begin a blue period."

Chapter Eight

Amadeo seemed to have decided that it was going to take all of us to select the red paint as a gift for Moishe, so we followed him out the door and downstairs, en masse. I had been curious to have a look at the little studio on the second floor that somehow contained, all in one room, the extensive life-energies of Amedeo and Diego and Angelina.

It turned out they really were painters, after all—and highly productive painters at that, each of them working in a different style. The narrow little room had two bed sheets hung up as curtains at opposite ends, to create a little privacy around the two mattresses on the floor, and almost all of the other available space was devoted to painting. There were three easels, arranged as far apart from each other as possible, and there were several tables covered with tubes of paint and open jars of solvent and palettes and brushes, both clean and unclean. And, leaning against every inch of wall, piled several canvases deep, were paintings, paintings, paintings.

Amedeo and Diego began rooting around the room by lamplight, turning up tubes of paint in various shades of red and handing them over summarily to the increasingly emotional Moishe. Meanwhile, I lit a second lamp and began examining the artwork.

Nothing in my two years of academic training had prepared me for this. For one thing, that was my first exposure to analytic Cubism and I found it rather disturbing. The style was so *intentionally* an affront to the eye and brain, so purposely uncomfortable to look at and difficult to interpret. I had been classically trained, with the tacit assumption that an artist's role is to give pleasure to the eye of the viewer. *Everyone* had been trained that way, for centuries. Cubism was the first stylistic convention that absolutely could not be interpreted in this way. It was intended to be an acquired taste rather than a natural one, and you were no more supposed to enjoy your first exposure to it than, say, your first mouthful of veal brains.

"That one is Angelina," Diego told me. He had come over to stand behind my shoulder as I browsed slowly through a thick stack of his works, completely aghast. The canvas he was referring to looked pretty much like all the others: a jagged mass of incomprehensible triangles, with here and there some recognizable feature, such as an ear or a row of buttons. If this was supposed to be Angelina, it looked rather as if she had been skinned, and then random patches of her hide had been sewed back together to make a patchwork quilt.

"How *horrible*," I said, forgetting that Diego was right there beside me.

Instead of being offended, he chuckled as if I had said something witty. "Yes, and it's all the rage. It took a genius like Pablo to realize the beauty in something so hideously ugly."

The works of his two roommates were more palatable, particularly those of Angelina. Her portraits were not entirely to my taste, but she had a series of colorful still lifes that I enjoyed. Her sense of color seemed garish to me, but the academy had prepared me for that, and I don't think *any* excess of color could have shocked my trained eye. After all, the world had had fifty years of Monet and Renoir and Cezanne by that time, and even the outrageous colors of Matisse had had a few years to wend their way from Paris to distant outposts like Cherbourg.

And then there were the Modigliani paintings: of all of the La Ruche artists—even Chagall—his paintings were the one I liked the most at first sight. But standing there that evening, with my lamp, browsing through dozens and dozens of Amedeo's finished boards and canvases while he wandered around the studio somewhere behind me like a drug-addled wraith, I admit I didn't recognize his brilliance. Those sad and elegant figures, stylistically elongated and posed in sweeping curves. The muted, moody colors. I thought the outlined, cartoonish forms had a certain kitsch quality about them, a little too much homey comfort and not enough draftsman's brio to justify it. I don't really understand why, but I connected with the sensibility of his paintings in a way that I didn't with the others.

Eventually, it proved to be impossible for the two wastrels to give away every speck of red paint that they owned to Moishe, no matter how much they insisted. He thanked them with great humility, carefully selected a couple of small tubes in hues that he preferred, and left the rest by the door. By the time he escaped, the poor man looked perfectly exhausted.

Irène followed him upstairs, but I lingered for a while, still examining the scores of paintings in the crowded studio. I was learning a difficult lesson, and I needed to drink the cup to its dregs. Strange as it may sound, before that evening I had been sure that my academic training had fully prepared me to launch a career as a painter. But if one judged by the paintings that I was seeing that night, an academic training was only a first, elementary step—one that placed an aspirant onto the well-beaten main road. The three painters in this studio were all of them clearly trying to beat their way *off* that road, into the wild brush where they would forge paths of their own. I found it a most sobering thing to apprehend. Was this the only way to gain public attention in Paris? Was it the only way to earn a living as an artist, nowadays?

The hour was late indeed when I plodded up the stairs and quietly slipped in through the door of my new home. I carefully checked the room before locking the door behind me. Irène was asleep, and the studio was lit only by a milky patch of moonlight on the floor. I sat on my cot and removed my boots, still feeling very pensive—the vessels of my mind overflowing with all those unfamiliar images I had just drunk in. I was feeling quite overwhelmed at the outrageous implications for my own incipient career.

At some point when my eyes had adjusted a bit to the darkness, I noticed a strange green glow coming from the little Arabian table that now stood beside Irène's bed. Irène was apparently sound asleep, and all that could be seen of her was a raft of golden brown hair spilling out from under her new and heavy red velvet comforter. I crept quietly over for a closer look at the source of the light, taking care not to awaken Irène after her strenuous day.

The glow was coming from the side of her white silk purse. At first I wondered if perhaps some burning thing had become lodged in there, an ember of some sort, but there was no smoke or odor of burning. I scrupled for only a moment or two before opening the purse to look inside.

The glow was coming from an object wrapped in a delicate white handkerchief. When I pulled it out and unwrapped it, the thing proved to be a stone, rough-edged and about the size of a small biscuit. About half of the stone's surface consisted of patches that were glowing in a pallid, sickly shade of green. When I carried it into the direct moonlight for a closer look, the weak glow became all but unnoticeable, and the thing looked like a plain stone that one might have picked up by the roadside.

I was dying to ask Irène what this remarkable object was, but of course I was far too embarrassed to admit that I had been rummaging in her purse. Reluctantly, I began to wrap the stone again in the handkerchief, when I noticed that there was a monogram worked into the cloth's embroidered edgework.

I leaned in more closely under the moonlight, and made out the monogram: "ISC."

With surprise, I glanced over at the small sleeping form and then checked the monogram once again. Irène's last name, then, was *not* Langevin at all! This meant that she was almost certainly running from something or someone. Any number of explanations began elaborating themselves in my mind, and many of them were very disturbing. Perhaps the most benign was that she had made an unhappy marriage and was running from her husband.

Arranged marriages were still quite common, especially in the small towns and countryside, and a teenage girl from a poor family might find herself saddled with a lifetime of unhappiness very suddenly, if she was unlucky. But Irène didn't have the bearing of a woman who had been raised in poverty. The latter conviction led me to darker lines of thought. The next most likely thing for a young woman to be running from, if not a husband, was the law.

I hastened to wrap the stone back in its cloth. I was carefully placing it back where I had found it, when I noticed a strange cylinder, about as long as my palm, sitting in the purse among her currency and makeup. Somehow, I think I knew what this object was, even before I touched it. But even if I did not, then by the time I lifted it, its weight clearly identified it as gold.

The cylinder was covered in a roll of heavy paper. When I carefully unfolded one end under the moonlight, a fat minted coin of Swiss gold plopped out into my hand. I gasped a little at the sight of it, particularly since my head was full of theories about the secret nature of Irène's past and her relationship with the law. The coin on my palm must have weighed about an ounce, and it seemed to me that there could be ten or twelve of them in the roll. That was enough to pay a lifetime's rent at a place like La Ruche. I slipped the coin back into the roll and folded the paper tightly with trembling fingertips. Then I placed it back in the purse where I had found it.

I stood staring at Irène's sleeping form for some time, my curiosity now thoroughly piqued. Irène had made no pretenses to me, or none that I knew of. She had simply been a young artist like myself, looking for lodging. I had taken to her naturally enough and through no artifice or deception on her part, save in the matter of her surname. By now, she had earned my admiration in many little ways. I felt certain that if she were truly fleeing from someone, it must be due to an injustice or a misunderstanding. If Irène wasn't afraid of the assassins who were supposedly pursuing *me*, then I refused to be afraid of whoever might be pursuing her.

I began undoing the buttons on my dress, and recalled Irène's alarmed response to my suggestion that I contact the local gendarmes about my concerns for our safety. That put the matter to rest for me: I would not risk Irène's safety by contacting the authorities.

Even then I was not destined to get to bed as soon as I had hoped. It was a warm evening, and the window was open. I became aware now of an annoying sound coming through the window: someone was plucking incompetently at a stringed instrument out in the yard. The sound was only vaguely musical, and though I tried to ignore it, I felt certain it would keep me awake. I had no desire to close the window and block out the fresh night air, so I fastened my buttons again, went to the window, and leaned out to see who was out there disturbing the neighborhood's sleepy peace.

It was Armand, the young man from the Souris Trempés who had brought my father's letter the previous day. He was sitting on one of the large stones among the flowering weeds under my window, with his back to the building. He was holding a battered old Spanish guitar on his lap, and he was hunched over it in a posture of great concentration. Unfortunately, the intensity of his attention to the instrument didn't do anything to improve the quality of the sounds coming out of it.

My first reaction was to pick up my boot or something that I could throw at him. Then I began to reflect on what he might be doing there, and it dawned upon me that he may have come around because he had become worried for my safety after I had related to him my father's warnings.

I pulled myself back into the studio, and thought for a moment about what to do. I resolved to go downstairs and talk with him, if only to dissuade him from playing that guitar. Then, I thought to myself of how thin he had seemed, and how comfortless must be the conditions of his chosen life on the margins of society. I remembered that Irène and I had brought back some bread and wine from our dinner trip, so I quickly collected a bottle, a glass, and half a loaf, put on my boots and carried the food downstairs.

Armand smiled as I walked up to him, as if he had expected that I would come down. "Leaozinha," he greeted me quietly. Then he set down his guitar and moved himself to a smaller stone nearby, in order to give me the better seat.

I wasn't about to address him by the silly name "Sabot," so I just frowned and said as sternly as I was able, "What are you doing here, Armand?"

He made a casual gesture with his right hand, as if the matter required no explanation. "I had to meet some Prussians tonight, over in the Fifteenth. The walk home took me right along your street, so I thought I would sit here for a moment and rest. I hope you don't mind?"

I wasn't about to respond to this unlikely (or at least incomplete) story, but he seemed not to mind my skeptical silence at all. I took advantage of the quiet moment to examine him in the moonlight. I was pleased to see that he had dressed himself a little better than the previous day. For one thing, he was wearing leather shoes rather than wooden sandals, which was a big improvement. Also his shirt, though still of a simple peasant cut, was made of broadcloth rather than canvas.

Armand hadn't so much as glanced at the wine and bread in my hands, but I suspected that he was hungry, so I handed them to him with no more preamble than to say, "Perhaps you would like some bread."

He shrugged slightly, as if it were of little matter to him, but once I had placed the loaf in his hand, he continued eating at a steady pace until it was all gone. I poured him a small glass of wine, and continued to refill it for him as he drank between bites of food.

"Were you playing guitar with the Prussians?" I asked, making myself comfortable on the larger stone and eyeing the offending instrument, where it lay among the weeds.

"Of course not!" he said, as soon as his mouth was clear enough to speak. "But I carry it with me in the evenings. Paulo gave it to me, and I'm trying to learn how to play."

"Isn't it supposed to have six strings?"

He already had another bite in his mouth, and nodded his head while chewing. When he was able, he replied, "So they say. But for the moment, I'm having enough trouble learning to play on just four."

We shared a laugh over that. I was surprised at how cheerful my own laughter sounded in my ears. Feeding Armand had put me in a good mood. I wished I had brought him some cheese.

As soon as his hands were free, he brushed them against his trousers, thanked me again for the bread, picked up the guitar and began plucking clumsily at its badly tuned strings. I listened for a while, despite myself. The noise wasn't as offensive as it had seemed from up above. At least he was playing very quietly, and one could hardly doubt the sincerity of the effort.

After watching him struggle through a couple of bars of some nearly unrecognizable folksong that he had memorized, I asked, "How long have you lived in Paris, Armand?"

"All my life, Leaozinha." He stopped playing and turned to look up at me. His large dark eyes were luminous in the moonlight. I was struck by how handsome his face was, with beautiful lines and a remarkably sensual mouth.

"But you have not been a Souris Trempé all your life."

"I have not."

"If I may say so, Armand, it is evident that you were raised in better circumstances. Good breeding is nothing to be ashamed of."

He continued to gaze directly into my face, almost unblinkingly. "Perhaps it's not, and then perhaps sometimes it is. You may be surprised to hear that some of the finest men I've ever met would be inadmissible to polite company. For example, Paulo. And I have often seen the lowest rogues riding tall carriages and dressed in the height of fashion."

There was no arguing with that, but I also did not intend to agree. I was afraid that if I did so, he would go back to wearing that canvas shirt. So I said, "If you wish to say that true nobility is not confined to the aristocratic classes, I accept your point. But I think that, at every stratum of society, I have seen both saints and devils."

He nodded politely, smiling to himself, and leaned forward over his guitar again. I suspected he wished to avoid arguing with me.

"*Here* is an injustice," I said firmly, causing him to look up from his instrument and meet my eyes again. "You have apparently known the details of my family tree since before we met. While on my side, though this is our second meeting, I don't even know your family name."

Armand's face became very sad for a moment, and he leaned his head down to avoid my eyes while he placed his guitar among the weeds at his feet. When he looked up again, he had buried the sadness behind a simple smile, a false and concealing expression that I thought suited him poorly. He told me, "I prefer not to go by my family name. My name is Sabot now—at least, to those like yourself who are awake to the flow of history. To all others, I am content to have the single name Armand. A single name is enough for the country peasants, and I need no more than they."

What an infuriating young man! But I was very curious so I continued. "I do not wish to pry into your personal affairs. But of course I wonder if some tragedy has befallen your family and left you alone in the world. Or, what may be worse, if your family has committed some offense against you that has caused you to disown them."

He dropped his eyes. "Neither is true," he admitted. "My family live, and I will speak no ill against them, save that they choose to remain blind to the injustice and hunger that are rife in their nation and their world." And then he seemed to make up his mind, and lifting his eyes to mine with a certain very agreeable attitude of defiance, he said, "My full name is Armand Jacques Marie Fontaine. I tell you this only because, as you say, I owe it to you in the spirit of fairness. I will thank you not to repeat it to others."

Naturally, there was something in me that thrilled at this personal confidence. "And your family are Parisians, you say?"

"There are Fontaines on Île Saint-Louis, and also in Versailles. I am the son of Maurice and Josephine Fontaine, of Île Saint-Louis."

This would place his parents' house no more than a mile or so from where we sat, on an island in the middle of the Seine that was crowded with the homes of Paris's oldest moneyed families.

"Very well. It is a pleasure to make your acquaintance, Monsieur Fontaine," I said with a formality that was only half in jest.

Armand blew out a despairing breath between his lips, caving in to the necessity of giving an equally formal answer. He grumbled, "The pleasure is entirely mine, Senhorita Sarmentos."

It was tempting to give him my hand to kiss, but I restrained myself. Nonetheless, while I had him at a disadvantage, I couldn't resist saying, "It seems to me that your solidarity with downtrodden people needn't prevent you from wearing decent clothing. In fact, don't you think that whenever you find yourself speaking out publicly in support of the disadvantaged, a well-tailored suit would add some gravity to your delivery?"

Even by moonlight, I saw his face harden and I clasped my hands in alarm. I had only meant to tease him a bit, not to give any offense.

But, as always, Armand gave me a level and considered reply. "Before I committed myself to the general cause of justice," he told me, "I lived every day among people dressed in the sort of clothing that you describe. And during all those years, not once did I hear someone speak out, as you say, to support the disadvantaged. Quite the opposite. I seem to remember an awful lot of them railing against the dirty people in the streets, and blaming society's ills upon those who were quite obviously the greatest victims of those ills. So no, in answer to your question, I believe that rather than adding gravity to my words, such clothing would be more likely to identify me as a hypocrite."

It was tempting to drop the conversation, but it seemed like such a shame. The more I looked at Armand, the easier it was to imagine him in a colorful silk blouse with brass cufflinks, as was popular with the young men of the boulevard at that time. With a proper haircut and a pair of high leather boots, it seemed to me he would cut a dashing figure.

"My *father* does not wear rags," I pointed out. "And there are few who would call him a hypocrite."

But Armand just waved this aside. "Your father is no hypocrite, Leaozinha. He is a hero to all free-thinking men. But I'm sure you perceive that France is not like Portugal. Here, we have already had our revolution, long since. Now we have other problems. Instead of a king, we must overthrow the longstanding prejudice of those who have been raised in the families of privilege."

"Such as ourselves," I said, in a tone of heavy irony.

"Yes," he replied with perfect simplicity. "Such as ourselves."

What was there to say to that? I was too tired to argue further, and especially over anything as dry as politics. A few minutes of silence passed between us, during which we both turned our heads to the southern sky to gaze upon the spectacle of the comet for a while. I didn't even notice when Armand retrieved his guitar again. When he began to finger the strings, I found that I was content to listen to him now, despite his lack of skill. At the least, he could certainly capture the *cadence* of a simple old ballad, and somehow also its ineffable sadness, though the melody might elude him. I was exhausted from my long day, and yet I couldn't find any will to get up and leave. So I sat there for perhaps half an hour, following along with the music in my mind as Armand's fingers made their guileless errors.

At last my head nodded to my chest, and I knew I had to go inside. I stood up and straightened myself carefully, then turned to Armand where he stood, holding his guitar in one hand, politely waiting to say good night.

"Thank you for your conversation and your music, Armand," I said.

"The pleasure was entirely mine."

"Let me add, though, that if you were sitting out here in the darkness tonight with some intention of watching for my enemies, then I should warn you that my father is prone to exaggerated drama. He is, when all is said and done, much more of poet than a revolutionary."

"I think you should not be flippant in the face of such warnings," Armand said immediately, though in a gentle tone. "I would be very distressed if I heard that any harm had come to you." He added, "And I'm sure your father would too."

I let my eyes meet his fairly boldly then, and found him gazing back, as if curious to see how I might respond. Staring up at that handsome face I wondered to myself what it would be like to kiss him. I only said, "Thank you for your concern. You are very much a gentleman."

He smirked a little, and I suddenly felt rather foolish. Then he bowed graciously, and I took my leave. I could sense him following me to the door, but I didn't look back. Clearly he was very concerned for my safety, and I was touched.

Back in the studio, I fairly collapsed with exhaustion as soon as I had pried myself loose from my corset. I lay down on my narrow cot, expecting the blackness of sleep to overwhelm me instantly, but it did not. I lay there in the moonlight for several minutes, as if suspended in space and time, with all the memories of that long day swirling through my mind, and I was afraid my thoughts were not going to let me sleep. My eyes rested in deep contemplation upon the old daguerreotype of Mother and me that rested on my bedside table, showing us during a trip to Paris many years before. We were posed in front of the statue in the Place des Pyramides, when I was twelve. It seemed to me that she had swum through this city as naturally as a fish through water. How I envied her—I had been in Paris for less than forty-eight hours, and my life seemed already to have been spun around and turned on its head.

Then I heard the quiet plunking disharmony of Armand's guitar start up once again, wafting in through the window from the nightlit yard outside, and I felt peace begin to spread through my tired muscles. A few seconds later, I drifted into sleep.

Chapter Nine

T he next day I awakened very late, feeling strongly disinclined to do much of anything. It wasn't only me; the entire building seemed to cautiously nurse itself through that day. Amedeo and Diego and Angelina barely even showed themselves. As for Irène, she was arranging her sculpting area when I awakened, but after that she lost momentum and spent most of the afternoon lying on her bed, reading a book. I believe it was *Le Fantôme de l'Opéra* by Leroux. Everyone in Paris was reading it.

I assembled a few wildflowers for my planned still life, but the morning light had already passed, and eventually I gave up and spent the afternoon cooking up a big pot of *provençale* chicken-and-vegetable soup in the communal kitchen. I had been most alarmed at the smell emanating from the kitchen when we first arrived, but it had been cleaned recently and was well stocked with pots, saucepans and utensils of all sorts. Irène and I carried some bowls of this to Moishe's studio, knowing we would certainly find him at home. In those days, Moishe almost never left his studio. We found him working hard on a big red canvas of imaginary flowers and farm animals, presumably set at his family home in the Russian countryside. He was absolutely delighted to see the soup, and as we all sat around eating, he struggled charmingly to contribute to the conversation. I think frankly that, since Moishe didn't have any money, he might not have eaten anything at all during his first weeks in Paris if Irène and I hadn't fed him. But he was a very pleasant person to feed, so we developed the habit of going over to his studio to eat, any time we weren't having our meal out.

Anyway, that was Tuesday. On Wednesday, I finally got around to sending cryptic messages to a few people of my old world in Portugal, letting them know that I had arrived in Paris. I also jotted down and sent letters to my new friends and contacts in London and Cherbourg, telling everyone that they could reach me through my bank's Paris office. Due to my father's warning, I felt obliged to keep my street address secret, and at any rate I had my doubts that the French post could be relied upon to deliver letters to La Ruche with any regularity. I suspected I was likely to receive my mail quicker through the bank.

Also on that day, I tried to contact my father's friends in Paris. I stopped by the campus of the Sorbonne, looking for Professor Almeida. His secretary said he wasn't in his office, so I left a sealed note for him. In the note, I let him know that, although I would prefer not to write down my street address, I would be stopping by at the same hour on the following day in the hope of meeting with him. He had fled Portugal a few years before, to evade the same wave of persecutions that had brought down my father, so I knew he would understand my reticence to leave more exact information in writing. I also felt sure that he would be discreet.

That was Wednesday, and the next day was the fateful Thursday that may have been the most dramatic turning point of my life.

Thursday morning passed peacefully enough. I finally put in a few sincere hours of painting in the dawn light, while Irène breathed peacefully beside me on her bed, deep in her usual long morning's sleep. When she awakened, we had a breakfast of hot croissants and coffee in Moishe's studio, which gave us a chance to admire the big red pastoral still life that he had completed sometime the night before. Irène absolutely adored this painting, and I too was beginning to warm more and more to Moishe's style.

In the afternoon, I headed back to the Sorbonne to keep my appointment. Professor Almeida was out again but had left me a note sealed with wax, as mine had been. His secretary handed it to me with a very peculiar look, which suggested to me that the exchanging of sealed notes was not a typical part of her day-to-day chores. The exchange made *me* a little nervous, too. I had been certain that the professor would want to see me.

The note did nothing to allay my worries. In it, he gave the street address where he lived with his wife and two children, just a few blocks from Place de la Contrescarpe, and asked me to visit them at eight o'clock sharp that evening. He emphasized that it was a matter of grave importance.

I stopped at a *tabac* shop as I left the campus and bought a box of sulfur matches. I set fire to the professor's note in the gutter of a quiet side street near the Panthéon. The Almeida family had been friends of my father's since before I was born. I wasn't close to any of them personally, and I had only intended to fulfill a formal social duty by paying them a visit. So why would the professor send me such a terse message? For the first time since receiving my father's letter, I found myself really nervous. All I could think was that he bore bad news about my father.

I had nothing to do with my early evening, so I returned to La Ruche for a few hours. Irène immediately recognized my agitation and began to ask me questions that I found awkward. She was sculpting while she interrogated me. The evening was always the time when Irène's creative impulses took over, so she was sitting primly at her worktable, surrounded by the smoke and odor of molten wax, carefully roughing out the hollow core of a small figurine that she said would be a faun when it was completed. She was working without a model, but she had a number of illustrated Greek classic editions scattered on the floor around her, opened to engravings of various dancing nymphs and fauns, to provide inspiration.

After I had evaded several of her questions, her hands stopped what they were doing for a moment, and she turned her bland, pale face to gaze at me over her shoulder. Her mirrorlike eyes darted quickly over my features, probably collecting all the answers from me that her questions had failed to elicit. After just a few days of living with Irène, I was coming to realize that, although she might be full of secrets that I couldn't guess, I myself was generally unable to keep any secret from her.

"You shall be going out this evening, then?" she asked, as if innocently. She turned back to her work, once again arching her narrow torso over the table. Although I hadn't said as much, I allowed now that, yes, I would be out for a few hours. She worked quietly for another minute or so, then said, "If you really must go, then please be careful."

"I shall. Thank you."

A bit later, I set out into the fine evening, and I gladly walked the mile or so from La Ruche to Place de la Contrescarpe. Once one was past the pedestrian bridge that stretched over the dozen or so parallel tracks at Montparnasse Station, the rest of the route was delightfully entertaining. The streets were already working themselves into a festive spirit as Paris's nighttime denizens emerged to enjoy another spring evening. Every restaurant, café and brasserie had their windows and doors open at the street level, allowing noise and the glow of gaslights to spill out unchecked across the cobblestones of every narrow street. The sounds of countless guitars and violins and accordions trickled out into the air from all directions. By midnight, the voices of most of those instruments would be sounding airs that were either seductive or maudlin, but at the moment they were all ringing out their most festive tunes.

The roads steepened and narrowed as I approached Place de la Contrescarpe, which sits near the top of a hill. I had to ask directions twice to find my way to the little street where the Almeida house was located. Finding the address took me some distance off the main roads of the district, onto unlit passageways that were too narrow for most carriages.

But when I arrived at the Almeida family home, I discovered it was a pleasant-looking building. It was one of a short row of tall and narrow brick townhouses that were built along a ridge, with a view looking down over the treetops and chimneys, past the sprawling Halle aux Vins wine market to the winding Seine. Through the obscuring foliage of the linden trees that lined the narrow street, I could see a couple of windows that were lit in yellow gaslight, and, for a moment, all my worries were abated. Though the tone of the summons had been rather foreboding, and the alley that led here had been dark, still this house seemed a cheerful enough destination. I was looking forward to being welcomed into the home of people I knew and I was convinced that my earlier concerns were unwarranted.

I approached the stairway to the front door with good spirit and I was about to place my foot on the first step when something caught my eye. Emerging from concealment behind the building, I saw a large figure lurching toward me.

My breath caught in my throat and I clutched the wrought-iron rail to keep myself from stumbling onto the flint stairs. The large man in the shadows was moving toward me with a strange and grotesque gait, extending one stiff leg at a time and then seeming to fall forward with each step and barely able to catch himself.

I had just resolved to make a dash for the end of the street and the glow of the first lamp on the corner, when I realized that the bulky figure was none other than the obese Professor Almeida himself. As he came out from under the lindens, the moonlight caught him fully in the face, and I gasped with surprise. His broad, fleshy face seemed to be formed of wet clay, his cheeks unnaturally blotchy and covered in shiny rivulets of sweat.

After another step, the big man nearly fell upon me. He caught himself heavily by dropping both of his large hands on my narrow shoulders, almost knocking me off my feet. The sight of his face at such close proximity was truly horrifying. His eyes looked like black and yellow balls of glass in the dim light, and they rolled this way and that, as unseeing as the eyes of a panicked horse.

"Professor Almeida," I managed to say in a dry whisper. "Are you . . . can I . . ."

"No time," he said to me in Portuguese. The words were so quiet that I could barely hear them, though there was no other sound in the street at all. The air in his throat seemed to come bubbling up through thick fluid, and I believe he could barely breathe. "Listen! He will return. No . . . no time."

I couldn't get words to form in my mouth, nor give him any reply. I tried to guide him over to the stairs so that he could sit, but he was surprisingly tenacious in resisting me. He held me firmly in place by my shoulders and wouldn't let me go.

"Listen," he said again, but then it seemed there was no more air in his lungs, and I feared no further word would come. But he leaned close to my ear, and with a final cough of air, he managed to say, "Under . . . the bench."

His hands loosened then, and they slid down my arms, and he toppled dead at my feet. The only sound I could hear now was my own panicked breathing, and the warbling noises that I was emitting in lieu of outright screaming.

The professor had been in his shirtsleeves, and I saw now that the entire back of his white silk shirt was soaked from collar to waist in blood. Jutting out of the center of his back was the handle of a slender stiletto. My hands flew up to my mouth to stifle my cries of horror.

I crumpled to the flagstones with my skirts about me, unable to stand a moment longer. But the murderous stabbing could not have happened more than a few moments before I wandered up the alley, and I realized that the villain who had committed it was surely close at hand.

Though I was only paralyzed with fear for a few seconds as I sat on the ground beside the fallen professor, it was ample time to take a good, long look at the handle of the dagger that had slain the poor man. The handle was glowing fiercely in the moonlight, and it appeared to be wrought entirely of silver and gold. It was made in the form of a crucifix, a cross that was planted now in the blood-drenched Golgotha of the professor's corpulent torso. The anguished form of the Savior was wracked upon that little cross, in the Iberian style, but—as if to add one further horror to the Passion scene—the cross and the figure upon it were both decked in gouts of flame, sculpted in gold.

At last I managed to stagger to my feet, and I immediately turned to flee. But I had taken no more than one step, when I noticed something that made me stop and hold my ground, uncertain.

Around the corner of the building, in the narrow yard, I could see a small wooden garden bench covered by a tangled bower of bougainvillea. With his dying breath, Professor Almeida had begged me to look beneath that bench. I realized that his words could have no other meaning. And so, though I hardly felt I had enough courage even to keep my feet under me, I began to cautiously move, one small step at a time, toward the shadows that fell behind the house.

The yard, thank God, was empty when I peered with terrified eyes around that corner. I sprang over to the little bench in two quick steps and fell clumsily beside it, groping around in the uncut grass beneath it. My fingers closed upon a cold, cylindrical object.

I lifted the thing cautiously and stared at it for a moment in the moonlight. It was a copper tube or pipe, about the thickness of my wrist and the length of my arm, and its ends had been beaten down flat and rolled, sealing it tightly closed. Its surface was dry and clean, suggesting that it had been thrown under the bench only recently.

I wasted no time in further examination but clutched the thing to my chest with both hands, ran out of the yard and into the alley, and dashed away as fast as I could in my bustle and corset and high-heeled boots. I didn't stop until I had reached the corner of the road, with its blessed glow of lamplight from above. There I paused and tried to gain control over my breathing, and to silence the little sobs that were still coming unbidden out of my throat. I realized only now that my cheeks were wet, and I made haste to take out my handkerchief and dry my face. The few passersby gave me curious looks, but fortunately no one stopped to ask me what was wrong. How strange that there are such moments in life, when we're *glad* of a certain lack of caring kindness in our fellow man!

I looked carefully around, but I seemed to have escaped the professor's house unobserved by whatever villain had murdered him. I began walking purposefully down the hill, tracing my steps back the way I had come and clutching the copper tube with both hands as if it were the greatest treasure on earth.

When I came to a big intersection and saw a Hansom cab waiting at the curb, I hailed the driver and climbed aboard. Taking a cab would mean that I must skip a meal sometime in the coming days, but it was well worth it. The cab would take me home swiftly, safely and in concealment.

I told the driver where I had to go. Then I sat back and took out my handkerchief and began to weep copiously, but as silently as I was able.

Chapter Ten

I had the cab let me off a block from La Ruche and took myself off the main street immediately. There was a system of alleyways that wound among the courtyards in the center of the large block, used mainly for deliveries to the kitchens of the largest houses. I was in two minds about whether to keep to better-lighted places or to favor concealment. If my father's terrible warnings were coming true, then where was there any protection for me, in all the world? I hardly dared even to approach my studio. But I had nowhere else to go.

I pressed my way through a gap in the hedge that separated the yard of La Ruche from the small walkway among the buildings behind. Looking out fearfully from the hedge's shadow, I could see no sign of trouble. Most of the windows that looked out from the back of the building were wide open, with lamplight and voices and snatches of music drifting out. This was all very comforting. If I was really a target of some ruthless assassin, then it was great good luck that I lived in a community as vigorously populated as this one. I doubted that in the entire ten years of La Ruche's existence, there had ever been a moment when there wasn't at least one person awake somewhere in the building.

I was just about to burst out from the hedge and trot across the yard, when it occurred to me to worry about the strange copper object that I was carrying. It was clearly of great importance, and very possibly it was a thing of some particular use to my father. I had to ensure its safety and it would probably be impossible to carry it through the building and into my studio without someone asking what it was. Not that I had any idea.

So, before I left my place of hiding, I slid the long tube under the exposed roots of the hedge, and concealed it well under fallen leaves and branches. Then I mustered my courage, looked around one more time to make sure I was unobserved, leapt forth, and walked briskly to the shadows at the edge of the building.

I hadn't gone very far when I nearly ran headlong into Armand. He was rounding the corner of the building in the opposite direction, entering the courtyard. I was startled for only the briefest moment. Even in the dark, I recognized him instantly, and felt almost as if I had expected to see him there.

I wasn't sure, however, that I wanted him to be privy to what I had seen that night. I needed some time to reflect on the matter first. So I straightened up, drew a breath, and prepared to address him with a formal greeting.

Then, to my dismay, I leaned my face on his lapel and began to cry like a child. He held me gently, and it felt such a relief to be in his arms. I felt safe at last. He waited patiently until I had control of myself again. As this took several minutes, I suppose it took admirable forbearance on his part to withhold his questions so long.

"Come with me," he said at length, and began leading me by the hand.

I was afraid he was going to suggest we sit in the yard, since I was unwilling to linger in such an exposed location. But he led me to a gap that I had never noticed before, at the end of the hedge, and through it back into the system of little alleys from which I had just emerged. He led me around the corner, and into a small circular court that must have been used for laundering by women of the neighborhood. It had a wellhead and a pump with an iron handle, and there were stone benches against the walls. There was great privacy here, as the walls that faced the court had no windows. I sat down and put my face in my hands and Armand sat beside me quietly and patiently until I had composed myself.

"Please speak to me," Armand said gently in my ear, after I had quieted. "Has someone attacked you, Florbela? Have you been hurt?"

I shook my head vigorously, biting my tongue to keep from telling him everything. Then I went ahead and told him anyway. "My father's friend was killed! He was stabbed . . . there was a dagger! He was stabbed in the back," I blurted incoherently.

Armand was sitting very close, but of course he was not touching me now. I was still very distraught, and I unreasonably wished that he would put his arms around me and hold me for a while longer. I hadn't seen him in three days, though I had awakened in the middle of the previous night and had seen a figure sitting in the shadows, on the broken wall of the yard, and I thought it might have been him. Later, he would admit that he was out there every night.

"This happened in Portugal?" he asked quietly.

"No!" I cried irritably, wishing he was a little better at reading my mind. "I *saw* it! Just now. Over in the Fifth, near Place de la Contrescarpe. Oh, Armand, it was horrible."

He stood up abruptly, as if stung by an insect. "You *saw* it? You have seen a man murdered, tonight?"

I nodded, losing my voice again for a moment. I buried my face in my handkerchief for several seconds, then at last answered him. "Yes. No. Not the actual murdering. He was already stabbed when I arrived. But I . . . I watched him die." The awful vision of Professor Almeida laying on the cold stone path and covered in blood came back to me, and tears welled up in my eyes again.

Armand knelt before me, and I looked into his face, expecting sympathy. But his expression was extremely purposeful, and the hardness of his look brought me back into control of myself at last. He said slowly, "Did you see the face of the man who did this?"

I shook my head firmly.

"Now listen, Florbela. Did the murderer see *your* face?"

"I don't think so. I worried that he was hiding in the shadows, but I never saw him, nor any sign of him. I hurried home by cab and was coming in by the back way when I encountered you."

Armand touched his jaw, as if he were thinking hard. "A

dagger, you say."

"Yes, a stiletto. Right in the middle of his back. It was . . . so horrible."

"But why should you think it was a stiletto, if you didn't see the murderer?"

"The thing was still there! He had left it in Professor Almeida's back."

Armand gazed up at me from where he knelt on the flagstones, and his dark eyes seemed very hard and calculating. He repeated thoughtfully, "The murderer left his weapon, right there in the body? So he meant it to be found. But then . . . Florbela, describe it for me. What did the knife look like?"

Now, it was only then, as I described the ghastly thing to Armand in careful detail, that I realized the significance of a murder weapon in the shape of a flaming cross.

Armand rose purposefully to his feet, crossed his arms over his chest and frowned with great seriousness. "The Ordo Crucis Incendio. They have come. Exactly as your father foretold."

I could hardly breathe. It felt like someone was choking me.

"What am I going to do?" I whispered hoarsely. "Oh, Armand, I cannot stay here!"

He glanced around at the little court, apparently mistaking my meaning. "This place is fine, for the moment. No one will find us here. The weapon that you describe, if it was made of precious metals as you say, well, that is a special symbol of terror that is used only upon the most important victims, and only by *that order's* most highly ranked assassin. This assassin is a loathsome man, a sort of human insect who can climb up walls, and slither into the narrowest chink of stonework to vanish in its shadow. He has killed many who are mourned by the Souris Trempés, and at least one good man whom I knew personally and admired. This assassin calls himself Onça do Papa."

My heart was knotted in my chest at this terrifying news, but my lips repeated the strange Portuguese name: "The Pope's Panther."

Armand dropped again to one knee before me, so that he could look me earnestly in the eye. "You mustn't panic, Florbela. There is no reason to conclude that this awful man, this devil who walks the earth, is seeking you. Let us be frank. If you were his real target tonight, then it would have been you whom he killed."

I kept my eyes dry and my lips from trembling, which cost me some effort, and I nodded once to accept the logic of this proposition. I didn't attempt to reply aloud.

"Now, one of two things is surely true," Armand continued. The easy, reasoning tone of his voice began to slowly infect me with some of its confidence. "Either *that order* is not looking for you, and the events that you witnessed tonight were merely coincidental with your father's warnings, or if they are looking for you, then they don't yet know how to find you."

I nodded again, and managed to say without my voice breaking, "I suppose you must be right. Do you think I should go to the police?"

"No!" he said with real force, "You must not go to them. They will certainly have spies in the police and gendarmes."

Armand rose from the ground and set himself beside me again on the bench. "Still, it would be most imprudent to send you directly home to your studio. My comrades will want to look into this matter very closely, I assure you. I believe they will also feel that you are deserving of protection. Let us wait for an hour right here, since the air is dry and warm tonight, and that way we can be more certain that the street is free of observation. Then we can exit this block through a quiet route that I will show you, and go together to pay a visit to the headquarters of the Souris Trempés."

I had to smile a little at the silly nickname adopted by his group, but, all things considered, I would have been glad of any suggestion for a place to go other than home. "Very well," I said, and then had an unpleasant thought. "It shan't be *too* damp, shall it? Must I change my shoes?"

"The front room is quite dry," he assured me quickly. "You will be quite comfortable there, and those shoes will be perfectly adequate." He gave me a quick, nervous look. "You do not suffer from allergies? To mold?"

I laughed and shook my head. "Armand, why don't you move to an apartment above ground? You could spend the whole day, every day, with your friends, and then go home to a room that is free of stagnant water."

He lifted one eyebrow ironically, though it wasn't clear whether it was directed at me or at himself. Either way, I suppose he might have been relieved to hear me laughing a bit. "This is my expression of commitment to the cause!" he joked. "And besides, we pay no rent at all. Just a tiny gratuity to the gendarmes who patrol our block. Their rates are very reasonable, though they make rather *laissez faire* landlords."

"Heavens, how tawdry it all is! Well, if it is so, then I hope at least these corrupt officers of the law let you off for free during the week of the Great Flood."

"Alas, no. We suggested as much, but they pointed out that the flood was no fault of theirs, and insisted on their usual sweetener. Actually, they were in a foul mood that week, as I recall. *Their* headquarters had been inundated, too."

A slender crescent moon had risen above the wall opposite us, and also a smudge of pale light that I realized now was part of the rising comet. The comet was getting larger by the day. I had read that the astronomers anticipated that our world would fly right through its tail in a week or so.

I felt my head nodding heavily, and I forced my eyes wider open. I hadn't realized how exhausted I had become, after all the wild emotions of the past few hours. To stay awake, I looked Armand critically up and down and said to him, "At least you're beginning to dress properly. These trousers suit you much better than your workman's pantaloons."

He folded his hands on his knee and sat up stiffly, as if preparing to endure whatever opinions I intended to sling at him on the familiar subject of his appearance. "Pantaloons are good enough for France's common man," he said, predictably enough, "and they are quite good enough for me. But I have no objection to a simple cut of trousers, upon occasion."

"Well, I feel they suit you quite well. And say, do you know what would go very well with them? A silk blouse in white or blue, with cuffed sleeves and a nice high collar."

He laughed, not entirely in good humor. "Oh, certainly! That would be perfect—if I meant to mix with all the vapid dandies in Marais! Imagine *me*, wearing a silk blouse."

"Cotton, then. And if you don't like blue, then green should do just fine. Actually, green might better match your eyes."

"A fine partisan I would make," Armand grumbled under his breath, as if speaking to himself, though I was only a foot away. "There are far more important things in life, you know . . ." He began uttering incomplete sentences too quietly for me to fully understand the words, and he went on in that way for a while.

His grumbling struck me as entirely *pro forma*—I didn't really believe that he was irritated at all, and I felt that quite a bit more such advice would probably do him a lot of good. I began to imagine him in a dark red blouse, a deep maroon perhaps. That might do nicely, and also appeal to his revolutionary instincts. I decided that, grumbling or no, I would recommend it to him, but right around then I must have fallen asleep with my head on his shoulder.

Chapter Eleven

rmand awakened me some time later. It must have been around dinnertime, because not long after we set forth, my stomach began to growl. I would miss dinner that night, but I was too nervous to eat anyway.

As promised, Armand led me through a secret route that brought us out between two buildings, in the dark neighborhood that faced away from Rue de Dantzig. He began leading me through the web of small streets, some of them not even paved in stones, weaving among the small, rude dwellings of a very poor neighborhood. I would not have walked through such an area by night alone, so I stayed close to Armand while he navigated the maze.

"We'll keep the moon on our right. That should get us to the tracks, and we can cross them on the second bridge—the little one. From there, we will walk east and avoid the main roads, until we come to the river," Armand explained confidently.

I made no argument, but was glad he thought he knew the way. The fresh night air began to revive me, and my good spirits were returning, all of which was fortunate because the walk would cover a good two or three miles along tiny, potholed roads.

We emerged at the palisade fence above the train tracks, and we followed it through the darkness until we came to a skinny bridge over the rail yard, one that I had never crossed before. After that, the rest of our nighttime ramble was like a dream to me, because we were passing through the city in a manner that I had never tried, advancing block by block through the tiniest of

streets within the most obscure of neighborhoods, the rich ones
and the poor alike. One generally finds one's way in a large city
using the boulevards and the largest roads. But we were avoiding
all such roads, navigating by the moon and stars as one might do
in a wilderness. Each time we came to one of the giant boulevards,
we crossed it as one might cross a river, slogging across it lane by
lane until we came to the other side, then entering into yet
another little neighborhood through some inauspicious gap
between the buildings.

Armand was very thoughtful and stopped frequently along the
way to let me rest, so our walk was punctuated by little
conversations taken in any number of pleasant places: a moonlit
stoop, the base of a sculpted fountain, a bench under trees that
overlooked the Place d'Italie. In fact, I enjoyed the journey much
more than the prospect of either what lay behind or what lay
ahead, and would just as soon have continued strolling the back
streets of Paris with Armand until the sun came up.

But at last we crossed an ugly trestle bridge over the tracks of
the Austerlitz train station and came down upon the Quai
d'Austerlitz, a lonely place far from the city center. The quay
stretched along the bank of the Seine, ugly and inauspicious, and I
found it an alarming place to walk along by night. The stonework
along the bank was filthy and the river itself was lined with ugly
freight barges, each of which was apparently guarded by a
drunken sailor or a mangy dog on a rope. Armand led me briskly
along the tug-path, exchanging prolonged and silent eye contact
with each man who turned in the shadows to watch us pass. I
suspect that, if he had not done so, I might have received any
number of rude comments.

Armand stopped before a double-plated trapdoor set into the
stonework that covered the ground. It was held shut in the middle
by a large padlock, which he reached down and flipped open. Its
clasp had been sawed through, so the lock was apparently serving
only as a subterfuge. He lifted one of the two iron flaps, revealing a
stairway that led down into darkness. Everything about this
opening suggested that it must lead down to a most dank and

fetid place.

"Oh no," I told him, shaking my head firmly.

"It is *intended* to look inhospitable," Armand assured me, a little impatiently. "It isn't so bad as it appears." He glanced up and down the quay warily, then gestured firmly at the dark stairway with his open hand. "If you please."

Going down those stairs felt a lot like voluntarily descending into one's own crypt. Armand followed closely behind me, gripping my wrist while I held it above my shoulder so that he could stop me if I fell. The stairwell was too dark for me to see where it was leading us, which made me feel that I was on my way, like Orpheus, all the way down to the gloomy kingdom of the dead. And then, of course, I heard a resonant *clank* behind me, and the last shaft of moonlight disappeared as Armand pulled shut the trapdoor behind us.

I began to notice a yellow glow coming up the stairs from around a bend below me. I hastened toward the light.

My eyes adjusted as we stepped down the last few stairs and came into a long, low-roofed stone chamber built of intersecting arches in the same form as medieval wine cellars. The entire room was lit, albeit poorly, by oil lamps suspended from the ceiling by wire loops. A number of battered wooden tables of wildly clashing styles and sizes had been arranged into a single long table down the center of the room, and this was surrounded by perhaps as many as twenty equally mismatching chairs.

Three of the seats were occupied by men dressed in rough burlap clothing, playing a game of cards beside a couple of empty wine bottles. All three of them stared at us stonily as we came into the chamber. Armand made haste to move a little in front of me in order to make the introductions, and I imagine also to suggest a tone of conversation among his rough companions that would be suitable to a female visitor.

"Comrades," Armand said briskly. "I have the pleasure to introduce you to Senhorita Florbela Sarmentos, known among us as Leaozinha. Senhorita, these three men are my personal friends, and fearless partisans of free men everywhere. Barbade is on the left, and this is Thierry, and against the pillar you see Le Roque."

There was silence for a moment. Then, the one called Thierry spoke up in a gravelly voice, to say, "That's great, pretty little Lord Fauntleroy. Did you bring back any wine?"

Armand turned an uncertain smile to me from over his shoulder. "He jests," he explained. "My comrades find it entertaining that I've lately taken to wearing linen trousers and leather shoes." He turned forward to face the chamber again, lifting his hands a bit at his sides as if in dramatic oratory. "Let us not judge a man by the cut of his clothes, comrade Thierry! Don't you imagine that, when we are speaking out in support of the disadvantaged, a well-tailored suit might add some gravity to our delivery?"

"Haw! I wasn't judging you by the cut of your clothes, comrade Fancy-Breeches." Thierry shared a grin with his two companions, displaying a sad absence of teeth for a man so young. "I was judging you by your lack of wine!"

The other two howled with laughter, and I really do mean howled.

Armand seem to be unfazed by all this badgering at his expense, and he continued his introduction. "Comrade Leaozinha is the daughter of the people's hero Hermes Tiago, the immortal writer who now languishes in the dungeons of Portugal's execrable King Manuel."

As you might imagine, I was preparing to leave by this point. But these last words from Armand really did seem to improve the tenor of the exchange of words. The three men dropped their eyes to the tabletop, and one by one laid their cards face-down, as if apparently deciding at last that our entrance was worth their full attention. Meanwhile, the loud voices had apparently awakened several other men, some of whom I could see now had been sleeping on mattresses in the shadows of the stone arches along the edges of the long room. More of them would gradually filter in from the various dark entrances that opened off the chamber in all directions.

"Your father's got courage," the one called Barbade said to me.

The look that he flashed at me might have been mistaken for a leer, but his words seemed complimentary enough. I nodded my thanks.

A scrawny old man was wandering over from one of the mattresses, scratching at his clothes and yawning. The old man glanced at me briefly and said, "Well met, little missy. Your father and his friend Braga are the last brave men in Europe." Then he loudly pulled back a chair and dropped himself heavily at the head of the table.

"Leaozinha," Armand announced with heavy import, "I wish to introduce you to our leader, Libreterre."

"We don't have a leader," the one called Le Roque inserted immediately. His drawling voice suggested that this was a hackneyed issue, and that it was tiresome to have to repeat something so obvious. Le Roque was a very nervous-looking little man. He seemed to be rapidly losing hair despite his young age, and unfortunately he was doing so in an extremely asymmetrical fashion.

"That issue hasn't been decided yet," Thierry replied quickly. "It has still to be put to a vote."

"We are not a democracy," Le Roque replied in a sneering tone. "Voting is for the bourgeoisie. No revolution was ever achieved by *voting!*"

Barbade threw both hands in the air dramatically, and looked upward as if calling upon God for strength—which I suspect he was not doing. "How do you expect for us to *agree* on anything, you fool? Shall we settle each issue with a fight to the death?"

"True consensus arises from direct apprehension of the truth, by every citizen," Le Roque said firmly, tapping his fingernail on the table to emphasize each word. "This is the only basis by which a true and enlightened anarchy can arise."

"Exactly," Thierry exclaimed, quite a bit too loudly for the enclosed space. "And that is why communist revolutions will succeed and anarchism will fail!"

Two or three more people had wandered into the room during this conversation, and now I saw Paulo appear in one of the doorways. Despite his appearance of a muscle-bound cutthroat, which I still found unnerving, I was nonetheless pleased to see a familiar face and one that I knew belonged to a man capable of basic civility.

When Paulo saw Armand and me still standing on the bottom stair at the entryway, he moved around to an unoccupied region of the long composite table and wordlessly pulled back two chairs for us. The others at the table seemed to have nearly forgotten that we were there, and they watched Paulo curiously as he performed this simple act of welcome. Several of them seemed to turn a bit sheepish as they watched us come quietly over and take our seats. I suspect that Paulo commanded a lot of respect among this lawless bunch, due to his formidable size.

After a moment of embarrassed silence, the old man, Libreterre, spoke up. "Pardon our coarse ways, little mademoiselle. We are none of us much accustomed to lady visitors."

"I appreciate your hospitality, monsieur."

"Comrades," Armand spoke up, apparently deciding that the preliminaries had at last been successfully negotiated. "We have pressing news." There were perhaps a dozen people seated at the table at this point, about a third of whom looked so alarming that I may very well have crossed a street to avoid passing them in broad daylight. I was pleased to be sitting between Armand and Paulo, whom I now took to be my protectors—protecting me as much from my father's supposed friends as from his stated enemies.

Armand then related to them, secondhand, the story I had told him of poor Professor Almeida's murder. Revisiting the horror of just a few hours before brought me to tears again. He glanced at me a couple of times as he recited the details, and I was afraid he might yield me the floor to recount the story directly. But when he saw that I was daubing my eyes again, he simply finished telling the story for me, and I was most grateful.

When the story of the murder had been told, that underground chamber of reformers in rags was left in meditative silence for a lengthy spell. It was the elder at the head of the table, Libreterre, who first spoke into that silence. "The thing falls upon us once again," he said with an old man's bitterness. I glanced at him and was surprised to see that his wrinkled old countenance was surprisingly resolved, even commanding. "These murderous vermin, these thugs who kill in the night, and who have the temerity to pretend they work under a religious charter! We must *kill* this cockroach! Bring me the head of Onça do Papa."

Unfortunately, he delivered this last sentence, which had such dramatic potential, in a mumbling undertone, as if he had run out of air. At any rate, no one seemed to take the order very seriously.

"His power is stealth," Paulo said in his firm baritone. "We will not be able to kill him. Not until he makes a mistake."

"Perhaps we can hunt down his master," said a man to whom I had not been introduced. He had a thick Russian accent and a blond beard.

No one replied to his proposal directly, but a number of small conversations broke out around the table, many of them in argumentative voices. Armand turned to me and said quietly, "We know but little of the structure of the Ordo Crucis Incendio. But it is said that the most sensitive assassinations, such as the one that was performed tonight, are always commanded by a single man who is the order's secret leader."

A pounding noise made me jerk my head up. Barbade had taken his wooden clog from under the table and was pounding it against the rough wood of the tabletop for attention. "Comrades!" he shouted. "The lady hasn't come to us to listen to us dreaming about assassinating the man! We all know that it has been attempted many times, with no success."

"Unfortunately," Armand quickly inserted, standing to take the floor before anyone else could respond, "our friend Barbade is right. The question is not how to track down this Onça do Papa in his lair and eliminate him, but how to protect this daughter of Hermes Tiago who sits here with us tonight. Her noble father has written to warn that she is in immediate danger, and she has this very night walked in the shadow of death."

"Where are you living, Mademoiselle Sarmentos?" Libreterre

asked from the head of the table. In the ensuing silence, all heads turned to me for the first time.

"I am living at the artists' residence called La Ruche, in the Dantzig Passage."

There was a moment of surprised silence, followed by renewed murmuring of a louder and perhaps more hostile nature. I made out phrases such as, "bourgeois flunkies," and "self-indulgent aestheticists," and "decadent bohemians."

Then Thierry stood up, so abruptly that all eyes turned to him. The way to get the floor in this assembly seemed to be by surprising everyone through some dramatic gesture. He said, "Comrade Vladimir Lenin of the supreme people's Bolshevik revolution has his residence in that building." He threw his hand in the air and pointed a shaking finger at the stone ceiling. "Even if that place housed a thousand parasitic artists for a thousand years, it is still a sacred edifice for giving shelter to that living martyr of the people!"

Again, after a moment of thoughtful silence, each of them turned to his neighbor, and the room was filled with murmured comments. "Revolutionary throwback," "pathetic loser," "political has-been."

Armand took his feet amidst this chaos, and very purposefully brought up his hand and placed it gently on my shoulder. This violation of my personal space, which didn't particularly bother me, had the same galvanizing effect upon the room as the pounding of wooden shoes, and suddenly everyone became silent.

"There is only one question," Armand said clearly, just loud enough to make his words fill the room completely. "Do the Souris Trempés have enough backbone to protect this lady—this key personage of tomorrow's Portuguese Republic—or do we not? That is the question, comrades. And how do you answer?"

Although it may seem sad, in retrospect, to think that the only protection available to me was that roomful of rebels, nonetheless I must admit I fairly melted to see how this brief speech of Armand's brought the men there entirely around to my protection. All conversation for the next half hour, with only a few brief digressions, focused upon the question of how it would be possible, in a building as utterly unfortress-like as La Ruche, to safely house a young woman who might conceivably be the target of a terrifying and efficient assassin.

It was decided unanimously (and thus without encountering the embarrassing question of whether voting was or was not a valid method of settling disputes) that the Souris Trempés would place a rotating guard, around the clock, outside my humble building in the hope of catching Onça do Papa red-handed. During one of the more chaotic moments of this long conversation, when it seemed no one was listening, I drew Armand close and whispered in his ear, "But only consider! Many of these men here, if they are seen lurking in the shadows even in *my* neighborhood, they shall be arrested immediately!"

Armand assured me in a low tone, "Leave that to us, Leaozinha. Evading the arbitrary persecution of the law is our best-honed skill. I assure you that some of the men here have been slipping out of the hands of the gendarmes since long before you were born."

Chapter Twelve

It was nearly dawn by the time I finally came home to my studio, dragging my tired feet up the stairs. Armand and Paulo had accompanied me, and Armand, who might well have been as tired as I, did a fine job of keeping up my spirits during the long walk across the city. He told me some very entertaining stories of the past exploits of the Souris Trempés, some of which were so outrageous that I'm sure they were made up on the spot in order to amuse me.

I awakened in the early afternoon and Irène had kindly left me to sleep. The heavy drapes were drawn, and upon first opening my eyes I was quite disoriented, and couldn't tell if it was day or night. Then, a slight clattering noise coming through the thin wall informed me that Irène was making tea for Moishe next door, in his studio. I had slept fitfully, often waking from nightmares in which I tried to save poor Professor Almeida from the assassin.

Still rather shaken from the previous night's events, I wandered over to the washstand and splashed my face. While I was dressing, I remembered with some alarm that the copper tube—that mysterious object that had apparently been worth Professor Almeida's life—was still buried under the hedge in the backyard. I hurried downstairs and out the front door. I half expected to see Armand and Paulo marching around the premises, but instead I saw only a man seated under one of the chestnut trees, keeping well out of sight of the street, with a woolen blanket pulled over his knees. He greeted me with a small wave, and I realized that it was Barbade, presumably taking his turn at guard duty.

I hurried around to the back, and found the tube exactly where I had left it. I pulled it out from under the roots and carried it inside.

Irène heard me coming up the stairs, and looked out from Moishe's studio. "Good morning," she greeted me cheerfully. "You must have had a late night! But you're just in time for some Russian tea and sugar, if you'd care for some. What is that thing you're carrying?"

I paused for a moment. Then I made up my mind, on the spot, to share my secret with Irène. I had never stopped worrying that I was placing her in danger by continuing to live as her roommate, and so I felt that she had the right to be informed of the previous night's alarming developments.

Moishe's studio now contained three cane chairs and a little round table. Irène had insisted on buying these for him, once it became clear that we'd be spending a great deal of time there, lingering over meals. When I came in, Moishe was seated on one of these chairs before his easel in his usual attitude, clutching a handful of brushes loaded with various colors of paint in his left hand, while his right hand delicately held a long brush with a bit of yellow paint poised an inch or so from the surface of a large, half-completed canvas. Moishe often puzzled for many minutes before he would apply a particular daub of paint to one of his pictures. I had been in the room for a little while already when he abruptly came out of his trance, noticed that I was there, then jumped up and bowed politely. Then he forgot about me again and went back to his work.

"Is it some sort of container?" Irène asked, glancing at the copper tube while pouring me a cup of tea from the little pot that was serving as her samovar.

"I'm assuming as much," I told her. "But its contents are as much a mystery to me as they are to you." I sat down and quickly recounted the details of my night's adventures.

By the end of the story, Irène's eyes were fairly starting out of her head. Moishe had lowered his brush, and he too seemed to have become engrossed in the story. Noticing this, I had spoken very slowly, for his sake. His competence with French was improving by the day, but his ear was still far from tuned to the language.

"A *murder!*" Irène marveled. "You're so brave! I'm sure I should have fainted."

"I nearly did," I confessed. "It was a terrifying sight. And it took all my courage to collect *this* strange item, as the professor had requested of me."

"Wait a moment, I think I read about the professor's murder in Le Figaro. I just bought the afternoon edition." She pattered next door and came back with the newspaper.

Sure enough, at the bottom of the front page was an article saying he had been murdered outside his home. I read through a couple of times and there was no mention of the gruesome murder weapon, nor any indication as to why.

"And does this mean that one of Armand's friends is outside, right now? Guarding the building? Oh, how romantic!" Irène had yet to meet Armand, but naturally I had described him to her on more than one occasion.

"May I open this?" Moishe asked, with his usual careful enunciation.

"Yes," I told him. "But if there is something dangerous inside— some message perhaps—then we must all three of us swear to keep it as our secret."

I repeated this entreaty in various wordings, to make quite certain that Moishe knew what I was asking of him. He and Irène readily promised to keep the secret, if it turned out there was one.

Moishe pried one of the crimped ends of the copper pipe open with the back of an iron spoon and rounded the opening by holding it against the floor and pounding at its edge, using the heel of an old boot as a mallet. Then he peered inside, inserted two of his delicate fingers, and drew out a roll of canvas.

It was a painting! Irène and I quickly cleared the table so that Moishe could unroll it on a flat surface. Even while it was still rolled tight, I could tell that it had been roughly pried loose from its frame, because the edges of the canvas were frayed and still showed signs of the regularly spaced holes that had been made when it was tacked with brass nails to its stretchers. The violence with which it had been unframed suggested that it might be a stolen artwork.

When the thing was unfurled, all of us leaned over the table to examine it. Then, just as quickly, all three of us recoiled back with exclamations of shock and disgust, as we realized what sort of scene we were looking at.

The image showed a festive occasion outdoors, with pleasant, comfortable summer lighting under a rich blue sky, depicted in a Rococo style. Beautifully ornate walnut bleachers, such as those that are erected for royalty to observe a horse race or other sporting event, filled nearly half the canvas. The bleachers were populated with careful portraits of long-dead notables of Portugal's church and state, most of whom I could easily identify by name. All of them were dressed in their finest outdoor apparel and wore pleasant, well-fed expressions that harmonized with the jaunty scenario and cheerful color scheme. The top tier of the bleacher was devoted to a pair of spacious thrones, inhabited by the familiar figures of Portugal's King João V and, upon a somewhat taller throne, Pope Clement XI. Given the monarch's apparent age, I immediately guessed the painting to be set in 1720, give or take a few years. I don't know if the pope ever actually visited the court of João V, and I suspect this was a conceit on the artist's part.

The cheerful nobles were looking down over an arena in which dozens of nearly naked men, chained tightly to large stakes, were being burned to death. A number of thoughtful-looking soldiers and workmen strolled about the arena, banking the flames around the feet of the condemned or adding sticks and kindling to keep the fires burning steadily. With the good taste that marked the classic works of the time, the artist had chosen to place patient, stoic expressions upon the faces of the burning men, and to depict the skin of their limbs as uncorrupted—as if the painting had captured the moment when the spectacle began, and the flesh had not yet begun to cook.

Irène turned quickly away and began to weep quietly. I placed a comforting hand on her shoulder, but I continued to stare at the image of the auto-da-fé with the same transfixed horror with which one might regard a poisonous reptile that one had just found under an overturned stone. At some point, I happened to glance at Moishe. To my surprise, he looked furious, with his cheeks bright red and his small hands clenched into whitened fists. It was later that someone, perhaps Angelina, would tell me about the atrocities of the Tsar's ongoing pogroms against the rural Jews of Russia. The truth was that I rarely even thought of Moishe as Jewish, though he looked as Jewish as could be. He was so completely an artist that it was hard to remember he had other qualities as well.

"We'd better put it away again," I said grimly.

Irène turned around and faced the table again, patting at her eyes with a little handkerchief. "No, I'm all right," she said bravely. "It was just a shock. It is so . . . so horrible! I must seem very silly to you. But honestly, I've never seen anything like that. I suppose I am . . . sheltered."

"They are *Jews*," Moishe said, his nostrils flaring.

I nodded and reached out to touch his arm gently. Although there were many of these mass burnings during the high years of the Inquisition in Portugal, and all sorts of heretics were put to the stake, I knew that by the eighteenth century the effort had become highly focused on the elimination of Jews who had been accused of flaunting their mandatory conversions to Christianity.

"It's unsigned. Where do you suppose it comes from", Irène said in a flat tone.

"I suspect it is from the school of Ouro y Colón," I said after examining it for a while.

"How can you tell?"

"Look at the playful quality of the foliage and the way the painter has added small flowering shrubs in unlikely places. Over here, by the arena gates . . . and here, in the shadow of the bleachers. And see, this odd little blue basilisk, sunning itself on this rock? Little bits of graphic fancy like this are typical of the pastoral schools of northern Portugal in the early eighteenth century. Then also, the heavy use of cerulean blues in the clouds." I was reveling in the opportunity to at last be more expert in a subject than Irène, but she still managed to surprise me with her knowledge.

"These webs of surface cracks over the earth-toned shadows," she said, pointing to a corner of the painting, "if I recall correctly that means the varnish was applied a few months too early, while the deeper layers of paint were still curing?"

"Indeed," I agreed. "So it was definitely painted by Javier de Ouro y Colón, or by someone in his workshop."

"But what do you suppose all these odd little symbols mean?"

We gathered around the table and looked where she was pointing. The wall that enclosed the ghastly arena was covered densely in small symbols that I had taken as merely ornamental. They were quite regularly spaced, arranged in twelve rows that passed along the full length of visible wall, which is to say over half the width of the painting. There must have been hundreds of them, and upon close inspection there seemed to be very little repetition among them.

"Some kind of heraldry," I proposed.

"None that I have ever seen," Irène replied.

"This school of painting was much given to fanciful and arbitrary ornamentation?" I reminded her.

"These symbols don't strike me as fanciful," Irène said stubbornly. "They strike me as odd."

There wasn't much arguing with that. The more I examined them, the odder they seemed. Now that I was inspecting them closely, I could see that many of them were, in fact, repeated in various places, some of them many times. But there was no pattern that I could discern in the repetition.

"I think they are alchemical," I said, pointing to one symbol I recognized.

"Some of them are," Irène said. Her voice was just a bit patronizing, as though she expected that all of us had perceived *that* much at a glance. "This one, for example, and these two over here. Others are astrological, such as these, and this one over here is the Phoenician letter *sadhe*. The question is, what are all the others?"

At length, she raised her head and, in her bright, piping voice, told us, "This is some sort of cipher, in my estimation. Very likely it is unbreakable, if one does not possess the key."

Chapter Thirteen

ince I had already missed breakfast, I went out with Irène for lunch. I spoke excitedly with her about the alarming developments of the past day, while she ate and ate and ate. I was so engrossed in my babblings that I barely remembered to pick up a baguette and an orange on the way home, as offerings to my brave protector from the Souris Trempés.

We found Barbade napping under the tree when we got home, which wasn't terribly reassuring. I tucked the food into the blanket on his lap so that he might find it when he awakened.

Back in our studio, we looked at the painting again and pondered together the question of where it should be stored. I had it laid out on my cot, and as I gazed at it I was suddenly struck with an inspiration.

"Perhaps the symbols have only just been added on!" I exclaimed. "Even though the painting is two centuries old, the enciphered message might have been written onto its surface just last week, or last month."

"I believe that to be impossible," Irène replied. "You see that the varnish covers the symbols, as it does the rest of the paint." Nonetheless, she came over and had another look, and eventually she grudgingly admitted, "I suppose it is *conceivable* that a new layer of varnish has been added, to conceal the modification. Come, help me carry it into the light."

We stretched it across Irène's worktable near the window. She unscrewed the end cap from the brass body of her little telescope and removed the large, convex lens to use as a magnifying glass.

Then she spent fifteen minutes examining the surface of the painting with great care.

She set her lens down on a folded cloth and turned to me. "I suspect that you're right, Florbela. There is a layer of varnish that is flaking off the surface of this painting, and it seems to me to be of a better grade than that beneath. Still, if this canvas has been modified, it did not occur last week, nor even a month ago. The top varnish is brittle and yellowed, and I would guess it has been there for many, many years."

We rolled the ugly thing up then, and shoved it back into its tube.

"You should store it next door, in Moishe's studio," Irène proposed.

I was a bit shocked at the suggestion. "Irène! I don't wish to endanger Moishe. I feel guilty enough endangering you."

"Moishe will be in no danger whatsoever. The painting can be well hidden, and we shall tell no one where it is. Also, we shall swear Moishe to secrecy. If ever a thief comes searching for it, he may search our studio to his heart's content, and never find it. To find it in Moishe's studio, he would have to search the entire building!"

What she said made sense, so after some deliberation I agreed that we should take the painting next door. It took some time to get our idea across to Moishe, but when he understood what we were asking of him, he immediately agreed. We slid the copper tube up into the rafters above his ceiling, through a loose tile. Then we swore him to secrecy and let him get back to work.

I spent a couple of hours painting that afternoon, but my heart wasn't in it. I finally retired onto one of the seductively comfortable silk-upholstered wingback chairs that Irène had purchased and spent the early evening curled there, reading one of her books.

That was the night I had promised to dine with Brian Torrence Grimm. Since I was bored and unoccupied, I suppose I spent an hour or more primping and selecting clothes before the mirror. Naturally, that meant that when eight o'clock finally rolled around, I wasn't even *nearly* ready to go out and ended up rushing to get dressed at the last minute.

"Florbela, you look so beautiful," Irène said when I finally finished.

"You are sweet," I said and gave her a kiss on the forehead.

Brian had warned me that he was going to show up in his carriage, but I had been expecting a small cabriolet with a hired driver sitting on the roof. Instead, I stepped outside into the evening air to find him waiting in a handsome black barouche, with the driver's seat way up in front behind two lovely white stallions. To my relief, Brian was dressed exactly correctly: in a suit that was elegant and well tailored, but not so expensive as to make me feel underdressed. I had no doubt that he had some suits in his wardrobe that were worth more than my year's expenses. Brian stared at me for a moment and then said, "Senhorita Sarmentos, it's delightful to see you again." He stood beside the step to help me up, extending a gentle hand that was about as large as both of mine put together.

It had been several years since I had been in circumstances that would allow me to settle back on soft leather upholstery under the broad canopy of a fine carriage and watch the city roll by. But it is amazing how quickly one can adapt to circumstances like those! By the time we reached the lights and bustle of the Fifth District, I'm sure I was gazing out at the pedestrians with the nonchalant elegance of a noblewoman, having consigned my youthful La Ruche period to the distant past of ten minutes ago.

Brian was charming company. I never would have guessed it, from his rather formal and lofty presence back in his office at the embassy, but he managed to be precisely formal and hilariously funny at the same time, which is a difficult balancing act. His sense of humor only emerged after I began insisting that he speak in English, a language in which I had rarely had opportunity to indulge since leaving England two years before. The French language simply doesn't lend itself well to the English sense of humor, and I suppose the opposite is also true. Even a bawdy circus clown in England would probably tell stories too dry to draw a laugh from a jaded Parisian audience.

We dined at La Tour d'Argent, spiraling up its seemingly endless red-carpeted stairwell to the lofty dining room.

"This is a restaurant where you must prove yourself by trial before they will give up their food to you," Brian quipped as I struggled up the last few steps. "Though I understand they have a dumbwaiter in the back, to haul up the serious gourmands."

That evening was the first time in my adult life that I ever ate in truly elegant circumstances. Of course, as a child in Lisbon, I had dined that way: at a table covered in lace and linen, carefully arrayed with fine china and nine pieces of silver and three crystal glasses at each setting, with formally dressed waiters hovering a step behind one's elbows at all times. But I felt very different now than I had as a child. I had not been dragged by grown-ups into that chamber of elegant ritual; I had arrived.

We had the *caneton à la presse*, the pressed duck for which the restaurant is justly famous, together with an 1896 Pinot Noir from the Côte-d'Or. Brian kept up a patter throughout the first three courses that was so funny and yet so precisely correct for the circumstances that I was in a state of continuous delight. I don't know when I started calling him by his first name, but certainly well before dessert. And whenever our eyes would meet, I could tell that he too was having a great good time, which of course I took as a high compliment.

"You haven't eaten here before," Brian said, asking the question in the form of an observation.

"Oh no. The only fine place I have dined in Paris, up until now, is Maxim's. I was only a girl, then."

"Ah, but Maxim's!"

I smiled sadly, remembering my trip to Paris with Mother many years before. "My mother took me. She was good friends with a man who kept a table permanently reserved there. He dined at Maxim's at least once a day, I believe."

He blinked at me, astonished. "But that could only be . . . the aviator, Santos-Dumont!"

I nodded. "Mother was quite an avid believer in flying

machines. I feel that they were the only thing in this world that she envied of men."

Brian smiled tentatively. "Ah . . . but you say she *was* avid . . . may I ask then, is she . . .?"

"Mother was taken by consumption, five years ago."

"I am so sorry."

"Thank you," I murmured. "It took me a long time to recover. You see, Mother and I were very close." I picked up my knife and fork, and ate another mouthful as I recalled those painful memories. My mother was diagnosed while I was at boarding school in England. I briefly returned home to Portugal but she had already been admitted to a sanatorium and I was not allowed to visit her.

I finished my mouthful and forced myself to smile. I said, "But it is long past, so let us speak of happier things."

After a tactful pause, Brian noted, "He is still there, if you would care to meet him. Your mother's friend, Monsieur Santos-Dumont. He still keeps his table at Maxim's."

"Really! And does he still fly dirigibles over the city streets, with mobs cheering below him?"

"He has moved on from those days. Now it is aeroplanes."

"Aeroplanes! Really, what a world."

Just then another course arrived, interrupting us at this fortunately cheerful juncture. We ate in silence for some minutes, and then Brian sat back from his plate and gestured to the waiter to top up my glass. "Now then," he said. "This is all so jolly that I hate to bring up matters of a practical nature."

Please don't, I thought.

He turned those brilliant blue eyes of his at me and said, "I shall try to keep this brief, Florbela. I have made inquiries into the conditions and circumstances of your father but without success." Then he added, "I will continue to purse diplomatic channels through my contacts. But since our last meeting, I have had some notable concerns for your safety. May I ask you, then, if *you've* had any further word from your father or his associates?"

And there it was. The question was so direct that I could

hardly evade it and remain honest. Besides, my father had effectively told me to place some trust in this man.

Though it took all the strength of my will not to cry as I told him about Professor Almeida I recounted everything to him. The murder that I had witnessed, just twenty-four hours before; the suspicious coincidence of my scheduled meeting with Professor Almeida and his death at the same hour; his dying request that I should collect the strange copper package from beneath his bench; the even stranger painting that it proved to contain; and finally, the vow taken by the Souris Trempés to stand guard over my home.

Predictably, this last part rankled him visibly. "Are you sure you want *them* hovering about your neighborhood, night and day?" he asked in a rather stiff tone.

I was careful to keep control of my temper this time. "I admit that I don't know the men of the Souris Trempés very well," I said, matching his stiffness with my own. "But then, Brian, I suppose that I know them as well as I know you. It continues to be my opinion that you dismiss them too categorically, and overlook their redeeming features."

He smirked a little and bit back a reply. This was fortunate, as it probably would have been quite witty, but would have tempted me to admonish him more firmly. After a moment, he straightened his features and said, "So how many people know of the events of that night? Whom have you told?"

When I explained, he asked "You didn't go to the police or the gendarmes?"

"No, Armand said it was likely the . . . *that order* has spies who may be trying to identify the recipient of the painting."

"Yes, indeed. Now, this painting. You still have it in your possession?"

"I do."

"Then I should very much like to see it, if you would permit me."

I turned away from him and gazed out through the broad windows at the sparkling vista of Île Saint-Louis, across a channel of the Seine. Long river barges passed in stately silence under the stone arch of the Tournelle Bridge, beneath our window. But even indoors and on the third floor, one could hear the occasional muffled roaring of some gigantic motorcar passing along the street below.

"I'm afraid that transporting it to your office might pose me some real inconvenience," I told him.

"Oh no!" He started a bit, and his fingers touched mine for a moment as if to restrain me from such brash action. "Let me beseech you not to carry the piece out onto the street. I am assuming that you have it concealed somewhere safe? Good! The less it is exposed, and the fewer who know of it, the better. With your permission, I will come to your premises and examine it personally on Tuesday. I only regret that I cannot come sooner."

I was about to raise an objection, as a matter of propriety, to the notion of an unescorted bachelor visiting me at my private room. But what was the point? With characters as disreputable as Diego Rivera and Amedeo Modigliani barging in at all hours without even bothering to knock, the only thing that preserved my reputation from ruin was Paris's legendary tolerance and willingness to look the other way.

So we agreed that he should visit on Tuesday evening, and our conversation turned thankfully back to less weighty topics. My mood quickly recovered and elevated through dessert, then the cheese, then the coffee, then a lovely glass of port that made me both homesick for Lisbon and a little bit giggly.

During the ride home, Brian did a great deal of staring at me, and he also made a conspicuous effort to guide his smooth and clever conversational skills toward matters romantic.

"Florbela," he said at one point, "I have not taken so much delight in a woman's company in many years. In fact I had almost lost hope of doing so . . . until tonight."

"It it has been a fine evening for me too, thank you Brian," I conceded, and then turned to practical discussion. "I particularly loved that marvelous dessert—what was it called again—oh yes, Soufflé Rothschild. Do you think it really did have gold leaf in it?"

"Indeed, I believe they use Goldwasser."

The man impressed me yet again, by working the conversation back around to that topic *exactly* the right number of times, before tacitly acknowledging that I was not ready to speak of such things, and giving it up. If he had continued in that manner any longer, I would likely have become irritated; but on the other hand, naturally, if he had given up any easier, then my feelings might have been wounded.

As he helped me down the steps of his carriage onto the rough cobbles beside the Dantzig Passage, our eyes met, and there was a sort of spark, an electricity in the blue of his knowing eyes that made my heart leap in my chest.

I gave him my hand and said, "I had a lovely evening Brian, thank you."

He smiled, then turned and retreated under the shadow of the leather canopy.

"Until Tuesday, senhorita," he said. His driver whipped up the horses, and the barouche pulled away and headed quickly back toward the wealthier quarters of the city.

As I approached the front door, I faintly heard the strains of Armand's old Spanish guitar coming from around the corner of the building. I knew that he must be sitting in the yard below my window. I stood listening for a while, and was pleased to hear that his guitar had six strings now, and that his fingers seemed to be learning how to find a melody. I almost went around to speak with him, but somehow I couldn't, not right then. So I made my way quietly up the steps and slipped into my studio, carefully locking the door behind me. I found Irène at home as usual, working on her little sculpture with great concentration. She barely glanced up at me when I bid her good night.

I lay there in the mingled light of lamp and moon for a long time, surrounded by the familiar smell of the molten wax and the clumsy airs of ancient ballads wafting sadly in through the open window. It had been a grand night for me, and I was too excited to sleep.

Chapter Fourteen

Saturday was a very easy day. In fact, I think I forced it to be easy—to be a plain, normal day. I spent the early morning painting, and at last made some real progress on my still life of wildflowers and wine bottles. Then I went out with Angelina, shopping for groceries and other little things at the myriad of tiny stores that lined the Rue de la Convention. I bought a newspaper and tried to find news of the events in Portugal. The few articles did not give me much cause for optimism. In fact Prime Minister de Sousa had recently warned that a coups d'état was imminent.

It rained in the afternoon, so Angelina joined Irène and me for our usual afternoon tea in Moishe's room. Moishe had only been in town for about a week now, and he was already completing his third canvas. I envied his productivity, but I was also very glad for it. I had finally come around to adoring Moishe's beautiful artworks like everyone else, though I still couldn't see *why* we all found them so beautiful. Perhaps it was only that he seemed so unfettered—he simply painted any way he pleased. Everyone spoke a lot about "freedom," but our lack of freedom wasn't only due to tyrants and social strictures and poverty. Whenever he had a brush in his hand, Moishe's soul was already freer than the rest of us would *ever* become.

That was also the morning that I found the announcement of Professor Almeida's funeral in the newspaper. It would be the next day, at a large cemetery not far from the city. My heart was heavy as I explained to Irène that I planned to attend the funeral, as a representative of my family.

"Oh, Florbela," she said in a serious tone, "that sounds like a very bad idea. Surely if some organization was watching the family they would send spies to the professor's funeral to see who attends."

This thought hadn't even crossed my mind. I felt very foolish for even thinking of attending, once the danger had been pointed out to me.

"Of course, you're right—thank you." I said glumly and gave her a hug.

The following day I was painting once again but couldn't concentrate. My mind was distracted by thoughts of Professor Almeida's funeral and I recalled the last funeral I attended—that of my dear mother five years before. I still felt the loss acutely, particularly as I was never able to say goodbye in person. I wrote to her during her confinement but I never saw her after she became ill. I wondered how Mrs. Almeida must be feeling and couldn't help wondering whether the professor's death had anything to do with me.

It was during one of these depressing diversions from my canvas that I heard the boisterous voices of Amedeo and Diego coming up the stairs, and others with them. I was in no mood for empty festivities, being determined to work at my painting until it was done. But I was certainly surprised when the chattering and the clumping of boot heels passed right by my door, heading for Moishe's room.

This was strikingly unusual, as Amedeo and Diego no longer went into Moishe's room unless Irène and I were there. I actually think they found the little fellow intimidating. After a while, my curiosity got the better of me, so I splashed my face with water, patted it with a towel, then went out into the hall to have a peek into the studio next door.

The first person I saw there was Irène. She rushed over to the door to greet me, shouldering her way among the others. There was a pretty good-sized mob of people in there.

"There she is!" she cried out, her voice unusually effusive. "Mr. Apollinaire, this is my roommate, Florbela Sarmentos. She is also a painter. She is undiscovered, but of most notable talent." I had to cover my mouth to hide my amusement when I heard this, since Irène had never seen even one finished work by my hand.

The others in the room were Moishe, Angelina, Amedeo and Diego, plus a short, broad-shouldered man of about thirty with dark hair and a long, pointy chin. This man glanced my way with sly, amused-looking eyes, seemed to decide that I was worth a moment's digression, and stalked slowly over to the door.

"I am enchanted to meet you mademoiselle," he said. He took my fingers, bowed, and kissed my fingertips with greatly exaggerated formality.

"It's a pleasure to meet you, Mr. Apollinaire."

"You may call me Willie," he proposed, pronouncing the W hard, as if it were a V. His accent was mildly Italian. "The pleasure is entirely mine. I cannot tell you how I enjoy meeting new . . . talent."

I had, of course, heard of Guillaume Apollinaire. It would scarcely have been possible to have lived among the young artists of Paris for an entire week without hearing of him. Apollinaire was a legendary kingmaker among the young Parisian artists. He was a clever, even brilliant, critic who was known for his spectacular eye for spotting new talent. He was also a social gadabout who had the remarkable ability to get along not only with the half-mad people who were making all the interesting art, but also with the wealthy people who were buying it. Knowing all this, I was surprised indeed to be confronted with the man's actual presence, unannounced and practically in my own home.

"Is that what brings you to La Ruche, Mr. Apollinaire?" I asked. "Searching for new talent?"

"He came here to drink our wine!" Diego howled, in mock outrage. "Success hasn't changed him a bit. He still has the nose of a bloodhound for an open bottle."

"You see, ladies?" Amedeo put in. "The valuable skills that one acquires at La Ruche shall never desert one."

Mr. Apollinaire was quietly glowing under this affectionate ribbing, though he maintained an aloof look, affecting not to realize that the words referred to him.

I asked, "Did you once live in this building, then?" Now I thought that I might vaguely remember having heard something of the sort.

"I was one of the first tenants," he told me. "On this floor, too, just around the other side. I may as well warn you that, come August, the heat up here is unbearable."

Then, to my astonishment, Irène began chattering to him at high speed in a language I couldn't even identify. He chuckled a little and replied to her in the same tongue, and fluently. She began to laugh quite merrily, so much so that she put her hands over her mouth.

"I asked him in jest if he could arrange to have all of our works shown in the Louvre," she told me. "And he said that it would be a bad idea, as he intends to burn it down someday."

"Burn down the Louvre?"

"Yes," Mr. Apollinaire answered, raising two fingers pontifically. "It is the only noble way to herald the new era of art, don't you agree? It shall be like storming the Bastille, but much more satisfying. I consider it my sacred duty. Besides, no one goes in there but foreigners anymore. And of course, the very old, who drag themselves in there to die."

Irène again said something in the language I couldn't identify. She caught me staring and told me, "Willie's mother is Polish! His real name is Wilhelm Kostrowicki."

My head was spinning a bit by this point. "I . . . I'm sorry, but I don't think I can say that name. May I continue to call you Mr. Apollinaire?"

"Willie," he repeated.

"But *you*, Irène! Where on earth did you learn Polish?"

"My mother is Polish, too," she replied. Every day, it seemed, there was some new surprise from Irène. I had never met a person so prone to secrets.

"He's going to start painting again," Amedeo warned us all, from his position behind Moishe's chair. Poor Moishe looked quite overwhelmed at all of this loud and uninvited activity in his studio, and indeed he seemed to be drifting back into his painterly trance, staring at the canvas with brush poised and gradually forgetting about the rest of us.

"What, shamelessly creating art, before our very eyes? We can't have that," Willie said. He stepped over toward the window to place himself in front of the easel, for his first look at Moishe's work. Angelina said something to Moishe in Russian, and Moishe seemed to come to his senses, looked around with a startled expression, then reluctantly backed away from the canvas.

I, of course, had already seen this near-completed picture, so I knew it to be a complex scene depicting the village or *shtetl* where Moishe had grown up. Some of the figures were inexplicably flying around overhead like ghosts or angels, and there was an upside-down cow. There was also a lot of pink and ultramarine and viridian, placed according to a logic that only Moishe could really understand. It was his biggest painting so far, and his most ambitious. I liked it, myself, but the excesses of the composition seemed to me so unjustifiable that I was afraid it would be badly received by others. I rather imagined that people were soon going to become bored with all this wild and senseless liberty, and move on. But that, of course, would never happen—not to Moishe.

Willie stopped with his back to the window and stared hard at the canvas. He began making odd choking noises, like a cat trying to disgorge a ball of hair. I had seen several people go through stunned first impressions of Moishe's artworks by now, so I took all this in stride. But in this case, there was more to the matter. Willie was in the throes of a visceral process that was more or less unique to himself: he was struggling literally to *cough up* the words to describe what he was seeing.

Out of his mouth came the word, "Sur-natural!" Then he took a deep breath, as if producing this word had cost him a fair amount of effort. I remember thinking that he looked as if the appearance of the new word had surprised him as much as anyone else in the room.

That done, he pried his gaze away from the painting momentarily to look around at the rest of us with a little smile, blinking rapidly, to see what we thought of his word. We all of us spoke up quickly and said that it was pretty good, which was true. Amedeo and Angelina in particular praised Willie up and down for the clever wordplay. As it turned out, we would all repeat the word a lot, and so it would end up making the rounds, spreading around the Left Bank in the way these things do, and over the coming months and years any number of painters would find themselves called ur-natural by critics and admirers at one time or another.

The term sur-natural was eventually forgotten when Willie coughed up the even better word "surreal," a few years later, describing someone else's paintings. *That* word was so well-freighted that it eventually trickled out from the Sixth to spread throughout France, and eventually into all the languages of Europe. But sur-natural was not a bad first effort, and we certainly all agreed that it described Moishe's paintings well enough.

"He needs to sell something," Diego said firmly. "He lives on nothing but air, like a sort of plant."

"It's true," Amedeo confirmed. "I have even seen him refuse free wine, the artist's staple food." He switched to Italian, and I followed along with some difficulty. "How can any man live like that? He is like a machine that turns oxygen into genius. But you listen to me, if this amazing little monkey starves to death up in this atelier, the whole world is going to collapse under the weight of its shame." He placed his hand on Moishe's fluffy head as he said this last sentence, an ignominy that Moishe bore with good-natured stoicism.

Willie shrugged, as if these problems were almost too trivial to warrant discussion. "Take him to the Steins'."

"He won't go!" Irène, Amedeo and I all said, in chorus.

Willie looked stunned at this news. "He won't? Why on earth not?"

There was a pause as all of us tactfully withheld our various opinions and explanations, allowing Willie a few moments to look around the studio and draw his own conclusions. He drew them readily enough.

"Let us speak somewhere else," he said abruptly, in Italian.

"These ladies share the studio next door," Amedeo replied, also in Italian. He looked at me and added, "*Con il suo permesso.*"

"*Certamente,*" I managed to say, after a moment's mental struggle to recover the proper reply. And with that we all ambled over to Irène's and my studio. I had a quick glance at Moishe as I was leaving, but if he wondered where we were going or why, he gave no indication. He was already leaning in toward his canvas again, brush poised.

Chapter Fifteen

Willie had a good laugh when he saw the way Irène and I were living. I must admit that the contrast between our home and the abject austerity of Moishe's studio was quite a shock to the eye. Willie suggested that perhaps we could get Gertrude Stein to come and visit *us*, instead of the other way around. Diego snorted mightily at that suggestion, and proposed that it would probably be easier to get her to leap over the Himalayas and have a tour of the painting studios of China. Meanwhile, Irène and I fussed about, pulling up chairs and trying to make our guests comfortable.

"So. He doesn't wish to be corrupted," Willie proposed, looking slowly into each of our faces, to confirm his theory.

"Well . . . I think the word 'corrupted' has such a negative connotation," Amedeo objected easily. "I'm sure the little fellow doesn't think that we would take him anywhere that was bad for his spiritual or mental health."

Willie responded with a wicked smile, so wicked that I was a little bit shocked. "No," he agreed. "How could he be so foolish as to imagine anything of the kind?"

"But the *Steins'*!" Diego interjected. "There is nothing to corrupt anyone at the Steins'. Unless you count success and money, that is. But why did he come to Paris, if he doesn't want to succeed?"

"There's Pablo," Amedeo pointed out, in a tone that suggested he regretted the necessity of making a contrary observation. "He really is a corrupting influence. I think anyone would agree. And he's *always* there."

"Plus one might see you there," Diego added.

"Or you," Amedeo promptly countered, holding up three fingers to give the tally so far.

"Plus also," Willie put in, "there are Leo and Gertrude Stein themselves. And, often, myself and a number of other shockingly bad influences. And then, of course, there are the *ladies* at these affairs."

A small groan emerged from everyone in the room, except Irène and myself, who were still naive in these matters.

Willie pursed his lips thoughtfully and brought his fingertips together in the delicate manner of a man who is plotting something subtle. "Hmm. Do you imagine that those ladies might be brought to bear as an incentive? Are they necessarily detrimental to the cause?"

A much louder groan emerged, by way of response.

Willie waved his hands around in frustration. "Very well, never mind then! The man's heart is perhaps already spoken for?"

Diego threw his head back and whimpered at the ceiling, "Bella!"

"Enough," Willie said in distaste. "I don't need to know the details. But listen to me, I'm quite serious. The Steins will not come here. I don't mind carrying some of his canvases to their salon, if need be, but you understand that they will want to *meet* him before they will open their purses to him."

Irène was on the edge of her chair, I noticed. She seemed nearly distraught at these complications. "Well, they *must* meet him! Of course they would love him. How could they not?"

Willie nodded, as if that went without saying. Then he looked at me. "You will bring him."

"I?"

"Both of you. He trusts you, does he not? So there, do you see? If you tell him that *you* are going, and tell him that he must go with you, then he will go. Very simple! Modigliani, listen here. On Saturday the Steins will have their usual salon. I shall arrange invitations."

"Don't bother! The old cow won't have me in her house

anymore, not since I vomited on her hideous little Braque canvas."

"It is a *glorious* little Braque canvas," Willie corrected him gently. "I selected it for her. But a truly strong composition like that one can only be improved by sincerely expressive reactions—and that is precisely what you gave it."

"I suppose I did. That, and some questionable fish I had eaten at lunch."

"At any rate, Amedeo, I was not proposing to arrange an invitation for you, but for your charming neighbors here, and for their shy friend next door."

"Then why are you speaking to me? Tell them!"

"Because, you nitwit, if I asked Mademoiselle Langevin, she would politely refuse me, no matter how I phrased the invitation. And if I ask . . . the beautiful Spaniard," he said, clearly forgetting my name.

"Senhorita Sarmentos," Amedeo inserted.

Willie nodded and continued, "She will certainly say no unless Mademoiselle Langevin says yes. In short, I can obtain three invitations, but I cannot actually invite anyone. You, on the other hand, cannot go, but you can invite them, and if you handle the matter tactfully then I suspect they will say yes."

"I'm Portuguese," I corrected him. I was at an absolute loss, whether to be amused or offended.

"A thousand pardons."

Amedeo actually looked like he was working himself up to apply all the charm at his disposal, which could be considerable, to carry out Willie's wishes. I held up a hand to prevent him.

"Never mind. We will go," I said firmly. "Irène?"

She looked uncertain. "Who shall be there?"

Willie told her quickly, "I will be there. Other than myself and your roommate and your talented neighbor, I'm afraid that you are unlikely to recognize anyone. But I promise you it will be a small affair—a drawing room affair. And quiet. The Steins are Americans, it's true, but they are not without civility."

"I think we have to do this," I told Irène. "Moishe will just sit in there and paint forever, until someone comes and discovers him."

I thought, but didn't add: *Or until he dies and they discover his body and his paintings, both.*

She nodded, not without reservation. "Then I am willing."

"Excellent!" Willie said, and got to his feet quickly, before we could change our minds. "I'll see if I can arrange to have the Steins send us around a couple of cabs. We'll be carrying the paintings wet, I suppose, so don't forget to gather up some oilcloth and canvas so we can carry them on our laps. Don't worry, it's a short trip from here into the Sixth."

"Come with us now," Angelina said impulsively, getting up to move with the others toward the door. "We are go out now, and we eat, and we make some conversation. We get real merry, and this evening we go to open house at Delaunays'. Is big fun!"

Irène and I both smiled and shook our heads, following our guests to the door. It really all sounded like quite a bit more fun than could possibly suit our tastes. As Irène rarely used the studio for her sculpting work before evening, she went out on some errands and left me brooding by the window.

When evening approached, I went out for a long, pensive stroll, leaving Irène an undisturbed environment for her work when she got in. It was a beautiful night, and when the comet rose, I admired it for a long time. Halley's Comet was, by now, growing into a truly dazzling sight. I spotted one of the Souris Trempés following me from a distance and waved to him to indicate that I appreciated his discreet protection. I dined alone, and though I didn't linger over my meal, the evening was well advanced by the time I returned home. I had the restaurant package up a small meal which I handed to my patient guardian when we passed through the yard of La Ruche.

The studio was empty when I came back, but I could hear voices through the wall. When I peeped in at Moishe's studio again, I was surprised to find Mr. Lenin there, together with Alfred Boucher and Irène. Mr. Lenin was sitting on one of the cane chairs in front of Moishe's easel, leaning forward with his elbows on his stocky knees, gazing at the canvas with great intensity. But then again, he had a face that was broad and heavy and at the same time very angular, and this always made his gaze seem frighteningly intense, even if he were only glancing at a crust of bread on the floor.

They all looked up and nodded pleasantly when I stepped in.

"I didn't know you were a lover of the arts, Mr. Lenin," I said, coming over to stand behind Irène with my fingertips on her shoulder.

"The workers of Russia must stick together," he replied in his gravelly, thickly accented French. He gave Moishe a wolfish smile and said something in Russian, presumably repeating the comment. Moishe smiled and nodded, perhaps a bit too vigorously. Sitting there beside his large, brooding guest, practically shoulder-to-shoulder with him, poor Moishe looked rather like an angora rabbit posing for a picture beside a bulldog.

"The painting is finished," Moishe told me, enunciating slowly. I came forward to admire the canvas by lamplight and found it looked much the same as it had earlier in the day, though it now sported his *Marc Chagall* signature.

"It really is beautiful, Moishe."

"Tomorrow, I will paint again."

Mr. Lenin nodded with satisfaction. "It's good to see a painting of *shtetl* life, here in this western country. The troubles suffered by the Russian Jewry under Tsarist oppression . . . I think these troubles are not well known outside our country. Often the Tsar orders pogroms, to massacre these Jewish villages. Now, what is to be done?"

I was surprised at these remarks, because I had been of the impression that the Russian rebels were themselves anti-Semitic. "Are there Jewish Bolsheviks, Mr. Lenin?" I asked.

He frowned and shrugged his heavy shoulders in a slow and nuanced way. "*All* the workers of Russia stand together, though perhaps a few don't know this yet. As for me, my own grandfather was Jewish." He clapped a big hand on Moishe's shoulder, startling the little painter so much that he dropped a couple of brushes. "Come the revolution, my brother, you return home to Mother Russia! When I seize control of the empire, perhaps I'm going to make you commissar of arts!"

We all had a pleasant laugh. It was nice to see that even a man whose grandiose plans had fallen as deeply into ruin as Mr. Lenin's could still make little pleasantries at his own expense.

"Say!" Boucher inserted, still chuckling, "If you ever conquer Paris, Volodya, be sure to put Moishe in charge of the juried Salons. That ought to freshen things up a bit."

Even as I laughed at this, I examined my shaggy little landlord with renewed curiosity. His own sculptures were famous for their graceful, classical realism, and yet he was so tolerant, so supportive of the art movements among the radical young.

"Are you a *French* Bolshevik, Mr. Boucher?" I asked him with an arch smile.

"Ha! I'm a worker. Does that count? And I do share Volodya's belief in the rights of man. But I don't think the Bolsheviks invented these things, did they?"

"Mr. Boucher grew up as a farmhand!" Irène told me. From her tone of voice, she might have been relating a miracle. Then again, after a few moments of reflection I realized that it *was* something of a miracle for a farmhand in nineteenth century France to grow up and win the Grand Prix du Salon.

No longer laughing, I turned to look into his twinkling little eyes. "Is that really so?"

"It is," he told me. "As a boy, I tilled the fields by my father's side, a peasant like any other. To be a peasant of the fields is a good, honest life, but there is no hope in it that one might rise above the station that one is born to. Except perhaps by a life of crime."

"Tell her how you became a sculptor, Mr. Boucher," Irène demanded excitedly.

He gave her an indulgent smile. "Ah, I was very lucky. In the summers, I used to work in the gardens of van Zanten, the sculptor, whose summer cottage was just down the road a bit. Once, he let me take some clay to play with, and I copied one of his sculptures. I felt that the thing came out well, so I left it on his patio as a gift. After that, I became his apprentice for two years, and then he passed me on to Auguste Rodin."

I was speechless. What a story! It was like a fairy tale. Now I began to understand why Mr. Boucher had such a fanatical sense of support for society's underdogs.

"And how are *your* paintings going?" he asked me, with his elfish little smile. I must have dropped my eyes and blushed, because he added, "Ah, never mind, young mademoiselle, never mind. The muse will visit you in her own time, just you wait."

Irène and I drifted back to our studio not long after that. I changed into my nightclothes as she warmed the wax at her worktable. When she pried open the window, the familiar sound of Armand's guitar wafted up from the yard. I pulled a shawl around my shoulders and went to the window to look down at him. He was sitting on his favorite stone, his back to the window, strumming quietly. He was getting better. The tune he was playing was a simple one, but he carried it well.

"That man is in love with you," Irène commented, without looking up from her work.

"Don't be absurd," I said, blushing.

I tucked myself under the bed covers, and the faint strains of Armand's simple old melody, endlessly repeated, carried me gently to sleep.

Chapter Sixteen

I devoted myself with real intensity to my painting during the early days of that week. For one thing, Irène's statuette of the faun was taking form by now, and the parts of it that she had detailed were exquisitely beautiful. I admired her talent, but the presence of this formative work of art made me feel considerable pressure to hurry up and create something. So I put in some long mornings painting but making only modest progress on my project. One real disadvantage of working in the classical styles is the immense commitment of time that these styles demand of their practitioners. Any Modern painter worth his salt could have slapped down a still life in half the time, I have no doubt. It also provided me with distraction from troubled thoughts of my dear father and his friend Professor Almeida, and all that had transpired since my arrival in Paris.

At six o'clock on Tuesday evening, Brian Torrence Grimm arrived in his fancy barouche. I hadn't exactly *forgotten* our agreement that he should come and see the mysterious painting of the Inquisition that evening, but nonetheless his visit caught me completely by surprise. We hadn't set a time, and somehow I had imagined him arriving a few hours later, around dinnertime. I can't imagine why I would have thought this, but at any rate the sight of his carriage at the curb caught me unawares. Irène and I were both in our work smocks, and I had been wearing mine all day. My hair was in wild disarray, and in general I was completely unprepared for a visitor, especially one as sophisticated as Brian.

While I was making hasty preparations to receive company, I

glanced out the window obliquely so that I could see the front curb and check on his progress. To my great surprise, he emerged from the carriage door bearing a bottle of wine and a box that looked like it might very well contain chocolates.

Irène, perceiving my startled reaction, looked up from her work and leaned out through the window to observe the street front, around the side of the building.

"Ah ha," she said in the aloof manner of a scientific observer who has just acquired some new data. "I believe that *that* one is in love with you, too."

"You say the most preposterous things," I snapped. My irritation, however, mainly stemmed from the discovery that I was wearing a frumpy house dress under the smock, and would thus have to change my clothes completely before I could open the door to a foreigner bearing wine and chocolate. "Mr. Grimm is not the sort of man who falls in love," I explained to her, undressing myself with all haste. "He is much too . . . serious."

Irène began to hum to herself, as if implying that she had a ready rejoinder but was tactfully withholding it. This was so irritating that I was preparing to say something quite snippy, but I was interrupted by a gasp from Irène who was still looking out the window. I raced over to see what was happening.

Mr. Grimm's progress along the path to the front door was abruptly halted by a man who walked quickly out from the yard below me, almost running, following a course that was clearly intended to intercept the Englishman. Aghast, I realized that it was Armand.

Because I was dressing, I had to stay well back from the window, but from what little I saw, the two men greeted each other in a manner that was stiff and unsmiling, but sufficiently civil nonetheless. What I wouldn't have given to be able to hear the words they were exchanging!

"Interesting," Irène noted in that same tone of clinical detachment. "Do you suppose that now they shall fight with each other?"

"Of course not! But here, please help me with these buttons, quickly. Oh, I wish it didn't take so long to get dressed!"

As soon as I had my dress and boots buttoned up, I dashed next door and told Moishe that I needed to retrieve the copper tube from his ceiling immediately. This communication was mainly achieved with a little pantomime of hand gestures, which was the usual way I communicated with Moishe when I was in a hurry. I pulled the tube down, took it quickly back to my studio, and was at last preparing to go out and greet my guest, when I heard him coming up the stairs.

I was amazed to see Armand stomping up the stairs right on Brian's heels. To the best of my knowledge, Armand had never set foot in La Ruche before, although by now everyone in the building was accustomed to seeing him sit out in the courtyard with his guitar. Both men were a bit breathless and red-cheeked with what appeared to be barely contained hostility. They did, actually, look like they were using considerable effort to restrain themselves from having a fistfight.

"Good evening, senhorita," Brian greeted me shortly. "Would you please be so kind as to tell this young man that I am an invited guest here?"

"Good evening," Armand said to me, stepping around Brian and shouldering his way in front of him. This was actually a much better arrangement in a practical sense, since the top of Armand's head was not quite as high as Brian's chin, so I could now see both their faces at the same time. "I apologize for intruding, but I feel that my organization has a right to know what business this man has with you. If you would please enlighten me, senhorita."

I couldn't help raising one eyebrow at Armand, but I think I managed to withhold my smirk. He was certainly expressing his viewpoint in a somewhat fatuous manner, by suggesting that his interest was *political* in nature. After all, he had already confessed to me that he despised Brian for personal reasons, including what seemed to be a general prejudice against Englishmen—something I found hard to abide. Then there was the matter of the wine and the chocolates, which I imagined might also have had something to do with his confrontational mood.

"Why don't you both come inside, and we'll talk." I ushered them into my studio with a gesture that was somewhat too brusque to be polite. "This is all quite scandalous," I whispered to them as they slipped past me. "Fortunately for us all, this is La Ruche, where scandal is as commonplace as wallpaper, and draws little more attention. Still, go in, go in, and let me shut the door!"

"Is that it?" Brian demanded, pointing a long finger at the copper tube. "Because I must insist that you not display it while this young man is in the room. This may be a matter of official concern for the Grand Lodge of Freemasons."

"Freemasons!" Armand snorted. "Whatever that copper pipe may be, I think that Senhorita Sarmentos may show it to whomever she chooses, and I fail to see what any *Freemasons* have to do with the matter. Also, I am here as an official representative of the Bande Liberté du Monde, and I strongly doubt that the senhorita has any secrets to keep from *us*." He turned to me, and his angry eyes abruptly revealed a certain frightened look. "Have you?"

"It's not a secret," I said hastily. "At least . . . I don't think it is. Oh, Armand, how can I know if it's a secret when I haven't found out yet what it *is*?"

This guilty little outburst of mine caused an awkward silence that stretched on for several seconds. Irène, bless her, broke the spell by pivoting around in her chair, as if noticing all of us for the first time.

"Oh, Mr. Grimm! Are those Debauve and Gallais chocolates? How wonderful! Do you mind if I have one? I haven't had a bite since breakfast, and I'm absolutely ravenous."

This, of course, was a flagrant lie, since Irène never ate breakfast and had in fact devoured the equivalent of about four lunches just a few hours earlier. But everyone in the room took advantage of the opportunity to shift the mood, and to slip into the pleasantly civil ceremony of opening the box of chocolates and the bottle of wine, and serving them.

"We will *all* look at the painting now," I said firmly, drawing it out of its metal tube. "Armand, Professor Almeida gave this to me just before he died. I'm sorry now that I didn't tell you about it before. It's just that . . . I don't yet know what it means, or why it was given me." The truth, of course, was that I had told Brian about it and not Armand because Brian seemed like he might know a thing or two about abstruse and occulted matters, whereas Armand surely did not. Still, I was feeling very sheepish. "Perhaps it *is* a secret, Armand, I don't know. Please be careful whom you tell."

"You can trust me in all such matters," he said simply, and I had no doubt that it was the truth.

I unrolled the ugly canvas across a table, and Brian and Armand leaned in to look at it. After a couple of seconds, both of them started back a little and gave out noises of surprise. Then they leaned in again and began studying it in earnest under the lamplight.

I found myself effectively alone, since all three of the others in the room were now leaning studiously over their respective tables with their backs to me. Brian had handed me the chocolate box after offering it around. I was starting to feel extremely uncomfortable to be holding it, especially with Armand standing there. I walked around the studio, offering the chocolates and topping off all our glasses with the delightful wine that Brian had brought.

When I returned to the table, I slipped one of the chocolates to Armand, and he promptly ate it, barely even bothering to look up from the painting. A few moments later, I slipped Armand another chocolate, and he ate that one, too. This seemed an excellent resolution to my dilemma, so I kept at it, feeding him chocolates at a slow but steady pace.

"Many of these symbols are alchemical," Brian commented authoritatively. "But it is surely some form of code." He looked up just in time to see me feeding the last of his chocolates to Armand. He frowned at me, and I smiled back at him as innocently as I could, then placed the empty box beside him on the table. He stared at it coldly for a long moment, then looked up and asked, with no change in tone, "Do you know the provenance of the painting? Who was its previous owner, and how did it fall into the hands of Professor Almeida?"

"I haven't the slightest idea. He seemed to be keeping it concealed."

"Hmm. Breaking ciphers of this nature without some sort of key is notoriously difficult, I can tell you that much. But I know a couple of men who are very good with this sort of thing. Indeed, one of them is a don of mathematics. With your permission, I will take this canvas to these men and we shall see what can be done about it."

I was about to agree to this—in fact I was quite eager to see the painting leave the premises. But Armand interrupted.

"You're not taking anything!" he exclaimed, while still chewing the last of the chocolates. "This painting doesn't belong to the English Freemasons. It was handed over to Senhorita Sarmentos and the free people of Portugal, for reasons currently unknown. For all we know, it might be of great value in some way or another."

To my distress, the two of them began arguing the matter heatedly, and at considerable length. Brian at first claimed that he would only keep the painting for a very brief period and would return it promptly and undamaged. But under pressure, he did in fact eventually admit that if his brotherhood determined the painting to be of special significance to them, then it might be a long time before anyone outside their closed membership saw it again. I wasn't sure how I felt about that, but it was evident that Armand would have none of it. He went as far as to place himself bodily between the table and the door, as if concerned that Brian would snatch the painting and try to run away with it.

"Very well," Brian eventually allowed, with an exhausted sigh. "I shall simply describe the painting to some friends, if I may have your permission to do so. Here, let me also copy down a sample of the cipher, if that's indeed what it is, so that my acquaintances can consider the possibility of its decryption." I gave him some paper and ink so that he could copy a dozen of the symbols. When he finished, he folded the paper and turned to me, "I'm afraid that these circumstances may make it necessary for me to visit your quarters here again for a closer look at the encoded sequence, depending upon the opinions of those learned men. Again, with your permission, senhorita."

"Oh no," Armand exclaimed firmly. "I shall take this painting in its sealed container to the secure headquarters of Bande Liberté du Monde. You may visit me there, Mr. Grimm, if you wish to look upon it again. It's much too dangerous to leave such an object *here*."

"Outrageous," Brian growled, and went so far as to ball his large and bony fists. "This, I shall not allow."

"It's all right, Armand," I hastened to insert. I explained that the painting wasn't stored right there in our studio, though I refused to tell him exactly where I was keeping it. I felt that, if it were an object that people might die over, then the fewer who knew its whereabouts, the better. "It is quite secure, I assure you. And since it isn't kept here in the room, I believe there is no reason to remove it from the building."

And with that, I reached between them and hastily rolled the painting up again, then slid it back into its tube. I glanced pointedly in the direction of the door. Both of them reluctantly took the hint and let me herd them slowly back out into the hall.

"I'll see your visitor out, Florbela," Armand told me rather stiffly. "If you need any further assistance, you know where I am to be found."

Brian, ignoring Armand completely, gave me a small and formal bow from the door and said, "Thank you for accommodating me into your schedule, senhorita. As soon as I have any news, I will be in contact once again. I hope you will be so gracious as to do the same for me."

And with that, both of them walked stiffly away down the curve of the dim hallway.

Chapter Seventeen

T he invitations to the Steins' arrived the next day. They were hand-delivered by courier, which was still a common alternative to the unreliable post. The courier simply dropped them just inside the La Ruche front door and then left, unseen by anyone. It was Irène who spotted the envelopes there and carried them up the stairs.

To everyone's surprise, Apollinaire had not only wrangled invitations for Irène and Moishe and me, but also for Amedeo.

"She has forgiven me!" Amedeo exclaimed, as Irène placed the invitation into his hand. "I really would have thought that this was impossible. Unless . . . do you suppose she has come around to my point of view, concerning her Braque canvas?"

He began to argue the question with Angelina and Diego, so Irène and I slipped away from their studio and went upstairs. Moishe received his invitation in a predictably placid and tranquil fashion, for which we teased him, and then pulled him out of his chair so we could all dance around a bit in his studio. We were going to the Sixth!

The other big event of the week, for me, was finishing my still life on Friday. I caught the last of the morning light that day and used it to glaze some subtle highlights onto the reflections on the wine bottles. Then I pronounced the work done and proudly signed my name. Irène adjudged it a minor masterpiece, which probably inflated my head a bit, but it felt very good to be done. Then she called in Moishe, who examined it from various angles with happy smiles and told me again and again how pretty it was.

After that, Irène apparently felt obliged to dash downstairs and drag Amedeo, Diego and Angelina up from their studio to let them admire it as well. That put a halt to the festivities.

To say that their reaction was *crestfallen* would be an understatement. Amedeo refused to comment aloud, but the sight of my little "masterpiece" certainly made him look like he had been hit on the side of the head with a sack of potatoes.

Diego was more verbose. "But *why?*" he demanded of me, almost pleadingly. "Why would you *paint* such a thing?"

So. The early reviews did not seem entirely promising for my career as an artist among the Moderns.

At any rate, the next day was Saturday, and Irène and I spent the afternoon preparing ourselves for our grand arrival in that refined and desirable northern apex of Montparnasse, the few blocks of it that are wedged into the Sixth District. The Steins' Saturday salon was always held in the early part of the evening, so that at 8:30 or so the guests could disband and make their way to dinner somewhere else. It was odd to be dressing up in our evening finest so early in the day, but the peculiarity merely added to the thrill.

Apollinaire arrived in a pair of cheap, hired coaches at around six o'clock, and he came upstairs to help Moishe select the paintings that he would take with him to the salon. Knowing the shabby state of Moishe's wardrobe and finances, Willie had brought with him a smoking jacket and silk cravat—the smallest that he owned, he told us. The jacket was nonetheless too wide at the shoulders, and its sleeves draped down over Moishe's knuckles. While Willie made his selections from among the paintings, Irène and I struggled with great haste to sew up the sleeves on Moishe's borrowed jacket.

After only two weeks in Paris, Moishe had already completed five paintings, and none of them were fully dry. Eventually, Willie selected the two that were largest and most intricate. He and Amedeo each carried one of them carefully out to the carriages, with Moishe following close upon their heels, wringing his hands like a father watching his babies carried off by the authorities.

THE SIXTH

Though it wasn't very far, there was still plenty of opportunity to enjoy the brisk ride along the boulevards. We headed straight toward the center of the city, and when we crossed the Boulevard du Montparnasse and entered the Sixth, I was gawking shamelessly through the windows. I was disappointed to find that it was a staid-looking neighborhood, if a prosperous one. I don't know what I had expected—probably wild nightclubs and painters with their easels at every corner, or something of the kind. But at first glance, Montparnasse's northern tip appeared to be not only its wealthiest corner, but also its quietest.

The Steins lived behind a massive wooden porte cochère, in a stone house of modest size that shared a courtyard with two others. There was a very sleek two-door automobile parked in front. "That is Gertrude's new Model T Ford. She has only just had it delivered," Willie explained. "It is the touring model," he added. It was the first American car I had ever seen, and it added a great deal of glamour to the street.

The Steins' salon was a single large room, and as it was the only part of the house that was open to visitors, the arrival of the five of us with Moishe's two paintings rather filled the place up. Leo Stein rose from a big armchair near the unlit hearth to greet us and to help with the paintings. He was a slender man, already balding in his late thirties, and looked very much like an American banker or financier. His sister Gertrude, who barely glanced up from her chair at our arrival, was a stout and dour woman with very short hair, dressed in velvet and satin in muted tones. They both spoke good French, with strong American accents. There were two other couples in the room, the Ekdahls, who were blond and Swedish, and the Vincents, who were small, reserved people and almost never spoke. I eventually learned that both of these couples were neighbors of the Steins', and dilettantes in the arts.

But the thing that completely dominated the salon, at least at first glance, was not the people who inhabited it but the paintings. Every bit of available wall space was covered in art, with sometimes as many as four canvases arrayed in columns between the ceiling and floor. And what paintings!

"Absinthe?" Willie asked me, handing me a glass. He stood beside me as I pored over an almost unbelievable collection of Renoir canvases, which was spread out across the wall beside an almost unbelievable collection of Degas canvases. "This is only the tip of the iceberg," he told me quietly. "The rest of the collection is in storage somewhere. The Steins have been buying Impressionists for years, and now they have begun with the avant garde. They bought a lot of Matisse, as you can see over there. Now it's Picasso. Who knows? Perhaps you'll be next."

I smiled sadly at this friendly little joke, remembering the dismal reception that Diego and Amedeo had given my still life, the day before.

When I turned my attention away from the art and back to the room, most of the conversation had turned to Moishe's paintings. Amedeo had propped the two wet canvases up against the stonework of the hearth so that the Steins could examine them at leisure from their comfortable chairs. Moishe himself was slowly circling the room, examining the artworks on the walls with great attention. Everyone else was gathering gradually into a semicircle around his two paintings, to hear the Steins make their pronouncements.

"How extraordinary," Miss Stein remarked in her husky voice. "I wonder why some of the figures are upside down?" She leaned toward her brother and added, *sotto voce*, "Do you suppose it would be rude to ask him?"

"Mr. Chagall," Mr. Stein called out. Moishe didn't recognize his adopted name and continued staring fixedly into a small Monet.

"His French isn't very good yet," I told them. "I'm afraid you might find it difficult to convey the meaning of your question."

Miss Stein smiled at me dryly. "And no doubt even more difficult for him to convey the meaning of his answer. Well, that's just fine. He doesn't need to entertain us—his paintings are quite entertainment enough. What do you think of them, Leo? They are certainly colorful."

"Willie, who's collecting these?" Mr. Stein asked.

"Nobody, yet. Mr. Shagalov just arrived from Saint Petersburg, two weeks ago. He's staying at La Ruche."

"He's awfully young," Mr. Stein noted. "Fresh out of the Petersburg academy, I would guess. I suppose we'll keep an eye on him for a few years, and maybe start buying his pieces if the style catches on."

Amedeo folded his arms, and both of the Steins shifted their eyes over to look at him, rather nervously. I suppose they were wondering if he was about to make them regret having invited him into their home again. "*Somebody* ought to buy *something*," Amedeo told them imperiously. "As you might guess, Mr. Shagalov is utterly penniless, and just look at his work! We can't send our most original talents out to starve in the street, can we?"

The Steins continued to stare at him coolly for a few moments, then let their attention drift away. "We'll keep an eye on him," Mr. Stein repeated. "Thank you for bringing him to our attention, Willie."

This exchange would have gone farther, and probably too far, if not for the arrival at that moment of the Picasso household. Mr. Picasso came charging in through the front door without ringing the bell or bothering with any other formality, and close at his heels was his girlfriend or helpmate, Fernande Olivier. Their arrival increased the liveliness of the room substantially, but they also brought a fair amount of emotional tension with them, as if they had perhaps been fighting. Pablo immediately went over to talk with Amedeo and the Steins at the hearth, while Fernande took herself to the other side of the room and plopped down on a sofa to begin an animated conversation with the Ekdahls.

"Ah, Modigliani!" Pablo exclaimed, with carefully modulated elation. He and Amedeo clapped each other on the back like old friends. It was evident enough that their affection was natural and unfeigned, but despite that, I took an immediate dislike to Mr. Picasso even before we were introduced. He was a handsome young Spaniard with fierce eyes and arrogant demeanor, the kind of bravo that I knew all too well from my Lisbon childhood. Here he was, visiting the home of wealthy foreigners in his collar and tie, but it was just as easy to imagine him wielding a knife in a brawl or compromising some helpless housemaid.

Amedeo introduced us, and the way that Pablo flashed his black, bullfighter's eyes at me immediately told me that he was a merciless seducer.

"Mademoiselle, I am delighted to make your acquaintance," he said in a tone that, despite myself, made me catch my breath. I gave him my coldest smile and let him touch my fingers for only a moment before I withdrew them and broke eye contact.

"Are you all right?" I heard Willie saying, from somewhere close at hand. I glanced over and saw him supporting Irène by one arm and looking at her face with great concern. He asked her something in Polish.

She shook her head vigorously and gently removed her arm from his grip. "No, I . . . I just turned my heel on this rug, that's all. It's these . . . new shoes." Her face was strangely pale, with red patches below the cheekbones. She turned away from us, and moved toward the back of the room. I leaned in that direction, thinking to follow her.

"What are these?" Mr. Picasso asked abruptly and very loudly. He had apparently been turning to the Steins to pay his respects, when his eye had fallen upon the two canvases down on the hearthstones.

Amedeo pointed out Moishe, who was still exploring the artwork on the walls, and he began explaining how the two wet paintings had arrived at the salon. During this explanation, Pablo gradually crouched down lower and lower to look at the two paintings from a more propitious angle, and it eventually became clear that he wasn't hearing a word. Amedeo finally gave up the effort and stopped right in the middle of a sentence.

"Well, *Pablo* seems to like them," Gertrude said to her brother. "That's something, anyway."

Mr. Picasso was indisposed for conversation for quite some time—perhaps half an hour or more. He eventually folded up his legs and sat Indian-style on the carpet in front of the two paintings, his elbow on one knee and his chin on the palm of his hand, apparently oblivious to any activity around him. As a friend of Moishe's, I naturally found this very charming, though I was still inclined to dislike Mr. Picasso on a personal level. Also, I admit to a certain odd jealousy that was beginning to prey upon me. It was becoming clear that there were certain people who were immediately stunned by something or other in Moishe's paintings, and then there were the rest of us who warmed to them more slowly. Part of me hated to admit that this dressed-up street hoodlum on the floor was a member of the elite group, while I was not.

I noticed that Irène had wedged herself onto one side of an old loveseat, where she sat alone, staring broodingly at the carpet in the most distant and shadowy part of the big room. I went back there and sat down beside her, then put my hand on hers. "Are you feeling all right?" I asked gently.

She nodded absently. Then she looked up from the rug and turned to me with a startled look, as if suddenly realizing I was there. "What do you suppose he sees in her?" she asked me quietly.

I shook my head, having no idea what she was talking about. Then it dawned on me that she was speaking of Pablo and Fernande. I glanced over at Fernande, who was sipping a cloudy green glass of absinthe, apparently rapt in a deep but quiet conversation with the Ekdahls. She had the round face of a peasant girl, but large eyes and pretty, sculpted lips, and perfect white skin. It was certainly easy to see how any man might be attracted to such a woman. True, it was also evident that her manners were a little unrefined, but I imagined that even that might seem attractive to a young man of Mr. Picasso's sort.

"Well, they don't seem to be getting along very well, do they?" I replied quietly. Amedeo, who knew them both quite well, had gossiped to us extensively about Pablo and Fernande in recent days. The couple had been living under a single roof for several years now, though it was said that she was still legally married to some other man off in the countryside somewhere. So she was a woman with an extensive and scandalous past, though she was certainly not yet thirty years old.

"Anyone can see that she is coarse," Irène said, speaking close to my ear. "Coarse not only on the surface, but through and through. Whereas he . . . *he* . . ."

She apparently couldn't find words to complete her description of Pablo Picasso. I looked at her sharply, in great alarm. I had finally divined her feelings. I couldn't have been more dismayed if she had just told me that she had been diagnosed with an aggressive tumor.

"That man is a rake," I said to her, speaking quietly but enunciating each word with great care, to make it clear that this was my considered judgment. "He is an arrogant opportunist. That type of man brings nothing but misery into the life of any woman."

Irène withdrew her hand from under mine and sat up very straight. After a moment's silence, she said, "You are quick to judge, Florbela. I suspect that he is misunderstood." Then she got to her feet with careful dignity and crossed the room to engage in a conversation with Willie.

I sat there alone for a few minutes, letting my eyes discreetly move in a circuit from Pablo to Irène to Fernande and then back again. Each time I did this, I became more distressed and unhappy, so at last I got up and moved back to the hearth, placing myself bodily between Pablo and Irène.

Just about then, Pablo at last snapped out of his trance and rolled up to his feet with easy grace. He looked around, blinking, as if awakening from a long dream.

"What about it?" Leo Stein demanded. "Is this the next big thing? A new style?"

"Hm? Oh, no, no," Pablo replied offhandedly. "No. No one can paint like this."

"Do you really think not?" Gertrude demanded archly. "Not to belabor the obvious, Pablo, but I believe one might make a case that at least one person *can* do it."

Pablo looked around for Moishe, and spotted him ogling a Matisse odalisque near the group where Fernande was sitting. He stared pensively at the back of Moishe's head for a while. At last he admitted reluctantly, "I suppose so."

"It doesn't look so hard," Leo mused, peering down at the two canvases.

Mr. Picasso didn't grace this comment with a reply.

"Mr. Shagalov," Leo Stein called out. Moishe turned around, startled. Leo smiled and beckoned, and Moishe quickly trotted over. He stood at the edge of the group around the hearth, giving each of them in turn a polite little bow of the head.

"This is Pablo Picasso," Gertrude said, flipping a hand in the air. "He likes your paintings. Do you understand me?"

Moishe nodded.

Pablo stared at him for a considerable period of time, the expression on his face troubled and rather puzzled, as if he were observing some inexplicable and potentially ominous change in the weather. At last he said, "You painted these?"

Moishe looked at his paintings, then at Pablo, and nodded vigorously. "I painted these."

"You understand color, don't you?"

I knew that this question was well within Moishe's range of comprehension, but nonetheless he hesitated for a moment. He was thinking about it. Then he gave a single definitive nod. "Yes. I understand color."

Pablo gave a sigh that was sad, almost despondent. "I wish I understood color," he said. "If Matisse dies, I suppose you will be the only painter left who understands what color is."

Irène had moved over very close during this conversation, and I glanced at her several times with great consternation, expecting her to say something witty or brilliant to capture Mr. Picasso's attention. To my relief, she seemed to be completely tongue-tied. She simply stood at the edge of our group, hanging on his every word, her eyes as wide and bright as those of a doll. As for Pablo, he hardly seemed to notice she was there. When Irène wasn't speaking, I'm afraid that she cut a very unimpressive figure: skinny, insubstantial, childish. He may very well have even thought that she was the daughter of one of the two dilettante couples.

Amedeo had a strange wobbly look about him, which

suggested to me that he might be drugged, but his speech was clear and he seemed to have his wits about him. He and Pablo launched into a long and amusing conversation about recent events in Pablo's shabby Montmartre residence, which was nicknamed Bateau-Lavoir. Amedeo apparently spent a lot of time over there, and I gathered from the conversation that he planned to move there as soon as his circumstances would allow it.

"But why would you want to move so far away from the Left Bank?" I demanded. I was aware that a small colony of poor artists had recently accreted at Bateau-Lavoir, but I couldn't imagine why they would want to live there instead of here. "It seems such a strange place to go. I believe it is literally as far from Montparnasse as you could be without actually leaving Paris."

"Blame it on Cubism," Amedeo said, and the comment extracted a knowing laugh from almost everyone within earshot, except Irène and me. Amedeo noticed that I had missed the import of his remark, and he explained, "Pablo and Braque were living there when they invented Cubism. Now, whenever one of the avant garde converts to the Cubist religion, he makes the pilgrimage across the city and appears on bended knee outside Pablo's door." This image got another chuckle from the listeners. "But listen, Pablo, even if I move to your neighborhood, don't imagine that I'll adopt your idolatrous ways!"

"We can tolerate the occasional backslider," Pablo assured him.

"So then, Mr. Picasso," I persisted, "how did you and Mr. Braque first come to move into such an unlikely neighborhood?"

He looked a little embarrassed to be asked this question, and I wasn't surprised to see a small spark of anger in his eyes. I also noticed that others standing around us were watching him, and I adduced that they were wondering if he would give an honest answer to what was, after all, an innocent question. I admit that I enjoyed discomfiting him.

He straightened his shoulders a bit, gave me a particularly arrogant glance, then said, "Matisse was living there. In Montmartre, that is. Not in Bateau-Lavoir, obviously."

Understanding dawned upon me. Henri Matisse had no doubt

moved into the fancy hills north of the Right Bank when he had achieved wealth and success, several years back. It was all too easy to imagine the young Picasso arriving in Paris, envying the great man, and choosing to go live in Matisse's shadow rather than in the Left Bank with the rest of us. Now, amazingly, a substantial portion of the Left Bank artists seemed to be migrating over there to join him.

"Well, I have no doubt that you will soon be as famous as Mr. Matisse," I said, deciding to smooth his feathers a bit. "You certainly seem to be as well represented as he is, here in the Steins' collection."

"Have you admired his portrait of Gertrude?" Willie asked. He gestured at a painting beside the mantel, not far from Gertrude Stein herself. I hadn't realized that the painting was done by Pablo, because it wasn't in the style of Cubism—in fact, it was more or less a piece of classical portraiture. I was strongly struck by the crudity of its rendering. It featured a large nose, much more like Picasso's own nose then Miss Stein's.

"I hope you don't find this news troubling, Mr. Picasso," I said. "But she does not look like her portrait."

Pablo smiled at me and raised one eyebrow. "She will."

The rest of the evening rolled out without any disaster, much to my relief. The conversation became louder and livelier as we all drank more of the Steins' wine and absinthe. I did my best to corral Irène away from Mr. Picasso. I think that eventually Fernande's feminine instincts informed her that there was a potential rival in the room; at any rate, halfway through the soirée, she got up and went to Pablo's side, and remained there steadfastly until the party dispersed.

As dinnertime approached, Willie, with his remarkable faculty for extracting value from ambient social resources, gathered up Moishe and his paintings and those of us who had come with him, and told us we were all going out to dinner with the Vincents. This rather mousy dilettante couple, who had hardly said a word all evening, seemed more than happy to take us all out for a lavish meal at a small but pleasant restaurant just down the street. So we bid good night to the Steins and their other guests, and went out for a good, long meal at someone else's expense. For the first time in my life, I felt like a genuine bohemian.

The whole experience would have been completely perfect if not for one ominous detail. Irène merely picked at her dinner. She engaged in the table conversation no more than required by civility, and hardly ate a thing.

When Willie dropped us off at La Ruche, it was close to midnight. Irène avoided me, staying a couple of steps ahead of me as we went into the building and climbed to our studio. She undressed quickly behind her screen and went straight to bed. Such behavior was extremely unusual for her.

Myself, I was completely exhausted from the long evening's activities, but I felt too excited to sleep. I lay on my cot for some time, glancing over surreptitiously now and then at the bony lump that was Irène hidden under her quilt, and worrying about her. But I can't say that her silly distress was the main thing on my mind, and besides, I assumed she would soon get over it.

Simple strains of music began to drift up from the yard, outside the window. Armand was out there, playing a folk melody on his guitar. I listened closely and noticed that his skill was still improving markedly, night by night. I followed along with his tune and imagined him sitting out there, bent over his guitar in concentration. The image was very comforting. I began to think about going out and telling him all the details of my exciting evening, but before I could do so, his melody lulled me to sleep.

Chapter Eighteen

I was awake at the crack of dawn the next morning after fitful sleep, punctuated by horrible dreams. As I sat eating an orange for breakfast I recalled the remarkable experiences the previous night at the Steins'. My determination to paint something of significance was greater than ever before. I pulled on my smock, tied up my hair, and prepared my palette in the first cold rays of morning light, then set up a fresh canvas on the back of the chair that was still serving as my easel. I would paint a light-soaked interior, perhaps emulating the style of Matisse. I would capture the pastel light playing over the red drapery and the wood-paneled studio wall, and I would be wildly free with my colors. I was going to paint something that would shock the professors back at my academy, and earn me a little attention from my new friends at La Ruche and the Sixth.

But as soon as I saw that blank white expanse of stretched and gessoed fabric in front of me, I simply couldn't force my hand to put a single mark on it. I sat meditating glumly as the light slowly shifted around the room. I vividly imagined a dozen ways that I might begin the project. Twice I even made a small and tentative mark upon the canvas, only to realize upon further reflection that the first stroke had already ruined the composition. I carefully cleaned away all traces of these marks with turpentine. By the time the shaft of morning light had abandoned the studio, I found myself putting away the same blank canvas that I had set up hours earlier.

The noise of my miserable retreat from artistic stardom briefly awakened Irène, and she turned over to examine me from beneath her quilt. She looked like a frightened rabbit peeking out from a forest burrow.

"I believe I'll be going out for coffee soon," I told her. "Would you care to join me?"

"No, thank you," she replied in a tiny voice. "I am not feeling well today. I believe I shall just stay in my bed."

I had immediate suspicions as to the nature of her infirmity, but I asked her politely to describe her symptoms. The symptoms, as far as I could ascertain, were that she was feeling unwell and didn't want to get out of bed. I convinced her to sit up long enough that I could brush her hair, and that seemed to soothe her a little bit, though without brightening her mood. After that, she refused again to come out for coffee, slid back down under her quilts, and disappeared.

I walked to a crowded cafe and had a light breakfast and sat reading the news of my homeland. The recent elections had returned a number of prominent republicans and this made the monarchists very nervous. I longed for news of my father and these dramatic events always made me very worried for his safety. As I walked home I recognized the familiar form of one of the Souris Trempés. I had noticed recently that in addition to watching the house, one of them would often follow me from a discreet distance. In some ways it felt a little uncomfortable because I was certain it was unnecessary.

I was out for a couple of hours, and returned around noon bearing two little cups of black coffee and a couple of small baguettes. I left one cup and a baguette with my Souris Trempé guardian and delivered the other to Moishe. I found him, as always, sitting in his studio before a canvas. It appeared he was doing another portrait of Bella today, this one a full-length figure in a spring dress that was apparently going to be lilac or violet. He thanked me profusely, drank his coffee and managed to eat half the bread before forgetting all about it and drifting back into his work. I sat in a chair behind him, watching him create his strange image and feeling a vast and irremediable envy.

There was always a lot of commotion at La Ruche in the early Sunday afternoons. The people who had gotten drunk the night before—which was almost everyone—were emerging blearily from their dens and staggering around the building, colliding off one another, both figuratively and literally. Out of the general din, a more particular commotion began to grow in volume outside Moishe's studio and reached a crescendo as Willie, Diego and Angelina came rollicking in through the open doorway. Willie was looking much as I had seen him the previous evening, but Diego and Angelina both had the pale and heavy-lidded look of the severely hung over.

"Ladies and gentlemen, the latest sensation!" Willie exclaimed merrily, throwing open both hands in Moishe's direction. "The toast of Paris."

I assumed at first that he was joking, and I may have chuckled a bit, but something in his tone caught me. I gave him a puzzled look. "Then . . . has there been a message from the Steins? Have they decided to buy one of Moishe's canvases after all?"

"No, no," Willie said dismissively. "Nothing of the kind. Ah, you are so *new* in town! But surely you can see that we made a spectacular triumph last night. Moishe has been presented to the Steins, and his art has fascinated them."

"And he didn't vomit on any of their canvases," Diego added hoarsely. He looked like he needed a drink.

"I thought their reactions seemed rather lukewarm," I said. "They didn't buy anything."

"But they will," Willie replied confidently. "They, and all the other collectors. Surely you see how it is. The Steins are investors, not philanthropists. They never buy anything until they are sure that its value will go up in the future."

I shook my head helplessly. I had no understanding of how such things worked, and I was left wondering what sort of "triumph" it was that could leave Moishe still with nothing in his pockets but the three rubles he had arrived with.

"What is most crucial," Willie said, gazing upon Moishe but evidently speaking to me, "is that we get him to the Delaunays' tonight, for their weekly party. The Steins naturally hesitate to open their purses because they are wondering if our new celebrity is simply going to vanish into obscurity. We mustn't let that happen."

"He won't go to a party," I opined. Moishe was watching our conversation with an expression of neutral interest, holding his brush poised for action, if we would ever let him get back to his work. I'm not sure how much of our discussion he could understand.

Angelina said, "Oh, you make him come, Florbela. Is wonderful party, big fun!" She spoke a couple of sentences to Moishe in cheerful and animated Russian. A sulky look appeared on Moishe's face, and his head seemed to retreat a little into his shoulders. He gave her a brief reply, which didn't sound at all enthusiastic.

Diego, observing this exchange, began ushering Angelina out of the room. "Come on, you," he said. "Florbela will do better without us. If you want to be useful, come help me raise Amedeo back from the dead."

Angelina, already halfway out the door, gave me a pitying look over her shoulder and shook her head. "That poor man."

A few seconds after they left, to my surprise, I saw Irène look in the doorway, fully dressed now and apparently restored to robust health. I was about to ask her how she was feeling, but before I could do so she asked, "Did I hear Diego?"

"He just left," I told her. "I'm sure you can find him in Modigliani's studio."

Irène immediately disappeared. I wondered to myself what she might need from Diego, but Willie distracted me by placing a hand on my forearm.

"I'm going to go look in on Amedeo now," he murmured, close to my ear. "Listen, Senhorita Sarmentos. If you love your friend, you will convince him to come to the party at the Delaunays' this evening. Offer to act as his chaperone, if that is what he needs. Every hour that he spends up in the Sixth brings him one step closer to earning a living wage." Having said this, he left me alone with Moishe.

I didn't feel I had much choice. I took a deep breath, seized a chair, and slid it so close to Moishe's that he had to turn his attention to me rather than his painting of Bella. I spoke to him slowly and carefully, and in great earnest. I explained to him that it was very important for *me* to attend the Delaunays' soirée that evening, and that I absolutely needed him to come along as my trusted escort. He put on a good face as he received this duplicitous demand, and he tried not to show how disappointed he was that he was once again to be dragged away from his work, and he reluctantly agreed. I smiled and patted his hand, then left him to his work. I hoped that Willie was right, and that this gambit on my part was to Moishe's benefit. I felt pretty treacherous, truth be told.

I returned to my studio to find it empty and I was just considering going downstairs and sticking my head in at Amedeo's room to find out what Irène wanted down there, when through my window I happened to see Willie leaving the premises via the yard. It occurred to me that I might learn more from him than from the others. I dashed down the stairs, and when I came out through the front door, I was in luck: Willie had paused to tie his shoe, so he was still on the path outside.

"Moishe will come to the Delaunays'," I told Willie as I approached him.

He gave me a friendly, conspiratorial smile. "*Excellent* news." There was something about Apollinaire's face that made anything naughty or transgressive look like a great good time. He added, "Invitations are not needed; they will be expecting you. I suppose that I won't even try to guess how you tempted him into accepting the proposition, but believe me, you won't regret it. The Delaunays throw a rousing bash."

"Do they? Well, I imagine that Moishe and I will try to find the quietest corner and just ride the thing out. But I wonder if I could ask you a question, Willie. If I may do so in discretion?"

"Of course!" He leaned a little closer, perhaps a bit too eagerly.

"What was it that Irène wanted to ask of Diego?"

He leaned back, not bothering to hide his disappointment. "Ah. Nothing, really. I believe she had overheard our conversation, and knew we were planning to go to the Delaunays' tonight. She asked if Pablo Picasso was going to be at the party."

My heart sank like a stone in my chest. "And what did you tell her?"

He cocked an eyebrow. I suspect that Willie had a very keen nose for detecting even the first sweet whiff of scandal. "We told her it was unlikely, but that there would probably be a few rising stars of even greater magnitude. She seemed unimpressed, and went back upstairs."

I thanked him and bid him farewell. Then I trudged slowly up to the studio.

I found Irène buried under her quilt again, pretending to be asleep, so I decided to leave her be. I selected a book and went out to the park, to spend a few hours strolling and reading on park benches among the song of courting starlings under a gorgeous spring sky. By the time I came home, I was in a truly fine mood.

No amount of coaxing would persuade Irène to come to the Delaunays'. Her moping was really beginning to worry me now, so I did my best to rouse her out of her funk, but to no avail. Apparently, if Mr. Picasso wasn't coming to the party, then neither was she. I felt a bit betrayed, since I could have used some moral support if I was going to serve as Moishe's guardian at some sort of lawless bohemian festivity. I certainly doubted that Diego and Amedeo could be relied upon to spend the evening keeping an eye on my wellbeing.

There would be no carriages sent around for us tonight, so if we couldn't scrape together cab fare, we would have to walk all the way. I dug into the last of my supply of pocket money and sadly counted out enough for a Hansom cab, there and back. Angelina and Amedeo between them managed to match this fund, and so, after a few last-minute preparations, we grabbed Moishe and the five of us went up to Rue de la Convention and hailed a pair of cabriolets. Angelina and I took one of them, with Moishe squeezed between us, and Diego and Amedeo led the way in the other. Amedeo was still looking half dead, but Diego more than made up for any lack of liveliness. He leaned out the cab window periodically, waving a fresh bottle of wine that he had opened for the trip, grinning back at us with his silly, fat friar's face, or howling up at the moon and the rising comet.

The neighborhood that we clattered into was no more than two blocks from the Steins', but much more satisfying in terms of bohemian character. *This* was what I had expected the Montparnasse Sixth to look like. The small block had at least half a dozen bars and dancing clubs, all of them competing to fill the air with music and noise, and there were couples and groups spilling out onto the sidewalk in fancy dress and festive poses. It was early on a Sunday evening, but nonetheless that was the first place I ever saw people literally dancing in the street. Diego leaned out the cab window, gave a whoop, and pointed up at a third-story window. There, I could see into an apartment that was glowing with pink light and crowded with people, some of whom appeared to be dancing riotously. I realized with some alarm that this apartment must be our destination, and I glanced quickly at Moishe, to make sure he hadn't seen it yet. I was afraid I wouldn't be able to get him up the stairs, if he knew where he was going.

I became progressively more alarmed as we made our way up the stairs. If the street was loud, the stairwell was louder, and the closer we came to the Delaunays' door, the greater the din became. Diego led the way up the stairs, taking them two at a time with huge enthusiasm. Amedeo also seemed to be coming back to life at last, as the aura of the party grew stronger and stronger.

We entered without ceremony into the loudest room I had ever been in in my life. The apartment was not large, but every square foot of its floor was covered with people. Most of them were young and looking a little drunk, about half of them dancing, many of them dressed very oddly, and everyone looking terrifically excited. At one edge of the crowd, I could barely make out the musicians: a clarinet, a Gypsy violin, and some sort of hand-drum from Northern Africa. The gaslights had been shaded with patterned red silk, giving the room an ambience that was exactly halfway between a nurturing womb and a vision of hell. The apartment was also rife with art and bric-á-brac of every description.

Amedeo and Diego immediately disappeared into the crowd, predictably enough, and Angelina drifted off after them. I looked at Moishe and to my relief found that he was wide-eyed with fascination rather than terror, at least for the moment. I was thankful that I had not succeeded in dragging Irène along. Even without Pablo Picasso, I could hardly countenance bringing my sixteen-year-old roommate into this sort of bedlam.

Willie appeared out of the throng, carrying in one hand a stack of small glasses that resembled the Tower of Pisa, and in the other a bottle of brandy. He spotted me near the door just as I was spotting him, and he came straight over.

"Welcome!" he cried, with obvious delight. I immediately suspected that he had not believed we would really come. He had to lean in very close to our ears so that we could hear him at all. "Here, take a couple of glasses off the top, and I'll pour you each a drink."

The brandy looked quite good, so I cheerfully complied, placing one of the glasses in Moishe's passive hand. "Are you moonlighting as a waiter, Mr. Apollinaire?" I teased him.

He laughed and filled the glasses. "Everyone who can afford to bring something to the Delaunays' parties, does so," he called into my ear. "When you are successful, Florbela, you will do the same. The Delaunays are not rich like the Steins, but they are truly a national resource."

Willie set down his stack of glasses on an end table that was already crowded with empty wine bottles and overfilled ashtrays, and he poured himself a glass. We all exchanged a toast. The first glowing drop of cognac that touched my tongue spread through me like warm gold, and oddly enough I almost immediately began to feel some of the boisterous joy that filled the room.

"Where are the Delaunays, Willie?" I shouted, leaning close. "Will you introduce us?"

"Of course! That's what you're here for." He looked around.

"They're never far away. . . . Ah, there's Sonia. Wait here, I'll steal her away."

Willie squeezed into the jostling crowd, and I shared a smile with Moishe. He no longer looked wide-eyed or at all overwhelmed. Like myself, he seemed to have absorbed some of the room's delightful and ambient madness.

"Are you happy?" I asked him.

"I am happy."

Willie returned a moment later with a positively radiant woman, a few years older than I. She had round, plain features and thick dark eyebrows, but her eyes were big and luminous, and she had a smile of unfeigned contentment that suggested a deep and truly peaceful soul. I immediately wanted to be her friend.

"Sonia Delaunay, Florbela Sarmentos, Moishe Shagalov," Willie said, making perfunctory introductions. Then he handed Sonia a glass, and filled us all a round of cognac.

Sonia blinked at Moishe, as if startled. "Your name is *Moishe*?" Then she quickly rattled off a question in Russian. He smiled bashfully and replied. She gasped and began to speak rapidly in that Eastern tongue of which I knew not a word. With a sinking feeling, I saw that I was not likely to have much chance to converse with her that evening.

As if to confirm my deduction, I felt Willie's hand gently pressing at the back of my elbow, guiding me away. "Come along," he said into my ear. "Our work here is done. They are both Russian Jews and both from the academy at Saint Petersburg. Your friend has just become a permanent part of Paris society, whether he likes it or not."

Chapter Nineteen

I followed Willie through the crowd blindly, letting him lead me passively by the arm like a pet on a leash. I was too short to see where we were going, and since many of the guests in the living room were large and leaping around rather wildly, I would not have dared to attempt to cross the floor on my own.

"Sonia used to be married to Wilhelm Uhde, the gallery owner," Willie shouted back at me over his shoulder.

"Very convenient," I joked when he turned around to see my reaction.

He laughed. "Convenient for both of them, really. I don't think Uhde has much interest in women, if you follow my meaning. Anyway, they were divorced a few months ago so that Sonia could marry Robert." I absorbed this information without gaining a lot of clarity. In fact, I was still trying to assimilate the fact that Sonia was Jewish. I would never have guessed the name Delaunay to be a Jewish name.

We emerged abruptly into a sort of clearing in the crowd, where three or four young dandies were listening with rapt attention to a young blond man with a pipe and bow tie. The speaker was a little older than I, perhaps twenty-five, and he had an unmistakably aristocratic bearing. He stopped his monologue in midsentence as Willie approached, and turned to us with an air of studied politesse.

"Robert Delaunay," Willie called out to me triumphantly, giving a flourish with his hand as if he had just produced the man out of a hat. "This is Florbela Sarmentos, of Portugal, London and

Cherbourg."

Robert gave me a heavy-lidded smile, managing to look boyishly charming—even innocent—while hinting at vast reserves of arrogance beneath his surface. "*Bem-vindo à minha casa, senhorita.*" He leaned forward to kiss the air just above my hand, a remarkably elegant gesture. As far as I could discern through the din, his pronunciation of the simple Portuguese formality was almost perfect.

"Florbela has managed to bring us that remarkable new Russian talent I told you about, Robert. He'll be around, by and by. We've left him in Sonia's care."

"I hope he doesn't need a place to stay," Robert replied, in a tone that suggested he didn't care much one way or the other. "The sofa and the rug are already taken. I suppose he can sleep in the kitchen, as long as he doesn't eat much."

Willie shook his head vigorously. "He has a studio at La Ruche."

Robert gave a small, knowing smile. "Ah! Then that's all sorted out." He turned to gaze at me with a look that was perhaps a bit superior, but too gentle to be a source of offense. "Are you also a resident of La Ruche? I lived there myself until quite recently, you know. Then marriage, *et cetera*, and now here I am."

By this point, I had deduced that Robert had probably been raised in some provincial château, or one of the grand old townhouses in Versailles. This made his marriage to a foreign, Jewish divorcée so extraordinarily unlikely that I had to take great pains to avoid letting my curiosity show on my face.

Nonetheless, Willie read my mind and pronounced, quite loudly enough for Robert to hear, "The Delaunay marriage has been the most engrossing scandal of the year."

Robert smiled indulgently, perhaps even modestly. "It's still only April." He puffed thoughtfully at his pipe. "There's plenty of time left to top the act."

I had no idea what I could possible say at such an awkward juncture in the conversation. I stammered, "Your . . . your wife seems like a *darling* woman, Mr. Delaunay."

"His parents all but disowned him when he married her," Willie remarked, shouting the news out to the room. "They cut him off without a *centime*."

"That's terrible!" I found myself shouting back, carried away by a moment of outrage. Then I had another thought and turned to Robert. "But in that case, how do you pay for all this?" I waved a hand vaguely about, indicating the general festivities.

"Ah. We are still working on that. That and the rent, of course."

"Come with me," Willie said abruptly, leaning away once again into the crowd. "I'll show you what Robert has been working on."

Although I would have preferred a few more minutes to meet the man himself, there was no polite way to refuse this invitation. Robert was already discreetly turning away from us, to resume the story that he had been telling to his friends, so I grabbed the tail of Willie's coat before he could disappear, and let him lead me once again into the hurly-burly.

We squeezed through a crowded hallway and into an adjoining room that was apparently Robert's painting studio. It was nearly as crowded as the front room, but much quieter and more sedate, filled with people chattering in small groups. The easels and furniture had been pushed against the walls.

"Over here. This is the series he's been working on recently." I followed Willie as he shouldered his way to a stretch of wall displaying a series of over a dozen canvases, all of which looked quite similar at first glance. "The ones by the door there are the early ones, from last year. Then the series advances to the right."

The moment that followed was one of the most eye-opening experiences of my life. It took me some time, perhaps even several minutes, to really understand what I was seeing, but for once, no one had to explain to me the import of what was before my eyes. The first canvases, on the left, consisted of stylized and rather festive images of the Eiffel Tower. As the series progressed to the right, the tower remained recognizable for a while, but its details were gradually lost and its outlines disappeared, and large regions of the canvas flattened out into simple fields of color. Finally, the last two canvases showed nothing but flat, geometric patches of paint: jumbled triangles and rectangles. If those two paintings had been shown by themselves, few viewers would have guessed that they represented the Eiffel Tower.

"How *bizarre!*" I exclaimed, standing in front of the last canvas in a sort of aesthetic epiphany.

"He calls it Abstract art," Willie said proudly, as if he had painted the series himself. He was clearly delighted at my reaction. I'm sure I was looking quite comically flabbergasted.

"But is it even . . . I mean, can you even really call it . . ."

"Is it art? Of course it is! Just wait and see, senhorita. One day, this will be bigger than Cubism!"

"Let's not exaggerate, Willie," a voice said from behind our shoulders.

We discovered that we had been joined by a man in his late twenties, with very dark hair and eyes, a strong chin and a long Gallic nose. He was dressed casually, but at the same time impeccably and even a bit conservatively, and he was extremely handsome.

"Ah-ha, at last! A real artist," Willie exclaimed. "Someone who can correct my errors in these matters." He glanced at me with a quick, almost invisible wink. "In fact, someone who inevitably *will* do so."

"You could spare me the trouble," the man replied in a droll tone, his expression deadpan. "If only you would lose the habit of holding so many incorrect opinions."

Willie gave a hooting laugh and clapped the man on the shoulder. "Allow me to introduce you to my upstanding friend, Fernand Léger. Monsieur Léger, Senhorita Florbela Sarmentos. I suspect you'll like Monsieur Léger, senhorita, as he is by no means a rogue. Indeed, I believe that of all my personal friends, he is the only one who cannot, in all fairness, be called a rogue."

Monsieur Léger bowed his head slightly. "You are too kind."

"Though he does hail from La Ruche," Willie hastened to add. "And you've seen what sort of riffraff inhabit those quarters."

I turned curiously to meet Léger's warm, dark gaze, which was regarding me unwaveringly. "So then, you once maintained a studio at La Ruche, Monsieur Léger? What induced you to move out?"

He opened his mouth to reply, then shut it. A moment later, he opened it again and said, "I had the good fortune to find an atelier elsewhere that provides better light."

Willie snorted with mirth at this comment, which was obviously a fatuous civility of some sort. I would have assumed that Léger was actually saying that he had moved out to escape the noise, chaos and disreputable company. But Willie explained, "He moved out because he became a success. Everyone who becomes a success at La Ruche moves out immediately. Didn't you know that?"

I turned back to Léger, my curiosity piqued even further. "Are you, then, a successful artist, Monsieur Léger?"

He shrugged modestly. Before he could reply, Willie cut in to say, "He is the *only* person in all this crowd who makes a steady living through his art."

"You are exaggerating again," Léger rebuked him.

Willie craned his neck comically, panning slowly around the room, then leaned out through the door to stare for a few moments at the crowd in the front room. Then he faced Léger again. "No, I'm not."

"There's Brancusi," Léger offered.

"He's not here tonight."

Willie might have noticed an unintentionally crestfallen look on my face at this frank accounting of the appalling odds that faced a young and untried contender in the field of the fine arts. He quickly added, "But they *will* succeed! Many of them. If Léger can do it, anyone can, isn't that so, Léger? And Léger appears to be doing quite well indeed, senhorita; in fact, he has a flat of his own, just a block or so from here."

"Oh! Do you live in the Sixth?" I asked, a little more quickly than I had intended. The northern tip of Montparnasse was coming to seem like the center of the universe to me, and I envied anyone who lived here.

"I do indeed," Léger replied, showing neither pride nor irritation at my abruptness. Though his eyes were warm, he evidently had a habitually cool demeanor.

"I hope you don't mind if I slip away," Willie said suddenly. "I have to make a few social calls." He gave me a glance, feigning sternness. "Don't get him started on politics, senhorita! He's a rabid communist." And with that, he stepped away into the crowd.

I smiled uncertainly, left so suddenly alone with Monsieur Léger. "Is that so?" I asked him politely. Communists, as I have mentioned, were almost completely unknown to me at that time, and still struck me as an exotic breed. I would certainly never have guessed this man for one, with his carefully combed hair, his staid and academic-looking blue cardigan, his impeccably polished shoes.

He rolled out from under the question. "I believe in social equality. I believe in the rights of workers. If that makes me a communist . . ." He let the thought trail off, but his tone made it quite clear that the answer to my question was simply yes. He changed the subject smoothly, inquiring how I had come to live at La Ruche, and what I thought of the place. I found myself giving a few words of description, particularly of Amedeo and his permanent houseguests. We shared a good laugh.

Monsieur Léger was a stunningly handsome young man, though he already had a few stern lines that gave his face rather a stolid and foreboding character. Still, chatting with him that first time, as every time after, a great deal of what made him attractive to me was not so much his appearance as the fact that one could tell at a glance that he was unaware of his own physical beauty. He was cool and emotionally aloof, it's true, but what a contrast with the aloof manner of Pablo Picasso! Rather than seeing himself as some sort of special treat that had been bestowed upon the women of the world, Léger seemed to regard himself as simply outside the world of women, self-sufficient, and probably too busy for a lot of romantic nonsense. For these reasons he made a very positive impression upon me, from the start. He was a serious man, but a charming one for all that.

When I asked him if he was a Cubist, he smiled dismissively but without condescension, and said, "Come with me."

He led me through the crowd and showed me one of his small canvases, hanging on Robert's studio wall. The composition was strangely formalized and had been stiffly outlined, so in those two ways it did in fact resemble Cubism a bit. But the fields of color had been painted using the tidy but naive techniques for the rendering of curvature that we see in engineering diagrams. The effect was almost childish-looking. Of course, the same adjective could be applied to Moishe's work, but this painting lacked the charm and freedom that we see in the works of children, before they have been trained by teachers. I silently adjudged the painting to show a truly original style, but one that was certainly not to my taste.

I realized that Monsieur Léger was watching the side of my face; indeed, he almost seemed to be holding his breath. Surprised and flattered by this unexpected attendance upon my opinion, I must admit that the first words that came out of my mouth were, "I like it . . ." Then I saw his brow lower just a bit, and I realized that I could not deceive him in such a matter. So I quickly appended: ". . . much more than Cubism." We shared a chuckle over that, and I believed that I had passed some sort of test.

Almost despite myself, as our conversation moved to other matters, I found my voice developing a soft tone of encouragement, drawing him on. I certainly kept the drift of the conversation intellectual and a bit abstract, but I admit to being a little flirtatious nonetheless. He effectively cornered me at one end of the room, behind the backs of the chattering crowd, but I felt certain that he had no idea that he was doing so, and I let him do it without protesting. His eyes watched me almost unblinkingly as we spoke, and I think that if they had been cold blue eyes like Brian Torrence Grimm's then I would have felt oppressed and perhaps offended by his stare. But there was a deep softness in Léger's eyes, despite the hard lines defined by the bones of his face, and this made it pleasant to be the object of his scrutiny. He was absolutely charming company and I felt flattered that someone as important as he was paying me so much attention.

It was as we were laughing over some amusing story he had recounted that he visibly caught himself and held back some comment or other, his lips slightly open, as if the words were still on the tip of his tongue. He gave me an asymmetrical smile and said, "You know, if I may say so, this is quite odd. I really never *do* this."

I looked at him sharply, on the verge of asking what he meant by the remark, but something in his face made me certain that he was merely stating the precise truth. He was a thoughtful and serious man, and despite his attractiveness, I believe he was no womanizer. I suspect that the sudden intimacy of our conversation had been as rare and unexpected of a thing for him as it was for me.

"I suppose I had better give you back to your friends," he said. "But perhaps you will do me the honor of accompanying me to a charming restaurant that I have recently discovered? Some evening soon?" He watched my face and seemed to be biting his lip.

Though I admit that I was very pleased, I nonetheless thought that the suggestion was a bit too sudden. "I'm not sure . . ." I began.

"Perhaps tomorrow?" he proposed easily.

"*Not* tomorrow."

"Tuesday?"

I laughed and relented. "Very well. Tuesday."

No sooner had we made our arrangements than Sonia appeared from out of the crowd, dragging Moishe by the wrist. I almost laughed when I saw Moishe's face. He was agog, eyes bulging, and he had a silly, amazed smile; he was evidently having the time of his life. Sonia hesitated, intuiting that she might be interrupting something, but I pulled her over to join us. I was glad that our pleasant conversation was ended with an equally pleasant interruption.

Sonia introduced Moishe to Léger, and the two men shook

hands and bowed slightly. To my chagrin, I noticed Léger observing Moishe superciliously down the length of his nose. When Sonia indicated Léger's painting on the wall, Moishe turned to examine it with apparent amazement. I was embarrassed to see Léger adopt a tight, superior smile as he watched Moishe's reaction, like a professor overseeing a young student during some elementary exercise in art appreciation. He placed himself behind Moishe's shoulder and murmured words of explanation, pointing authoritatively at various parts of the canvas.

Sonia turned her attention to me and lifted a small piece of paper that she had been carrying carefully between her fingertips. "Look! Moishe painted this." She had a mild Russian accent, which gave her French a mellifluous, rather smoky sound. The picture turned out to be a tiny gouache in richly saturated colors, and I quickly perceived that it was a crudely rendered portrait of Sonia herself, unmistakably in Moishe's style.

"He just did that?" I asked, surprised to think of him as the kind of man who might produce a work of art as a party trick. But then it occurred to me that Moishe almost never went two whole hours without painting *something*.

"Give me that," Léger said imperiously, and he fairly snatched the painting from Sonia's hand. He leaned closely over it, grumbling something under his breath, then, apparently dissatisfied with the illumination, took two steps away and stood under a nearby gaslight. We waited to hear his pronouncement, but he simply continued staring at the little painting, his eyes burning as if he intended to pounce on the image, kill it with his teeth and devour it. Occasionally his eyes darted left to give the nervous little Moishe a piercing glance.

Having seen people react to Moishe's work before, I knew just what this was about, so I did my best to distract Sonia's attention by commenting on Roberts' remarkable series of works. She beamed with pleasure. "Do you like them?" she asked excitedly.

"Well . . . I'm amazed by them," I told her. "But I don't know *what* I like anymore. I have only just arrived in Paris, and I worry that everything that I have ever learned about art may be wrong."

"Ah, yes! It was the same for me when I arrived," she assured me, leaning over with her hand on my arm. "It is overwhelming? Now, I love this Abstract art, but this series that Robert is working on, it's too angular for my taste. Honestly, what is wrong with circles?"

She turned away from me abruptly and poked Léger hard on his arm with her fingertip. "Well?" she demanded. "What do you think of this gouache that he has done for me? Isn't this delightful?"

But despite the probing, Léger refused to reply. He actually turned a few degrees to the right, showing us his back while he continued to brood over the little painting under the light.

Sonia rolled her eyes dramatically at me, then hooked my elbow under one arm and Moishe's elbow under the other, and began to guide us away. Léger, however, reached out abruptly and seized Moishe's sleeve firmly, snatching him from Sonia almost by force. He drew Moishe close and began interrogating him quietly in an intense undertone, pointing at the little portrait in his hand.

I had seen Moishe garner admirers before, so I was just as happy to let Sonia lead me away. She promenaded me around the main room, introducing me to several of her extraordinary friends and hangers-on. Eventually we joined the clique that surrounded Robert, who proved to be a witty and erudite speaker.

Sometime after midnight, I noticed that Diego, Amedeo and Angelina had vanished from the party. Although I was a little irritated at them for wandering off without saying goodbye, it was easy enough to surmise that they had been caught up in the vortex of the Paris night, and whisked away to yet wilder entertainments. In a certain sense, it was perspicacious of them to sneak off without mentioning the matter to Moishe and me. It certainly would have been pointless to try and invite us to come along.

Indeed, it had come time for us to get ourselves home, and so I shouldered my way back through the crowd, looking for Moishe. To my surprise, I found him still cornered in the back of Robert's studio, engaged in intense conversation with Monsieur Léger. The two of them were talking animatedly, Léger bending close to listen with great care to Moishe's broken French. As I paused to watch them, I saw them both suddenly burst into loud, uninhibited laughter. I stopped where I stood, unwilling to approach closer and interrupt such a prodigious and unexpected meeting of creative spirits. Who would have thought that two men so different in nature could enjoy each other's company so much?

Willie had appeared at my side, unnoticed. "He doesn't know what's good for him."

"Who doesn't?"

"Your friend Moishe. Remember how we almost had to tie his hands and feet to get him here? And look at him now."

"True," I allowed. "But I'll bet that next week, he won't want to come again, despite all that. He'd rather stay home and paint."

Willie shook his head in wonder. "The whole world is just the light in his eyes. And all of us are nothing but loud and tiresome distractions."

We were silent a moment, considering this observation. Then I reminded him, "Except Bella."

I asked Willie to help us find a cab on the street outside, and he did so with practiced efficiency. He insisted that I let him pay the driver, and though I was reluctant to accept, I must admit that I was secretly glad of his generosity. Moishe was still beaming with excitement when we climbed up into the compartment, but we had barely gone a block before he began to nod his head. By the time we arrived outside La Ruche, he was sleeping like a little boy, with his head on my shoulder.

Upstairs, I wasn't surprised to find Irène wide awake, sitting up in her bed and reading by lamplight. She nodded and murmured hello to me in a sulky tone, very unlike her, and furthermore she didn't quite make eye contact as she did so. After a few minutes, I approached her side of the room on some pretext or other, in order to examine her more closely. I found that she was reading what appeared to be a children's book and nibbling on chocolates.

"Have you had dinner?" I asked her.

She turned the page without looking up. "I am not hungry."

I frowned at this news and almost said something more. As far as I could tell, Irène hadn't had a real meal in at least twenty-four hours, and she surely couldn't afford to start losing weight. Still, it was hardly my place to criticize her eating habits, so I let out a long breath of frustration, intentionally audible, and turned away to prepare myself for bed.

I had barely begun to undress, when I heard the soft plunk of Armand's guitar through the window. My fingers hesitated on my buttons. I closed my eyes, imagining him sitting out there: my dogged, self-appointed protector, keeping watch through the night outside my home while I was out kicking up my heels. I tried to remind myself that I had certainly never asked him to take on such a role, nor did I wish to find myself feeling imprisoned by his kind intentions. Still, I found myself fastening my bodice back up again, then rummaging about until I turned up what meager bits of food were laying around the studio. These turned out to be a sad, stale roll and half a bottle of wine.

As I stepped toward the door, I heard Irène's clear, piping voice say, "Florbela." Barely lifting her eyes from the pages of her book, she extended her slender little hand to give me her half-eaten bag of chocolates. I added this to the other offerings, kissed her on the forehead, and trotted down the stairs and out to the yard.

I found Armand leaning over his guitar in his intense, one-minded fashion, as if he were trying to bolster his fledgling skills by the application of exaggerated attentiveness. When he heard my footfall, he looked up and smiled as if he had been expecting me.

"Leaozinha."

He stood up to offer me a seat and accepted the food and wine with a nod of thanks.

The comet was hidden behind trees, but I watched the big, luminous moon while Armand ate, and I could feel his eyes drifting over occasionally to glance at me. My mood had changed, and I no longer felt at all guilty for living my life as I pleased while he and his comrades played their game of guard duty outside my home, but I was glad that I had decided to come out and sit a while with him. Two or three times, as he ate, I could feel that he was about to say something. I hoped that he would not, because I was very tired. He seemed to read my mind, and remained silent.

When he was done, he brushed his hands, leaned over his guitar again and began to play.

Chapter Twenty

Two days later, it was one of those cool, rainy days you get sometimes in the Paris spring. The dim sky hung low over the city, relentlessly dumping fat drops of cold rain, hour after dismal hour. Though we were close to May Day by now, winter seemed to be entertaining the notion of a reprise.

I puttered about the studio all afternoon, feeling trapped, glumly failing to work on my current canvas or for that matter anything substantial. The obscure and oppressive illumination from the rain-spattered window converted my half-finished still life into a morbid spectacle, but I made a few game stabs at its shadows and receded spaces, hoping the grim light might bring out some of the nuances in those gloomy corners.

The gloomy weather coaxed out my troubled thoughts and I often found myself thinking of my father, and of his old friend the professor. My mind replayed those terrible visions of the dying man and his instruction to search for the ugly painting under the bench. Why would he want *me* to have such a horrid thing?

Irène spent the whole day hunched on the chair at her worktable, her bent shoulders and the back of her head buried under a huge knitted shawl, slowly turning the pages of an immense book on the history of ancient Persia and Mesopotamia. Occasionally, I tried to engage her in conversation, and she did her best to pay me off with grunts and monosyllabic replies. This was her third day of moping, and I was by now quite worried for her health of mind and body.

At some point during that long afternoon, there was a sharp

click on the windowpane, causing both of us to jerk our heads up and look around. After a moment's pause, I recalled that this was a signal. Armand had proposed a simple collection of signs and warnings to allow my Souris Trempés guards to communicate with me. A piece of gravel bouncing off my windowpane meant that I should cautiously look outside.

The rain had relaxed into a misty drizzle and I could see, around the edge of the building, Brian Torrence Grimm unfolding himself out of a black-and-brass automobile, almost certainly an official vehicle of the British Embassy. I stared through the slit between the curtains, feeling alarmed and startled at his unexpected arrival. He said a few words to his chauffeur, then tucked some sort of leather folder or portfolio under the lapel of his jacket, pulled his collar up against the rain, and began bustling toward the front door.

I noticed a movement in the dripping, untrimmed shrubbery in the yard beneath my window and barely made out the bedraggled anarchist Thierry, waving to me from cover, struggling to get my attention. Clearly it was he who had thrown the pebble, and it occurred to me that he was awaiting instructions, and might be considering some defensive action against the suspicious intruder, who was after all both a Freemason and an Englishman. I waved my ragged protector away and turned to the mirror to check my hair.

I had been remiss in my dealings with Brian over the past week. He had sent me an invitation by courier on Friday, proposing that we attend the opera together on Saturday evening. I would have enjoyed seeing the performance, which was the hit of the season—a staging of Kálmán's *The Gay Hussars*—but alas, by the time the invitation arrived I had already promised to take Moishe to the Steins'. Being in a hurry at the time, I had been forced to hand the courier a brief response, saying that I would be busy on Saturday evening but would respond shortly. Since then, however, given the long evening at the Delaunays' and my ongoing concerns for Irène's emotional well being, I had as yet sent no word. Still, it was difficult to believe he would pay an unexpected personal visit merely as the result of impatience born of a three-day wait.

I hurried down the stairs to meet him, and found him standing diffidently, just inside the front door, sheltered from the rain but unwilling to advance further without an invitation.

"Mr. Grimm," I hailed him as I clattered quickly down the last flight of stairs. I used a tone of cool formality. "What a surprising pleasure." I inflected this civility in such a way as to suggest that the element of surprise might possibly exceed the element of pleasure.

He bowed his head as I stepped up to him, politely accepting my implied chastisement. "Please accept my apologies for the abrupt intrusion, Senhorita Sarmentos . . . but this is not a social call, and the matter may just be of some urgency."

My hand, of its own accord, groped blindly for a moment until I found the newel at the base of the stairs and clutched it for support. For a terrible moment, I was certain he was bringing news of my father.

Seeming to sense my tension, he raised his eyebrows and quickly continued, "Though there is certainly no emergency . . . no cause for alarm."

I let out a breath of tentative relief. Remembering my manners, I said, "Please," and turned, gesturing to propose that he come with me and find a comfortable place to sit and share his news. But as we were in the neglected common space of the building, there was no such place at hand, so I was forced to leave the word hanging.

He gave no sign that he had noticed this awkward gesture, but continued to speak formally, as if in an official capacity. "I received word," he murmured to me very quietly, "less than an hour ago, that certain experts of my lodge are all but certain that the *special object* in your keeping is of key importance to the monarchists of Portugal."

My eyes must have widened, but I think my initial reaction to this news was less of amazement than incredulity. "*Key* importance?" I demanded.

He simply nodded. "That is their judgment. And of course, that means it is of equal importance to the republican partisans of your nation."

Now, in a way, this news came as no surprise. After all, poor Professor Almeida would not have given me the painting as his dying wish if it weren't an object of some usefulness to my father's cause. I suppose that I had imagined it was a treasure of some monetary value, something that might one day be sold at market to provide funds for a Portuguese rebellion, or perhaps even specifically to negotiate my father's release from prison.

I leaned closer and whispered, for clarification, "So then . . . the symbols truly are some sort of enciphered message?"

He nodded once, firmly.

I looked at him skeptically for a few moments, but I could detect nothing in his face except an attentive seriousness, and then, also, he *had* arrived in an embassy car, which suggested that he really did feel himself to be on legitimate business.

"I don't think I can let you take it," I told him. I was surprised at my own firmness in the matter, but it seemed to me that if the painting were really of some special importance to my father and his cause, then Armand had been right in saying that I couldn't simply hand it over to the English Freemasons, however much I might trust Brian's personal intentions in the matter.

Again, he nodded just once. "I anticipated as much," he said frankly. "I'm prepared, if you'll let me, to copy the entire sequence of the cipher onto these sheets that I have brought with me." He drew forth a leather folder he was holding tucked under his jacket.

I was about to point out that, given the large number of intricate little symbols, that would take quite some time, but the look on his face made it clear he was prepared to work at the task for as long as necessary. Impressed at last with the gravity of his visit, I held up a finger and said, "Please give me just one moment." Then I turned my back to him and ran quickly up the stairs.

I stopped first at my studio to poke my head in the doorway and whisper a warning to Irène's back from across the room, letting her know that we were about to receive a visit from Mr. Grimm. She turned to give me a long-faced expression over her shoulder, but she raised no objection. I closed the door and moved on to Moishe's studio, next door. I found him, as usual, deeply absorbed in his current canvas. I communicated to him that I was going to start prying at his ceiling once again, and he nodded assent.

I left the painting in its metal package just inside the door of my studio and was pleased to observe, in passing, that Irène was at the mirror and preparing herself for company. I rushed back down the stairs and ushered Brian up.

He entered our studio deferentially, ducking a bit at the doorway to get himself inside. He bowed stiffly to Irène. She had already taken her seat again and gave him only the faintest of nods in return, her face expressionless, then turned her back to the room and peeled up another page in her thick book.

Brian leaned down and snatched up the copper tube where it sat near the door. I helped him to extract the canvas and to spread it over a table under a lamp; then I offered him our modest stock of refreshments, which he refused. He produced a few large pieces of linen rag paper, carefully set up his pen, blotter and inkwell, and began carefully copying the first of the symbols.

I returned to my makeshift easel, where my moribund still life was propped soundly against the back of a chair with my palette on the seat in front of it. I sat facing it, toying with the grays and blues of the darkest regions of the canvas in the poor lighting, waiting, perhaps a bit expectantly, for Brian to say something to me—to call me over on the pretext of showing me some little discovery. I was to be sorely disappointed. Hours rolled by, literally hours, and the three of us simply sat there with our backs to one another, forming the corners of an elongate triangle that spanned the narrow room. Speaking for myself, I was certainly not as interested in my work as I was feigning to be, and I strongly suspect that the same was true of Irène, but I feel quite certain that Brian had nothing on his mind but the careful transcription of those arcane symbols. I have to admit that I was a little offended that he ignored me so thoroughly.

The gray afternoon faded gradually and imperceptibly into gray evening. At some point the rain stopped, and then a little later the clouds simply blew away, leaving a cool, clear evening. I opened the window and the fresh spring air rolled intoxicatingly through the stuffy room. I leaned out a bit to fill my lungs, and the world outside had that bejeweled look that comes after long spring rains: all the fresh greenery and unexpected flowers gleamed with shimmering beads of water.

A few minutes later, back at my easel, I heard some busy clattering behind me on Irène's side of the room, and this was followed by a faint odor of hot wax. I felt a real surge of pleasure to think that Irène was working again and perhaps at last emerging from her funk. I got up and wandered casually across the room to gaze over her shoulder and admire the familiar, skillful manipulations of her narrow fingers as she tooled her wax.

It took me a few moments to realize that Irène wasn't working on her faun. My first thought was to worry that she had abandoned that project or had somehow spoiled the delicate little statue during her days of depression, and this struck me as a terrible shame, since it had been a beautiful piece and had seemed to be very nearly done. She was hard at work on a new project, one that she must have been keeping hidden under her dust cloth during the past day or two, roughing out its basic form at times while I was away.

It was the bust of a young man, and although it was still in an early stage of development, it seemed to stare back at me haughtily through its hollow eyes. With horror, I began to think I might recognize the face: that long nose, those wide cheekbones and arrogant lips. With alarm I realized she was making a bust of Picasso.

Irène continued sculpting as if I weren't there, perhaps defiantly, her hands continuing their deft ministrations. Now she demanded of me, in a neutral voice: "Well?"

I glanced back over my shoulder to make sure that Brian was too far away to overhear. Then I whispered sharply in Irène's ear,

"What on earth do you think you're doing?"

She replied with her usual clear enunciation, and with a complacency that chilled me. "I've decided to essay a bust of Theseus. Or perhaps it shall be a young Adonis. I haven't yet decided."

I felt my temper rising; so much so that I might have been driven to shake her by her bony shoulders if we had been alone. I glanced again at Brian, and was relieved to see that he was too busy to notice the urgent whispering coming from our corner of the room.

I leaned close to my roommate again and hissed in her ear, "It looks to me more like Narcissus."

Irène's hands paused only a moment at her work. Then they carried on, gently sculpting an earlobe. She replied in a harsh whisper, "I should think it's a bit early to judge."

I ground my teeth only for a moment, then forced myself to relax. It was certainly true that if Irène insisted on finishing such a project and displaying it to one and all, then there was going to be some scandal, albeit probably a small one by Paris standards. I sealed my lips, turned my back on her, and walked across the room to sit at the table near the door, where I could watch Brian finishing his painstaking transcriptions.

Barely had I made myself comfortable when I heard rapid footsteps approaching my door, followed by an urgent rapping of knuckles on the door panels. I opened the door cautiously and found Armand standing in the hallway, his cheeks flaming red and his broad brow pinched low over his eyes. I was surprised to see him there, to say the least.

Armand gave me a perfunctory nod and said, in uncharacteristically stiff tones, "Please forgive this intrusion, senhorita, but . . ." He looked past my shoulder and gave a lethally pointed stare at Brian Torrence Grimm.

"Oh dear," I said, holding the edge of the door firmly between my fingers to block him from entering the room. I glanced over my shoulder and found Brian looking blandly up from the table, his upper lip twitching a bit as if he were barely holding back some irate and no doubt inflammatory comment. I frowned at him and he turned slowly back to his work, his shoulders rolling in an almost imperceptible shrug.

When I turned again to Armand, I found that he was crowding me in the doorway, almost touching me. He noticed the irritation on my face, and stepped quickly back to a polite distance, where he adopted a rather hurt and self-righteous pose. "I arrived a few moments ago, to take my evening shift," he said quietly but with crisp formality, "and I was informed by the man whom I was relieving that this . . . *lodge member* . . . had insinuated his way into the building."

I interrupted him, speaking with careful precision to emphasize the anger that was building up under the facade of my civility. "Then you were misinformed. I admitted Mr. Grimm personally. He is working in this room at my invitation. Unlike you."

I was somewhat surprised that Armand didn't back down from my hostility, as he usually did. Rather, he seemed to stiffen further, digging in his heels, as it were. He said, "I must demand to know, on the part of my people, and on the part of all just partisans everywhere, what exactly *that man* is doing in your room." He closed his lips with a nearly audible snap, but then couldn't resist parting them again to add, "And what exactly you think *you* are doing."

I forced myself to wait the space of one breath, to avoid saying something I might really regret, and I still just barely managed to suppress a tremor of fury in my voice as I replied, "Mr. Grimm is working, as I've already told you. He is trying to help my nation's cause. Have you already forgotten that this was my father's express wish?"

Armand actually sneered when he heard me formulate the situation in those words. "If he is actually *working* on anything, I think we can be fairly certain that it's some nefarious Masonic plot." He glared over my shoulder at the side of Brian's face and added, "If his kind have their way, the flag of Portugal will one day bear an armillary sphere!"

At this remark, Brian emitted a nasty laugh, probably involuntarily. Unfortunately, this forced him to abandon the noble pretense of simply ignoring our conversation.

Realizing that I wasn't going to get rid of Armand easily, I blew out a puff of pure frustration, grabbed him by the lapel and tugged him into the room so that I could close the door behind him and stop sharing this ridiculous little fracas with my curious neighbors.

Brian turned around fully in his chair, looked Armand slowly up and down, tugged up the creases of his trousers at the knees fussily before crossing his legs, and drawled in English, "I say, aren't you supposed to be out watching the yard?"

To his credit, Armand ignored the baiting, though I suspect he understood it well enough. He crossed his arms and spoke down his nose at the seated Grimm, apparently making the most of his momentary advantage in altitude over the seated Englishman. "These premises are under the official protection of the Bande Liberté du Monde," he pronounced, "as ordained and contracted by the true republican government of Portugal. If you have business with that government, through the person of its consul, Senhorita Sarmentos, then you will make arrangements with us in advance. Is that understood?"

I probably emitted some inarticulate sound of outrage before exclaiming, "*Consul?*"

His eyes flickered at me for only a moment before returning to the face of Brian Torrence Grimm, whose cool blue eyes were gazing up at Armand with an admittedly infuriating arrogance. "*De facto* consul."

I turned my back and walked away to the window, where I found Irène putting away her working materials. Behind me, I heard Brian begin speaking in the honeyed-yet-poisonous tones that express the pique of a lifelong diplomat, proposing that Armand clarify his outrageous demands, while Armand tried to speak over him, suggesting a formal meeting between the senior members of the Bande Liberté du Monde and of the secrets chiefs of the Grand Lodge of Freemasonry.

"Are you getting ready to go out?" I asked Irène bleakly.

She gave me a wan smile, one that was not without sympathy. "I believe I will find a quieter place to spend the next hour or so. Perhaps you would care to join me?"

"Thank you, that's very thoughtful. But I have other plans."

She raised her small voice slightly to make herself heard over the increasing din behind my back. "Oh, shall you be going out, then?"

"I shall."

"That is very fortunate."

I gazed over to Armand and Brian, who were still in a heated exchange that I feared might degenerate into physical violence at any moment. Something occurred to me as she turned her attentions back to her preparations, and I asked, "What was the meaning of that odd comment about the sphere? Do you know?"

"The armillary sphere," Irène informed me, arranging a short cape over her shoulders in the mirror. "It is an archaic astronomical device, and a symbol of the Knights Templar. They were an ancient order, long disbanded, with whom the Freemasons claim some sort of kinship."

I thanked her for that, and then, seeing that she was ready to leave, I chaperoned her the length of her own studio to get her safely past the fractious men who stood between us and the door. Armand and Brian had the minimal grace to cut off their argument in midsentence and bow slightly as Irène passed. But the moment she was out the door, they turned upon each other again, wagging accusatory fingers and disputing points of protocol with real vehemence.

By this point, it was getting close to eight, and it was my pleasure to turn my back on my bellicose guests and disappear into the screened corner of the room. I took a good long time preparing myself, probably longer than really necessary, with some hope that my self-styled protectors would finish ventilating their differences and come to some sort of peaceful resolution, given enough time. But although the topics of dispute changed frequently, the argumentative spirit never waned. They were still leveling bold, if vague, accusations and charges back and forth when I finally emerged.

I had decided to wear my showiest clothing, and I'm pleased to say that the sight of my emergence finally put a halt to the pointless squabbling, at least for the time being. I was glad to return Armand's and Brian's nonplussed stares with what I hoped was a self-satisfied smile. Then I stepped to the mirror to examine the effect. I had been holding this dress in reserve for a special occasion. It consisted of a pleated, midnight blue silk bodice over a grand and elaborately folded black-and-gold skirt. This latter piece was a family heirloom, but I had paid to have it redesigned a year prior, in Cherbourg, to lift the waistline to just under the bust in the contemporary style. The result, if I may say so, was the height of elegance.

There was a loud kind of silence coming at me from the other end of the room, but I refused to look in that direction. I made a few final, preening adjustments, then checked the clock. I had intended to waste as much time as possible behind the privacy of the screen, but to my surprise I saw that it was exactly eight o'clock, and that for the first time in recent memory I was precisely on time.

I went to the window and looked out, and sure enough I saw a rather elegant, if funereal-looking, rented cabriolet waiting in the road, behind a tall white horse. Léger was nearby, leaning back jauntily on the fender of Brian's automobile, smoking a cigarette and chatting with Brian's chauffeur. He noticed me leaning from the window, and we exchanged a quick wave.

"Who is outside?" Armand demanded in the same aggressive tone he had been using with Brian.

I turned around and gazed at him defiantly, arching my eyebrows as if to suggest that I was about to ask what business it might be of his. I held the moment long enough to see him brace himself for the worst, then told him simply, "It is Fernand Léger. He is taking me to dinner."

Chapter Twenty-One

I was rather amused when Armand and Brian both dropped their jaws in perfect unison. They looked as if they were about to break into lugubrious song.

After a pause, Armand echoed, "Léger?"

Brian chimed in, "As in Léger . . . the *painter*?" It was the first time I had ever seen him at a loss for anything intelligent to say.

I'm afraid I was still angry enough at their boorish behavior to enjoy torturing them a bit. I took a good long moment to admire their shocked expressions. "That's right. I'm surprised you've heard of him, Brian." I noticed Armand smirk just a little, perhaps perceiving that this jab at Brian concealed a tacit compliment to himself. Armand had a fairly exhaustive knowledge of life on the Left Bank, and although he may have regarded the creative spirits who lived there as decadent, he always seemed to be current with the rumors of their activities.

"Everyone in Paris knows Fernand Léger," Brian grumbled. He frowned, evidently getting a grip on himself, no longer willing to play the fool. "He's a good, solid man of the city," he opined decisively. "Not one of your . . . bohemians."

I took up my bag and walked the length of the studio, passing between the two men with a little flounce. This was the sort of dress that produced a devastating flounce. "Please hide the canvas behind the wardrobe, and lock the door when you go. You can leave the key with Moishe."

As I descended, I was vaguely aware of someone scampering down the stairs below me, in the gloom. When I came to the ground floor, I was delighted and amazed to find Moishe, of all people, clasping Léger's hands as he stood on the rope rug just inside the front door. It was an odd sight. Léger was in "smoking," meaning to say a man's formal evening ensemble, while Moishe was wearing rags, covered with a paint-streaked smock. Furthermore, Léger was nearly a head taller, and frankly gorgeous in comparison with the mousey little Russian. But despite their disparities, the two men were positively beaming at each other.

As I appeared at the base of the stairway, Léger patted Moishe's hand, turned to me and said with grave formality, "Mademoiselle Sarmentos, it is delightful you see you and may I say you look radiant this evening."

"Thank you Monsieur Léger."

But I had scarcely gotten out these words of acknowledgement when, to my surprise, he turned away from me again. He went right back to struggling to communicate with Moishe in that funny way that all of us relied on, which is to say, using a hundred words of monosyllabic French vocabulary and a great deal of miming gesticulation.

I might have been offended at losing Léger's attention so quickly, but it was impossible to be anything but charmed at the lavish and proprietary concern that he was displaying to this unassuming little man whom he had so recently met. "You have paint?" he demanded. "You have food? Yes? No? You need clothes. No, listen. You need clothes. Borrow this. No, take it. Yes. You pay me later. Take it, take it," he said as he shoved what appeared to be a wad of notes into Moishe's painting shirt pocket.

The door opened suddenly and Mr. Lenin walked in, looking, as he usually did, terribly serious and deep in thought. He shouldered his way around us, head ducked, hurrying for the stairs and making eye contact with no one.

Léger broke off his conversation with Moishe in midsentence and took two steps in pursuit of Mr. Lenin, catching him as he was placing his foot on the first stair.

"Vladimir Lenin!" Léger exclaimed, sounding suddenly rather breathless. "You are Vladimir Lenin!"

Mr. Lenin stopped and turned around very slowly, looking, I'm afraid, like a man who is well accustomed to being apprehended unexpectedly in public, and not necessarily by friends. Above his head, I noticed that in the dimness of the stairwell Brian and Armand were standing at the top of the flight, apparently halted there by the sight of Léger importuning Mr. Lenin.

Mr. Lenin's face, which was habitually dour of expression even in the best of times, sank down into a theatrically disapproving frown as he examined the unknown man who had halted him on the steps of his own home, and whom he now perceived to be dressed in that merry uniform of triumphant capitalism, the tuxedo. But Léger didn't seem at all put off by this silent and inauspicious greeting.

"It is a tremendous honor to meet you, sir," Léger said with rich enthusiasm. "Please excuse me for interrupting your evening, but I could hardly let you pass without telling you that I think you are mankind's greatest living benefactor."

Mr. Lenin arched one of his black and remarkably expressive eyebrows very high upon hearing this unexpected flattery, but still did not smile. He spoke in his heavily accented growl, and demanded in a challenging tone, "Are you, then, a member of the Party?"

"Oh yes!" Léger exclaimed, and reached immediately under his lapel, as if fishing for his wallet.

Lenin afforded himself a tiny smile and said, "Is all right, comrade. No need to show me your card. I am not police."

Léger chuckled happily and said in tones of glowing admiration, "This is a great day for me . . . a true benefactor of mankind! And the architect of Russia's revolution!"

Mr. Lenin dropped his chin a few degrees, as if sinking again into his usual brooding mood. "But I will not be remembered for this," he murmured.

"Of course you will!"

"No, comrade. I intend to be remembered for Russia's *next* revolution."

All of us who were present laughed politely at this turn of wit.

THE SIXTH

It was common for the scruffy, impoverished residents of La Ruche to joke about their absurdly optimistic hopes for the future, but I suppose that this comment pretty much took the prize.

Mr. Lenin reached out a broad hand and clapped Léger on the shoulder with his thick, scarred knuckles. "Thank you for such words of encouragement, comrade." He pointed beyond Léger's shoulder at Moishe without shifting his eyes, and added, "If you are a friend of this Russian worker behind you, I encourage you: please educate him. He is a man of the people, from the *shtetl*, but I fear he is now backsliding." He leaned in closer and added, *sotto voce*, "He keeps company with some very decadent *artistes*."

He left us there laughing and stomped his way up the stairs. Armand and Brian leaned back against the rails to let him pass.

Léger turned to me at last, his face glowing with pleasure. "We had better be on our way. And as for you, Moishe"—he leaned over the smaller man and kissed him on both cheeks—"go paint. Go paint."

I heard Brian Torrence Grimm clear his throat ominously as Léger helped me arrange my cape, and for a moment I was afraid there was going to be a row. But as Léger opened the door for me, I glanced up and saw Armand and Brian sitting side by side near the top of the stairs, their chins on their palms, watching our exit wordlessly. I blew them a kiss from the door, one kiss to share, and Léger whisked me away.

The carriage transported us through the streets, wet and sparkling, directly into the Sixth, Léger's neighborhood. If I had felt a little slighted by not receiving Léger's full attention when he arrived at my door, he more than made up for it once we were on our way. His boisterous mood was infectious, and he had me laughing and at my ease before we had gone a block.

He had the driver let us off outside a perfect-looking but unremarkable little bistro in the lively heart of Montparnasse's corner of the Sixth.

"Le Loir Rôti," I read as we passed beneath the sign. "I don't think I've ever heard of it." I admit that I was putting on airs. I had been scarcely a fortnight in Paris, but after all I had already dined at La Tour d'Argent, and I suppose I had high hopes of soon knowing my way around the top echelons of Parisian gastronomy.

"No one has heard of it, *ma belle*," Léger told me confidentially, guiding me to the door and leaning close to murmur in my ear. He had a perfect tenor voice, and it fairly gave me goose bumps. "But alas, I doubt that we can keep the secret for long."

He was evidently well known at Le Loir Rôti, and the lone waiter ran over to hold the door for us and give him greetings as to an old friend, in that delightful and timeless fashion of French restaurateurs with their favorite customers. The room was quite full, but they had a small table reserved for us by the window.

There we sat for a few delightful hours, working our way slowly through a great number of tiny courses, many of them quite clever, all of them delicious and exquisitely presented. With each course we were presented with a new glass of wine, though I was unable to finish most of them. I don't remember the contents of our conversation, and that in itself is perhaps testament to Léger's natural social talent. I don't believe that a practiced seducer like Mr. Picasso, nor for that matter a painstaking man of the world such as Brian Torrence Grimm, could have led me through an hour or two of cheerful conversation under such intimate circumstances without a single topic marring or at least punctuating my memory of the exchange.

Late in the evening, as we finished our main course—a truly memorable filet mignon *chasseur*—the chef came out to wander the room and look for familiar faces. He was a surprisingly young man, with a drooping mustache and wandering eyes that gave his expression a beatific and rather scatterbrained appearance. As soon as he spotted Léger, he came directly to our table.

Léger stood and embraced him, then indicated me with a flourish. "Senhorita Florbela Sarmentos, this is Chef Didier, Paris's newest rising star."

I thanked him for a wonderful meal and praised his cuisine, then asked him where he had developed his skills.

"In London, mademoiselle."

"London?"

"Didier was the sous-chef at the Carlton Hotel," Léger told me in lofty tones, no doubt intended for the pleasure of Chef Didier's ears. "Under Auguste Escoffier. Have you heard of him?"

I had, and I said so. "I lived in England for some time, Monsieur Didier. Monsieur Escoffier has a reputation as the best cook in Britain."

"This is quite true," Didier agreed, frowning gravely. "But . . . this is not, in itself, a hard mark to achieve."

I laughed in such a way that I must have indicated a certain perverse nostalgia for England's boiled beef and sausages. Soon, the young chef and I were sharing a quick series of reminiscences of the Island Nation.

"If you are considering options for dessert," Chef Didier said in parting, "let me recommend the peach Melba."

Léger smiled, boyishly happy. "Wonderful . . . and such a funny name!"

Chef Didier nodded in agreement. "One of Maître Escoffier's flights of fancy. I think you'll enjoy it."

By the end of dinnertime, around midnight, I had completely lost that guardedness one generally has the first time one is alone with a stranger—even if he is a charming stranger in a roomful of contented people who are talking a bit too loudly over coffee and brandy. I was chatting and laughing right along with them, enjoying a tiny snifter of cognac.

Things had been going so smoothly that I'm not even sure what the topic had been at the point where Léger interrupted it by suddenly becoming silent, his expression very intense and his eyes turned down at the tablecloth. Naturally, this gave me a worrisome moment, but I watched him and waited to see if he would recover himself, or at least tell me what might be the matter.

He looked up slowly and gazed directly into my eyes. "I've never done this before."

I had no idea what he was talking about. After a moment, I attempted a crooked smile. "Never . . . been out to dinner?"

"Never like this." He placed both hands flat on the table, and his eyes watched me without blinking. I shrank a bit under the intensity of his gaze, and I'm sure I blushed. He said, "How shall I put this? I have *played* at this sort of thing before, as if it were a piece of theater; I have worn my mask and recited my lines with all the other actors. But I have never simply sat here under the world's eyes, I, my very self, and simply *enjoyed* an evening in such close company. No, never. Not without some degree of pretense."

"Well . . . you flatter me, monsieur."

He shook his head emphatically. "I do not. I don't mean to importune, Florbela, but may I ask if you might say the same of yourself?"

This was the first time that he had used my Christian name. I'm sure I looked a little surprised, but after a moment I couldn't help breaking into a smile. I wasn't luring him on in some cruel fashion, I prefer to think that I was merely trying to burst the bubble of tension and restore the easy, rambling quality that had characterized our evening up till this point.

"I'm having a great time," I admitted.

He faintly reflected my smile, and he continued to stare at me with an almost desperate intensity. "I am not a man given to sudden impulse," he asserted abruptly.

Although it was tempting, under the circumstances, to tease him a little for this statement, I must admit that I felt that I already knew him well enough to see that this was true, at least for the most part. "I know that."

"To act directly, from the heart—that is not the same as impulsiveness."

I was thinking about how to respond to that, when suddenly Léger was down on one knee on the floor beside my chair, gazing up into my eyes with that same unwavering intensity, but now at very close quarters. I looked down at him, unable to move my eyes away, feeling a mixture of horror, excitement, and dreamlike disbelief. I was vaguely aware that the bistro had suddenly gone breathlessly silent, and I knew that everyone at every table must be watching us.

"Florbela, you would make be the happiest man in France—no,

in all the world—if you would consent to marry me?"

This unexpected turn of events almost knocked me right out of my chair. Certainly no one had ever proposed marriage to me before, and although I had expected that such a thing would probably happen someday, it took me completely by surprise that Fernand should choose such circumstances as these. I immediately assumed that he had drunk a little much and was indeed just being impulsive. He certainly cut a tragic figure, kneeling before me, but there's no denying that he was being very silly.

At any rate, I'm proud to say that I didn't do what I think many girls would have done at this panicky juncture, namely to deceitfully tell the man that I needed time to think the matter over. No, I gave him my warmest smile, but kept my voice cool and formal, and told him, "Monsieur Léger, that is the kindest and most flattering offer that anyone has ever made me. But it is my will to make my own way in this world as an artist, as you yourself make your way. In this resolve, I have my father's steadfast approval and encouragement. You are one of the most charming men I have ever met, but there is simply no room in my life for a husband at this time." I feel I had been doing quite well up to this point, but then, to my consternation, I found that there were tears on my face and I had to pause to pat them away. When I could speak again, I told him firmly, "Now, please take your seat, and let us drink our cognac."

He returned shakily to his side of the table. I noticed that the room had miraculously returned to its previous chatter and festivity, and that all eyes were averted from our little spectacle.

Léger was too graceful to sit in stunned silence, however much he may have felt like doing so. He immediately begin to speak about art, launching into the subject in a very technical and academic vein. It was clear enough that he was exploiting the subject that made him feel most confident, and behind which he could most effectively conceal his wounded emotions. Naturally, I listened with a great display of attentiveness, exaggerating my interest in the hope of helping him recover some semblance of balance.

I assumed that, as soon as we possibly could, we would be escaping from the restaurant—retreating from the site of the disaster. But Léger was a man of vast poise, and after a few minutes his voice and the subject matter of his conversation regained a bit of their habitual fluidity. He waved insistently at the waiter, who had been seeming loath to approach our end of the room. When the man finally sidled nervously over to our table, Léger made some small quip to force a smile out of him, then ordered us a second and much larger pair of cognacs. I could do no more than sip at mine, but he seemed stone sober by this point and much in need of a drink.

By the time we left the bistro, Léger seemed to have effectively bandaged his self-inflicted emotional wounds. Although I wondered how deeply he might be hurt, he certainly seemed to be acting like himself again. He clasped hands with the waiter at the door, cast his eyes confidently over the other diners, then stepped over to the curb to wake up his coachman and help me into the cabin.

We chatted fairly easily, if somewhat distantly, on the ride home. When we stopped outside La Ruche, he jumped out to help me down to the cobblestones, a perfect gentleman.

"I've been very silly," he said abruptly, distancing himself from the matter with an easy laugh. "But it was a fine evening anyway, wasn't it?"

"It was a very fine evening, thank you."

"We must do it again!" he exclaimed. "Shall we say, tomorrow night?"

I bit back a laugh, but couldn't help exclaiming, "Monsieur Léger!"

He patted his hands in the air, as if acknowledging that the request might have been excessive, but could be easily modified. "No, then, at your leisure, of course. Perhaps some day later this week?"

I tried not to show how uncomfortable I felt at his proposal and I certainly didn't want to hurt his feelings.

"I may, perhaps, attend the party at the Delaunays' on Sunday," I told him, in a firm tone intended to cut off any further propositions.

He opened his mouth, but, seeing my face, he closed it again. Then he dropped his eyes and murmured, "But you *will* really be there?"

I smiled and gave him my word. "Florbela," he said as he tenderly kissed my hand, "I live in hope that one day you *will* let me love you." I felt so touched by this sweet gesture and heartfelt show of affection, I almost relented and suggested we could meet later in the week. Then I caught myself—I really needed more time to think about my feelings for him. I felt his eyes upon me all the way up to my door, and I probably let out an exhalation of relief once I was safely inside.

I hesitated before climbing the stairs, remembering my rather harsh treatment of Brian and Armand earlier in the evening. I went out to the yard through the back door, and there I saw Armand sitting as usual upon the largest and smoothest stone, leaning over his old guitar with the moon and comet in the clear sky above him.

He stopped playing as I approached. I stood before him wordlessly, letting him examine me in my fine dress, letting him notice that my cheeks were still flushed with wine and excitement. The season's first crickets chirped around us as he looked me over impassively, almost impersonally. I felt that he might be about to say something bitter to me, even perhaps something unpleasant, and I felt he had the right to chastise me if he wished to do so.

But instead, after a few moments of examination, he let out a stoic sigh and dropped his eyes. He lifted his guitar and moved himself to a rougher stone, indicating with a wave of his hand that I was welcome to the better seat if I intended to linger.

"Good evening, Leaozinha."

I was deeply touched by his forbearance. I surprised myself by impulsively leaning down to kiss his cheek before taking my usual seat beside him. I was struck by how delightful he smelled—of sandalwood and bergamot—warm woodland aromas.

We sat side by side for some minutes, watching the comet together and saying nothing. Periods of comfortable silence like this one were by now commonplace between us, perhaps because it was so often the case that our moments together came in the middle of the night, at the end of a long day for me and in the midst of a long vigil for him. At some point, Armand began to play again, very softly. He could hold a tune by this point, as long as the melody was simple and the rhythm straightforward. I may have closed my eyes for a while, enjoying the peaceful plunking sound of his fingers on the strings. Then, to my surprise, I heard him begin to sing.

He sang very softly, and I was amazed at how pretty his voice was. Although he was quite new to playing the guitar, he would later admit that he had been singing since he was a very small boy, in choirs. He had the voice of an angel. His song was a romantic ballad with strange and alien cadences, and it took me some time to identify it as coming from the age of the troubadours, already six hundred years past.

No sooner could I dry
All the waves of the sea
Then constrain my own heart
From loving you

When he finished, I asked him to sing again, and he gave me another of those archaic ballads. But I knew that I couldn't stay awake through a third, so when he finished, I quietly took my leave and made my way up to bed.

I lay there with the window open and listened to him sing, as sleep gradually rolled over me. I was melancholy and wondered if I was proving to be a cruel woman: encouraging these suitors, holding them at bay, even perhaps breaking their hearts. The sound of Armand's sweet voice was just the comfort I needed, but at the same time I had to scold myself for encouraging him.

THE SIXTH

Oh, but in a way, they were all so infuriating, the lot of them! I was never going to become an artist if I married one of those pesky men.

Chapter Twenty-Two

O n Thursday of that week, I awakened quite early with the exciting knowledge that at last I might be receiving some funds. This was a matter of no small consequence: I had been budgeting in the assumption that my money would only have to last this long, and I was quite literally down to my last few francs. I sat up, and as I did so, I noticed that the early sunshine striking the walls and roof of the building had turned our studio surprisingly warm. I pattered groggily to the window to push open the panes, but as I was doing so I was given a rude surprise.

I was arrested by the sight of Irène on her bed. In the heat of the night, she had thrown off her blankets in her sleep; she was lying on her belly, covered only by her nightgown. Irène was so fastidiously modest that this was the closest I had ever come to seeing her unclothed, and the sight was truly alarming. She was so scrawny that there seemed to be nothing to her at all, just a few strands of sinew holding together a tiny skeleton.

I tiptoed over, my fingers pressed to my lips in horror, and leaned over her bed to examine her more closely. For the first time, it occurred to me that she might be dying of some wasting disease. In fact, I realized, that would explain so many things. What if these five days of moping, which I had so uncharitably interpreted as romantic malaise, were actually due to the symptoms of a wasting decline? I wanted to know immediately whether she was in need of medical attention, and I was tempted to awaken her. I might even have done so, except that I couldn't stand the thought of waking her up prematurely, when she seemed so badly in need of rest. As I stepped back from the bed, however, I begin to wonder why I should feel myself qualified to make a medical diagnosis. After all, her face wasn't hollow-cheeked or gaunt in any way; in fact, from the neck up, Irène always appeared red-cheeked and bright-eyed, the very picture of youthful vitality.

My worries for Irène completely filled my mind as I dressed in silence and prepared to go out. But I knew it would be several hours yet before Irène arose, so I left to attend to my banking errand, intending to return and speak with her around noon.

Once I was outside in the intoxicating warmth of the spring morning, I regained my earlier excitement and impulsively splurged on a cabriolet that took me all the way across the river and into the First District, delivering me at the Parisian offices of the Banco De Portugal. There I presented myself to first a clerk and then a banker, and after an hour or so of tedious proceedings I was duly given access to a modest but sufficient account of funds, as arranged by my family's solicitor in Lisbon. The banker was a plump, mustachioed little man, and seemed quite pleased to be the agent of my good fortune in this transaction, though he kept glancing at my face in a nervous manner. I suppose I probably looked like I was on the verge of bursting into tears of relief. On my way out, I also collected a half dozen letters that the bank had kept for me.

Outside in the brilliant spring sunshine, as I let the doorman help me up into my cab once again, I reminded myself sternly to spend this money with care so as to be certain that I might never find myself again so close to penury. But as soon as I was across the river and into the Sixth, I couldn't resist paying off my cab and strolling along the large boulevards for a while, relishing the tempting sights in all those huge windows, knowing that I could afford most anything now, if I really wanted it.

I stopped at Pâtisserie Ladurée for a lavish breakfast of coffee and pastries, while I read my letters from old friends. I also bought a couple of pear tarts to carry home in boxes for Irène and Moishe. That done, I hurried directly to my real destination: an art store where I had long since set my heart on a particular easel—a light and sturdy tripod model that would be as appropriate for *en plein air* painting as for studio work. My fingers literally trembled with excitement as I paid for this purchase. I carried it with the greatest care out onto the street, and loaded it into the nearest Hansom that I found along the curb.

When I arrived home with my purchase, I found to my surprise that Irène was not only out of bed but had already dressed and gone out. My earlier worries had become somewhat blunted by now, and I wondered if I might not be exaggerating the degree of her sickliness. I took her signs of activity as indications of improving spirits. After unwrapping the easel, I went next door to fetch Moishe so that he could help me set it up properly by the window. Then I sat and watched him slowly and attentively consume his pear tart.

Moishe was just finishing when Irène returned and I was pleased to see her looking far livelier than she had in the past five days. She had evidently been out shopping, too, and was carrying a large box and some parcels under her arms.

"You've purchased an easel!" she exclaimed. She stepped closer and gave it a quick inspection. "I should say that you have made a good purchase, there. It is certainly a very elegant easel, and I imagine it will prove to be quite versatile." But even before she had finished saying these words of praise, Irène had begun arranging her boxes on her bed, apparently losing interest in me and my easel.

"Would you care for a pear tart?"

"No, thank you."

I immediately became suspicious. There was something a little unnatural about Irène refusing food anytime after noon. "It's from Pâtisserie Ladurée," I told her.

"It is very good!" Moishe assured her from the table, indicating the crumbs on the plate in front of him.

Irène glanced at me with what might have been momentary impatience, then returned to the task of unpacking her boxes. "Thank you so much. Perhaps later." She took up several garments from the boxes, then disappeared behind the dressing screen. "I must show you this new dress!" she said excitedly, from her concealment.

Moishe took advantage of this moment to slip away and get back to his work, leaving me in a declining mood. I think I gave a little thought to the idea of simply gobbling up Irène's tart myself, if only out of spite, but I managed to restrain myself.

Ten minutes later, Irène emerged from behind the screen, wearing a pink and black dress. While I like to think of myself as fairly liberal I have to admit I was shocked at the sight of it. The bodice had laces rather than the traditional buttons, striking me as vaguely suggestive of a tavern wench—though at least the laces continued all the way up to the throat, rather than plunging into some decadent suggestion of the old décolletage style. I was speechless.

"Well?" Irène asked airily, spinning around to show herself from all angles. She stared at me with a cheerful expectation that struck me as almost aggressive.

"I . . . I think that . . ." I silenced myself for a moment, holding back the worst of my opinions. Then I simply remarked, "I suppose that I'm too provincial to be a true judge of Parisian fashions. But whatever the merits of such a garment might be, I cannot imagine to what sort of occasion *you* would wear *that*."

Irène's expression did not so much fall as harden. I took this to suggest that she had known full well that she might expect my disapproval. Her cheeks reddened darkly, but she didn't shift her eyes. She replied huffily, "Oh, such an occasion shall arise, I have no doubt."

I couldn't help but frown. "Perhaps to meet with Mata Hari."

I was very unhappy at these developments and left the studio without awaiting her reply. Some instinct made me suspect that there was more to this story than I knew, and that, one way or another, my neighbors on the second floor were sure to be involved.

I found Amedeo's door open, so I tapped once and walked in. The room was filled with a pungent, smoky odor, and Amedeo, Diego and Angelina were all painting, their easels lined up side by side along one wall in a big beam of early afternoon light that poured through their open window. All three of them looked over just long enough to give me the most cursory of greetings, then turned back to their work. I paused to watch them, amazed at the spectacle of these three bons vivants rapt, almost mesmerized, in a burst of obsessive productivity. There was a great brass hookah at their feet, and every now and again one of them would kneel down and draw loudly on one of its hoses.

"Come and paint with us," Angelina said, not diverting her eyes from her work. "Is perfect light . . . perfect!"

"Vernal . . . vernal," Amedeo said. He had beads of sweat on his forehead and spoke as if he were in a fever. "Pure liquid springtime."

I wasn't sure what to say to that, but I ventured, "It is a lovely day. Though I myself usually prefer to paint in morning light."

"And look!" Diego muttered excitedly, waving his free hand vaguely at the hookah while carefully detailing his canvas with his brush. "Last night, Gertrude Stein, that saint, gave us this big sack of Turkish tobacco mixed with hashish."

"Bring down your chair and join us," Angelina said again.

"I have an easel now."

"Even better! So, you go get this and put it over there; you put it there beside Diego. He is fat, but he can make room."

Diego grunted ambiguously.

Amedeo, who had been on his knees sucking at the hookah, stood up now and tipped his head back, blowing out great clouds of white smoke from his nostrils and mouth, looking rather like a locomotive. "Yes, yes, she is a saint. Saint Stein. I will never vomit on her valuable property again."

Now that I was beginning to appreciate the overall spirit of the occasion, it took some effort to remember that I had arrived there with a purpose. I bit my lip to avoid laughing, forced my face into the sternest expression that I could muster under the circumstances, and said pointedly, "Irène looks very happy."

"Good, good!" Angelina exclaimed.

"It's about time," Diego muttered. "She was on the verge of

becoming a bore."

"Yes, but *why* does she look so happy? Do any of you know?"

"Irène?" Amedeo said, looking over at me with droopy-lidded eyes that were as red as cherry tomatoes. "Your roommate, Irène?"

I stamped my foot, not loudly but with sufficient force to make them all look nervously over in my direction. "Amedeo! What *other* Irène do we know?"

"I suppose that she is happy because I promised to take her to a party on Saturday. Would you like to come along?"

I put my hand over my eyes. "A party where?"

"At Jean Cocteau's home, in Bateau-Lavoir."

I'm sure that I emitted some unbecoming and inarticulate sound of aggravation at this news, causing all three of them to cringe a bit. The image of Amedeo dropping my young roommate into the ravenous vortex of a Bateau-Lavoir party, her starveling body no doubt clad in that monstrous black-and-pink dress, was so infuriating that I felt like throwing things. I could well imagine that Mr. Picasso would be there.

"Swear you will not," I said sharply.

At last, all three of them lowered their brushes and turned to look at me with identical expressions of curiosity and tentative defensiveness.

"What?" said Angelina.

"Why?" Diego asked.

I shook my head, refusing to give any explanations. "Just swear it. Swear you will not take her to Bateau-Lavoir."

The three of them looked at one another, exaggerating their dismay, searching each other's faces for any sign that one of them might understand my reaction. This softened my mood a little, as it at least indicated that none of them had yet perceived the nature of Irène's infatuation.

"Swear it."

"All right, Florbela," Angelina said in a placating tone.

"Yes, of course," Amedeo hastened to agree. "I won't take her. I shall concoct some excuse. But why?"

"I would prefer not to speak of it anymore."

Diego frowned and squinted at me, putting one of his fat fists on his hip and turning to face me more fully. "You wish us to promise that we won't to take her out into the city?"

"Just not to Bateau-Lavoir!"

"I don't think this is right," Diego said, holding his ground. "She is young, and she wants to go out. Where's the harm? *You* do as you please; why shouldn't she? And besides, you're her friend, not her mother."

Of course, he was absolutely right. I was acting like her mother. But I couldn't countenance allowing her to fall into the clutches of Picasso. How was I going to make them promise not to take her?

Amedeo chewed on his lip, watching me as I absorbed this little harangue and considered my reply. He carefully added, "I think she stays in too much. I don't know—I don't know her so well as you do. But she seems pale and tired lately, don't you think? Shouldn't she go out? The stimulation will do her good, I should imagine."

Angelina put down her brush, wiped her hands carefully with a rag, and stepped over to stand beside me. She placed her fingers gently on my arm. "Maybe you worry too much. Irène, she is not a child. How can you or me say to her, 'You must do this, not that.' Is not right."

Tears of frustration came to my eyes, because this was, of course, precisely correct. "But *please*," I said, changing my tone, as I felt the high moral ground eroding away under my feet, "please, not to Bateau-Lavoir."

The three of them looked at one another again, and then Angelina suggested, "So how about you bring her to the Delaunays' on Sunday, yes? Big party, good time!"

Diego turned back to his Cubist canvas, warding me off with his thick shoulder. "Good idea. That sounds like a deal. We won't take her to Bateau-Lavoir on Saturday, but you'll bring her to the Delaunays' on Sunday. But I still don't understand why."

I nodded my assent and stood there thinking about it for a moment as Angelina wandered back to her easel. After a few moments, all three of them, as if of one mind, crouched down around the hookah, presumably trying to rekindle the mood of creative fervor that I had dampened. I backed glumly out of the room and plodded back upstairs. I found Irène tucked in bed once again, complaining of a headache, and the dress nowhere in sight. I sat on my cot with my head in my hands—I felt awful.

Chapter Twenty-Three

I'm not sure, to be perfectly honest, how I convinced Irène to come along to the Delaunays' that Sunday, but it did happen. Part of it may have been the overall sweep of events: the combination of my talking pointedly and happily about the party for three days, followed by the general festive excitement around La Ruche on Sunday afternoon. Amedeo, Diego and Angelina were rushing in and out of Moishe's apartment for hours that day, helping him to get ready and, I suppose, making sure that he didn't back out at the last moment. But I think there would have been little chance of that, as he really seemed to be looking forward to the event.

We arrived to find the party much more crowded than the week before, spilling out of the Delaunays' apartment and filling the stairwell so that we had to shoulder our way to the door. There was some sort of marimba orchestra, and although I never actually saw the musicians through the crowd, I suspect that they were numerous, as they were making a barbarous din. The music was further accentuated by a lot of rhythmic stamping and clapping among the dancers.

"This is going to be great!" I imagine Diego said to me, as we shoved our way into the salon.

We'd been standing there less than thirty seconds when, as if by a miracle, Léger appeared out of the crowd. He sidled directly up to me and leaned closely to inquire after my well-being in a rather intimate and proprietary fashion. I noticed my friends raising their eyebrows and winking at one another.

Léger then turned to acknowledge the rest of the group and to clasp Moishe's hand and kiss him on the cheeks. Then he turned back to me once again, offering to fetch me drinks and generally taking possession of me.

Around this time, Sonia Delaunay came over and joined our group, yelling inaudible greetings to us all. Then she threw an arm around Moishe's shoulder and fell into rapid chatter with him, presumably in Russian. Angelina wandered off with Irène to show her around the apartment and introduce her to some of her friends. Amedeo and Diego drifted off a step or two and huddled together for a moment. Then Diego leaned close to me and yelled, "We're going to go look for Willie! Maybe he'll have some brandy."

And with that, the two of them took a step into the crowd and vanished as abruptly as skilled conjurers.

"You look so very lovely this evening," Léger said in my ear, and took the opportunity to place his arm around my shoulders momentarily. His voice was deep and full of emotion, and I found myself catch my breath at his closeness and tender embrace.

I blushed and stammered, "Thank you." Then he took a small step backward and launched into a series of questions and I found myself engaged once again in a very comfortable conversation.

As much as I admired Monsieur Léger's strong qualities, and although I admit that I relished being the target of his charming compliments, after about an hour he began acting the part of suitor quite a bit too ardently for my tastes. It was becoming evident that he didn't feel very much restrained by the traditional fetters of convention. Whenever another man would try to converse with me, he would immediately become sulky and aloof. At one point he wrapped one of his arms around my waist and drew me to himself, ostensibly to move me out of the path of some lively partygoer. But instead of letting me go, he lent down and kissed my neck tenderly. Then he whispered seductively, "I have thought of nothing but you since we were last together Florbela." I was breathless and surprised once again at such intimacy. Pulling away from him, I looked around to see whether anyone had noticed. A few of the guests looked a little shocked and quickly turned their heads away. I was rather embarrassed, but Léger paid them no attention.

"Florbela . . ." he started to say and then hesitated.

I was half afraid that he intended to propose to me again, right there in front of my friends. I frantically searched for a formulation of words that would be sufficiently dissuading but wouldn't cause any wounds.

It was Sonia who came to my rescue. She apparently intuited the nature of my plight, and she abruptly dragged Moishe over, her arm still around his shoulder, then executed a deft tactical maneuver that placed the two of them bodily between Léger and me—no easy feat, I should imagine.

"Come with us," she yelled cheerfully in my ear, hooking her free arm under mine. "We're going to meet some people now." With that, she launched herself forward into the mêlée, dragging Moishe and me along with her. Léger followed us closely, practically treading my heels, but he had lost the romantic initiative, and so the crisis, for the moment, was passed.

We followed Sonia through the party for a while and indeed met some people who seemed quite interesting, though I can't remember exactly who they were. Then again, I could hardly make out a word that anyone was saying. At last, to my relief, Sonia led us into the deeper recesses of her apartment and showed us her studio. Angelina and Irène were there and chatting animatedly with some of the party guests. Sonia's studio was a bit smaller than Robert's, but had tall, south-facing windows, and must have received much better light during the daytime. The crowd was quite thin here, and the noise greatly reduced. Her paintings were all under dustcovers, and I was about to ask her if she would show some of them, when Diego and Amedeo excitedly burst in through the door, followed closely by Willie and a tall, bearded man.

"We found them!" Diego cried, cutting a broad wake through the groups of conversing guests, like a fat galleon wedging through cluttered seas.

"Eureka!" Amedeo agreed, from behind his shoulder.

Willie chimed in merrily, "Ah, Léger was sequestering all the ladies! Good evening, Sonia. Senhorita. Little mademoiselle. And Monsieur Shagalov, our rising star!" He bowed to each of us in turn.

"Please pardon the interruption," Diego said, with a huge and entirely fatuous smile, crowding in close to loom over us, while reaching behind him to pull the others up beside him.

"Yes, please excuse the interruption," Amedeo said. "But look, we have brought Constantin, to meet your new discovery—the *enfant terrible.*"

Amedeo and Willie parted slightly to make room for the tall man to step forward. "Constantin Brancusi, this is Moishe Shagalov, the most peculiar new painter of the season."

"And that's saying something," Diego added.

"You've met these others? Léger and Sonia, of course. And over here, Florbela Sarmentos and Irène Langevin."

I had certainly never met Mr. Brancusi before, and I found his appearance somewhat off-putting at first glance. I would imagine that he was in his mid-thirties, and he was nearly a head taller than anyone else in the room, with gaunt features and a lanky build, though he was somehow very strong-looking nonetheless. He had piercing, dark eyes with a jarring quality that suggested he was half mad: he had furthermore adopted a style of grooming that seemed intended to accentuate that impression. His straight hair was cropped short, but protruded wildly out of his head in all directions, and he had let his beard grow quite long while keeping it in perfect trim.

Mr. Brancusi gave us all the briefest of glances and a quick nod, then turned his riveting eyes down upon little Moishe and extended an immense, bony hand. He continued shaking Moishe's hand for quite a long time, not saying a word but staring down at him unblinkingly, like an eagle trying to decide whether some small and unfamiliar form of rodent might be edible. Moishe did his best to maintain his poise under this investigation, managing to smile most of the time, but forgetting occasionally and betraying a certain amount of quite understandable panic.

"Brancusi is our wild Transylvanian sculptor," Willie explained. "Have no fear! He is more than half tamed by this point. I believe he even uses tableware while dining, don't you, Brancusi?"

"Tamed?" Diego exclaimed. "Now that he doesn't live with *us* anymore, he is quickly descending into a fully civilized state."

I screwed up my courage and asked, "Were you once a resident of La Ruche, Mr. Brancusi?"

He pried his eyes away from Moishe for a moment. Moishe took advantage of the opportunity to extract his hand and take a full step backward, out of arm's reach.

"First floor," he said, in a rich Balkan rumble.

"But we never see him anymore," Diego complained. "Now that he's a success, he's forgotten all about us."

"He sold a couple of sculptures and moved across the river."

I was surprised to hear that Mr. Brancusi's recent successes would make him move to the Right Bank rather than to the Sixth, like everyone else, and I was about to ask him about it when I realized that he was staring fixedly at something just to my right. I glanced over and found that Irène was hiding behind Sonia and Moishe. She was literally cowering there, trying to hide her face behind their shoulders.

My first reaction was one of shock at seeing this man, whom I was beginning to imagine must be some sort of boor, intimidating my friend in her fragile state. But as I turned to glare into the face of the "wild Transylvanian", I was surprised to see that he had dropped his eyes, hooding them under his thick, lowered brows, and that his whole leathery face seemed to be turning inward with some sort of brooding concern. It occurred to me, abruptly, that he and Irène must have been previously acquainted, as unlikely as that might seem. And they certainly were not behaving like friends.

Diego and Amedeo continued chattering at the two sides of Mr. Brancusi's head while this brief and silent interaction between him and Irène played itself out. When Diego asked, "Is it a bargain?" Mr. Brancusi slowly emerged from his meditations, turned a baffled look upon Diego and said, "What's that?"

"Wednesday! Aren't you even listening? Our big party! Gertrude Stein's hashish!"

"You *must* come out to visit us at La Ruche," Amedeo insisted, "because I need you to see my new series of canvases. You're going to like these, I assure you."

"Yes, yes," Mr. Brancusi said absently. "Yes. Wednesday. I will come."

Mr. Brancusi appeared to recover some of his manners at this point, and in fact became rather charming, chatting with Sonia and Amedeo in a jocular tone and averting his rather disconcerting gaze from people's faces. But I suspect, looking back upon it, that he was only trying to get us all to drop our guard, because as soon as I had done so and allowed Léger again to lure me into a rather intimate conversation, I noticed from the corner of my eye that Mr. Brancusi was quietly sidestepping his way around our group. He advanced upon the tiny and cowering form of Irène very suddenly, confronting her in the darkened lair that she had arranged for herself behind the backs of the rest of us. This forceful intrusion seemed like such an affront to decent manners that I was on the verge of confronting him, but to my utter astonishment, Irène greeted him with a mincing and deferent smile. Certainly, she seemed mortified at his sudden and public advance upon her, but at the same time she received him with such uncharacteristic passivity that I was left completely baffled. As for Mr. Brancusi, though his expression was stern, there was nothing aggressive in his demeanor at all. Quite the opposite: his face had softened, and while speaking he leaned over her in a manner that was almost avuncular. To my further amazement, I saw him wave one of his big hands, apparently suggesting that she follow him away from the group, and she did so without the slightest protest—indeed, I think she curtsied slightly before letting him guide her off into the crowd.

For several minutes, I stood there with my curiosity growing, utterly ignoring the words of courtly adoration that Léger was whispering in my ear. Finally, I could take no more. I held up a hand to stop Léger in midsentence and said, "Excuse me Monsieur Léger, but I must see how Irène is." Then I shouldered off into the crowd.

When I found the two of them, Mr. Brancusi was hovering above Irène in the farthest corner of the room, gazing down upon her with that same stern but gentle—indeed proprietary—look. Irène was looking fixedly up into his face with her hands clasped behind her back. I intruded upon them as abruptly as I could, and stood with arms akimbo, looking up at Mr. Brancusi with what I hoped was a challenging glare.

Mr. Brancusi regarded me quite directly and coldly with those dark eyes of his, but after a few moments, he dropped his gaze from my face, gave a sideways smile, and said, "Ah, Senhorita Sarmentos. Don't worry, you are not intruding. Our business here is done."

"Business, you say? I wonder: what sort of business? In what capacity do you know Mademoiselle Langevin, Mr. Brancusi?"

"Irène is my student," he told me. "Or, that is to say, she has been my student in the past."

My arms fell to my sides, and I seemed to lose my breath at the sheer unexpectedness of this explanation. I'm sure that my face looked quite silly. "Your student?"

"I am a sculptor," Brancusi said, speaking French as clearly as he was able, as if trying to clarify a simple concept for someone who might conceivably be a bit thick-headed. "I taught her how to sculpt."

Now the first time I had met Irène, she had claimed that she had studied under some of the finest sculptors in France. But despite this claim, and despite her extraordinary aptitude as a sculptor, I had become so certain that Irène was a fugitive from some sordid past that I had simply assumed the claim had been a harmless ruse on her part. For one thing, up until this very moment, it had seemed that no one in Paris had ever *met* her prior to her arrival at La Ruche, and so I had come to assume that she had quietly slipped into town to start a new life, at about the same time I did. I turned to Irène, stung a bit by a feeling of guilt at having misjudged her, and also marveling at having once again discovered hidden dimensions of her life that she preferred to keep concealed. But when I saw Irène's face, I shut my mouth tightly and held back whatever I had been about to say. The poor girl looked absolutely mortified. She was wringing her hands, her eyes lowered toward the floor, and she seemed so crushed that she might be about to weep. Before I could even begin to guess the cause of these strong feelings, Irène dashed away from us and vanished into the crowd.

I made a move to go after her, but a hand closed on my shoulder, restraining me. I looked around and saw Sonia, watching me mildly and shaking her head. I don't know how much of these interactions she had seen, but I realized immediately that she was right and that Irène should be left alone for a while.

I turned again to Mr. Brancusi and said, "So! You were her teacher. You must be very proud of her. Her sculptures are wonderful."

Mr. Brancusi was still looking at the backs of the people nearest us, watching the spot where Irène had disappeared as if he hoped she would re-emerge. He nodded vacantly, perhaps understanding my words and perhaps not. I wanted to pry information from him, of course, but I felt that I had already overstepped my boundaries.

Sonia grabbed us both by the arms and said cheerfully, "Come back to the fold, you stray sheep! Willie is pouring brandy."

As we rejoined the group, the others were so engrossed in some pointless argument about the German Expressionist movement that they hardly noticed our return, with the exception of Léger, who stepped up to stand beside me the moment I appeared. I had expected Brancusi to position himself as far from me as possible, but he placed himself just beside me, opposite Léger. He leaned down close to my ear.

"You share a flat with Irène. No? Yes? This is true? How does she live?"

I glanced at him uncomfortably. "I'm not sure that I understand your question, Mr. Brancusi."

He shrugged his lanky shoulders, an absurd pantomime of flippancy, as if he hoped to convey that he didn't care much one way or the other. "Is she comfortable there? Is she eating well? What sort of company does she keep?"

I frowned and glanced around at the others and noticed, not surprisingly, that we were beginning to capture their attention. Léger in particular was developing a rather surly expression.

Sonia, who was close at hand, called over, "Now, Constantin! Behave yourself. It's rude to speak of a young lady who is not present, don't you agree?"

Brancusi barely glanced at her, and continued to address me. "I am only curious. Surely it is polite to inquire after our mutual friends, isn't this so? Is she happy and healthy? Is it my imagination, or does she seem to be in some low mood?"

I'm sure that my face betrayed my exasperation at this last question, and I told him sharply, "Yes, she is unhappy. I don't think that it takes much perceptiveness to notice that. But I shouldn't concern myself, if I were you. I'm sure that the mood will pass."

At that moment Léger touched my arm and whispered, "Senhorita, I must go. But I should like it very much if you would have dinner with me sometime later this week?"

"Thank you, I would like that."

"I will be in touch," and with that he kissed my hand, nodded to the group and took his leave.

"So then, she isn't always this way? Sometimes she is happy?" Brancusi said as soon as Léger was gone.

"It's *just* a passing mood," I snapped, wishing he would leave me alone. "She has only been this way since Saturday."

I could have bitten my tongue when I heard this overly specific comment escape my mouth. I glanced around and saw to my chagrin that, indeed, the others were exchanging quick glances.

"Saturday?" Amedeo echoed. "What do you mean? Nothing bad happened on Saturday. That was the day we all took Moishe to the Steins', remember?"

"I think she enjoyed herself there," Willie volunteered.

"Perhaps she ran into someone there who caused her some distress," Sonia proposed lightly.

For the space of several seconds, this suggestion didn't seem to make any impression upon anyone. But then, to my dismay, I saw first Willie and then Amedeo slowly widening their eyes, in a state of abrupt enlightenment.

"Pablo."

"Oh no, not Pablo!"

Sonia raised the tips of all her fingers to her lips and turned to look at me, searching my face to have the matter confirmed or denied. I did my best to make my face a wooden mask, but it was too late; she saw enough there to find certainty. "Oh, lord. That poor, dear child."

"So," I heard Brancusi say in his gravelly baritone, and then again, "So."

I glanced up at him and saw that his expression had fallen into a reflective sulk, and I heard him sigh deeply and with real emotion. I couldn't imagine what might be the relationship between this alarming man and Irène, and indeed I didn't even want to speculate on what gave him the right to pry into her affairs of the heart. After all, there was nothing at all between Irène and Mr. Picasso, or at least nothing beyond an idiotic fancy on her own part, which would hopefully dissipate someday soon. But I supposed that there might be any imaginable history between Irène and Mr. Brancusi. Whatever that history might be, I prayed it would stay buried in the past, where it belonged.

Willie, Diego and Amedeo, alas, all looked like they were struggling to hold back various bits of witty commentary on this juicy new piece of information.

Not surprisingly, it was Diego who first lost control of his tongue. "Well," he fairly hollered, "if the woman wants to break her heart over a man, she couldn't pick a better man to do the job than my dear old friend Pablo!" He threw back his head and roared with laughter. "Pablo won't just break her heart, he'll *pulverize* it!"

"Say, Willie," Amedeo said with a devilish grin, "didn't Pablo steal your girlfriend?"

"Good riddance," Willie replied, dismissing the matter with a backhand wave. He glanced at me, and I'm afraid he probably read the question on my face, though I was making an honest effort to ignore the conversation completely at this point. "Ah, you're probably the only one among us here—well, you and Moishe—who don't know that Fernande was my dearly beloved, at least for a few months back there somewhere. I forget the details." He smiled disingenuously, and I believe there was some hostile pleasure in finding this easy opportunity to dredge up Mr. Picasso's unsavory secrets. "Anyway, the essence of the matter was quite simple. Fernande loved me because I was wild and unscrupulous. But then she met Pablo, and how could I possibly compete with that?"

This drew a good hearty laugh from the crowd, so Willie cheerfully plowed ahead. "Oh yes! She likes to say that she would prefer a more orderly life, but I think one might find cause to doubt it."

The sordid stories about Pablo continued and I felt my stomach fluttering so badly from anxiety that I worried I was about to become physically sick. My eyes darted around the crowd, hoping to catch sight again of Irène. Surely there was some way to impress upon her the dangerous character of the man who had become the target of her infatuation.

My eyes happened to cross the face of Mr. Brancusi. With mixed emotion, I saw on his face a reflection of my own distress.

Chapter Twenty-Four

O ver the course of the next few days, Irène's funk dragged on and probably deepened further. She certainly didn't seem eager for a friend upon whose shoulder to cry, so I did what I could to leave her alone. Twice I made delicate efforts to get her to confide in me the nature of her acquaintance with the mysterious Mr. Brancusi, but she was reticent the first time and petulant the second, so I ceased my inquiries.

My dream of finding a personal creative style and generating my first real work of art seemed to be becoming more elusive. In the mornings, I worked with feverish attention but only sluggish progress upon my third canvas: another still life with flowers. I spent the evenings darning my old clothes and sewing new ones, activities that I was coming to find very relaxing, in that they gave me the opportunity to create objects whose value couldn't be denied, even by the most heartless of critics.

Irène had resumed the habit of sculpting in the evenings, though she too appeared to have lost her way. Night by night I watched the so-called "Adonis" bust lose its initially promising qualities of proportion and expressiveness, gradually becoming monstrous and ugly under Irène's overly fussy attentions.

We were thus engaged on one evening that week, sewing and sculpting respectively, while noises of festivity wafted through the door from the second floor. The distant voices and laughter grew steadily louder over the course of perhaps an hour, and then were joined by music and the thumps of dancing feet on thin floorboards. Neither of us paid a great deal of attention to the sounds, accustomed as we were to the revels that tended to erupt almost daily at Amedeo's studio. But my peaceful ruminations were finally disrupted by a rapping at our door, which stood ajar. I was surprised when I looked over and saw Moishe peeping in, his cheeks flushed, grinning in an uncharacteristically agitated manner.

"You would like to come downstairs?" he asked politely. His French was improving by the day.

"To the party?" I asked. "I think perhaps not, Moishe. What about you, Irène? Do you feel like going to Amedeo's party?"

"Mr. Brancusi visits," Moishe told us excitedly. "Diego says it is"—he paused, groping for the correct word—"reunion."

"It sounds like a lot of fun," I said mildly. "But I have a bit of a headache." I glanced over at Irène, trying to be discreet, but terribly curious to see how she had reacted to the announcement of Mr. Brancusi's presence in our building. I wasn't entirely surprised to see that she was already on her feet, hastily packing up her work area. I appended, "Unless Irène is going to attend. Irène? Are you thinking of going to the party?"

She replied over her shoulder, without actually looking at me, "I think that I shall not, thank you. I seem to have worked up an appetite, and I believe I will go out now for an early dinner."

Before I could reply to this, I noticed the sound of heavy footsteps in the hallway. I turned just in time to see Mr. Brancusi appear in the frame of our door, standing behind Moishe and towering above him. He stared at me with those mad eyes of his and fixed his lips instantly into a large but joyless smile.

"Good evening, ladies," he said. "This is where you live? I was actually looking around here to see this man's studio." Here he clapped Moishe on the shoulder with his knobby hand. "But I'm glad to find you. Ah, and look! You are sculpting, Irène. May I see your studio?"

I glanced back at Irène, and saw that she had turned to face the door and was eyeing Mr. Brancusi with a hangdog expression. She gave a small nod of acquiescence and he stepped inside, gently moving Moishe out of his way.

I was relieved to find that Diego, Amedeo and Angelina were just behind him in the hallway. They all crowded inside together, fairly packing the room to the walls. I bundled up my sewing and got out of the way, then watched from a distance as Irène played the reluctant host to this mob. She mutely showed off the ruined and fortunately unrecognizable bust that she had been working on, then dug out the impressive but unfinished figure of the faun.

"This is wonderful!" Diego said, examining the monstrous Adonis from every angle. "Is it Cubism?"

"Not precisely," Irène told him, concealing her feelings behind admirable poise.

"But this," Angelina said, gently touching the faun with her delicate fingertips, "*this* is truly beautiful. Don't you think so, Constantin?"

Mr. Brancusi's expression was aloof and judgmental. "The rendition is skillful," he said. "But the composition is academic . . . perhaps even just a bit . . . *trite*." He glanced down at Irène. "Isn't that so?"

She nodded once, without raising her eyes to his face.

Angelina scowled. "That is not fair, Constantin! Look again. This is full of life and expression. Just look!"

Mr. Brancusi glanced at the piece, then at Angelina, and then he made a quiet but perfectly audible snorting sound. "She can do much better than that."

This pronouncement, coming from the mouth of Brancusi, created a moment of complete silence, in which all three of our downstairs neighbors turned their heads to stare at Irène, as if seeing her for the first time. Irène's eyes were still cast down at the floor, but her cheeks reddened. After a moment, she spoke up, her voice unusually small, as if coming from a great distance, but still piping-clear and perfectly enunciated, as always. "I think that I need to speak with Mr. Brancusi privately for a few moments, if you please."

"It is quite so," Mr. Brancusi agreed, as if this were the most natural thing in the world.

"Please leave us," Irène said. "Please, all of you. We will come down and join you in just a few minutes. If you please."

Diego and Amedeo both widened their eyes a little, but said nothing as Angelina ushered them from the room. She gave my arm a little pat as she walked past me, and I felt that I had no choice but to accompany them out the door and into the hall, much as I disliked doing so. I took one last nervous glance into the studio as I stepped out, and saw Irène and Mr. Brancusi standing side by side, watching us go. Angelina left the door slightly ajar and ushered us all down the stairs.

Amedeo's studio was not nearly as crowded as one might have expected, given the amount of noise emanating through its door. There were two La Ruche residents playing music on an oboe and fiddle, and another four or five drinking and dancing erratically among the clutter of easels and canvases. The addition of five more of us was more than sufficient to crowd the room.

I accepted a glass of wine, but barely sipped at it. I moved gradually toward the darkest corner of the studio, nearer the door and out of elbow room, as far as possible from the center of attention. Angelina followed after me, while Diego and Amedeo, who were probably inclined to leave me alone, reluctantly trailed along behind her.

"Don't worry," Angelina said, patting me on the forearm. "I'm sure is fine. Drink some wine. Enjoy the party."

"I can't help but worry," I confessed. My voice caught a little, and I sipped some wine to conceal my confusion. "She's so young and . . . and vulnerable. I can't help it—I feel very protective of her."

"But Constantin's all right," Diego said encouragingly. "It's true, you do worry too much."

They eventually turned away and joined their more festive guests. I stood there for a little while, but then couldn't help setting down my glass and backing slowly and inconspicuously toward the door. I slipped quietly out into the hall, dashed back up the stairs on tiptoe, and set myself in position to eavesdrop outside the door of my own home. I don't know what I would have said if anyone had caught me there.

"I don't demand so very much," Mr. Brancusi was saying. His voice was low but had a resonant undertone that carried through the crack of the door with perfect clarity.

"I know, I know," Irène replied, with unaccustomed petulance. "You just want one thing. I have already agreed!"

"This is not precisely true, Irène. How clever you are with your words. Now, I want to hear you say this thing clearly. Please, you *promise* this for me."

There was a distinct pause, and then Irène said in a small but clear voice, "I promise you that I shall not go to Bateau-Lavoir. You have my word."

I can assure you that I was astonished to hear Irène making emotional concessions to anyone, most especially to this bizarre and enigmatic man. When Mr. Brancusi spoke again, his voice was more relaxed, as if he had been relieved of a substantial burden. "Excellent," he breathed. "Then that much, at any rate, is achieved. I can tell you that I am not satisfied with how things are, Irène, but I don't intend to interfere in your life any further. Well . . . not at the present time. But now, I must be going."

There was again a pause, and then Irène asked him, rather pointedly, "Are you going to come back up here, after the party?"

"I shall not return to the party," Mr. Brancusi told her flatly. "I am in no mood to banter with my young friends downstairs. I wish to go home, where I can have some peace."

"In that case, I suppose you want it now?"

"Yes, give it to me now! All of it. And then I will go away."

This last exchange was so fraught and confusing that I held my breath, leaned forward very slowly, and peeked around the frame of the door. What I saw was Irène reaching into her purse, which was open on her bedside table, while Mr. Brancusi hovered nervously above her. Her hand came forth holding a blue cylinder, which I recognized quite well. My jaw fairly dropped as I watched Irène place her cache of gold into the hand of Mr. Brancusi. He gave a perfunctory nod and dropped the weighty cylinder into the pocket of his waistcoat.

I hurried to pad away from the doorframe and hide in the

broom closet nearby. Less than a minute later, I heard him stride by and walk heavily down the stairs. I waited a few more minutes in the musty darkness, then emerged and walked as noisily as I could up to my own door and pushed it open with an audible thump, in order to announce myself.

Irène had already rearranged her sculpting supplies and was stirring her wax as it melted again in the pot upon her little stove. We exchanged a few minimal words of greeting, and then I settled myself back into my chair, took out my sewing, and pretended to engross myself in handiwork.

The next hour or so was pure emotional torment for me, and I imagine that Irène's state was even worse than mine—though you would never have imagined it, to see her sitting there. Each of us sat quietly in her place, pretending absorption in our work while I, for one, was seething with uncertainty. Should I confront Irène with what I knew? My guilt outweighed my curiosity and so we passed an hour without speaking, until dinnertime was approaching, while downstairs the sounds of the party continued unabated, not in the least discouraged by the disappearance of the guest of honor.

I certainly wasn't doing much sewing, and had fallen into something of a reverie over my needle and thread, when I was suddenly brought sharply to my senses by a fierce cry which sounded as if it had come from just outside the building.

Irène and I crowded to the open window and leaned out to stare into the dim space between La Ruche and the street. There was some sort of movement out there, but too deeply shadowed to make out. Then, for just a moment but with perfect clarity, I saw a black-clad man running at great speed and in perfect silence, captured momentarily by a shaft of light from the street, as if by a photographer's flash-lamp. For a few seconds after that, I could still vaguely make out the fleeing man moving against the mottled backdrop of the hedge. Then he must have darted through to the other side, because I saw no more.

At the very moment that he vanished, there came another loud shout and the sound of racing footsteps below us. We craned our heads downward to see Armand rushing at a full sprint from around the side of the house. He darted to the break in the hedge where the blackened figure had disappeared, and dived through in pursuit.

"Did you see?" Irène asked me excitedly.

"Unbelievable!"

"What on earth was that man wearing? He seemed to be dressed for the ballet, or perhaps for a circus act."

"All wrapped in black cloth. Even his hands and face!"

"It reminded me of those pictures that you see of Arabs in the desert . . . but all in black." We were still staring out the window as we exchanged these remarks, waiting to see if anything further would transpire. "Who could he have been?" Irène mused. "And how did he arrive in our yard? Surely he didn't simply stroll down the boulevard, dressed in those outlandish clothes."

As soon as Irène had posed the riddle in those terms, it was obvious that there could be no easy answer. How indeed could a man in such garb arrive outside a residence in a city as dense as Paris without making a general spectacle of himself? The most obvious answer was so outrageous that it bordered on the supernatural—namely, that this was a man who could pass at will through the streets of the night city, completely unnoticed, cloaked in shadows. I shuddered, rejecting the notion, assuring myself that there was a more rational explanation.

Irène must have been thinking similar thoughts, because she said, "Perhaps he can fly."

I glanced at her sharply.

"Like a bat," she added, then appended the tiniest of smiles to show that she was attempting humor.

I laughed dutifully but without mirth, seeing nothing funny in the situation at all. Then I said, "Excuse me," and strode briskly out of the studio and downstairs, hoping to meet Armand when he returned.

I stepped carefully outside, but kept myself shaded and close to the doorway, afraid to expose myself further to whatever might be creeping about out there in the night. Fortunately, I only had a few minutes to wait before I saw Armand come striding back. His fists were still clenched with tension, but his hanging head and brooding expression made it clear that he hadn't caught his man. I advanced into the light so that he could see me, then slipped around the back of the building to find a private spot in which to wait for him.

He put on a brave face as he approached me, but it was obvious that his mood was very grim. "Did you see?" he asked.

I nodded once.

He looked around, as if afraid there might be listening ears, then told me quietly but clearly, "Onça do Papa."

I shook my head, resisting belief, not wishing to give the thing credence. As the weeks passed since Professor Almeida had died, I had come to think of the presence of my Souris Trempés guardians as quite unnecessary. I certainly didn't mind bringing them bread and wine upon occasion, and I admit that I had grown accustomed to the sweetly naive strains of Armand's guitar as I fell asleep each evening. But the idea that I might actually be a target for political assassination had seemed less and less likely as time passed.

"Leaozinha," Armand said in a stern undertone, close to my ear. "You cannot stay here anymore. You see that, don't you? We cannot offer you real protection in a place as public and open as this. To be honest, you are lucky to be alive."

This dire assessment of my situation made a very strong impression upon me. I was half inclined to believe that this was the precise truth—that my life was in immediate danger and that if I didn't wish to end up like Professor Almeida then I had better place myself into the hands of others who were more skilled in stealthy tactics than myself. But the other half of me resisted this idea with great force, saying that living in a bustling community such as La Ruche was as safe as any place, and that it was cowardly to run from shadows. Armand had no proof that it really was the assassin. After a long moment's reflection, the latter side won out.

"I want to stay here," I said firmly.

"You must leave!"

"I've already told you that I will not. I shall not crawl under some rock."

"I don't ask you to!"

"You do. There is nowhere you can hide me where I can continue to live as a free person. You know that that's true. I have to choose either to live a life of hiding, or to continue to live my real life in the face of danger, as I have been doing in recent weeks. Once I start hiding, nowhere will be truly safe, and so I will hide myself away, deeper and deeper, until my life becomes a prison."

Armand raised his hands slowly up to the sides of his face, and I noticed with some alarm that his fingers were trembling with agitation. Suddenly he reached out and grabbed me by my arms, and he stared into my eyes with such intense emotion that I was afraid he was on the verge of either slapping or kissing me. "You are a living as if in a dream," he told me. His grip on my upper arms was so strong that I winced in pain. He let go and dropped his hands to his sides in resignation and turned away from me. "Just like your father," he added over his shoulder. He was quiet for a few moments and then turned to face me again. "I don't claim to understand such people, but I want you to note, truly *take note*, that I do not approve of such an impractical view of life. Still, history teaches us that revolutions cannot be won without the willful inspiration of dreamers, so I will not demand that you change your mind."

He reached down to pick up his guitar from the weeds where he had dropped it, and took his seat without meeting my eye. "You may count on the Souris Trempés to guard and protect you," he said, dismissing me. "As best we are able."

*　　*　　*

The next week was a test of nerves. I slept fitfully during those nights if I slept at all, and spent my daylight hours in the company of others whenever possible, returning always before dark and cloistering myself behind a locked door from dusk till dawn. The

Souris Trempés were quite heroic, intensifying their efforts to watch the property, and often there would be two of them prowling around outside, one in front and one in the backyard. I found Armand's attentions to this duty particularly touching. He seemed to practically live in our yard during those days. I made a point of visiting with him two or three times a day, bringing out snacks and sharing small talk.

Sometime during that week, I received invitations from both Fernand Léger and Brian Torrence Grimm, asking me out to dine. I refused them both, rather impulsively, following a nervous instinct that told me not to venture out of doors after dark. But when their invitations were repeated the following week, with new and even more tempting suggestions of restaurants they would like to share with me, I accepted them both. I felt that I was in danger of becoming a prisoner in my own studio, and the only way I was likely to feel truly safe out on the night streets of Paris was in the company of an attentive escort. Brian and Léger were certainly that.

I fell into the habit of dining with each of them on alternating weeks, and these dinners were great highlights of the late spring and early summer for me, as they were an opportunity to get to know each of these two charming men a little better, and to sample the finer things of Paris. Other than one night a week when I dined with Fernand or Brian, I hardly ever left the studio in the evening for nearly a month.

I believe that it was the second week after our sighting of the black-clad intruder that a rumor came to us, courtesy of Willie and Amedeo, that Fernande had left Pablo Picasso and moved away to parts unknown. To my utter chagrin, this news conspicuously dragged Irène up out of her marathon bout of depression and lifted her high into the air, like a songbird riding the draft of a spring breeze. Or perhaps a better simile would be to say that she floated lightly off her feet as if her head had been inflated with hot air.

Despite my irritation at the cause, I must admit that Irène was delightful to be around in this new and vernal mood. Suddenly I had a friend willing to join me on my brief excursions during daylight hours, wandering through the gardens and boulevards of the city or gathering some tasty food from the many specialty stores in the Fifth and Sixth districts. We also habituated the Left Bank art galleries, where an increasing number of new and baffling styles were appearing in the back rooms, competing for space against the Impressionists and Symbolists whose works commanded most of the wall space. One of the Souris Trempés would always follow us close by and this made me feel much safer.

Naturally, I was afraid that Irène was secretly planning some way to place herself in Mr. Picasso's way—but she was true to her word to Mr. Brancusi, and never once visited Bateau-Lavoir. And since Mr. Picasso never came to La Ruche nor the Delaunays', and since Willie knew that he would incur my wrath if he arranged an invitation for Irène to the Steins', the weeks went by and she had no opportunity to encounter Mr. Picasso.

Irène was very productive during this period, not least because neither of us dared to go out much after dark. To my profound relief, she melted down the ruined bust of "Adonis," and during two or three days of intense work she finished her beautiful little faun and sent it off to a foundry to be cast in bronze. Angelina arranged a party, and Irène simply glowed as the guest of honor. It was one of the happiest evening of the spring for me.

The next day, as I was dressing and chatting with Irène, she suddenly stopped in mid-sentence and said, "Florbela, you have such a beautiful body. Has anyone mentioned that you are the perfect model for a classical sculptor? Would you consider posing for me? "

"Well . . . yes of course, " I said, surprised.

"In the Grecian style perhaps? I shall braid your hair . . . and we can use this fabric I bought the other day," she said as she rummaged around in a bag.

I agreed to pose with only Irène's fabric lavishly draped around me, and she completed the wax sculpture quite rapidly, during three long sittings over the course of less than a week. The bronze figurine that resulted was delivered from the foundry even before the faun arrived. She showed the result to Willie, and he took it to Wilhelm Uhde—the gallery owner who was Sonia's ex-husband—who sold it to an anonymous buyer almost instantly. Again, we had a rather wild party down on the second floor, this one generously funded by Irène from the modest proceeds of her sale.

As pleased as I was at Irène's sudden and entirely predictable success, the comparison with my own listless progress was demoralizing. I had finished five still lifes by this point, and was working on a cityscape based upon the dawn view over the treetops as seen through our window, which was very pretty. Willie had graciously agreed to carry my completed canvases around to galleries, acting as my agent. Surely no better representation was available for an unknown artist, probably in all of France. But not long after Willie sold Irène's figurine of me, he returned my canvases, encouraging me to try again.

Meanwhile, next door, Moishe's studio had become positively crowded with works. He seemed to finish something or other every day or two. He was never at a loss for materials, and by now I was perfectly certain that Léger was consistently lending or perhaps simply giving him money. Sometime in June, Willie was able to sell one of Moishe's paintings for the first time, as well as some small pieces by Diego and Angelina. This, of course, left me alone among my friends as the only one who had never sold a piece.

And then, during the first week of June, Irène and I were sharing a lunch in a little café overlooking the Seine with Willie and a couple of his friends when one of them mentioned that Fernande had returned and was living once again with Pablo Picasso. I wonder if any news has ever struck me with such ambiguity of feeling. On the one hand, I was vastly relieved to hear that the danger—the sword of Damocles that had been hanging over Irène's head for the past few weeks—had passed, and that no chance encounter with Mr. Picasso on some boulevard might lead to a situation that would destroy my friend's life. But at the same time, as I looked at her across the table from me with her

THE SIXTH

shoulders gradually slumping, her gaze falling to stare at the cold bowl of soup that sat in front of her, I knew what was in her heart. And I could feel only immeasurable pity.

Chapter Twenty-Five

O ne Friday evening early in June, when I carried out the usually pleasant errand of delivering a simple meal to Armand in our backyard, I found that he was very agitated and not at all himself. He returned my nervous greeting in a most perfunctory manner, then accepted the covered bowl from my hands and simply put it aside.

"I think that you should sit down, Leaozinha."

"What is it, Armand? You're worrying me. Has something happened?"

"Please sit; come, take a seat here. We have to talk."

By the time I was settled, he had me so worried that it took an effort to avoid clasping my hands together. He looked at me sternly and told me, "I have an admission to make. A confession of sorts."

"Confession?"

"We have been reading the private mail of Brian Torrence Grimm for some time now."

"You've done *what*?"

"Not me, personally. My comrades. We were able to compromise a courier at the British Embassy and make an arrangement to divert Mr. Grimm's mail before it is delivered. There is one among us who has a knack for opening and resealing letters without cracking the wax seal."

"But that's outrageous, Armand! Why would you do such a thing?"

"I think you know that we feel little trust for the Freemasons, and none of us have been entirely comfortable with your father's decision to involve them in his cause." He frowned, still not letting his eyes waver from mine. "No, wait a moment before you speak, Leaozinha. I can see that you are displeased, but perhaps you will feel differently when you hear the rest of what I have to say."

I really didn't want to hear any news that might have been obtained through such devious pathways, but my curiosity overmastered me, so I dropped my eyes, took a deep breath, and said with some apprehension, "Please be brief."

"Today, Mr. Grimm received an enigmatic and unsigned letter, summoning him to a secret meeting in the Bois de Boulogne, this very night."

"Are you sure of that?" I reflected for a moment further, then added with stronger skepticism, "A meeting out in the *darkened woods*?" This was so unlike the Brian whom I knew that I was at a loss to imagine what it might mean. The Bois de Boulogne, which was so pleasant by day, was generally reputed to become in the hours after sunset a haunt for cutpurses and other rogues, as well as a venue for the lowest types of romantic trysts. "Why would he meet with someone in such a ghastly place?"

Armand nodded once, firmly, as if agreeing that this was indeed the key question. "We believe that the likeliest explanation is that he and his Freemasons have deciphered some message hidden on the painting. We suspect they are preparing to take some secret action without your blessing—something that might affect the political situation in Portugal."

I sat in stunned silence for nearly a minute. Armand watched me, giving me a chance to let the turbulent thoughts in my head settle into some sort of order.

How well did I *really* know Brian Torrence Grimm? Not so very well, I confessed to myself now; certainly not well enough that I could weigh the relative measures of his divided loyalties among his nation of England, the Grand Lodge of Freemasonry and me. But still, was it really possible that he had been toying with me for political ends all this time, like a pawn on a chessboard? That he had lied to me, and perhaps even machinated against the interests of my father and my country? It seemed improbable in the extreme, and yet it distressed me that I hadn't in any way guarded against the possibility of such things. *I am such a child in these worldly matters!* I thought to myself.

Armand continued, "I haven't actually come here this evening to guard your home. Rather, Barbade will arrive shortly to take my shift. I came here to let you know that I will go to Mr. Grimm's appointed place of meeting tonight, in the Bois de Boulogne, where I shall investigate and perhaps confront the conspirators. I felt you had the right to know."

"Then I shall come with you."

Did he smile a little? It was hard to tell in the moonlight. "I thought that you might say as much. I admit that it is your right to do so, but I must point out to you that the enterprise is bound to involve certain dangers."

"You must take me along, nonetheless."

He gestured to me with his palms up, as if to say that he understood the futility of trying to change my mind. "It would be wiser for you stay here. But if you insist on coming along, I admit that your presence might be useful. Mr. Grimm and his collaborators will certainly be more easily obliged to acknowledge the justice of your claim in this matter, if you are present."

"Just so."

Armand paused, then shook his head vigorously and allowed himself the indulgence of saying, "I warned you about this, Leaozinha. These Freemasons will not help your father's cause unless they have some assurance that they will be able to install themselves in a position of power in Portugal, once the issues there are settled."

"I'm not sure if this is the time for you to be scolding me, Armand."

"Fine. As you say."

"For one thing, nothing has been proved, and we would both do well to leave our minds open until we have further evidence." He rolled his eyes up to gaze off at the rising comet, which was still faintly visible on some evenings, among the stars. I found his silence infuriating, but kept my tone moderate and asked, "In order to intercept them, what time will we have to leave?"

"Quite soon. We might get started even now, in fact."

"You don't propose that we walk all that distance?"

"Of course not. I've hired a carriage for the evening."

I'm sure that my eyes opened quite comically wide at this unexpected revelation. Armand glanced my way, and for a moment his face relaxed into the broad, boyish smile that I liked so much. "How can you afford a carriage?" I demanded. "I have always been under the impression that you can barely buy sufficient food to avoid starvation."

He held up a hand to stop me, then reached under his lapel and took out a bright object which, when he angled it to the moonlight, I saw to be a fat silver coin. "I have certain funds at my disposal, Leaozinha."

I nodded. "I see. You have some family money, hidden away somewhere?"

"Yes, that's correct," he informed me flatly. "An inheritance. But as far as I'm concerned, that money now belongs to the cause of the people. I merely guard the funds, in the role of steward, preserving them against the day when some crisis places my comrades in immediate need."

I was tempted to point out to him that one ongoing crisis among his comrades was an immediate need to purchase some food, decent clothing and a few basic amenities. But I simply shook my head in exasperation and held my tongue.

He led me out to the street and half a block toward the city center, then stopped along the curb of the boulevard. At first I didn't realize that he was indicating we had arrived at our means of transport.

"This? Armand, you can't be serious!"

He had halted, posing in his shabby broadcloth shirt and canvas trousers beside an elegant black landau carriage with gilt trim and two tall white horses. In addition to the coachman there was also a footman standing on the back, and both wore velour livery. The footman jumped down to the curb to open the door for me. I noticed as I climbed aboard that his uniform, though fine, bore no insignia that might suggest what house or family he worked for.

"Where did you get this?" I demanded as we started off toward the west, horseshoes clattering on the cobbles. I was almost laughing, despite the gravity of our errand. "Does it belong to your family?" The seats were upholstered in finely polished leather, the armrests were kid, and there was a set of crystal glasses on a brass rack, presumably in case we had thought to bring along a bottle of Champagne.

"I hired it for the evening."

"Unbelievable! The rental must have cost a dozen times as much as simply hiring a hackney."

"More like a hundred times," Armand informed me glumly. "But I have my reasons, as you might imagine."

"Oh, I'm making no objection! For myself, I would prefer to become accustomed to this sort of transportation. But please, do admit that you would feel more at ease now if you were dressed just a little differently."

He shot me a brief look of great impatience. "I'm glad that you are enjoying the luxury, Leaozinha, but this is not to the point. One of the things I learned in my parents' home, for better or worse, is that hired stables of this particular sort can be relied upon for impeccable prudence, both during and after any given event. Which is certainly *not* true of regular cabdrivers."

I nodded slightly to indicate that I understood. I had heard of such outfits: rather shady businesses that leased fine carriages to the rich for the purpose of keeping clandestine assignations and similar affairs where family crests must be kept out of view. Now that I thought about it, I realized that such companies must surely exercise absolute discretion, as a basic service to their clients.

I enjoyed the evening ride through the night streets of Paris so much that I nearly forgot the sobering nature of our mission, until we passed abruptly through the unguarded gates of the Bois de Boulogne. We paused for a minute while the coachman lit the two lanterns at the front of our carriage. The gaslights of the street were all behind us now, and although the packed gravel roads that laced the immense park were maintained in fine condition, there would be no light from here forward except the glow of the rising moon.

Through the window, I nervously watched our progress into the heart of the dark and looming woods. Armand had a crumpled piece of paper that he referred to by lamplight, calling out occasional instructions to the driver through the front window. I didn't know the Bois de Boulogne very well, but as nearly as I could make out we were now winding our way up along the unsurfaced roads that formed a labyrinth above the Upper Lake.

At last, Armand called to the driver to hold and the carriage came to a stop. The footman opened the door for us and Armand climbed out and then helped me down. "Wait here," he told the coachman. "Speak to no one."

I could see a faint glow among the trees that crowded the curve in the narrow road ahead of us, and I followed Armand in that direction. We came around the bend to see one of the many tiny, hidden lawns scattered around that region of the park. The glow proved to be coming from several lanterns, some of which had been placed on the grass while others were held in the hands of a few men who were milling about the field.

"Wait," Armand said abruptly, barring my way with his arm. "This is not . . ." He paused. "I think that this . . . wait a moment. What *is* this?"

My eyes were well adjusted to the moonlight by this point, but I too was baffled at the tableau spread across the lawn. I had expected to find a clutch of conspirators talking together among the trees, or perhaps huddled in darkened carriages, not a scattering of men spread widely over a lawn with bright lanterns. There were only four men whom I could see: two close at hand, and two who were a few dozen yards away, near the edge of the forest. All of them seemed very busy.

"What's happening?" I whispered emphatically to Armand.

He turned to me and placed a hand behind my elbow, attempting to guide me back in the direction from which we had come.

"Come along, Florbela," he whispered. "I've made a mistake. We must leave."

"No!" I exclaimed, somewhat louder than before. "What is happening? Tell me! Look over there, that is Brian Torrence Grimm! Right over there."

"Come along, come along. Hurry now. We shouldn't be here."

I placed my feet more firmly under myself, and yanked my arm from out his grip. I was beginning to get angry at this brusque treatment. "I shall not go! And you shall stop trying to lead me away. I demand an explanation." I suppose that my voice must have been loud enough to carry a bit, because when I looked again, the two men who were closer to us were gazing in our direction. We, of course, were in near darkness, so perhaps they couldn't make us out, but now that they were facing us I could see clearly who they were. One of them was Fernand Léger, and the other was Robert Delaunay. Robert was holding a brilliant lantern at waist height, and by its light I could see that Léger was holding a pistol.

For a moment, I was probably immobilized by the sheer improbability of this vision. I could hear Armand continuing to hiss vainly into my ear that I should come away, but I pulled my arm away from him again and strode directly onto the lawn. I headed for Léger and Robert, because they were closer to us than Brian and his companion.

"Oh God, no!" Léger said, by way of greeting.

Robert, remembering his manners a little better, bowed to me slowly and said, in a tone of uncharacteristically brittle formality, "Senhorita Sarmentos. How extremely unexpected."

"What on earth is going on?" I demanded. I glanced over at Brian, who by now was striding rapidly in our direction. His companion followed close upon his heels, lantern in hand. I paused long enough to look more carefully at Léger's pistol. Indisputably, it was an archaic, muzzle-loading variety: the sort that is kept, in matching pairs, in the drawing rooms of every old family in Europe—duelling pistols.

"This is completely outrageous," I said loudly. "Aren't you ashamed of yourselves?"

Léger coughed into his hand, keeping his eyes averted from my face. Robert opened his mouth to reply, then closed it, thought for a moment, then opened it again to say quietly, "Oh dear."

At this moment, Brian and his companion joined us. "This is most improper," he said in stiffly formal English, speaking not to me but apparently to Léger and Robert. He added, in French, "This is not at all what has been agreed upon."

"I didn't *invite* her!" Léger snapped irritably.

"Well, someone did," Brian snapped back at him. "You don't expect me to believe that she was simply strolling by. And who on earth is that, over there?"

Armand, with extreme reluctance, was shuffling closer to the group on the grass. By now he was close enough to be half visible in the glow of lamplight. The men all turned to regard him with lowered eyelids under arched eyebrows.

"Oh, good lord!" Brian said after a moment of careful scrutiny. "It can't be."

"Never mind that," I said sharply, waving to Armand to hurry him closer. "Have you all completely lost your minds?"

"Mademoiselle," Brian's companion said, his French bearing such a thick English accent that it was almost incomprehensible. "This is an affair of honor. It would be most gracious if you would clear the field." He was a burly young man in an English officer's uniform, with one of those unfortunate curled mustaches that men of the British foreign service sometimes affected.

I glared at Brian, who had been conspicuously hiding one hand behind his back, and he grudgingly brought it forth, revealing a pistol identical to the one that Léger was carrying. "We really *have* to go," Armand murmured, close to my ear.

"It isn't merely a matter of your gender," Robert explained, apparently trying to be helpful. "It's best not to be a witness to these affairs, if you can help it. Technically, you know, this sort of thing is terribly illegal."

"That's true," Armand chimed in. "And the newspapers love to treat these things as a great scandal, if word happens to get out. They wouldn't scruple about printing your name."

Brian added, with a nod at his second, "Indeed, Captain Struggles might face a court martial if this were reported to his superiors. So, please, it's quite important that you make haste to leave, and forget everything you have seen."

I was so angry by this point that I think that I raised my fists; at any rate, I certainly noticed everyone rearing up a bit in alarm. "This shall not go any further," I said, quite loudly. I suppose that I may have been shouting at this point. "There is no reason for you to fight! You don't even *know* each other."

Léger and Grimm exchanged poisonous glances. "Oh, we know each other well enough," Léger said, drawing the sentence out very slowly.

Grimm stiffened and frowned. "I shall exchange no more words with you, monsieur," he said down his nose. "Let us proceed."

"Brian, Fernand, please . . . this is insane. Please don't do this," I begged them.

"Impossible. It must be done," Brian's second said decisively.

Robert had moved to my side and spoke to me in that calm, reasonable tone that is used to coax horses over icy bridges. "Certain *words* have been exchanged," he explained to me. "Words of . . . shall we say, unfortunate zeal. Some of these words have seemed most injurious to sentiments that these two men hold dear. *Patriotic* sentiments, for example."

I made an inchoate, sputtering sound in my effort to construct a reply to the insanity that I was hearing. The noise that I produced was ugly even in my own ears, but I was incapable of clear articulation by this point.

"She must be taken from the field," Captain Struggles said in English, perhaps unaware that I spoke his language. "I don't wish to place hands upon her. Could you gentlemen . . .?"

Suddenly, Robert and Armand were holding me firmly, each by one of my arms. As I began to kick and shove at the ground with my feet, they lifted me nearly into the air and began walking me toward the edge of the field.

"I don't believe we have met," Robert said mildly over my cries of outrage. He leaned around me to look at Armand. "Robert Delaunay, at your service."

"We have met before," Armand told him in a small voice, as if loath to admit it. "I am Armand Fontaine."

Robert stopped, forcing Armand to do the same. As I growled and kicked the air between them, he leaned further around me to examine Armand more closely. "My God! Can it be true? Someone told me that you were in Germany. Or dead. Or perhaps both."

"Yet here I am."

"Well then, I'm very pleased to see you again, despite the circumstances. May I ask, though, what on earth was on your mind, bringing Senhorita Sarmentos to such an affair?"

"I was grievously misinformed."

"I should say so! Well, listen. I don't wish to carry her any further, if I can help it. Her boots are chopping trenches into my calves. But if I let go, then I fear she will bite."

"I believe I can restrain her," Armand volunteered. "At least briefly. It appears that this business will all be over in a very short time, wouldn't you say?"

"Oh yes. We're loaded now, and the field has been paced, and so on. But how do you propose to keep her from crying out and distracting the shooters?"

"That might be difficult."

They stood there, holding me just high enough that my feet couldn't really touch the ground. I was still breathing hard, but I had stopped growling so that I could listen to them.

"We could gag her," Robert proposed.

"Just put me down," I told them.

They paused.

"Please put me down. I doubt if I will forgive any of you for this as long as I live, but I promise that I shall not interfere any further."

They hesitated a moment longer, but then they set me down, released me, and stepped away to a polite distance.

"Please forgive me for placing hands upon you," Robert said, bowing to me slowly and deeply. Then he looked at Armand. "You will stay here and keep her company?"

"I will."

I was getting tired of these two speaking of me in the third person, but that was the least of my aggravations. I swallowed my pride, touched Robert's sleeve to detain him for a moment longer, and asked in a humbled voice, "Are they serious, Robert? Will they kill each other?"

"Oh, I doubt that," Robert said in a consoling tone, patting my hand. "Well, I suppose *one* of them might. They're both extremely good shots, you know. But on the bright side, it's in the nature of these events that at least one of them is likely to end up more or less uninjured." He bowed again and walked rapidly away to rejoin Léger, who was standing between the lanterns at the near end of the lawn.

"Oh, Armand, is there not something we can do to stop this," I said turning to him and burying my face in his shoulder. He put his arm around me gently.

"I'm sorry for bringing you here tonight Leaozinha," he said tenderly. I began to weep copiously

I wiped my eyes with my handkerchief and prepared myself to witness the awful spectacle.

The preparations were indeed complete. Brian had resumed his position at the far side of the lawn, and I saw now that two lanterns were positioned on the grass just in front of him, to illuminate him like footlights on a stage. Léger was still checking his pistol as Robert joined him, but now he straightened up and placed himself behind two lanterns in a similar fashion.

"Are you ready?" Captain Struggles shouted from across the lawn, in his guttural French.

Robert was backing away from the line of fire, as he called back, "We are, sir."

"Well, then. You won the toss. First shot is to you."

Watching my dear friend Léger turn and prepare to point his pistol in the direction of my dear friend Brian was one of the most horrifying moments of my life, and I had to put my hand over my mouth to keep from crying out. Brian, however, affected not to notice. He appeared to ignore Léger completely, looking at the gun in his own hand and turning it slowly over, this way and that, as if checking it for flaws.

Léger raised his pistol and fired, all in one movement, taking no particular pains to aim his shot, and possibly not even sighting before pulling the trigger. The noise was shockingly loud in the stillness of the night. Simultaneously, there was a disturbance in the foliage of the trees just behind Brian's head, and a moment later a shower of fragmented leaves came twinkling down through the yellow lamplight onto the grass.

I couldn't breathe as I waited and watched. For the longest moment, everyone was silent, staring at Brian. But when he failed to collapse to the ground or show other signs of injury, Robert cupped his hands and called across the lawn, "You may take your turn."

My heart was pounding so hard I thought it would burst through my chest, and I felt like I was about to faint. Armand had his arms around me and was holding me up. All I remembered feeling was his strength and his warmth in the cool loneliness of the forest. I recovered and looked again at the two men I loved trying to kill one another. I felt ill.

Brian shifted his stance, placing one foot forward, and lifted his pistol very slowly and carefully, squinting along its length for a long moment. Léger spread his legs apart and placed his fists on his hips, holding his elbows akimbo and staring disdainfully into Brian's barrel. Again, the night air was torn by a powerful crack as Brian discharged his pistol, and the lantern by Léger's left boot exploded and winked out.

I burst into tears, and turned my back on the dreadful scene.

As appalled as I was by these proceedings, I was doubly shocked to hear Robert chuckle in the darkness.

"How can he laugh?" I wondered aloud.

Armand replied, "Mr. Grimm is clearly very handy with a pistol. It was kind of him to spare his adversary."

"You mean to say that he missed on purpose?"

"I should imagine they both did."

I turned back to the lawn and watched the two combatants consult with their respective seconds. "Then what are they doing here?" I glanced over and caught Armand frowning at me.

"You're asking me?" He laughed scornfully, "I had imagined that *you* might have some explanation."

"What on earth are you talking about?" I sputtered. "How would I possibly know anything about it?"

"Would you care for another shot?" Captain Struggles called across the lawn. "If so, we should need a minute or so to reload."

Robert and Léger muttered together for only a moment, and then Robert called back, "No thank you. How about yourself? Care for another go? No? Then I suppose we may as well pack up."

I began to weep with relief. I followed Armand in a daze toward the light of the lanterns where the men were gathering. I was also trying to fathom what Armand was insinuating—did he think it had something to do with me? Of course, it was impossible—I knew about as much of the incident as he did.

Brian and the captain arrived a moment later, and Robert began packing the pistols away into a velvet-lined walnut case.

Captain Struggles held up a lamp and gazed hard into the darkness in all directions. "We probably shouldn't tarry," he commented.

While the seconds packed up the gear, Brian and Léger stood by impassively, their arms crossed in front of their chests, close enough together that their shoulders were almost touching, but angled in such a fashion as to avoid seeing each other's faces. I continued to weep for some time, unable to say a word. How could two such beautiful men sink to such an ugly act of self-abasement as trying to murder one another? Despite what Armand had said, I refused to believe that all of this had anything to do with me.

"I suppose that I could do with a drink at this point," Brian remarked. "Anyone else?"

Captain Struggles shook his head firmly. "Sorry, sir. I've got to get back before I'm missed."

"A small nip does sound like the thing," Robert said hesitantly. "But I'm afraid I'd better not. Sonia will think that I'm having an affair."

Brian glanced over his shoulder at Léger and said formally, perhaps merely because he felt that civility required it, "How about you, then? A glass of cognac? You live upstairs from some sort of bistro, don't you?"

Léger turned to face him slowly, with a deep frown. "I suppose I do. But they close their doors just after dinnertime, and, at any rate, I'm heartily tired of hanging around the Sixth."

Brian shrugged. "Well, in that case . . ."

"Let's go over to Pigalle," Léger suggested. "Do you know Le Chien Ivre? It's a filthy place, but the cognac is as good as anyone's, and quite a bit cheaper than most."

"You don't say."

"Additionally, they are bound to be open until dawn, at the very least."

Brian nodded thoughtfully. "That has merit. Speaking for myself, I doubt that I'm likely to sleep anytime tonight." He cocked one eyebrow. "Perhaps this will give me an opportunity to demonstrate that an Englishman can drink better than he shoots."

The corner of Léger's lip flickered slightly. "Another challenge," he murmured. "But I believe I can uphold the honor of France on that front."

"Well, that's settled then," Struggles said, making an impatient gesture toward the road.

The four men bowed their heads to me momentarily, and murmured self-conscious good nights. While three of them stepped away into the darkness, Robert hesitated long enough to ask Armand and me if we would care to ride with them back into the city.

"We have a carriage of our own waiting, Monsieur Delaunay," Armand told him.

"That's good. But please, call me Robert." The two of them

shook hands. "Now that I know you live here in Paris, I hope we shall meet again under more auspicious circumstances. Perhaps you could come around to my home on Sunday night? My wife and I are having a bit of a get-together."

Armand smiled politely. "I've heard tell. Thank you, but I'm afraid that I am previously engaged."

"A shame. Perhaps sometime soon, then."

By the time Robert trotted away in pursuit of the retreating lanterns of his company, I was weeping again, though I refused to accept Armand's assistance back to our carriage. I felt that I would never stop being angry about what I'd seen that night, and I was also terribly confused. Both Brian and Léger had always seemed so exemplary and mature in my eyes, prior to that evening. Now I was left to wonder: are *all* men such barbarians?

Chapter Twenty-Six

Armand and I were almost certainly not the only people who had witnessed the duel. Over the next week or two, word of it spread quite widely around the Left Bank and my name, alas, wasn't spared. Some of these traveling stories were even more outlandish and lurid than the events themselves.

Although I kept to myself for several days after that unsettling evening, I did attend the Delaunays' party the following week. There, I had the oddly bittersweet experience of finding myself a celebrity for questionable reasons. I had never expected to experience notoriety, but I found to my surprise that when it comes, it brings with it certain rewards. The women at the party all wanted to be seen talking with me, the men to dance with me, and I found myself making only moderate efforts to wriggle out of the limelight. After all, as nearly as I could tell, I hadn't personally done anything wrong.

For the following month, the Delaunays' weekly party became my only evening excursion and I relished the opportunity to leave the studio in safety of numbers.

As for Armand, he certainly did not follow up on Robert's invitation to that or any other party, though I did what I could to encourage him to come along. For a week or so after the duel, he was a bit stiff in his conduct with me, and reticent in conversation. Although he obdurately continued to carry out his duties as a sentry every night in the backyard, he rarely played his guitar, and never sang in the night. I admit that I felt a strange sense of guilt whenever I thought about him, though I can't see why. Perhaps for that reason, I found it was difficult for me to fall asleep without the sound of his music outside my window. I suffered at least a week of recurrent bouts of insomnia, as a result of his silence. Then at last, perhaps two weeks after the duel, there came a night when he began to play and sing again, though I hadn't noticed any other change in his demeanor or attitude. I was lying on my cot at the time and felt tears start to flow involuntarily from my eyes into my pillow. Within a minute or two, I was sound asleep.

I avoided Brian and Léger, if only to give them time to cool their heads. Brian continued to send his polite and extravagantly printed invitations to my door twice a week as he had always done, but I ignored them all. As for Léger, he stopped sending me invitations after the duel. And my only other point of contact had been the Delaunays' parties, but Sonia ceased to invite him as soon as news of the affair in the Bois de Boulogne reached her ears, so I simply never encountered him anymore.

After three weeks or so, Willie came over and mentioned in passing that word of the duel had reached certain authorities, and that legal proceedings were being mooted. Although he felt that the case was unlikely to go to court, I felt for the first time a certain amount of sympathy for Brian and Léger.

Meanwhile, Irène remained oddly obedient to Mr. Brancusi's stricture against going to Bateau-Lavoir. In fact, she made no effort that I could perceive to engineer any meeting at all with Pablo Picasso. Although I was pleased about that, I was also mystified at her uncharacteristic lack of initiative. As for her health, it didn't perceptibly worsen, but her low mood seemed to drag on interminably. She had stopped sculpting, continued to eat poorly, and spent most of her time moping around our studio and those of our neighbors, listening to the conversations of others or simply reading.

One day, I came home and found her absorbed in a thick, leather-bound book. The sober gravity of the heavy binding made me curious, so I moved closer and peeked over her shoulder. Imagine my surprise when I saw that she was reading pages written in German, densely arrayed with abstruse mathematical equations.

"Are you studying mathematics?" I asked her, flabbergasted.

"I'm just reading a bit of Riemann," she told me.

I shook my head. "What is that? I don't think I've ever heard the word before."

She glanced at me over her shoulder, looking a bit supercilious, or perhaps simply exasperated. "Really? He's quite a well-known mathematician. This book has been around for years."

"I'm afraid that I don't really keep up with current developments in mathematics," I told her, wondering if she might seriously imagine that I did so.

"You would probably enjoy this," she told me, in her clear, high voice. "This volume is quite a thorough analysis of n-dimensional curvature. I think you would find it compelling."

In the days following that, she seemed to give up on reading novels altogether, and absorbed herself in tomes of higher mathematics for days at a time. I mentioned it to our friends in the building, asking if they thought I should be concerned. They all laughed at me, but then each of them made excuses to come up and investigate for themselves. When they would find her sitting at her chair or lying on her bed, flipping slowly through pages of incomprehensible equations, the sight certainly seemed to give them pause. I remember Amedeo commenting, after a week or two of this, that she was indulging in mathematics like an addict indulging in a favorite drug. Given his proclivities, this was a poignant observation.

Eventually July rolled around, and hot days began trickling into Paris, at first one at a time and then in groups. Through the newspapers, I learned that Portugal's armed resistance, which was scattered here and there around the countryside, was taking its summer siesta. I was relieved to hear it. Though I naturally supported their cause, I hated to think of my people butchering one another.

When the first really hot days of summer came around, our studio on the top floor of La Ruche became unbearable, forcing almost all of us who lived up there to find other places to spend our days, from noon until dinnertime. I believe that Moishe was the only one on the whole third floor who stayed up there on hot afternoons, painting right through the day. Some days it must have been like working inside an oven. Irène and I would come home in the evening to find him sitting on his little wooden chair, leaning as always toward his easel, with a big wet towel draped over his head and shoulders.

When a month had passed since the duel, I felt it was time to restore my relations with my two wayward friends, who had raised no further trouble, or at any rate none of which I knew. The easiest bridge to mend seemed to me the one between myself and Brian, because he sent me invitations so very often. I replied to one of these, refusing its specifics but suggesting that instead we might meet in some public place for lunch.

One Sunday morning in early July, I arrived in my summer clothes at one of the popular floating restaurants arranged along the left bank of the Seine. There I found Brian wearing his favorite suit with a starched shirt and bowler, waiting for me stoically, holding a white carnation in his hand. We smiled and nodded to each other, and he held the flower forth, presenting it with crisp formality.

"Thank you Brian, how thoughtful of you."

Our greetings were drowned out by the rising yowl of an engine, which I at first took to be some new sort of automobile passing by. But those around us began to crane their heads upward, and I turned to see an aeroplane flying overhead, following the course of the river. I had never seen one before. I had somehow naively imagined that these devices would be about the dimensions of a man with outstretched arms, so I was surprised at its great size—it must have been twenty feet wide, and just as long. Sunshine gleamed through the wings, which seemed no more substantial than paper. The pilot sat below them on a flimsy open frame, exposed completely to the open air. My immediate impression was that the endeavor seemed insanely dangerous . . . an impression which the dirigible had never made upon me.

"The *Demoiselle*," Brian told me. His voice was oddly devoid of excitement, given the spectacle passing overhead.

"Is it Monsieur Santos-Dumont?" I asked breathlessly. It seemed so completely unlikely that this device was going to stay aloft for more than another minute or so that I was certain we were about to witness a horrible death.

"It could be anyone. He sells them now, you know."

I pried my eyes away from the receding aircraft long enough to glance at his face, thinking he must be joking. He was not. "He is *selling* aeroplanes?"

"They are quite reasonably priced. Seventy-five hundred francs, if memory serves."

I turned to watch it speeding off around the river bend. "Imagine that! A manufactured aeroplane . . . up for sale, just like an automobile. What a world we live in."

"Yes, the aeroplane is not a novelty anymore, Florbela. I believe that there may be dozens of them nowadays, worldwide. Perhaps more than a hundred." He took my arm and guided me onto the barge ramp. In a glum tone, he added, "Mark my words. Before the twentieth century is out, soldiers will be firing guns and dropping bombs from them."

"From aeroplanes? Heaven forfend."

We took our table on the long deck under a big canvas umbrella that was printed in festive shades of yellow and green. We took our time reading the menu and placing our order. I used the delay to examine Brian carefully, glancing over my menu as subtly as I could. He had seemed quite himself when I first saw him, though perhaps unusually reserved, but when he wasn't feeling my eyes upon him, I could tell that he was distracted and ill at ease.

After we handed the waiter our menus, we were obliged to look at each other and smile politely. I had missed his delightful company over the previous few weeks, more than I imagined I would. To try and put him at ease I said, "It's good to see you again Brian."

His calm facade returned. After a polite pause, he said, "You're looking as lovely as ever."

"Thank you."

He gazed out at the river for a few moments, as if gathering his thoughts.

"Now . . . I have something that I feel I must say. It seems to me that what is most important is that you judge me as a person, rather than in my . . . worldly role."

I puzzled over this comment for just a moment, finding it extremely obtuse. "I think I do so," I said at length.

"I mean to say that, however you may judge me as a man, I should hope that your feelings would not dissuade you—nor your father—from trusting me to represent the Grand Lodge, in whatever way you should deem fit."

So that was what was on his mind! Or at least, it seemed important enough to him that he wished to put *that* foot forward. "I don't judge you so very harshly as a man, Brian," I told him. "Sometimes I admire your actions more, and sometimes less. I imagine that you might say something similar in regard to me. And I do certainly trust you to represent your order with integrity. Any reservations I might have along those lines apply to the organization itself, not to its emissary."

He let out a small breath, obviously intentional and intended to express his relief. I must admit that I was dismayed at this display of English sangfroid. Was *this* all that had been on his mind, during these past few weeks? That I might fail to serve my role as the liaison between the Portuguese partisans and the English Freemasons, out of personal disappointment with Brian?

As I was brooding upon these thoughts, we were served. We ate with an unusual amount of concentration, commenting upon almost nothing save the excellence of the food, which I think we exaggerated in order to give us license to avoid all other topics. This gave us a stretch of time within which to organize our thoughts, and it occurred to me over a dessert of speck and melon that perhaps his personal emotions were running much higher than he let on. I'm not sure what sixth sense informed me of this, but whatever might be passing in his mind or heart, his face betrayed nothing.

As we were waiting for our coffee to arrive, I gave up on my effort to see into his secret heart and said, "See how hazy the summer air is over the Seine. It makes one wonder why so many painters today would wish to be anything other than Impressionists. Don't you agree?" I allowed a fair pause, then tried again. "Just look at it! Doesn't the view invite the sort of treatment that Renoir or Monet might give it?" But he would not be baited into small talk, and there was only silence from his side of the table. His business with me was apparently over, and he didn't seem to want to speak to me at all. I was so disappointed that our meeting had turned out this way—I had been looking forward to seeing him again.

The coffee arrived, and Brian nodded the waiter away without quite looking up. In the next moment, I watched in disbelief as his left hand slipped up, as stealthily as possible, and wiped the corner of his eye. I watched him carefully, holding my breath. He turned his face away, to look at the roiling, gray-brown waters of the river.

"I shall not make a fool of myself over you," he said, his low voice construing a remarkable facsimile of cool detachment. "I know that you will never marry me, Florbela. But . . ." At this point he paused for a lengthy time, and I saw his lips tremble slightly.

I could hardly breathe. I loved him dearly, but he was right: I was not ready to marry anyone. I never expected that our friendship could cause him pain.

"Brian. . ." I said hesitantly, my hand reaching to him across the table. I wanted to comfort him, but I didn't know how.

His hand lifted a small distance toward his face, but as he regained control, he dropped it back onto his knee. He took a careful breath, then continued, "I have never known that I could want something so very much. I suppose I have discovered a thing about myself that I didn't know. I owe that to you." His eyes flickered in my direction for the first time since the food had arrived, then darted away once again to gaze out over the swirling currents.

I had to force myself to breathe, and withdrew my hand from the table. I was afraid that, despite his denial, he was about to propose marriage to me. My fists squeezed my napkin into a bunch, under the table. If he had asked me, I am not sure what I would have said.

But Brian had no intention to propose. He was, despite occasional appearances to the contrary, deeply wise in worldly matters, and I think he understood my heart very well . . . perhaps better than I.

"Excuse me if I seem maudlin," he said, attempting to lighten his tone, but still apparently speaking to the cold and rolling Seine. He gave a sad semblance of a smile. "Perhaps I have been drinking too much lately."

"*You*? That's hard to imagine. Do you drink alone?"

He shook his head. "No. No one ever has any reason to drink alone in Paris. The fact of the matter is that I most often drink with Monsieur Léger."

This surprised me so much that I had to stifle a laugh. "I'm glad that the two of you have found a rapport," I said. "But who could have imagined that you and he should become friends!"

"I suppose that the thing *is* odd, from a certain point of view." Brian continued to gaze across the waters. "I can offer no explanation."

"You certainly needn't offer any explanation to me—nor to anyone I suppose—regarding your friendships. I'm sorry that I laughed. But"—and here I hope that I wasn't needling him unduly—"what about your conflicting points of national affinity? I had the impression that there were some . . . *patriotic* conflicts between the two of you."

Brian shook his head and laughed through his nose, without humor. "Patriotic? That's an odd way to put it." He glanced at me quickly, not letting his eyes communicate much before flicking them away again. "Léger is really too much a communist to be any sort of genuine nationalist."

"Very well, but then . . . communism? Are you really more comfortable with communism than with French chauvinism?"

Brian lifted one of his long hands to brush this criticism out of the air. "I suppose that you have spent as much time with Léger as I have. How often has he spoken to you of his communist beliefs? I only bristle at his political notions when he brings them up, and I can't even remember when that happened last."

Our meal ended affably enough, though without any real rapprochement between Brian and myself. We parted ways on a street that overlooked the river. After he kissed my hand and turned his back to me, I looked over my shoulder several times, but only saw him walking away, head bowed. My heart was heavy and I shed quite a few tears as I walked slowly back to my studio, carrying the white carnation that he had given me.

Chapter Twenty-Seven

T hat evening, as every Sunday, there was a party at Robert
and Sonia's home. I joined Diego, Amedeo and Angelina in
their studio as they cultivated a festive mood in preparation
for the outing. I made a perfunctory effort to get Irène to come
along, but it was obvious even before I asked the question that the
answer would be no. I left her propped up in bed as usual, paging
slowly through one of her unfathomable books of equations.
Moishe, however, was eager to come along. He had become fast
friends with Sonia Delaunay and had fallen into the habit of
coming along with us on our weekly venture into the Sixth.

We arrived fairly early, before the main crowd. While Angelina
helped Sonia to move the furniture to the edges of the room and
Diego engaged Robert in loud conversation, I allowed Amedeo to
lead me around the apartment, showing off the works of art.
These were always on display, but they were rarely as visible as
they were at this time. The collection of art on permanent loan to
the Delaunays was one of the most remarkable *de facto* private art
collections in the world, containing Picassos, Riveras,
Modiglianis, Chagalls, Légers, Brancusis, and of course of the
works of Sonia and Robert Delaunay themselves.

Later, as the room was beginning to fill, I heard a familiar voice
at the door and turned my head sharply. There was Léger,
standing at the entrance. Robert was speaking to him quietly,
apparently neither inviting him in nor sending him away.

"Florbela?"

I turned and saw that Sonia was standing beside me.

"May I ask you about Léger?" She cocked her head, watching my face carefully. "He has been gone a long time, and he is a dear friend to us. I think perhaps we will let him come in. Would you mind?"

Although I had intended to arrange a meeting with Léger sometime soon, I would not have chosen a big party as the venue, since I knew him to be a man who didn't care much for conventions and propriety. Still, it was Sonia's home, not mine, so I nodded my accession. Sonia gave me a reassuring smile, then slipped away.

Léger hadn't been in the room for more than ten minutes before I observed him working his way toward me, under the scandal-hungry eyes of the assembled guests. Sonia, bless her, appeared abruptly in his path, dragging along Moishe by the wrist rather like bait on a fishing line. Naturally, Léger could not let Moishe pass by without giving him an enthusiastic greeting. I watched Sonia apply her considerable charm to the project of keeping Léger's attention focused upon Moishe, and I felt a great affection for her.

Nonetheless, it was only a temporary interference. A few minutes later, as I was chatting with one of the theater people from the Ballet Russe, a woman I barely knew, I observed from the corner of my eye that Léger was again slipping away from Sonia, headed in my direction.

"Excuse me," I said, and moved away toward the studios in the back of the apartment.

I entered Robert's studio, placed myself directly in the center of the room. Soon enough, Léger appeared at the door, paused, and stepped sheepishly inside. This stopped every conversation in the room. Léger came slowly toward me, his eyes downcast. "Senhorita Sarmentos," was all he said.

"Monsieur Léger."

Over the next few minutes, everyone in the small room drifted out the door, leaving us alone.

I expected a loud scene and was prepared to be very wrathful, but I was surprised to find that Léger was in a quiet state and perfectly sober. When the room was clear, I leaned toward him a bit, "Monsieur Léger, I have the feeling you have something you need to say to me." Beyond his shoulder, I could see and hear people outside the open doorway, only half pretending not to spy.

"I'm afraid that I do. I apologize for being forward with you, but I would appreciate just a minute of your time." Considering how determinedly he had been pursuing me, his voice was strangely meek, almost an apologetic murmur. I'd never heard Léger speak meekly before, and the sound of it set me back a little.

"You know how I live," he told me quietly. "I feel myself to be an island in the sea of mankind, and I prefer to live as such. I have beliefs regarding conduct and I hold to them firmly . . . perhaps even a bit too rigidly. I remain aloof from the hearts of others. This has been true even from my childhood. I prefer it so!"

I hadn't expected a confessional; not at all. I began to chew my lip, worried about where this might be going. I'm afraid the statements that he was making were all plain truth. Whatever his faults, Léger was certainly no philandering socialite or spoiled playboy. Although his passion for me might, at certain moments, have lacked temperance, I had never doubted his sincerity.

"But when I met you . . ."

At that moment, to my distress, his voice broke. He had to stop and breathe before starting again. He said, "The day we met, I lost that precious autonomy. The freedom and the clarity of vision that belong to any man whose heart is his own possession . . . all of that, I lost."

I was wringing my hands by now, and no longer felt at all in control of the situation. The sadness in his voice was almost more than I could bear. If he had proposed to me again at that moment, I might not have had the emotional wherewithal to refuse him.

"You needn't worry," he said, as if reading my mind. "I know that I will never possess you, Florbela." His eyes flickered up to my face, as if he needed to see me assure him that this were true. "And yet, I also cannot imagine what else in this world could possibly be worth having." He was leaning his head now, so that I couldn't see his face. I wanted to kiss his cheek and to apologize for causing so much grief.

Léger quickly took hold of himself once again, daubing his face with his hand and then slowly straightening up his shoulders.

"You are so very dear to me Fernand," I told him, as tears welled in my eyes. "But you must understand that I have no intention to marry at this time. My sincerest wish is that we should become friends once again. Do you think that would be possible?"

"Not today, I fear," he said quietly. "Perhaps in the fullness of time."

I nodded, watching him recover his composure. I was glad now that he had forced me to hear him out, and I was no longer afraid of him. I told him, scolding mildly, "I've been worried on your account."

He glanced up at me. "Worried? Yes, I admit that I have been drinking."

"With Mr. Grimm?"

"Yes, yes. With Brian. The man has many faults, and often enough he drives me to fury. But I prefer to drink with him rather than with others, nonetheless." He paused, as if trying to account for this contradiction. "It seems that he's the only one who understands how I feel."

Oh, how monstrous I felt at that moment. To be the cause of so much pain to two people whom I loved and whose company I delighted to share.

His eyes dropped, and his face pinched for a moment, but then quickly relaxed. When he looked at me again, his features were under perfect control. He bowed to me slightly and said with gallant formality, "Thank you for allowing me to speak my mind."

I opened my mouth, unsure of how to reply, and no words came out. But he was done speaking. He looked at me for a moment, then simply bowed again, turned, and left the room with dignity. He must have headed straight back out to the street, because I didn't see him again that evening. I stood there alone for a long time, staring out the window at the nightlit street to hide my tears.

Over the next few hours, I tried to lose myself in the evening's chaotic entertainments, and was more or less successful, but I never really recovered from my meeting with Fernand earlier in the evening. The party spiraled its way up to ever greater heights of noise and cheer until some time after midnight, and then began slowly winding its way back down again. It was a trajectory with which I was well familiar by now, and had learned to enjoy. I stayed there quite a bit longer than I did most weeks, and missed my ride back to La Ruche with Angelina and Moishe.

I found myself in the cold, small hours, standing outside on the cobbles with the richly inebriated Diego and Amedeo. Only half of my mind was following their semi-coherent conversation, as they considered their next move. The other half of my attention was again obscured under a glum cloud as I remembered my sad and painful meetings with Brian and Fernand that day.

"So how about that?" Diego slurred. I realized that he was speaking to me.

"What's that?"

"You're not even listening." He turned to Amedeo to repeat this observation, which was probably prudent, since Amedeo didn't seem to be in a state that would facilitate understanding much of anything the first time it was said. "She's not even listening."

"Going *that* way," Amedeo told me, clarifying his meaning by waving a hand in the general direction of the city center.

"Come along," Diego said, hooking his chubby arm under mine. "The night is young and who knows what recreations await us!"

I extracted my elbow. "You two go along and enjoy yourselves. I'll take a cab home."

I watched them swagger off into the misty night, feeling very fond of both of them. Then I turned to start in the other direction, toward the cab stand a couple of blocks away. I didn't have any money on me and so I would have to borrow the fare from someone at La Ruche.

I had been walking rapidly for perhaps a block, when I observed a ragged young man detach himself from a lamppost not far from me. My heart leapt, but the figure moved to place itself squarely in the light, and I realized that it was Armand. I smiled with relief and walked over to him.

"What a remarkable coincidence," I teased him.

He smiled and gave no reply, but fell into step beside me, letting me continue on my way.

"Were you waiting long?"

"I am accustomed to exercising my patience, Leaozinha."

"I suppose you must be. But usually you have your guitar with you, to while away the hours."

"The streets of Paris always provide entertainment, if one is paying attention."

"You should have told me that you were coming to meet me. I wouldn't have stayed so late."

"Ah, but if I had told you, you would have insisted that I leave you to your own devices. Isn't that so?"

I couldn't deny it. "Well, you're very sweet. And the walk will be far more pleasant in your company." I smiled at him in all sincerity, and he looked quite pleased.

"I wish that I could offer to hire us a cab," he said. "But I'm afraid that I am down to just one sou."

I laughed. "That's one sou more than I have." I took his arm and walked close beside him. He was my hero at that moment. A terribly unlikely hero, I'm afraid, and not the least because he was dressed like a ragamuffin. But there he was, strong, warm and dependable, and making me feel safe, as he so often did. Perhaps precisely because of this feeling of safety, I soon let the conversation languish. I fell into deep brooding as we walked briskly along, and I meditated upon the day's distressing encounters with Brian and Fernand.

After the best part of a mile, Armand laughed gently and complained, "You are squeezing rather tightly."

"Am I? I'm sorry!" I forced my hands to relax.

"Is something bothering you? I believe you may have riven a gouge into my arm."

He was joking, but I apologized again. Suddenly I was dying to tell him everything: to try to explain somehow, to place Brian and Fernand into a context that he could understand. I suppose that I wanted to confess myself to him and have him absolve me of the guilt I felt for their pain. But of course, this was all a ridiculous fancy; perhaps the wine I had consumed was making me self-absorbed.

As we approached the Rue d'Alésia, I was struck by the sight of a young flower girl under the gaslight, nodding, half asleep beside some baskets of tulips and roses, waiting for the dawn. In my mawkish state of mind, she seemed a symbol of how empty life could become, of how hard it was to be alone. I furtively wiped my eye, composed my face and glanced at Armand.

"In my opinion," I declared, "not all of God's fancies are equally good, and the worst of all is love."

"Really?" He smiled at me tentatively. "You think that that's the worst?"

I said emphatically, "Love and romance. The very worst of God's conceits."

His studied me carefully. "I suppose I can see your point. It certainly has struck me that, without all that sort of thing, everything in life would be simple and clear, as it is for children. Love muddies everything."

I nodded, "My point exactly."

We came abreast of the flower girl at that moment, and Armand stopped. The nodding child, perhaps ten years old, awoke abruptly and rolled her eyes up at us in surprise.

"Will this buy a rose?" Armand asked, holding out a sou with gentle formality.

"Yes, monsieur, if you don't mind a short stem." She selected a small and perfect red flower and handed it up to me, beaming into my face with her bright eyes. "What a gentleman is your beau, mademoiselle!"

Chapter Twenty-Eight

By that point in the summer, I had developed a greater sense of self-discipline with regard to my artistic regimen. For a few weeks, I worked on one canvas or another during a few hours of every single day, often pushing myself to the point of emotional exhaustion. As for Brian and Léger, I didn't run into them at all during those weeks. I missed each of them at times, and sometimes terribly, but I tried to keep myself busy so I couldn't think about them too much. On the other hand, I made a point of visiting Moishe twice a day in his studio, attempting to absorb some of his fixity of purpose. There was an ambience of monastic devotion to the muse in Moishe's room, and I would almost always leave there feeling revitalized and ready to give the work another hour of my heart's labors, however frustrating and disappointing the resulting canvases continued to look, even in my own eyes.

Irène also spent most of her time in the studio those days, reading her books. On many occasions, I became sufficiently enthused with my own creative efforts that I tried to encourage her to sculpt again. Occasionally I managed to infect her with a brief zeal, and she would seem on the verge of attempting a new piece, but unfortunately these short spells never amounted to anything.

Then came the night when I awakened in the very darkest and stillest hour, as abruptly and completely as if responding to some ancient instinct of danger. Although the room was as silent as a crypt, I was in some way certain that a tiny noise had awakened me. In an effort to fool whatever ghost or fantasy might be lurking in the unlit room, I held myself very still and kept my breathing regular, feigning sleep but paying the closest attention to the space around me through wide eyes. I wanted to cry out but I felt too foolish, since nothing had actually happened.

For the space of at least a minute, this endeavor seemed like a silly and childish game I was playing with myself, because despite the pitch darkness it seemed clear enough that the only person awake in the room was me. I had almost decided to turn over and go back to sleep, but then I began to perceive suggestions of movement, black on black. At first they seemed no more than tricks of the eye, or phantoms of a mind that was relaxing back toward sleep. At last, however, I really did see a moving form, vaguely defined but definitely real—and surely too large to be Irène.

My hands and feet suddenly went cold, as if my blood had stopped its circulation. I moved my head as subtly as possible, to stare in unblinking terror down the length of the darkened room. In the meager starlight, I could perceive that there was something moving near the far end of the studio, near the side of Irène's bed. It seemed to be a man, moving with a weird fluidity, in and out of shadow. His near invisibility confused my eye, seeming to suggest supernatural properties, until I remembered the night, months ago, when Armand had chased the man through the yard—a man wrapped in black cloth from head to toe.

I formed the words silently in my mind: *Onça do Papa.*

I opened my mouth to take a deep breath but before I could, the terrifying shadow was looming immensely above me. In the space of a heartbeat, I was suddenly pressed down firmly and my body was rolled over the mattress with force, leaving me wrapped in my own bed sheets as tightly as a fish in a newspaper. The whole process was accomplished with astonishing speed, leaving me sheathed from head to toe in a cocoon of fabric, bound so tightly that I couldn't move my limbs nor breathe, let alone cry out for help. I only managed a whimper instead of the scream I had imagined.

A moment later, I felt myself lifted roughly from my cot and lugged across the room like a rolled carpet. I was placed on a hard surface which later proved to be one of our wooden chairs. In darkness and panic, I struggled vainly to take a breath. I felt myself being quickly wrapped around with coils of cord, looped right over the sheets so as to tie me to the chair, leaving me with no freedom of movement whatsoever.

Just as I felt I was about to faint from suffocation, suddenly there was air. My assailant had uncovered my head with a single deft movement. For a second or so, my mouth was free, and I drew in a desperate breath, determined to scream with all the force and volume I could muster. But no sooner had I drawn the air into my lungs than a broad, silken strap was drawn across my mouth and knotted tightly behind my head. Suddenly, there was perfect stillness in the room again. I attempted to wriggle and shift my weight, hoping to bang the legs of my chair against the floor in order to awaken my neighbors, but even that amount of movement was impossible.

I was in for one more surprise, even before the darkness of the room was finally broken. There was another chair directly beside mine, and I saw that Irène was tied to it in the same manner as myself. The thought that our intruder had been capable of subduing and binding Irène so quietly as to avoid waking me chilled me to my bones.

Onça do Papa extracted a tiny candle from one of his pockets, primed its wick with a drop of spirits, and ignited it with a single strike of a flint on steel. Its small flame created a modest sphere of light, within which the three of us were illuminated in awful proximity.

He was a small and wiry man; smaller than I had imagined from my glimpse of his fleeing form, weeks ago. But he was indeed wrapped completely in tight-fitting black clothes, just as he had been that night. The costume reminded me of that of a circus acrobat, or perhaps one of those outlandish Arab assassins depicted in the illustrations of *The Thousand Nights and One Night*. Even his neck and head were hooded in black fabric, or rather, not so much hooded as wrapped, as if with bandages. Only his face was exposed, and nearly half of that was obscured behind a set of elegantly trimmed black whiskers. His eyes, too, were so dark as to appear jet black, and in the poor light they seemed almost like wells bored into his head. He was wearing an oil cloth packet strapped to his waist, about the size of a small folio. When my eyes noticed this accoutrement, they couldn't help returning to it again and again for closer examination. I suspected it to be a set of knives and daggers, and so the sight of it gripped me with terror.

I was so thoroughly bound in place that I couldn't turn my head far enough to see Irène's face directly, but in my peripheral view I could see the twinkling of the candlelight upon her cheeks, and deduced that they must be wet with tears. I could feel the tears running down my cheeks as well. I was terrified.

Our captor looked at us attentively and frequently, but never met our eyes. He seemed hardly to notice that we were living people at all, but rather to be investigating us as objects in the room, albeit objects that might be more problematic or potentially useful than the other pieces of furniture. He checked our bonds, confirming our complete immobility, then picked up his candle and began moving about the room. He examined every drawer, nook, shelf, crevice and hidden space with practiced efficiency. He performed this energetic and occasionally violent process in eerie silence, making no audible sound even when he produced a small carpenter's knife and began disemboweling the ticking of our beds, the paintings on our walls, and every pillow and cushion in the room.

He worked at this process for a half hour, which seemed interminable, and when he was finally done, every loose object in the room was laying on the floor, most of them broken or cut into bits, and every piece of furniture had been turned over and examined thoroughly. The studio might as well have been stricken by a typhoon, but the entire destructive process had been carried out with such feline grace that if my eyes had been closed, I might not have known that it was happening at all. I had never in my life imagined that stealth of such degree was possible.

Having completed the task of destroying almost everything we owned, Onça do Papa abruptly stopped his efforts, brought the candle back over to us, and sat himself down lightly on the edge of Irène's bed, facing us in the small glow. At last his eyes fell directly upon our faces, and his expression seemed so careless that one might have mistakenly thought that he was inclined to friendliness, though he did not smile. By now, however, I was beginning to understand that his casual demeanor was simply the outer expression of an absolute disregard for what might happen next, particularly to the two of us.

"I'm here to collect a certain work of art that does not belong to you," he told us. His voice was surprisingly deep for such a small man, and he spoke in French with a mellifluous and aristocratic Portuguese accent. He modulated his speech to a low murmur, almost a purr, and I soon noticed that he also elided his hard consonants. It occurred to me that he was controlling his voice in a manner intended to make it inaudible through walls.

"I am quite certain that you are in possession of this work of art, *demoiselles*, and attaining that certainty has cost me no small effort." He waved gracefully at the ruins of our home. "You have evidently hidden the object in question quite well, but I'm nonetheless certain that it *is* here." He paused for a moment, letting his eyes play loosely over the faces of Irène and myself in turn, as if expecting us to somehow answer him through our gags. "The work of art of which I speak is the property of my sacred order." He leaned closer—so closely that I could feel his warm breath upon my face. "My master cannot be disappointed at the outcome of my mission tonight. Do you understand? He *cannot*, and shall not. So you see: I will have satisfaction tonight, one way or another."

This threat was delivered into my face from such close distance that I felt I could see into an echoing cavern behind the blackness of his eyes. He didn't seem at all perturbed—neither disturbed nor excited—at the prospect of whatever foul deed might be on his mind. At that moment I realized that, however purposeful and efficient this man's actions might be, he was nonetheless, in a very real way, a madman. I believe that Onça do Papa was not bound by any of the standards I had taken for granted all of my life in regard to conduct. I felt that I might have been staring into the eyes of a spider.

He leaned back a bit and, with a casual gesture, produced a gleaming dagger. He may have taken the thing out of the kit that was strapped to his waist or from some other recess in his clothing, I don't know—it seemed to simply appear in his hand. I was bound so tightly that I could barely tremble as he extended it delicately toward me and touched its edge to the side of my throat. The blade felt like that of a razor, and if not for the extreme precision of his control, I believe it would have cut through my skin as easily as butter.

With his other hand, he reached up and tugged the gag away from my mouth. "Speak," he ordered me, in a mild undertone.

I don't know if courage contributed in any way to the silence that I returned to him, though of course I wish that I could boast of my heroic defiance. But the truth is that I was simply too terrified to speak. Any reply that I might have hoped to give him simply dried to dust in my throat. He stared at my mouth for quite some time, as if waiting to see if anything useful might come out of it, but he didn't seem at all surprised when I made no sound at all. With a perfunctory gesture, he pulled the gag back into place, then took the knife away from my throat and set it on the bed beside him.

He turned now to Irène. He reached down to grasp her left arm, which was the only part of her that I could see clearly from where I sat. With a few efficient gestures, he cut away the sheets and cords that bound her forearm, exposing it well above the elbow. Then he produced two buckled leather straps, similar to dog collars, and bound her elbow and wrist firmly to the arm of her chair. With a prestidigitator's flourish, he produced an ugly, curved knife. It so happened that, from my time in the port city of Cherbourg, I was able to recognize that this was a flensing knife—the sort used by sailors to peel the hides off seals. He moved it into his left hand, then poised it over Irène's tiny, fragile arm, touching its hideous steel blade lightly onto the surface of her pale and delicate skin. I heard Irène make an inarticulate sound of the utmost horror, muffled through her gag. I dreaded what he was about to do to my dear friend, and desperately tried to get his attention by making as much noise and movement as I could—which was effectively none at all.

Holding the knife lightly poised on Irène's arm, Onça do Papa turned his attention to me again. In a single movement, his right hand pulled my gag away from my mouth once more, then came to rest wrapped around my throat so that I could no longer breathe

"You will speak to me very quietly. Do you understand?" I could feel the firm pressure of his thumb and fingers, ready to crush my windpipe if I tried to cry out. "And now we will waste no more time at all. Speak to me now, Senhorita Sarmentos."

It was at that moment that the door opened behind me. In the dressing mirror, I could barely make out the dim reflection of Moishe, leaning into the room timidly with his small bedside lamp in his hand. Onça do Papa went completely rigid, like a marble statue. He seemed to be built entirely of muscle and bone, and the fingers that were locked around my neck suddenly felt like an iron collar.

It must have been very difficult for Moishe to see anything in the room with clarity, and I'm sure that he was confused. I tried to make a noise but Onça do Papa must have sensed it because his hand tightened so hard I felt near to fainting. My heart nearly stopped when I saw Moishe begin to retreat back into the hall once again, but he had only halfway extracted himself from the room when suddenly he popped his head back in through the door, wide-eyed, thrusting his lamp out in front of him to illuminate the studio.

His mouth fell open, and he began to bellow at the top of his lungs in Russian. "*Pomogitye!*" he shouted, or at any rate something that sounded roughly like that. He threw back his head and howled the word, over and over. I'm sure that very few of the people who heard him understood what he was saying, but the volume was certainly sufficient to awaken pretty much everyone on all three floors.

Onça do Papa unhanded me, while emitting an extraordinarily vulgar exclamation in Portuguese. He sheathed his knives in the blink of an eye, then leapt to the windowsill as lightly as a cat. Already there were voices and footsteps behind me, coming from the building's interior. I burst into tears of relief and looked over at Irène, who was sitting in stunned horror. "It's okay Irène," I said, "We are saved."

Crouched in the open frame of the window, Onça do Papa paused and turn to look me coldly in the eye. "*Je reviendrai*," he hissed. "You have not seen the last of me." Then he turned and leapt out into the darkness, appearing to take flight and vanish into the night air like a bat.

It took Moishe, our savior, just moments to find my sewing scissors and began cutting away our bonds. By the time I was able to turn myself far enough in my chair to have a look behind me, there was a confused crowd of half-dressed men jamming our doorway. I found myself glad that Irène and I were wrapped in sheets, as we had only our nightclothes on underneath.

As Moishe was cutting the cords that bound Irène's legs to the chair, I saw Armand elbow forcefully through the mob and burst into the room. "What are you doing, there?" he shouted at Moishe, making a forgivable error, considering that Moishe was wielding a pair of sharp scissors in the immediate proximity of two bound women.

I babbled some sort of mangled explanation, probably not making much sense but managing to convey to him that Moishe was saving our lives, not threatening them. Armand quickly produced a small pocket knife and helped to free me. When the bonds were removed, he gently helped me up and then impulsively he threw his arms around me and kissed my cheek. Then realizing what he had done, he let me go and stepped back, patting the air to show he meant no harm.

"Florbela . . . Senhorita, are you hurt?" he blurted out. It was clear that Armand was very distressed by the sight of Irène and me.

THE SIXTH

Then suddenly, Irène was free too, and we were standing there wrapped in sheets like Roman senators, or like ghosts in a mummer play. We hovered in place for a moment, wobbly on our shaking knees and unable to believe we were truly out of danger. Then we fell together and sobbed on each other's shoulders for a good long time.

Chapter Twenty-Nine

A few hours later, not long after dawn, I was sitting in the still confines of a parked carriage, staring blankly at the thin shafts of sunlight that gleamed through gaps in the heavy curtains obscuring its windows. The warm light of dawn offered an ironic invitation to good cheer and hopefulness—feelings that found no resonance in me. Though my tears were long since dried, my heart was unquiet in the extreme. I clutched the painting in its copper tube, but it felt more like I was transporting a serpent.

I was with Irène and Armand. Irène's arm was bandaged where that gruesome blade had lightly touched her skin and drawn blood. We had long since determined that Onça do Papa had broken into our room by dismantling the lock on the door. That is why Armand had never heard him, and how Moishe had been able to rescue us simply by opening the door and walking in. It was clear that Armand had been right: La Ruche was not safe even though it was full of people that hardly slept and was under constant surveillance by the Souris Trempés. It was not a comforting thought—if La Ruche was a dangerous place to live then where was I to go?

Our coach was at the curb outside the British Embassy, waiting for business hours to begin. Armand had dipped once again into his secret reserve of "the people's money," in order to hire this carriage from the discreet and anonymous livery service that he preferred. Apparently, providing unscheduled service at three in the morning was part of their standard offerings.

THE SIXTH

"That's him," Armand said, peeping out through the curbside window.

My heart sped a little, and I leaned forward to have a look for myself. Sure enough, Brian was approaching his embassy's front stairs, wearing a bowler, carrying a leather attaché in one hand, and holding a completely unnecessary umbrella in the other. He kept his back and neck preposterously stiff, in what struck me as a staged effort to convey solemnity. Despite his rigid posture, it was evident from his irregular pace, as well as a near stumble, that he was still a bit drunken from activities of the night before. *Oh Brian, what are you doing to yourself?* I thought sadly.

"I'm going," I announced, and I grasped the handle of the door and pushed it open. Armand was whispering something to me urgently, but I ignored him. I hopped down to the curb, clutching the copper tube tightly under my arm and began walking rapidly toward the embassy door. I heard footfalls behind me, and suddenly Armand was at my side. He tried to take my arm, but I pulled away impatiently. "You should go back to the carriage," I told him. "I believe this will be easier without you."

"No, I must come along," he told me. Before I could raise any objection, he reminded me, "It was into my care that your father remanded you, not into the care of Brian Torrence Grimm."

This was perhaps an imprecise statement of the facts, but it was close enough that I couldn't refute him without elaborate argument, and there was certainly no time for that now. We hurried together up the steps of the building. As we approached the great doors, the guards on either side eyed us warily and might very well have stopped us, had I not called out, "Mr. Grimm!"

Brian was already crossing the center of the immense and empty lobby, but he stopped abruptly on the broad expanse of terrazzo floor. He slowly turned. It seemed to me that his face went pale, though that may merely have been the effect of the dim lighting. He raised a shaky hand in a gesture that resembled a greeting closely enough that the two guards turned back to their posts and let us pass.

"Florbela," he said hoarsely, as I strode quickly to approach him. Then he remembered himself and added, "Sarmentos. Senhorita Sarmentos, you are here!"

Although Armand was directly beside me, Brian didn't seem to have noticed him. He stared at me almost as if he were seeing a phantom. He looked very wobbly for a few moments, and I worried that he might not be fit to transact the business that I required of him. Then, suddenly, he seemed to compose himself and leaned a few degrees forward, squinting to examine my face more carefully.

"Something has happened?" he asked. He straightened up again, frowning, and his eyes darted down to assess the copper tube in my hands. "Ah!" Now, at last, he glanced at Armand. He made an offhand gesture toward the row of chairs that was arrayed along one side of the lobby. "Wait here," he told Armand, then turned back to me and said, "Come with me senhorita."

"I will *not* wait," Armand said angrily. "You shall conduct your business in front of me, or not at all."

Brian's nostrils flared, and for a moment he looked a bit dangerous. But then he relaxed his features, flicked a hand in the air as if to suggest that this were a matter of no consequence to him, and turned his back. "Then come along," he said over his shoulder, and led us into the building's inner recesses.

As soon as we were in Brian's office with the door closed, I began blurting out my message as quickly as I could. "I cannot stay for long," I announced. "I think you know what I am carrying here. I need to leave it with you for some time. I trust that you can keep it secure for me until we meet again."

Brian sat down heavily behind his desk and settled into his chair in a manner that suggested he was taking a great burden off his feet. "Something has happened?" he demanded, for the second time.

I nodded emphatically. "I'm afraid it has."

"I *knew* that trouble was imminent. But you are all right? I mean to say, you have not been injured?"

"I have not, but only by great good fortune."

He shook his head vigorously. "I warned you. *Didn't* I warn you that you were being unwise?"

"I suppose that you may have, but it's hardly a useful observation at this point, wouldn't you agree?"

He closed his eyes and put his hand over his face for a moment, rubbing his eyelids, then leaned forward over his blotter to stare at me. "I would *not* agree, no. It is more relevant now than ever before. I must take you under the protection of my lodge, where you can be concealed securely. Surely you are not still thinking of carrying out your preposterous pretense of attempting to become a professional artist, despite everything? You are simply too *important* to be an artist."

Before I could frame a suitable reply, Armand spoke out. "She is not under your protection, Freemason." He spoke this sobriquet in a manner that seemed to insinuate that he was delivering an obscenity. "She is under the protection of the Bande Liberté du Monde, and you would do well to remember it."

Brian gave him a look across the carpet that was snide and patronizing in equal measure. My guess was that he thought this opinion was not even worth rebuttal, but that he was considering delivering a fairly offensive rebuttal nonetheless.

"Be *quiet*," I ordered them.

For a few pleasant seconds, there was complete silence in the room, allowing me a brief opportunity to weigh my options. I had little doubt that Brian and his colleagues could give me honest and complete personal protection, which was certainly untrue of the Souris Trempés. For the sake of both Irène and myself, that one factor loomed so paramount that I was sorely tempted to accept Brian's offer. But at the same time, I knew that doing so would render me into a state of indefinite confinement, as thoroughly and effectively as if I were a prisoner. Furthermore I greatly doubted that, as a confined guest of the Freemasons, I could maintain any certain access to real information about what was happening to my father and his cause, back home in Portugal. Brian would have strong opinions about what I should and should not hear.

All of these thoughts flew through my head in a brief moment, and then I said, "It is the painting, and not I, that needs your protection."

Brian immediately waved a hand dismissively in the air and said, "Oh, of course I am more than happy to do *that*, but—"

"I'm sure you are," Armand interrupted him, practically snarling.

Brian affected to ignore him. "—but if you have become an active target for assassination, then I don't believe you should walk out through that door unprotected."

Armand released a loud sound, a sort of parody of a laugh. "She is hardly unprotected!"

"I appreciate your concern," I told Brian, "but let me reassure you: I do not intend to return to my studio at La Ruche. I have plans for my own protection."

The corners of Brian's mouth turned deeply downward. "You're surely not taking up residence in that boggy anarchist grotto under the Quai d'Austerlitz?"

Before Armand could make some heated reply, I inserted quickly, "No, I do not plan to stay at the headquarters of the Souris Trempés. I have other plans. Accept my assurance that I will be quite invisible and well cared for over coming days."

I held up the copper tube in both hands. "I'm giving this to you. But you understand that it does not belong to you."

"I do understand that," Brian replied quickly.

"I cannot entrust this to you unless I have your word as a gentleman that when I request its return, you will comply."

He paused. "Of course, but . . . that will be a decision that may not be entirely mine to make."

I withdrew the tube, clutching it again to my body—though in my heart I longed to be rid of the horrible thing.

He added quickly, "But I will make arrangements! I shall, I swear it. Listen, it is possible that the Order will send it to England or Germany for inspection by certain experts. In that event, the best that I can promise you is that it will be returned to you within the space of a month—no, let us say a fortnight—after the day upon which you request it. Will that suffice?"

"Think carefully!" Armand hissed in my ear, making no effort at all to keep Brian from hearing him doing so. "He *wants* it."

"I accept those conditions," I said, and I stepped forward to place the tube on Brian's desk. He placed his hands upon it and stared at it for a long moment, indeed looking as if he had just acquired a great and unexpected treasure.

I pinched Armand's sleeve and quickly turned him toward the door, but Brian rose to his feet and called after us. "Wait! Please wait, Florbela. *Please* don't go." His businesslike mien seemed to have collapsed, and his voice was suddenly so plaintive that my heart ached to hear it. He walked around the table, looking completely sober now, and took my hand in his. "I promise you, I can offer you complete security." I might very well have turned to him and placed my fate in his hands, if Armand hadn't been right there at my side.

Armand certainly perceived my hesitation. He made a quiet growling sound in his throat, then hooked his arm through my free arm and guided me firmly out of the room.

We rode our carriage with curtains closed directly across the Concorde Bridge and into the heart of the Sixth. The Delaunays were waiting there for us.

Chapter Thirty

T hus, I found myself beginning a rather cramped life-style, sleeping on the small cretonne sofa in Sonia's studio and rarely venturing outside. Irène slept on a small cot that the Delaunays' borrowed from a friend and, unlike me, she would spend many hours at a time out walking during the day. As Irène left the apartment each day, I truly envied her freedom.

I made a date to meet Armand at La Ruche on Wednesday so that he could help me move my surviving possessions to the Sixth, in a hired cab. He was adamant about being included on this expedition, saying he wished to observe the streets behind us as we traveled, to make certain that we weren't followed and my new whereabouts betrayed.

I arrived at La Ruche an hour before the appointed time. Moishe leapt up when I appeared in his doorway and bowed to me in his charmingly ingenuous fashion. I was not eager to enter our studio even for the brief task of gathering my things, and I was certainly not looking forward to the spectacle of all my paintings slashed to ribbons and strewn about the floor. I lingered quite a while with Moishe, sharing simple conversation while he daubed at his newest canvas.

After we had been sitting together quietly for a rather long spell, I distinctly heard a sound through the thin wall, and I assumed that it was Irène. I found, however, that my door was closed, and imagine my shock when, upon opening it, I found Constantin Brancusi alone in the ruined studio! Moishe and I caught the "wild Transylvanian" *in flagrante*, stealthily pulling open one of the drawers of Irène's little secretary, which was propped up on two broken legs, in a corner of the room. As we stood there, gaping at him, he straightened himself to his full height and faced us rigidly. His pocked face was a mask of stony defiance, framed by his broad, thick-boned shoulders and his wild hair.

"Mr. Brancusi!" I exclaimed loudly, throwing the door wide open. "What are you *doing*?"

"As you see," he said in his gravelly accent, frowning grimly and folding his lanky arms in front of his chest, "I am looking for Irène's letters."

This bold admission left me absolutely speechless with indignation, and it was delivered in such frank terms that I think even Moishe understood it perfectly. I heard him emit a sound of outrage from behind my shoulder.

"Her *personal* letters?" I demanded, furious.

"That is right," he told me, with a firm nod. "I want to know if she is corresponding with Pablo Picasso."

Could he have said anything more infuriating? It was already bad enough, my having to worry that Irène might lose her head and throw herself into the clutches of a romantic opportunist like Mr. Picasso, but the idea that her obsession had excited the envy of a man as alarming as Mr. Brancusi was appalling to contemplate.

I raised my voice yet further, wanting to make sure that our conversation was overheard, just in case the situation got out of control. "Just what sort of interest could *you* possibly have in Mademoiselle Langevin's personal affairs?" I demanded. "And what could possibly make you think that you have the right to intrude into our home?"

He frowned at me, glowering through eyes as dark as cinders. "I am acting under the instructions of her mother."

That stopped me. "Her . . . her mother?"

"Perhaps you could lower your voice a little," Mr. Brancusi suggested. "I imagine that you are aware that Irène's surname is not Langevin, it is Curie. I am an old friend of the family, and particularly of Irène's mother, Madame Marie Curie."

I was speechless for a long moment. At length, I wobbled farther into the room and found my way to the nearest chair, where I sat down heavily and tried to compose myself. "Irène's mother is *Marie Curie?*" I had, of course, heard of the famous Polish émigré. She had been arguably the most famous woman in Paris, ever since she had won the Nobel Prize in physics several years ago.

Mr. Brancusi continued to frown down at me, with his chin somewhat elevated now. His expression suggested disbelief at my reaction. "I felt obliged to report to Marie that Irène has developed an unfortunate fixation upon Pablo, and that it's my impression that this fascination has gone on for too long. Marie was naturally *most* concerned. But come now, do you really claim that you didn't know who Irène was? That seems unlikely, I must say. She lives just a few blocks from here, in the south of Montparnasse."

I shook my head slightly. "Irène is not very forthcoming about her past," I told him in a meek tone.

He gave an exaggerated shrug, as if accepting my word grudgingly. "Well, I suppose that might explain your lack of concern with all of the school she has missed."

"Irène is enrolled in some sort of school?"

"Of course she is in school! I am one of her teachers. You are not about to deny that you knew *that.*"

I shook my head, not to make a denial but merely to express utter befuddlement. "Some sort of . . . academy?"

Mr. Brancusi made a rasping sound in his throat. "Academy! She's a schoolgirl! She attends the Cooperative. You have heard of it?"

I shook my head again, mutely. He tipped his head, as if allowing that this much of my story, at least, was likely true. "It's an experimental school for gifted children," he explained. "Established by a collective of parents, all of whom are well-established geniuses in their various fields. There are nearly as many professors in the school as there are pupils. I teach sculpture."

"Irène is not a schoolchild," I objected. "She is sixteen years old."

He eyed me intently, frowning like a judge who is pondering some unlikely utterance of the accused. The silence dragged on uncomfortably, and I found myself wringing my hands as if I were, in fact, guilty of something. At last he let out a breath and leaned back, sitting against the windowsill. He glanced once at Moishe, who was still hovering in the doorway, probably struggling to make sense of the odd conversation.

"I am not sure of Irène's exact age," Mr. Brancusi told me, in a more patient tone, "but she is certainly not sixteen—not even close. Your roommate is a schoolgirl, masquerading as a young woman."

"That's completely preposterous," I told him hoarsely. "It's just impossible. Listen, perhaps an adult could pretend to be a child, but a child *cannot* pretend to be an adult." He didn't reply, but merely watched me, assessing my sincerity, I suppose. I shook my head vigorously. "Think of how absurd the idea is! If Irène were a schoolgirl, she would have to be utterly *brilliant* to create the ruse of an adult life."

Mr. Brancusi nodded once, bluntly accepting my assertion, as if I had just articulated the essential nature of the problem. "Yes, that's correct. She is certainly the most brilliant child in France." He reflected upon this statement for a moment, then added, "Very possibly in the world."

I was left at a loss for words. Cast in that light, I supposed that the thing was just within the realm of credence—but my heart simply couldn't accept it. I turned and looked at the door to see if Moishe understood, but Moishe had left, apparently having realized that whatever was going on, it was a private matter.

Watching my reaction, Mr. Brancusi seemed at last to accept my innocence in the question of Irène's truancy, and his tone softened considerably. "Her mother has been very concerned," he told me again, "but she is an open-minded woman. Also, I think that she has great faith in her daughter's capacities."

I nodded mutely. There was certainly no denying that Irène was resourceful.

"I hope you understand," he added, "that until the evening when I encountered the two of you at the Delaunays', no one knew where she was. Marie had detectives out looking for her. The poor woman was so distraught that she could hardly get out of bed."

"How awful," I croaked.

"Irène pleaded with me not to reveal her whereabouts to her mother, and I told her that I might be able to arrange that for her, as long as she consented that I should report to poor Marie that Irène was well situated, and not far from home. Also, I told her that she must continue her studies on her own and stay away from the likes of Pablo Picasso."

I nodded mutely. That explained quite a bit.

"Also," he added, "she took some gold with her when she ran away from home. Ah, please don't misunderstand me; she didn't *steal*. It was a gift, from her great aunt. But I took that gold back to her mother for safekeeping, and I have been providing Irène since then with an allowance."

"Did you find any?" I waved vaguely in the direction of Irène's desk.

"Find any . . .?"

"Any letters from Mr. Picasso. I hope he hasn't been writing to her?"

Mr. Brancusi shook his head and smiled politely. "I felt that it was my duty to check about this for myself, but I never really expected that she would break her word to me. Irène was always a dutiful child."

I sat in stunned silence with my face in my hands. After a minute or so, I heard Mr. Brancusi moving awkwardly toward the door.

"Please forgive me for doubting you," he said, as he passed my chair. "I believe now that you are blameless in this matter, Senhorita Sarmentos, and I expect that Irène has been quite fortunate to have your companionship. She is a very troubled girl, but I think we all expect her to come to her senses shortly. Now, if you will please excuse me." He passed quietly out of the door, closing it behind him.

I stood up and paced up and down the empty room, unable to collect my thoughts. I found myself standing at the window, gazing out abstractedly at Mr. Brancusi's receding form as he loped out to the street on his long legs.

A young man was coming up the path toward the house, dressed in old but natty seersucker and polished two-tone shoes. He and Mr. Brancusi tipped their hats to each other as they passed, and as they did so I realized with some amazement that the young man was Armand. Armand's style of dress had been gradually improving for months, but this was nonetheless a major step forward.

I felt so distracted and distraught at these unexpected revelations about Irène that I hardly felt able to give Armand a civil reception, but there was no getting out of it now so I opened the door to receive him. Then I pulled my old valise out from under my cot, threw it open, and began rapidly filling it with the many necessities of life that I had been doing without over recent days.

Armand arrived in my open doorway and rapped diffidently with one knuckle to announce himself. Although his face was familiar to everyone in the building, he had only been up to my studio on a very few occasions, and never before unaccompanied.

"Please come in," I told him, pausing only momentarily before turning back to my packing. "I shall be ready quite shortly. Please sit." I glanced up from the clothes that I was folding, to look him up and down. "That's a very smart suit."

"I am in disguise," he explained. He tugged up the knees of his trousers and settled himself onto one of Irène's big wingback chairs.

I may have smirked, since this claim was unlikely in so very many ways. I was tempted to propose that he could do worse than to disguise himself in such a manner on a daily basis. But my mood was too gloomy to allow for anything as flippant as banter, so I held my tongue and kept working.

I suppose that he noticed my reticence. "Is there anything

wrong? Nothing has happened, has it?"

I shook my head without replying. Eventually, I would tell Armand everything I had learned that day, but this was not the time.

"You haven't seen anything . . . suspicious, have you?" he persisted.

"No."

Armand leaned back in his chair and relaxed. "Well, it's important to be cautious. Do you remember the fellow I told you about, the one from out of town? The wretch who calls himself Sapeur, and seems to spend all of his time flattering Libreterre? He keeps bringing the old man little gifts of tobacco and food, to keep himself in favor."

I muttered some sort of response, though I was barely listening. I suppose that the only thing that struck me as odd about this "suspicious character" about whom Armand complained so often in recent days, was that Armand thought it worthwhile to mention him. From my own point of view, almost all of his comrades at the Souris Trempés were suspicious characters.

"Everyone but me seems to think that he's harmless enough," Armand continued. "Libreterre simply adores him, the old fool. Me, I thought at first that he was a police informer, but now I worry that he is a spy employed by . . . *that order*."

I was sitting on my overstuffed valise by this point, trying to close it sufficiently to hook its latches. I eyed Armand's face carefully, wondering if he sincerely believed that a spy for the Ordo Crucis Incendio would bother to infiltrate the Souris Trempés. "I suppose that anything is possible," I muttered.

"Here, let me help you with that." Armand added his weight to mine, and we managed to latch the valise and buckle its straps. Then Armand took it up, and we left the studio.

We took it down the stairs and out the back way, intending to pass through the shrubs at the rear of the yard and leave La Ruche discreetly, through the alleyways. But when I glanced over my shoulder, I happened to see Irène around the other side of the building, approaching the front door.

"Wait. I must speak with Irène for a moment."

Armand seemed about to raise an objection, but he must have changed his mind when he saw the expression on my face. He nodded curtly and said, "Then I shall wait over there, in the alley. Please be brief."

I followed Irène upstairs, and was a flight below her when she entered our studio. I arrived to find her already sitting on her ruined bed holding a box of chocolates in one hand, and in the other a big, gloomy-looking volume of mathematics.

"Florbela!" She jumped up and we embraced. When she sat back down on the torn coverlet, I sat beside her with my arm around her bony and delicate shoulders. This unusual proximity seemed to alarm her a little, and I felt her pull away, but I didn't let her go. For a moment, I thought I might cry, but I tamped down my emotions and sat stroking Irène's hair with my fingertips until I had full command of my voice.

"Irène, how old are you?"

I felt her go rigid beside me, and I glanced at her. She was watching me with a calculating look, and I suppose that she was assessing the likelihood of a spinning a successful lie. But she dropped her eyes and replied, her voice an uncharacteristic mumble, "I'm fourteen and a half."

I thought I was fully prepared for this moment, but even so, the number caught me off guard. I leaned back and seized her by both shoulders, turning her to make her look me in the eye. "You're *not*! No! Could you *really* be?" I babbled. I closed my eyes firmly, then opened them again, trying to see her freshly, as if for the first time. Gradually I began to understand that it must somehow be possible that her words were true. "I can't believe it . . . and yet, oh! It explains so many things."

She dropped her eyes again, seeming acutely embarrassed at the uncanny success of her imposture. When she spoke, her voice was her own again: clear, high, and crisply enunciated. "I thought that you knew. That is to say, I thought you had guessed it, long since."

I certainly had not. I shook my head vigorously, trying to clear my thoughts. "Do you know, I was afraid that you might have some sort of *cancer*? And here: it was only adolescence."

"I know it was wrong not to tell you, Florbela. I meant to, honestly, on so many occasions! I'm sorry if I have caused you undo concern."

"But, Irène, *how* can you be so young? It strains belief."

"Well . . . I am unusually tall for my age."

"That's not what I mean! You *know* so many things."

She frowned and rolled her eyes away from me for a moment, as if pondering this conundrum and seeking a satisfactory explanation. "I'm very fond of reading," she said at last.

I sniffled and realized that tears were trickling down my cheeks. Irène quickly reached to her bedside table and found a handkerchief to lend me. "I wish that you had trusted me more," I complained. When she dropped her eyes contritely but made no reply, I added, "Listen, I know who you are—I know you are the daughter of Marie Curie. So you must tell me the whole truth now. You have run away from home, isn't it true? But why? Are your parents cruel?"

"Oh, no!" she replied quickly. "My mother is very kind and loving. My father was too, though he has been dead these four years now. But, then . . . you didn't know that my father was killed? He was struck down by a horse and carriage."

I offered belated condolences. I'm sure that Dr. Curie's untimely death must have been the cause of nationwide mourning in France, but four years previous I had still been at school in England, and I had no recollection of the news.

Irène went on to describe the difficulties of living in the shadow of her mother's greatness. I questioned her, but couldn't ascertain to my satisfaction the exact nature of her complaint, and perhaps she herself couldn't specify it perfectly. It sounded to me somewhat as if her mother neglected her, not out of any lack of affection, but rather because her mind—and perhaps her heart as well—was forever absorbed entirely in scientific researches. To make matters worse, it was apparently not in Madame Curie's nature to imagine any worthwhile future for her daughter, save following in her footsteps as a scientist.

"She only wants the best for me," Irène told me, in abject misery.

By now, my tears were dry, and it was Irène who was crying. Her tears were the only sign of her lost composure; her voice remained oddly clear and steady, her expression frank and neutral. It was as if only her eyes were weeping.

"So then, you don't want to become a scientist?"

"I don't know," she told me. "That is to say, I *thought* that I knew. I thought I had made up my mind to become a sculptor—something of which I'm sure Mother would never approve."

I interrupted her, still trying to grasp the nature of her grievance against her famous mother. "She would forbid it?"

Irène hesitated. "No, it's not that. But she would be . . . disappointed. Which is worse. I'm sorry that I can't explain any better. If you knew her, you would understand."

"But why didn't you tell me that you're fourteen years old? I think I can understand what you're telling me, well enough. Didn't you think that I would help you?"

Irène let her head sag. I immediately regretted scolding her, as she seemed positively mortified. But when she spoke, it was only to say, "I'm not fourteen. I am fourteen and a half."

"Very well, then, fourteen and a half. But, Irène, you told me that you were sixteen!"

She lifted her head and forced herself to look at me again. "You have treated me as your peer these recent months. Not only as your friend, Florbela, but as your peer. Would you have been able to do that if I had told you the truth?"

This left me rather perplexed, because of course the answer was plainly no. And yet, that being the case, it meant that if she had been honest with me then I would have missed out on our pleasant and memorable friendship. It occurred to me, confusingly enough, that I was feeling an absurd grudge against this new child-Irène, for depriving me of the cherished company of the woman-Irène who had been my best friend for months now. That thought, once formulated, was so preposterous that it threatened to give me a headache.

"Did Monsieur Brancusi tell you?" Irène was asking me.

"He did," I murmured. Then I realized that telling her so might suggest that we were conspiring behind her back, so I quickly added, "I forced the information out of him. He kept your secret as best he could. But, for one thing, I had seen you giving him your gold."

Irène hesitated. "My gold? You were watching us? But it was wrapped in paper. How did you know what it was?"

I didn't mind having made this little slip; in fact, I was eager to put all deceptions behind us now. I described to her the evening when I had searched through her purse, after having been drawn to it by the strange, glowing rock that she kept wrapped in her handkerchief. I asked her what that rock was.

"It contains radium," she told me.

I was, by this time, quite accustomed to admitting my ignorance to Irène. "And what is that?"

"It is a mineral that my mother discovered," she told me. The tone of pride in her voice was unmistakable. "It emits an invisible radiance that excites the sulfide of zinc, which is also found in the rock, and this causes it to emit light."

I tried to imagine that. "Rather like a firefly," I hazarded.

She smiled at me tolerantly. "No. I'm afraid it's not like that at all."

I smiled and embraced her again, and she allowed herself to be embraced. "I think you must go home to your mother," I opined. "But perhaps you are stronger than you give yourself credit for. I believe you will become a sculptor, if that is what you want."

"Oh, none of that matters anymore," Irène told me glumly. "I've stopped sculpting long since. I suppose that my heart is broken."

I did everything in my power not to betray any amusement at hearing a fourteen year old bemoaning her world-weariness.

"I was planning to go home anyway," she told me. "Recently, I find myself spending most of the day walking the streets of my neighborhood, in Montparnasse. Sometimes I stroll right past my house, and I have to fight the urge to just walk right in the door. I suppose that our neighbors must have seen me by now, and they have probably told my mother that I'm about. So I came here to pack up some of my clothes—those that are not destroyed. I think it's time to go home."

It was only at that moment that I realized the Irène whom I had known—the Irène who had never really existed—was gone now, gone with complete finality, leaving no trace behind her. All that remained was this extraordinary child, of whom I knew almost nothing. I felt tears welling up in my eyes again, and I daubed at them furtively, hoping to hide my grief.

But one could not hide much from Irène. I saw her hands and feet begin shifting and fidgeting nervously, as they always did when she was trying to conceal her agitation. "I'm sorry if I have caused you any difficulties," she told me.

"No, Irène," I said, kissing her cheek. "You've been a very good girl."

*   *   *

I proposed to Irène that, if she was planning to return home anyway, she might as well take advantage of Armand's presence to help her to move her things.

"In fact, it's very dangerous for you to be here at La Ruche alone. Onça do Papa could return at any time. He's probably having the place watched right now," I said. And then realized it was almost certainly true and shuddered at the thought.

After a certain amount of hand-wringing and agitated darting about the room, she agreed that what I said was sensible.

I went out to the alley to retrieve Armand. He grumbled quite a bit at this "breach in security," as he called it, but I hushed him. He came inside, and we all got to work helping Irène with the considerable chore of her packing. Though the furniture had all been destroyed, Irène had nonetheless managed to salvage a remarkable number of worldly goods from among the wreckage.

Through the window I noticed Alfred Boucher pruning the

trees in front of the building, so I went out to give him notice that both Irène and I were leaving, and that although I, for one, might well return, a considerable time might pass before that happened. I hated to give up my studio, but I didn't feel I had the right to reserve it for my use. He received this news with his usual good nature and proposed letting Diego and Angelina live there in our absence, rent-free, in exchange for cleaning up the mess and carting away the rubble. I bent down and embraced him gratefully, then ran back upstairs to finish our preparations.

We pulled up a couple of hours later in two overstuffed cabs at the front of a tall and narrow brick townhouse on the Rue de la Glacière. Even as we were stepping down to the curb, the driver of the front cab hailed the house with a voice of considerable strength, causing a curtain to be pulled aside. A moment later, a middle-aged woman came bolting out the front door, her eyes so wide that it seemed they might spring from her head.

I looked to Irène and saw her looking happy, really happy, for the first time in weeks. She leapt out of the cab, shrieking, "Mama!" All of us, including the drivers, watched raptly as mother and daughter clasped each other in ecstatic reunion.

Madame Curie was a woman of gravely defined features, with narrow lips and an immense brow, draped in the drab clothes of a widow. It took some time for her to calm herself sufficiently that Irène could introduce Armand and me, and I'm afraid that even then she barely noticed us.

A man was standing in the Curies' door, and eventually he ventured outside to join us. He was a bespectacled little man with pointy whiskers and close-cropped hair, and when Irène noticed him, she greeted him with affectionate formality. He patted her shoulder and welcomed her home, addressing her with dignified reserve, which I took to be reflective of his own nature rather than indicative of any lack of enthusiasm.

"This is my dear friend, Florbela Sarmentos," Irène told him. "And her friend Armand. This is my teacher, Professor Paul Langevin." Hearing this name, I glanced at the man with curiosity, wondering if he was aware that Irène had been borrowing his name. I doubted it, and to this day I suspect that he never knew.

As we watched the luggage being taken into the house, Irène and her mother stood aside, leaning together, touching each other lightly and murmuring. I was surprised when eventually Professor Langevin sidled over to join them. The three of them remained huddled there together, talking and laughing, like a happy little family. I even noticed Professor Langevin placing his hand briefly on Madame Curie's back at one point, as a man might do with his wife. I don't know what their relations were, but my time at La Ruche had already made it clear to me that very brilliant people—like the very rich—tended to flaunt conventional mores and habits.

As soon as they were finished unloading, Armand and I began to feel superfluous, so we bid our farewells and headed for the Sixth.

Chapter Thirty-One

These events had all taken place in the second week of August, just as the really sweltering part of the year was beginning to fall upon us. A few days after delivering Irène home to her mother, I awoke in the late hours of a Monday morning after a scant few hours of sleep, having just lived through one of the Delaunays' all-night parties, only to find that the apartment was too oppressively hot for habitation. I don't know how Sonia and Robert survived their Mondays generally, but in the heat of summer the prospect was daunting indeed. Their entire apartment was a shambles, and the air was as torrid and dense as the exhaust from a chimney. I spent a long while scrubbing myself with cool water, but simply couldn't make myself feel clean.

When I finished my ablutions, Sonia and Robert had yet to emerge from their bedchamber, so I turned myself to the Herculean task of tidying the place up. I had barely started when I was interrupted by a knock at the door, which stood ajar to allow some fresh air into the room. I was surprised to find Irène poking her head in.

She was dressed for school, and she was so nearly unrecognizable that I must have stared at her for an uncomfortably long time, eventually causing her to giggle and ask if she could come in. She was wearing the gingham frock and round, buttoned boots of a schoolgirl, and someone had bound her hair into a pair of stringent braids. She was indisputably, irredeemably fourteen.

"Shouldn't you be in school?" I asked her, as soon as I had embraced her and offered her something cold to drink. I hesitated, then added, "You haven't run away again?"

"Oh, no! I am taking my lunch break. I received permission to have the period extended today so that I might ask you to join me for lunch." She smiled sweetly. "I am content with my circumstances, for the time being."

"Good. I'm very glad to hear that."

I was certainly happy to abandon the chaos of the Delaunays' apartment, and to allow myself to be removed to the bistro downstairs. There, as I sipped coffee and ate some fresh fruit, I was further pleased to watch Irène eat a hearty meal, devouring a tureen of bouillabaisse and a large baguette, followed by a massive wedge of cake.

"Your health seems much improved," I commented. "It's good to see you hungry again."

She gave me a worried glance. "Please excuse me if I am not eating very daintily," she said, as soon as her mouth was clear enough to speak. "My tutors have insisted that I perform some extra and remedial studies since my return. The effort seems to have stimulated my appetite."

"Bon appétit," I encouraged her, and nibbled at a slice of melon.

We sat around lethargically after the meal, sipping iced drinks and complaining of the heat. "We usually go to our summer house for August," Irène told me. "In the hill country, near Chamonix."

"That sounds wonderful."

"Yes, it's very beautiful up there at this time of year. I imagine that Mother would have made the journey a week or two ago, if not for my absence." She looked down at her hands.

"So, will you be leaving now?"

"Mother will," Irène told me. "And Professor Langevin, and most of the servants. I have been ordered to stay behind and catch up on my studies, in preparation for a round of examinations." She smiled at me wanly. "I suppose that I am being punished."

"But then . . . you won't be left alone in the house, will you?"

"Oh, no. My old nanny, Berthe, will stay behind with me. She doesn't like to travel, and she claims that she doesn't mind the heat. Also, Mr. Brancusi has promised to visit every day or two." She had been picking nervously at crumbs on her plate as she explained these things. I watched her, marveling at the notion of Irène having a nanny. She looked up from her plate and said, "Actually, that is my ulterior reason for visiting you. I was wondering if you would like to stay for a few weeks in one of our empty rooms."

I tried to accept this offer graciously, rather than in an unseemly gush of relief, but I don't think I was entirely successful at hiding my elation. As much as I loved the Delaunays, spending another week embedded in their wild lives had been a daunting prospect, and I believe that enduring another Sunday night and Monday morning in their home might have been the death of me.

And so the next day I moved again, and I spent the next three weeks enjoying the quiet and spacious Curie home as Irène's houseguest. I hardly left the house, day or night, so those weeks were torpid and uneventful. I mainly remember them as a long series of sleepless nights listening for the smallest bump or creak, followed by days of groggy naps and cooling baths. I spent a few hours of each day painting and was rather pleased to find myself developing what I considered to be a fairly unique style. Irène was more active than I, and always seemed to be either studying or eating, while her nanny hobbled perpetually about the house, dusting and polishing things. Old Berthe was senile in a charming way, with a body that was nearly spherical and a huge gray bun at the back of her head. She muttered to herself incessantly, and whenever I was able to make out the words, they seemed to be utter nonsense.

In the evenings of those heat-addled days, as the night was settling in and bringing a luscious coolness to the air and as the cicadas finished their hysterical summer choruses in the trees outside, I would cross the street to bring food to Armand. He insisted on keeping his nightly vigils, though the townhouse didn't have a yard; thus, he was forced to sit on a bench in the little park across the street. It would have been impossible for him to loiter for hours on end in such a neighborhood if he were wearing the ragged garb that he seemed to favor, and so, to my delight, he was forced to consistently "disguise" himself in summer suits of linen or seersucker. I received another check from my family's solicitor during my first week at the Curies' and made Armand a gift of a set of colored silk shirts with big folding cuffs. He didn't refuse them, though his thanks were not exactly effusive. As soon as he had managed to obtain a set of cufflinks somewhere, he began to wear these shirts in the evenings as part of his disguise, and I thought that the effect was most pleasing to the eye.

I also read the newspaper each day from cover to cover in the hope of hearing some news from Portugal. The few articles that appeared over those weeks didn't give me much insight into what was happening but they also didn't report any major battles or retaliation by the king and that was encouraging.

As August came to an end, the worst of the heat wave passed with it. In anticipation of the return of Madame Curie and her entourage, I began making reluctant preparations to move back to the Delaunays' apartment.

Then one evening, just at sunset, there came a knock at the door. A moment later, Berthe came waddling into the drawing room where I was fanning myself and reading, and told me that there were two men who wanted to see me. I hurried to the door with some alarm, since very few people knew where I was to be found, other than Armand and Willie Apollinaire. I had deputized the latter to act as my go-between with the La Ruche community, but had sworn him to strict secrecy.

I peeked through the curtain at the front steps, and was surprised to see Brian Torrence Grimm and Fernand Léger. Brian was wearing a long black evening cloak, oddly enough—odd not only because the weather was far too warm for it, but also because the cloak didn't match his suit. I threw open the door and greeted each of them with a kiss on the cheek and urged them to come inside. I hadn't seen anyone whom I knew for three weeks, save Irène and Armand, and I had been missing Brian and Fernand for months now.

"I'm sure we're both terribly sorry for the inconvenience of this unannounced visit," Brian said, standing in front of the chair that I had offered him. He drew back his cloak, revealing that he was carrying the copper tube I had left with him. I was a bit shocked that he saw fit to carry the thing so openly, right there under Léger's eyes, but I waited to hear him out.

"Willie was very reluctant to tell us where you could be found," Léger added. He glanced at me only briefly. "We assured him that the matter was an emergency."

They refused my offer of iced tea, then asked that I send Berthe upstairs and otherwise make certain that no one might overhear what they had come to say. That done, we all sat facing one another at close range, leaning forward to speak in murmurs, like conspirators.

"We have solved the cipher contained within this image," Brian told me, touching the copper tube lightly with his long fingers.

"You . . . together?" I looked back and forth between them. "The two of you?"

"I know that I was not intended to be a confidant in this affair," Léger told me hastily. "The matter came to my attention quite by accident, and through no fault of Brian."

I looked to Brian, and he rapidly blinked his normally imperturbable blue eyes. "Well . . ." he said slowly, "perhaps I may have incurred *some* blame in the matter. I'm afraid that I made a small indiscretion while I was . . . rather drunk."

"Too drunk for any real blame to accrue," Léger quickly assured him, making a magnanimous gesture. Then he glanced at me. "At any rate, I believe it proved to be a 'happy fault', as the Jesuits might say."

"Indeed," Brian chorused. "It turned out to be quite a piece of good fortune. You see, Fernand has a phenomenal understanding of visual symbology. One of the mathematicians working on the code had uncovered a clue which he shared with me and between the two of us, we were able to unravel the mystery."

I looked back and forth between them, still not accustomed to the peculiarity of seeing these two men sitting side by side in the same room, apparently with all their differences reconciled, and now bosom friends. Also, now that Brian had put aside his cloak, it was possible to see that both of them were looking rumpled, unwashed and unshaved. It occurred to me that lately even Armand had been looking quite a bit more spruce than these two.

Léger noticed my eye making its furtive, critical investigations of his person, and lifted his chin slightly. "Please pardon our slovenly appearance. I'm afraid that we have neither slept nor rested since yesterday morning."

Brian added, "Once we had begun to unravel the cipher, its import immediately impressed us as grave indeed. The more we have come to understand it, the greater has seemed the need for haste."

He paused dramatically, and I jiggled impatiently in my chair. "Well, what is it?" I demanded. "What does it say?"

"The painting contains a message," Brian told me, "encrypted on behalf of old King Carlos and intended for the eyes of Sultan Abdulhamid of the Ottoman Empire. We believe that this painting was sent to the sultan as a gift, perhaps twenty years ago."

I frowned, considering the implications. King Carlos, the father of Portugal's reigning King Manuel II, had instigated the tyrannical and economically ruinous royalist policies that his son continued to maintain. I shook my head slowly. "The *king* sent a secret message to the Turkish emperor, in that painting? But why? I mean to say, why would he hide it in a *painting*, instead of giving it to an armed courier detachment? Surely it would have been safer if guarded by soldiers."

Léger and Brian glanced at each other, and Léger nodded. "You have cut right to the heart of the matter," he told me.

Brian said, "I feel quite certain that the whole point of selecting such an unconventional channel of communication was to circumvent the attentions of the Portuguese military. I believe that the king didn't trust his own generals and military advisers, and that he acted to deceive them."

"Very well. I suppose that might be possible. But what does the message say?"

"It offers terms for the forging of a secret alliance between Portugal and the Ottoman Empire."

My jaw must have dropped at this news, because I saw Brian smile slightly at the sight of my face. He added, *"There.* Now I think you understand our sense of urgency."

"The people of Portugal would never accept such an alliance!" I exclaimed.

"I imagine not. Nor, most certainly, would your generals," Brian agreed. "Though they would surely enforce it, once the alliance was already in place. This is the irony of national policy-making. Opposing a change in policy is often simply prudence; opposing an established policy is generally treason."

"But why would King Carlos have done such a thing?"

"I imagine that he hoped to expand Portuguese influence in the south of Europe, and perhaps to take some new territory, as well."

Léger inserted, "Perhaps the man was a bit of a megalomaniac?"

Brian tactfully ignored this broad summary, characteristically preferring to navigate the discussion according to the facts at hand. "This painting explains a number of matters that were already known to the Order of Freemasons, though not to the world at large. So, please understand, what I am about to tell you is not public knowledge and must be for your ears only, and those of your father. I share this information with you under the authority of the Grand Lodge, but under the condition that you and your father will use it with discretion."

"Of course," I agreed immediately. "What is it?"

"There was a large and secret transfer of funds from the Portuguese treasury to the Ottoman court in 1891. The action was kept secret from the public, and even those with privileged information regarding the affair believed it to be some sort of highly speculative investment scheme. But there seems never to have been any return on this 'investment,' and the principal funds simply vanished."

"Eighteen ninety-one!" I exclaimed. "The year before the

economy collapsed."

Brian nodded, watching my face to assess the degree of my comprehension.

"So," I said slowly, "you are telling me that King Carlos sent a secret message to the Turkish emperor, proposing a military alliance, without even telling his own generals. And then, when the Turks agreed to the plan, Carlos sent them some large payment out of the national treasury. But the Turks simply kept the money and reneged on their side of the deal?"

Léger and Brian nodded in tandem. "Precisely," Brian said. "Thus, a few months later, your nation of Portugal was forced to declare bankruptcy, and to default on its loans."

I fell back against the cushions of my chair, feeling as wrung out as a washcloth. Then, after a few silent moments, another question occurred to me. "But how did the painting get here, to Paris?"

"Ah, now, *there* is a very good question," Brian replied. "I certainly don't know, but I might hazard a guess."

"Please," I said sitting up again, eager to hear his theory.

"It seems to me that the Turks might have found certain obvious advantages in *purposely* sending the painting abroad, particularly if they could insinuate it into the hands of enemies of the Portuguese monarchy. That is to say: the republican partisans. If anyone asked, then the Turks could claim that the painting had been stolen—that it had simply vanished from the imperial palace."

"Yes," Léger added. "But you can see that the sultan's agents wouldn't dare to explain the *meaning* of the enciphered message, not even to rebels against the Portuguese throne. To do so would be to reveal the Ottoman Empire as an open enemy of Portugal. A rather treacherous enemy, at that."

"Yes, handing over the message itself might very well have served as a *casus belli*," Brian agreed. "It might actually have united the fractious people of Portugal behind their king, in shared outrage toward the Ottomans. It might have brought foreign allies to Portugal's aid, as well. On the other hand, if the partisans deciphered the message for themselves, that would be another matter altogether."

Léger gave a tight little smile. "You see the brilliance of the thing, I'm sure. By simply seeing to it that the painting became the property of the Portuguese rebels, the Turks admitted no blame of their own, nor confessed to any wrongdoing in the matter. They could plausibly claim that they had no idea the painting contained a message. So the message enciphered upon this canvas only proves the villainy of one man: the King of Portugal."

I closed my eyes as I tried to sort out the tangle of ramifications that sprang from this exposition. Brian and Léger sat watching me silently, giving me a moment to compose my mind.

"You have written out your translation of the text?" I asked at length.

"Yes," Brian assured me. "It is on a sheet of foolscap, which we have rolled together with the painting."

"We have also included an explanation of the cipher system," Léger added. "So that anyone who wishes to do so may confirm our interpretation."

I stood up and paced about the parlor. "Then this package must be conveyed to the resistance in Portugal, immediately."

"I agree entirely," Brian said quickly. "And so does my order. It should be placed directly into the hands of Teófilo Braga, or one of his top aides. I ask your permission to use the means at my disposal in order to convey this package to him in secret, and without delay."

I was anticipating that he would make this offer, and I immediately shook my head firmly. "That, I cannot allow."

"But, Florbela! You must!"

"No, Brian," I said. "I trust you, and I know that you mean well, but the Freemasons have done their part in this matter. Remember, you once told me that, when you and I converse, it is not only we who are meeting, but the International Order of Freemasons meeting with the People's Republican Movement of Portugal. You went so far as to refer to me as an 'agent' of my father's cause. I certainly wasn't comfortable with that description of myself at the time you said it, but I think that under the current circumstances I have no choice but to accept it." I was imagining my father very vividly as these words came from my mouth, and I simply couldn't believe that he would approve of my leaving this treasure of the Portuguese resistance in the hands of even the most well-meaning foreign power. And what would Armand say, if he heard of such a thing! I added, "However reluctant I may be to admit the fact, I represent Portugal at this moment—*free* Portugal—and so you must hand over the painting to me. I will find the means to convey it to my father's people, and you must trust me to do so."

Brian and Léger made a great fuss and show of objection after they heard me say this, but I could tell that the effort was largely a formality on their part. I think that it was likely that they had secretly expected this reaction from me and had discussed it in advance as a contingency. When Brian, in due time, placed the copper tube into my hands, his expression was glum and disapproving, but perhaps there was also a stratum of relief hidden beneath that mask. Certainly, he was ridding himself of a most burdensome object. I steadfastly refused his suggestions of ways in which he might still be of some help to me in the task that I was taking on; I knew that if I were to let him help me, then soon I would be completely dependent upon his aid. Of course, neither Brian nor Léger knew about Onça do Papa's nighttime visit a few weeks previous, or they would never have consented to let me transport the painting on my own.

Our business was done, so I escorted them to the door as quickly as decency would allow. I think that all of us perceived that time was very precious now. I thanked them both sincerely and gave each a kiss on the cheek.

Chapter Thirty-Two

As soon as I was alone, I ran upstairs and barged into Irène's room. I found her sprawled on her bedroom rug, engrossed in her studies. I told her, in general terms, what had occurred. She sat up as the story progressed and stared pensively at the copper tube in my hands.

"What shall you do now?" she asked. "Do you intend to carry it to Portugal yourself?"

"I believe that I must."

"When shall you leave?"

"I suppose I had better leave . . . immediately." Until she posed the question I had had no firm conception that this was so. I had vaguely imagined that the matter could be attended to sometime in the coming days, but I saw now that it was dangerous to linger for even an hour in this house while possessing such a dangerous and valuable object. I repeated, more firmly, "I suppose that I must leave Paris tonight."

She nodded agreement. "I shall come with you."

"Definitely not—it is much too dangerous!" I gave her a hard look as she sat there on the floor, dressed in her little frock and white stockings, with blue ribbons in her hair.

She didn't attempt to press the matter, but dropped her eyes and asked, "But how shall you travel?"

"By rail, I suppose. I probably have just enough for the fare." I was starting to wish that Armand would arrive so that I could ask him for his advice. In fact, I was about to pull aside Irène's curtains to peer through the darkness at the park bench across the street, when I heard a quiet rapping, downstairs.

"That's the kitchen door," Irène exclaimed, springing to her feet. "Armand must have come around through the courtyard!"

We ran down the stairs, and indeed found Armand standing among shadows at the back door. He had never approached the Curies' house before.

"I need to speak with you immediately," he said when we let him in, cutting me off before I could tell him my news. "Sapeur . . . do you remember my telling you about the spy, Sapeur? It was all true! Yesterday he asked any number of dubious questions of Thierry and Barbade, and then, when their suspicions were aroused, he fled and has not been seen since."

"It's no matter now," I told him impatiently. "Look!" I held up the copper tube and showed it to him.

"If you please," Irène interrupted. "I think that this news might have some bearing, Florbela." She peered around my shoulder at Armand. "This spy . . . this Sapeur person. Do you think that he might be in pursuit of this object?" She pointed at the metal tube.

"I cannot prove it," Armand told her. "But for my own part, I feel certain of it."

"And what do you think that he might have learned from your comrades?" she persisted. "Do you think that this man could have learned that Florbela is staying here at my home?"

"I don't know, but I fear that it is possible. That's what I needed to say." He turned to face me again. "I must insist that you let me move you out of the city immediately. I have already arranged a very secure location, at the home of a trusted cousin, not far from Versailles. If you will please take my advice, you should pack some things, and we shall leave this evening." His eyes dropped to the copper tube. "As for that, we shall conceal it in your luggage."

I interrupted him impatiently. "I'm not going to Versailles! And I'm not staying here either. Listen, Armand, this painting is much more important to my father's cause then we could ever have imagined. Don't ask me to explain, but trust me: this is a powerful weapon for the republican movement, perhaps even a decisive one. I must carry it to Portugal in secret and as quickly as possible—and by my own hand. So, please, advise me. I must leave here tonight, this very *hour*, if I am able."

Armand was completely nonplussed at this outburst. He stared at me silently, his expression blank, for several long seconds. Then, somewhat disconcertingly, a huge grin spread across his face. "Excellent!" he exclaimed. "In that case, naturally, I shall accompany you."

I hesitated just long enough to give him a chance to mute his enthusiastic expression to a more appropriate level, and then I accepted his offer without complaint. In truth, I had been hoping he would volunteer to escort me. I had grave doubts that I should have been able to carry out such a venture on my own, without falling directly into some sort of trouble.

Armand did his best to maintain a serious expression, but was not entirely able to suppress his boyish excitement. As he spoke, rapidly considering logistics aloud, his eyes wandered slowly off to stare unfocused at the wall. "We shall need a few men. Paulo certainly. No, maybe *just* Paulo; best if we travel light. Some of the roads are quite poor, so I'm afraid this is going to take us two or three weeks, especially if we stay off the main highways. Which we must, whenever possible."

"You could make the trip in three or four days, by either rail or ship," Irène inserted.

Armand shook his head, hardly seeming to hear her. "Much too conspicuous. We will travel on horseback." Then turning to me, he said, "It *would* be possible to travel by carriage instead, if need be, but naturally it shall be quicker to ride. If you are able."

"I can ride."

"Good. Bring whatever is necessary," he told me. "But no more than you can carry easily on your back, if the need should arise. Wrap your things in a light bedroll. It's good that the season is warm!" His gaze shifted to Irène, and he added, "Help her to pack, would you please? Be circumspect. Try to consider inclement weather, that sort of thing. Avoid anything superfluous."

I took a bit of offense at the implication that my fourteen-year-old friend could plan my travel kit better than I could myself. Admittedly, I had no delusions to the contrary, but it wounded my pride a bit nonetheless.

Armand's thoughts were already moving swiftly ahead. "For myself, I must go and fill my wallet. I shall return here in half an hour's time with a carriage, to take us discreetly to the edge of the city. There, we shall begin our journey. May I borrow some writing materials?"

Irène nodded and wordlessly left the room.

Armand explained, "Thierry came with me tonight, trailing a block behind me. We were hoping to trap Sapeur, if he should try to follow me here in an effort to determine your whereabouts. I believe that Thierry is still hiding in the shrubs of the park across the street, and I shall give him a message to carry back to Paulo."

I realized only now that my heart was pounding violently with excitement. I leaned forward impulsively on tiptoe to kiss his cheek, and said, "Thank you so much." He looked quite startled, but before he could reply, Irène hurried back into the room with a pen and inkwell and paper. He set to work immediately at the kitchen table, scribbling his message. When he straightened up again, folding the sheet of paper between his fingers, our eyes met briefly. His face was shining with excitement. "Be quick," he urged me. "I shall return in no time." With that, he slipped out of the kitchen door and vanished into the night.

Irène took me by the hand and led me upstairs, where she watched me select the bare necessities for a fortnight on the road. Then, to my dismay, she sorted through my selections, removed about half of them, and placed them back in the wardrobe.

"Where is that riding skirt of yours? Ah, here it is!" she said, as her hand fell upon my old equestrian split skirt where it hung on the rack.

"Oh, yes, I must have that."

Irène took the skirt down and quickly folded it, adding it to my supplies. We rolled everything up tightly in a woolen blanket and an oilcloth tarpaulin, then bound it all with leather straps.

"I don't think you should stay here alone in this house with only Berthe," I told her, as I hefted the bundle in my hands to feel its weight. It certainly seemed to me that I could carry quite a bit more than that, and if Irène hadn't been prodding me toward the door, I would have been tempted to repack the thing and add at least dozen more indispensable items.

"Don't worry about me," Irène replied, herding me toward the stairs. "I shall take a cab across the river to Mr. Brancusi's atelier. I'm sure that he will either have space for me there or will find safe lodging for me elsewhere until Mother returns."

In the kitchen, we wrapped up the copper tube in an old flour sack as well as we could, then bound it with twine. We were still trying to secure this awkward package when we heard the jingle of a harness out front.

I hurried to the door with my parcels clutched in my arms, then stopped with my hand on the doorknob to kiss Irène on both cheeks. Her slender fingers clutched my sleeve momentarily to stop me from rushing away. "Florbela," she said with great seriousness, "you must be very careful."

"I shall," I replied hastily.

Rather than letting me go, she narrowed her eyes, observing my face closely. "I think that perhaps you should let me come along."

I made a noise that was supposed to be a laugh, but didn't sound much like one in my own ears. I kissed her again, on the forehead, and said, "I shall return as soon as I am able. Promise me you will go immediately to Mr. Brancusi's house." I waited long enough to see her nod her head, then I pulled away and ran out to the carriage in the street.

Armand threw open the door for me and helped me up, without emerging from the shadows of the cabin. As soon as the door was pulled closed, he pounded on the roof to signal the driver.

Armand had drawn all the curtains, and for a few minutes he barely spoke to me, moving instead from one window to another to peek out as we clattered along the streets. Apparently spotting no signs of pursuit, he eventually settled back onto the seat facing mine.

"You've done very well," he said, gesturing at my tiny bundle of gear.

I saw that there was a lump in the shadows on the seat beside him, which I surmised must be his own bedroll, no larger than mine. He also had a leather pouch strapped to his waist, which would prove to contain several fistfuls of twenty-franc gold pieces—the little coins that were commonly known as "roosters".

"Where are we going?"

"To a post house that I know of," he told me. "Just outside the city, beyond the Porte d'Orléans where we can rent horses."

I patted my bundle. "I have brought riding clothes."

"Good. Then we shall start the journey in that fashion, at least. It's about a thousand miles to Lisbon, and I doubt if either of us has ever ridden so far before—especially not in a hurry. If you find yourself exhausted after a day or two, we can most likely hire a trap at some post house along the way."

"I imagine that I can ride as far as you can," I told him, feeling suddenly defensive.

In the dim light, I saw him once again burst out into a big, hearty grin, one that seemed grossly inappropriate to the circumstances. But he only said, "I do not doubt it."

It didn't take us long to get beyond the city limits, and we arrived a few minutes later at the big post house of Arceuil, at the head of the great highway that pointed to the southern cities. The stables were only lightly staffed at that hour, but proved to have a reasonably clean room where ladies of the gentry could change into their riding clothes. The clerk seemed fairly shocked that I wanted to use this room at such an hour but showed me to it nonetheless.

While I donned my riding apparel, Armand bargained for horses. I emerged to find that he had the grooms saddling up no fewer than three fine and solid-looking mixed Arabians.

"What is that?" I heard him demanding of a passing stable boy. He pointed at a strange and elongate object made of stitched leather that was hanging among other bric-à-brac on a wall near the entrance to the offices.

"That's an old saddle scabbard, sir," the boy told him, affecting a knowledgeable tone. "That's what that is. From the ancient times."

"Big, isn't it?" commented one of the grooms, who was standing nearby and puffing at a burl pipe. "They used that sort to carry them old flintlock scatterguns."

"I'll need that," Armand told him. "How much will you sell it for?"

The groom laughed, assuming that he was joking. But when Armand persisted, someone eventually invented a price, and Armand paid it. A few minutes later, while no one seemed to be paying us much attention, I noticed him discreetly slide the copper tube out from under our bundles and insert it into the oversized leather holster, where it disappeared completely. He carried the scabbard over to his horse and strapped it to the side of the saddle.

We started our horses off slowly on the empty highway, heading south and lit only by moonlight, leading the third horse along on a guide rope. As soon as we were safely alone, I began asking the several questions that I had been suppressing.

"The third horse is for Paulo," Armand told me by way of reply, "whom I hope we shall encounter shortly. And no, I do not think that Arabians are an unnecessary luxury. Indeed, we will require the finest horses that we can obtain for every leg of this journey, and we're lucky to have found these ones to get us started. I imagine they can canter on level ground for hours on end, though there's no need to rush things yet—not until we have rendezvoused with Paulo. Most of the rural post houses ahead of us will probably provide us with nothing better than light trotters. Now: can you keep up a faster pace?"

I told him that I could, and we cued the horses up to a slow canter.

I had never been for a long ride in the dark of night before, and the passing of the unlit road soon began to seem quite dreamlike. In the middle of the night, we came to the fork in the highway where the roads to Chartres and to Orléans branched apart. There was an inn at this junction, and we dismounted in the shadows beside the old wooden building. While I watered the horses, Armand pulled a light cloak around himself, attempting to shadow his face, then went inside to fetch us refreshments. He emerged some time later with a day-old loaf of bread, a small, cold roast, and a bucket of ale.

I followed him away from the building to the far side of the road. Armand didn't speak until he was certain that we were out of earshot of anyone who might be lurking or loitering outside the inn. Then he said quietly, "This is where we shall meet Paulo. Come along. Just beyond those trees there's a deer meadow—I remember it from years ago. I believe that we can watch the road from there, and also get some rest."

We tied up the horses behind a windbreak row of spruces, then sat on the shadowy grass to eat our simple repast. *Just like outlaws*, I thought to myself for some strange reason. I must have fallen asleep soon after eating, because the next thing that I remember was Armand shaking my shoulder.

"There he is," he whispered.

I peered between the trees and could see the hulking form of Paulo stepping firmly along the road, coming from the direction of Paris. The sweat on his face and burly neck gleamed in the moonlight. "What a steadfast man!" Armand effused, as we hastily unhitched the horses. "I think I have never known anyone who was more dependable."

Paulo spotted us emerging from the wayside and came over to clasp Armand in a comradely embrace. He inspected our third horse briefly and with an air of satisfaction, and then we all mounted up. Not a word had been spoken beyond a few mumbled greetings.

Once we were well away from the inn, however, and passing between empty fields in the moonlight, we all rode closely abreast for a while and Armand asked Paulo for the details of his journey out of the city. He told us that he had collected on an old favor, one owed him by a certain drayage man, who had ridden him out of the city on his wagon behind a plodding old mare.

"You wrote that I should meet you at the inn," he remarked. "So I told him that I was going to a farm, half a mile back. I waited until he was gone, then I walked the last bit."

"Well done," Armand said enthusiastically. "Everything seems to be going just perfectly! I think it's almost impossible that we have been followed, nor our route discerned by anyone."

Paulo nodded mute agreement. After a moment he asked, "So. Where are we going, then?"

Armand had, of course, omitted this detail from the brief note that he had sent to the Souris Trempés headquarters, and had then forgotten the omission. He laughed out loud and brought Paulo up to date on our situation. Paulo listened silently, nodding occasionally, and asked no questions.

When Armand was finished, Paulo brooded for a few moments, then pulled his foot out of the stirrup to kick lightly at the immense leather scabbard dangling from Armand's saddle. "Is this it?"

Armand told him that it was.

"This will bring down the king?"

Armand glanced at me, then answered: "Such is our hope." He had, of course, been amazingly forbearing in that he had not asked me for details on this matter, and he asked for none now.

Paulo simply nodded once. "Then we should ride quicker."

We coaxed the horses up to a canter and, marvelous beasts that they were, they fell into this quick pace as if born to it. They sped along the dark and empty highway for the next few hours, and when dawn came they hadn't even worked up a lather.

Thus began our grueling trip through the center of France and into the southlands. Over the next few days, we rode twelve or even fourteen hours a day, changing horses at post houses every morning, and sometimes again in the afternoon if Armand deemed it worthwhile. We covered most of each day's distance at a slow canter. By the end of the second day, my thighs and calves seemed to be nothing but knots of pain, and I worried that I could go no further. But when I awakened the next morning, my legs had recovered just sufficiently to let me raise myself back into the saddle, and away we went.

We stayed on the main highway as far as Bordeaux. Armand and Paulo adopted a strategy of splitting our group: Armand and I riding up front, while Paulo lagged behind us by half a mile or so, watching for suspicious traffic. I asked Armand if we shouldn't keep to smaller roads, as this one was quite crowded with carts and coaches, and even the occasional roaring automobile shoved its way through, scattering the horses with klaxon blaring.

"As long as we're moving quickly," he told me, "I think that we're better on the highway, where we can cover the most distance in a day. Let's see how things go."

But I was well aware that we were moving a little slower each day. Before starting this trip, I had thought myself to be in fine physical condition, but by the fourth or fifth day I felt that I was approaching the limit of my endurance. I would wake up well before dawn each morning, with Armand hammering on my bolted door at some small roadside inn, and I would have to pry myself by brute force out of the black depths of my few hours of comatose sleep. I always felt that I could happily have spent the whole day in bed. By force of will, I was able each morning to painfully climb back into my saddle and ride again, but I knew that I was holding back our progress.

We came at length to a farm road crossing that was within sight of Bordeaux. Armand stopped by the roadside there, and we waited for Paulo to ride up. The two of them discussed strategy, and soon agreed that our slow pace meant that there was at least a possibility that some sort of pursuit could be catching up with us by now. After a few minutes' discussion, they decided that it was too great a risk to pass through the city, and so we would circumvent it. Thus, we turned off onto the smaller road, heading into the countryside, and by evening we were passing along the anonymous, muddy tracks that spanned the wine country of Gascogne. It was much slower going but the scenery was beautiful and it did give me a little rest since we didn't canter the whole day. Once we were past Bordeaux we returned to the highway.

The next afternoon, as we rode our horses at a tired walking pace, Armand and I noticed Paulo galloping up the road to meet us again. We stopped to wait for him, and when he came within earshot, Armand stood high in his stirrups and called out, "Did you see anyone in pursuit?" There was no one to hear us in any direction, save the grapevines that spread out like a vast green blanket over the low hills.

"Perhaps," Paulo replied grimly, as he reined in his panting horse. He told us of a closed carriage that he had seen passing him on the road: a fast little calash drawn by a pair of expensive-looking Orlov trotters, driven by a stout man whose face was wrapped in a scarf, as if against the dust of the road. It had seemed an odd conveyance to find in this pastoral setting, so he had followed it at a distance. The carriage had stopped at a little inn that we passed quite some time back, and Paulo had seen a small and nimble man emerge from its closed cabin, dressed in a sleek, dark suit of fine cut, with a black silk hat. This man had visited the inn for no more than a minute or two before emerging again with his hands empty, carrying not so much as a bottle of wine.

"And the driver?" Armand interrupted. "You say he was stoutly built. Do you suppose he might have been Sapeur?"

Paulo turned his palm up in the air, allowing that this might be possible, then went on with his recounting. He told us that, as soon as the calash had driven off, he had gone inside, and the innkeeper told him that the peculiar man had spoken to him in a foreign accent and asked strange questions. In particular, he asked the innkeeper if he had seen a young man passing through recently, in the company of a foreign maid from the south. The innkeeper told him that he had seen no one of that sort, and the peculiar man tipped him and left.

"When he stopped at the next inn, I took a back route so they would not see me. They are not far behind us," Paulo added.

Armand and I both slumped a bit in our saddles at the weight of this bad news. "We have been tracked. But how can that be?" Armand muttered, shaking his head.

"He would have guessed easily enough that we were headed

south," Paulo reminded him. "And there is but the one great highway."

"Yes, but how did he find out that we had left the city at all?"

"There are a hundred ways."

Armand lifted a hand resignedly. "I suppose there are."

"We can avoid the inns and villages," I proposed bleakly, not at all relishing the increased hardships that lay ahead for us.

"Yes, to some extent we can do that," Armand replied absently, his mind obviously working on other problems. "But we certainly can't help but leave a few witnesses along our path, and the more we select untraveled roads, the more conspicuous our passage will be. On these country roads, any farmhand who happens to note our passing is likely to remember us."

"Also, we cannot avoid post houses," Paulo added, in his dour baritone.

"No, we cannot. I suppose there's nothing for it but to try to ride faster." Armand glanced at me, and I nodded firmly, determined to do better.

"But we cannot outrun him on the highways," Paulo said flatly, as if pronouncing sentence upon us. "We must take to the smaller roads in order to slow his progress in the carriage."

Armand shot him a quick glance. "But that will take much longer."

I sat up straighter in my saddle and said, "Perhaps it is time for you two to go on without me. I can hide, incognito, at some inn."

"Ridiculous!" Armand snapped, in a rare moment of pique. "It is *you* who bear this thing to Portugal. We're only here to guard your way. Anyway, he would find you."

Paulo looked at me very directly with his stolid face. "Senhorita, the two of us, traveling alone, we would like as not be shot as spies. By either one side or the other."

Armand added, "Our chances of getting through to the inner circle of Teófilo Braga would depend upon a roll of fate's dice. It is *your* name that will open the gates."

Chapter Thirty-Three

We turned our horses at the next junction and began to travel inland, intending to cross the Pyrenees at one of the passes around the Pic d'Anie. I found a new resolve, and tapped into reserves of endurance that I hadn't known I possessed, cueing my horse up to canter and holding that pace through the next few hours. We changed horses in the evening, rode through the night, and changed horses again in the morning. Thus, we rode for over twenty-four hours without rest.

By the evening, we were passing through the foothills of the Pyrenees, and the countryside was probably quite beautiful, but I could barely see it. My exhaustion had penetrated all the way to the marrow of my bones, and I felt flushed and delirious, as with fever. I could see nothing but the road a few feet in front of the plodding hooves of my tired horse.

Paulo was riding with us now, and he was quite merciless in his insistence that we maintain a steady pace, though I was already exerting myself far beyond any limits I had previously known. At last, Armand coaxed his horse closer to Paulo's and told him sharply, "Stop goading. We are all of us very tired."

Paulo frowned at him. "If we are overtaken, we will surely be ambushed."

"Perhaps so. But we have come a long distance today, and I believe that we have gained a good lead."

Paulo didn't look satisfied, but he did stop nagging.

Armand came over to ride beside me for a while, and I mustered my energies to make a show of good spirits, though I certainly felt none. "We must be nearly halfway to Lisbon by now," I commented. My throat was dry and my voice rasped.

"I think that's right," Armand agreed.

"Incredible. After only six days of travel."

"Here's an interesting piece of history that I recalled a few minutes ago," he said in a falsely cheerful tone, since I knew that he too was exhausted. "You know of the couriers of Darius?"

I shook my head, unwilling even to invest the effort of saying no.

"Darius was the emperor of Persia, twenty-five hundred years ago. He maintained a system of roads and post houses that was so efficient that a courier could carry a message from the farthest border of the empire to Persepolis in just seven days—a distance more than twice as great as the road from Paris to Lisbon."

My head was so murky that it took a considerable time for this claim to impress itself upon me. Even when its meaning was fully clear, it seemed outside the realm of the possible. I only shook my head again.

"Listen, I have a thought," Paulo called over to us. He had apparently been brooding on his conversation with Armand. "The sun is down, and soon it will be dark. Perhaps we could risk making camp for a few hours, once the night sets in."

"Good idea," Armand immediately agreed. "We will all move faster after two or three hours of sleep."

I barely remember the next hour, as we continued along the winding road that led up into the darkening hills, nor do I remember how we selected a secluded clearing off the road to serve as our campsite. And I certainly don't remember the pitching of our simple, fireless camp, because I left the others to do all the work. For myself, I lay down upon the ground almost as soon as I had stepped from the stirrup, and I was fast asleep within seconds.

* * *

I awakened very abruptly just a few hours later, sitting bolt upright on the ground and throwing off a blanket that someone had draped over me. Violent noises had awakened me, and all my grogginess of the evening was suddenly dispelled. My mind was almost preternaturally clear and alert.

I saw Paulo rolling and tumbling, most athletically, among the pale patches of moonlight in our little clearing. I realized that I must have been awakened by some brief cry he had made. I watched him for several seconds without moving, uncomprehending, imagining in rapid succession that he was playing some boisterous game, that he was trying to shake off some sort of biting insects, and that he had gone mad. But then I realized that he was not alone: he was in fact wrestling for his life against a silent and nearly invisible opponent—a small man wrapped entirely in black.

I let out a strangled cry and tried to get to my feet but my body was wracked with pain. I stood on my wobbly legs in a state of panic. I looked quickly around but didn't see Armand anywhere. I spotted a short sword laying on the ground near the two grunting, thrashing fighters, presumably dropped by one of them. Then I saw the flicker of another moving blade as it passed through a moonbeam, and I perceived that Onça do Papa was wielding some sort of dagger, while Paulo tried to hold back his arm.

In the next moment, with a mighty effort, Paulo threw the smaller man off him, literally hurling him through the air. As soon as he was free, Paulo bellowed out a huge and inarticulate shout of alarm. Onça do Papa landed on his feet, very like a cat, and seemed to simply bounce directly back at Paulo as if propelled by a spring, dagger flashing. I had never seen anyone move so quickly.

At that moment, Armand came dashing at me from the shadows of the trees, where I suppose he had been sleeping, and grabbed me roughly by the arm. He said nothing, but pulled me along with him in such a rush that I could barely keep my feet under myself. He dragged me toward our frightened and snorting horses.

In the darkness, he began fumbling rapidly at the knot that bound my horse to a trunk. I looked back at Paulo, who was again fighting for his life, and I said, "We cannot—"

"Paulo can take care of himself," Armand interrupted me in an urgent whisper. "Mount your horse! Do it now!" Then, suddenly, he dropped the reins and made a strange choking sound, as if he had been about to exclaim something but words had failed him. I had a foot already in the stirrup, and I had to step down in order to see what he was staring at.

I heard Armand hiss, "Sapeur!"

Paulo was on top of his opponent, and the fight might soon have been over but Sapeur, who seemed to appear out of nowhere, leapt through the air brandishing a knife of some sort. Paulo raised his arm in defense but Sapeur managed to drive his shoulder into the big man's ribs, bowling him over. No sooner was Onça do Papa released then he rolled fluidly to his feet, leapt over the two grappling men, and, to my horror, plunged his knife deeply into the back of Paulo's ribcage. Paulo fell to the ground with a boneless flop, all of his robust vitality suddenly gone, evaporated in a single instant. I was close enough to him that I heard his final words, delivered in a ghastly, gurgling voice that I shall never forget.

"Viva a república!"

All of these events had passed in mere moments, and I was left so stunned and horrified that I was literally unable to move my legs. Onça do Papa yelled something at Sapeur who was now going through Paulo's pockets. Then the black-clad assassin spun around, abandoning the fallen sword and darted into the darkness of the forest, presumably thinking that we had made our escape. Armand pelted after him at a full sprint.

"Armand, no!" I gasped, but he was in a fury.

Sapeur was a hideous little barrel of a man, short and thickly muscled, and even in the dim light I could see that his entire close-cropped head was webbed with ugly scars. He was on his hands and knees beside the fallen Paulo, and as Armand rushed into the clearing he got to his feet. They both spotted the short sword lying on the ground and raced toward it, though it was clear that Armand did not have time to pick it up before Sapeur would be on top of him. As Armand kicked the sword out of Sapeur's reach, the thick little man made a lunge and managed to grasp his ankle, sending him sprawling. Sapeur's other hand rose quickly above his head, and I saw that his thick fist was wrapped around the handle of a knife with a stubby, curved blade, probably intended for gelding livestock. I watched in horror as he made a vicious but clumsy slash with this ugly weapon at Armand's leg, striking him obliquely across the calf.

Armand cried out in pain, but spun himself around nimbly. He seized the wrist that held the knife and threw himself upon Sapeur. As the two of them began a desperate struggle, I turned away momentarily to look around me and grab the nearest heavy stick from the ground, hoping that I might strike a blow in Armand's favor. When I looked up again, Armand had bent Sapeur's hand back and forced him now to drop his knife. Armand let go just long enough to snatch up the weapon, but as he did so, Sapeur tipped him off balance, threw him over, and managed to lock his neck into the crook of his thick arm.

I ran over to them as fast as my aching legs would allow. Armand's neck was clamped so tightly that he wasn't even choking. His tongue protruded from his mouth, and his face was discoloring. I swung my makeshift cudgel hard, but the branch in my hands fractured into splinters over Sapeur's knobby head without effect. He turned his frightening gaze on me and growled. I was terrified, but I turned to race over to the short sword, which still lay on the ground a dozen or so feet further on.

Armand's eyes were rolling about blindly, and I knew that he was about to lose consciousness. Then, with a final burst of strength, he managed to turn himself a few degrees to one side, and suddenly he drove the knife into the side of Sapeur's chest, plunging the small blade all the way to the hilt.

I turned away from the ugly scene, unable to watch. Armand recovered himself very quickly, and then he was standing at my side, holding me by the shoulders. At our feet, the bodies of Paulo and Sapeur lay sprawled upon the soil and dry needles of pines.

"Your wound . . ." I started to say.

"There is no time," Armand croaked hoarsely. He picked up the sword and led me once again toward the horses, hobbling now on his slashed and blood-drenched leg. "He could be anywhere." We collected our things as quickly as we could and stuffed them into the saddlebags. He all but threw me up onto my saddle, then painfully mounted his own horse.

I followed Armand out between the trees to the road, and there we turned toward the high Pyrenees and took off at a full gallop. I felt as if I were in a nightmare as we hurtled through the darkness, and I remember sobbing inconsolably as I rode. The sounds of my grief and horror were lost in the rush of the wind.

We paused by the road after a few minutes, only briefly, to rinse and bind Armand's wound. It had been bleeding profusely, but the bandage stopped the flow. Then we rode on, pushing our horses to their limits.

Dawn came after a couple of hours and found us straining our way up a stony, winding road ascending a steep slope. Both the horses stumbled whenever a hoof landed on a loose stone, and from the way their nostrils were blowing I imagine that the animals were close to collapse. We had worked them hard for twelve hours the previous day, and then, after just two or three hours' rest during the night, we had raced the poor beasts at a gallop as far as they could go.

As for myself, my body seemed to have found yet another hidden reserve of strength, and I suppose that this was due to the shock of losing Paulo. Our mission now seemed to me quite plainly more important than life or death: Paulo's murder was invested in the endeavor, and I couldn't imagine that such a sacrifice should be in vain.

At the top of the rise we found ourselves facing a row of mountain peaks, with Pic d'Anie looming directly before us. The sun was just cresting the horizon in the east, and by its rays we saw to our great relief that there was a small post house not far ahead, with a few horses in its corral. We found the place barred and shuttered, but Armand hobbled over and pounded on the door until it was grudgingly opened by a roughly whiskered

Basque.

This man suggested in the rudest possible terms that we go away and return in two hours, or not at all. Armand handed him a large gratuity—an excessively large one, in my opinion—and the man's eyes immediately narrowed. He exposed his chipped and yellowed teeth in a venal grin, and threw open the door for us.

We ordered some food and while it was being prepared, we took a small room used for private eating where I cleaned and bandaged Armand's leg. It must have been extremely painful but he never made a sound.

Word of Armand's generosity apparently spread quite rapidly, and within minutes there were half a dozen ruffians running about the place, offering us not only horses and food but also whiskey, used weapons, and various forms of contraband. I had never been inside such a disreputable establishment in my life; even the headquarters of the Souris Trempés seemed charmingly civilized by comparison. Armand, however, was friendly and easy-mannered with them all, and examined their goods attentively. At last, he purchased a small revolver and a handful of brass cartridges. He loaded the little weapon with care, then tucked it into his belt.

"Be careful," I whispered into Armand's ear, the moment we were left alone. "These men look like cutthroats, every one."

"Patience," he whispered back. "We shall not be here long. I'm sure that few travelers come through these remote passes save smugglers and the occasional militiaman, so of course the traders up here are rather rough. Remember: we need their best horses."

The men seemed to do everything in their power to delay us, no doubt hoping to make a leisurely assessment of Armand's resources so that they could exploit him to the fullest. Although I could certainly see that Armand was agitated and as eager to get away from that place as I, he did a fine job of acting aloof and cordial with the louts who staffed the inn and stables, bribing them lavishly and repeatedly, and politely reminding them that we were in a great hurry. It irritated me to see these rogues bilking Armand of his money, but I admit that his strategy was effective, though expensive. In the long run, they let us have their very best pair of horses and a supply of perfectly adequate provisions, and we were on our way in a little under an hour.

It was a great relief to be away, and also to be riding by daylight after our harrowing race through the blackness of night. I rode up beside Armand for a while, and I asked him about the pistol he had purchased.

"It's not likely to serve us much use," he told me. "If we are confronted, it will almost certainly be by stealth, and likely under the cover of darkness."

I supposed that this was true, but I said, "Still, it's a comfort."

The road now became very steep, and it was clear that there would certainly be no cantering or trotting, not even with our fresh mounts. Also, though the sun rose higher and higher over the next few hours, we were ascending so steeply that the air around us grew colder rather than warmer. The wind picked up as well, and by noon there were small white clouds scudding by very rapidly, just above our heads, with gray wisps swirling and spiraling uneasily within them. Sometimes one of these clouds would engulf us, abruptly fogging the road and filling the air with such an opaque gray mist that our horses had to feel their way blindly up the narrow and treacherous road. These banks of fog would blow away and vanish as abruptly as they had arrived, leaving us once again bathed in sharp sunlight and the dry, crystalline mountain air.

During one of these moments of sudden clarity, after a fogbank had cleared, I heard Armand muttering something under his breath. I asked him what he had said.

"We're very exposed to being seen from below, when we're on stretches of road like this one."

I looked around and realized that it was so: a careful watcher could probably spot us from miles away, at that moment. I pointed up the road. "When we come around that bend, we shall be hidden again."

Armand hardly seemed to hear me. He was squinting down at the terrain from which we had come, shading his eyes. "I wish we had a spyglass," he muttered. "Then at least we should have some advantage from this high ground." A moment later he added, "I am sure that *he* is carrying one. I imagine he is watching us, even now."

I shivered at this unpleasant thought and tried to coax my mare to speed up a bit, but she was already struggling up the hill at her best pace.

We advanced very slowly, and I'm sure that we covered no more than a few miles that day. Sunset found us among the peaks in the true high country, riding so close to the restless and threatening sky that it seemed we could have reached up and touched it. Though it was only September, the evening bore a very wintry feel. We were riding with our blankets draped over our shoulders, and our breath came in little cloudy puffs. The gray canopy in the sky above us was unbroken now, and so dense and dark that it seemed it might burst forth with rain or ice at any moment.

By this point in the journey, my exhaustion was threatening to rob me of my wits. Every few minutes, I would fall into a fitful sleep in my saddle, despite the roughness of the trail and the hard weather. I suppose that only some innate stubbornness kept me from falling off my horse during these spells. I would awaken each time with a jolt, but find myself unable to fully clear my head of the sensation of dreaming. Even when awake, I saw the faces of cruel and laughing gods in the violent swirling of the clouds overhead, and the cairns by the roadside seemed like tombstones, though they were only meant to serve as markers for those times when the road was lost under snow. Armand rode close behind me, and although he himself seemed hardly able to sit his saddle, I think that he was watching me, in case I fell.

The night came on very rapidly, and then it began to rain. The temperature seemed to plunge mercilessly, and the wind whipped up until the raindrops felt like nails striking my face. I huddled deeper under my blanket and oilcloth, but they seemed no more substantial against the elements than lace curtains.

I don't know how long we endured this, but after what seemed like an eternity of suffering, I realized that, miraculous to say, there was a twinkling light in the wall of darkness ahead. We rode up to find a tiny mountain inn just off the road, a last refuge for travelers who were approaching the pass from the French side of the range. The light was coming from a storm lantern, which swung wildly from a post in front of a low and tightly shuttered building. Without the advertisement of this lamp, we might well have ridden past without even noticing the humble edifice in the darkness.

Armand beat at the door, and was soon answered by a bent and wrinkled old man, whose body seemed as lean and hard as the gnarled pines that dotted this high country. He said something to us, inaudible over the howl of the wind, then led our horses to shelter while we hurried inside. We came into a small and low-ceilinged room, dimly lit by tapers, but dry and wonderfully warm. An old lady, exactly as wizened and sundried as her husband, hobbled up to fuss over us, taking our soaked blankets from around our shoulders and hanging them from a wall that faced the wood stove. This splendid device consisted of a small and ungainly ball of crude iron, dented and blackened all over, and it was positively glowing with fiery heat. I had never seen anything so beautiful in my life. The only furniture in the room was a single ancient and threadbare sofa. I sat myself resolutely upon it, leaned forward toward the stove, and lost myself in the idolatrous worship of its warmth.

Armand sat down beside me and began unwrapping his wounded leg. His laceration looked terrible, but I suppose it could have been much worse. The gash was quite wide, and certainly should have been stitched, but there were no signs of infection, and the loss of blood didn't seem too dire. The old woman clucked and fetched him a clean rag, and he set to work redressing the wound.

It turned out that the old couple were the only people in the building. "You're in luck," the old man told us in a friendly wheeze. "You can have any room you like."

"Not that we'd turn you away," his wife added. "Even if the

place were full. Not in a storm like this."

"I'm afraid we can't stay," Armand told them. This pronouncement must have struck them both as perfectly insane, and they stared at him as one stares at a madman. "But if we could trouble you for a hot meal . . ."

"Of course!" the old woman replied immediately. "I've got a fine stew, if you don't mind rabbit. I'll heat some up right now. But you *can't* go out in this!" Armand just stared at the stove, slowly turning his hands to warm them front and back. The old woman lifted her arms at her sides, as if to ask the world at large what one could do with such a lunatic, and then she disappeared into her kitchen.

Her husband pointedly didn't say anything, but looked at me for some time and then looked at Armand's leg. Blood was already seeping through the fresh bandage. I suppose the old man was trying to figure out how this young man proposed to go out riding in a mountain storm with an exhausted woman and an injured leg. But Armand soon got him engaged in a practical discussion of the local terrain, and of the various roads and trails that were to be found on the other side of the pass. Not surprisingly, the old man was more than content to let the conversation be diverted into these pragmatic considerations of a subject he knew so well.

The stew arrived and we wolfed it down. I followed Armand's example in this, though I would have been happy to linger for an hour over a hot meal. Then, predictably, as soon as my belly was full, the temptation to stretch out upon the old sofa and sleep for a day or two was nearly overwhelming.

Armand touched my shoulder and murmured in my ear, "We must go."

The old man stood with us at the door, looking out into the storm as Armand paid him for the meal. "There's snow coming," he remarked. "I suppose you know that you are taking your life into your hands, and most recklessly. Hers, as well."

"I know that," Armand told him. "Thank you for your hospitality, and good night."

The old man touched Armand's elbow with a craggy old claw,

forcing him to hesitate. "Just one question, young fellow. Whatever it is that you're running from, I reckon that it will be coming up that road sometime pretty soon. So I want you to tell me: should Ma and I be worried?"

Armand looked him squarely in the eye. "A man will come up the road," he said. "He will ask you questions. Be courteous, and tell him everything he wants to know. Do you understand? Do not try to bar your door against him. Hide nothing from him, and he will not harm you." With that, we stepped out again into the driving rain, collected our unhappy horses out from under their shelter, and mounted up.

One more miserable hour brought us up to the pass. By then, true to the old man's word, the rain had turned to snow. A thick torrent of flakes sped by us, horizontal in the darkness, so that it looked as if we were deep inside a gray and rushing river. We traversed the crest, then descended along a series of icy switchbacks down a steep face. When we came to the bottom of that face, we rode out onto a broad plateau of some sort. The snow had stopped by then, and the air was dry, but the wind had strengthened even further and bit painfully at our faces. The icy wind dragged away any heat that my blanket might have trapped, and I shivered as if I were naked. The clouds were still thick and low overhead, completely obscuring the moon and stars.

We hadn't gone far along the high plain when Armand called me to a halt. To my surprise, he gingerly stepped down from his saddle and proceeded to limp about, exploring our immediate surroundings in the darkness. Then he approached and called up to me through the screaming of the wind: "We turn here." Without waiting for my reply, he limped back to his horse, mounted, and turned off the road.

I followed him because there was nothing else to do, but I prayed that he knew where he was going. There was scarcely any sign that we were on a trail at all, but I assumed that he was trying to follow some shepherd's path he had learned about from the old man at the inn. Gradually, this near-invisible trail began to descend, leading us down through the bitter wind and darkness toward the Spanish foothills.

The path, if that was what it was, took us at one point up a small hill, and as we crested the top of it, a flash of lightning over the peaks behind us briefly illuminated the terrain spread out before us. A deep and ragged mountain gorge was cut into the floor of the valley, and I thought I saw a bridge. There was intermittent moonlight by now, beaming through gaps among the rushing clouds overhead, and by this uncertain light we coaxed our frightened horses down the slope.

We were nearing the edge of the gorge when an immense flash of lightning startled us both, causing us to look back over our shoulders. Even as the crash of the thunder struck our ears, a second, smaller bolt lit the sky once more, and by its light we saw a rider, all in black, coming down the slope behind us, like a vengeful wraith. He was sitting high upon a tall black horse, and the wind whirled a great black cape about him.

My heart went cold as ice, and I came as close to true despair as I have ever been. Armand and I turned, as if of one mind, and urged our horses up to a gallop, dashing over the wind-flattened grass in the moonlight, straight for the ravine. We turned to follow the edge of the precipice and rode along its edge until we came upon an old rope bridge that was strung across the abyss. The span of the ravine was not great, but its depths were so black that they might as well have been bottomless. We could hear the angry roar of the torrent, and it sounded like it was far, far below.

The wind threw the deck of the bridge around mercilessly, flipping the loose rope structure from side to side, and sometimes even tossing it up into the air as if it were weightless. Our horses balked as they approached it. I followed Armand's lead as he jumped down to the ground, grabbed his horse firmly by the reins and began dragging it toward the bridge by main force. But when the creatures came close to the abutment, they dug in their hooves and screamed in fear, and would go no further.

"There's no time for this," Armand shouted close by my ear, over the howling elements. He was tugging at the gear around his saddle, though I couldn't see his hands. He shouted to me again,

"Drop the reins! Do it! Just let the animal go. Now here, take this." He was handing me the scabbard. I looked inside and saw the copper tube, container of our precious cargo. I tied the scabbard across my chest. Armand extracted a knife from his gear: a long dagger or dirk of some sort. He unsheathed the blade and simply threw the sheath away onto the ground.

"Go!" he shouted. But my hesitation was not because I was unwilling, nor had I any alternative action in mind. I was simply, physically unable to embark onto those leaping planks; my feet would not obey the commands of my brain. It looked like certain death to step out upon that bridge.

I felt Armand throw an arm around my waist, grasp me tightly, and begin forcing me bodily out onto the suspended deck. "You must go first," he yelled in my ear, pushing me out onto the span. "When we've crossed, I will cut the anchor ropes on the other side."

This crossing was so horrible that my mind and body recoiled at the sight of it. The planks of the bridge's deck were very old, some of them rotted away entirely. Every surface was slick from the night's rain and there were patches of gleaming black ice. The nauseating thrashing of the ropes and planks became more powerful with every step we took toward the center of the span. I clutched the scabbard against my body and clung to the rope beside me with my free hand; Armand had his arm around my waist, goading me forward much more rapidly than I was willing to go. The wind seemed like a living and malevolent force, endeavoring to pry us loose and launch us into the black maw of the depths. I remember screaming each time I lost my footing, but my voice was lost in the greater shriek of the wind.

The distance was, however, mercifully small, and once we were past the center of the gorge then the lurching and tossing of the bridge became milder with each step. I ran the last few yards, and with a final leap I planted my feet upon solid, stony ground, feeling that I had just survived a crossing of hell.

I turned shakily to look behind me and found that Armand had stopped on the deck, still a few steps from safety. He had his back to me, and his loose clothing was flapping about him like rags on a scarecrow. In the scant moonlight I could see the dirk dangling in his left hand, and I wondered if such a small blade would really suffice to cut the thick ropes that carried the bridge's weight. Seconds passed and he did not move, and it occurred to me that he might be stuck, perhaps with his clothing snagged on a nail or his foot caught between loose boards. I opened my mouth to scream at him to hurry, though I doubt that my voice would have carried through the gorge's frenzied winds.

Then there was the flicker of another distant bolt of lightning, and in its brief flash I saw that Armand was holding his small pistol in his right hand, staring along its barrel at the wet glint of a dark form that was coming toward him across the blackness of the ravine. Onça do Papa had left his cape and horse on the far side, and he was creeping across the bridge, crouched low and all but invisible in his assassin's wrappings. He was no more than three or four steps away from Armand. I saw the brief gleam of a curved blade twinkle in his hand, catching the moon's pallid light. He was wielding a short scimitar. The flicker of light vanished, and an instant later I heard the faint crack of Armand's gun over the howling wind.

If the bridge had not been heaving so violently I believe that Onça do Papa would never have escaped the bullet at such close range. I cried out in horror as he lunged at Armand and slashed him across his wrist. I think Armand might have lost a hand from this blow, had he not jerked his arm violently away. The revolver flew from his grasp and vanished into the night and storm.

Armand leapt back and moved the dirk to his bleeding right hand, then sprang at his attacker. The two men simultaneously made slashing feints at each other, their blades cutting silently through the howling air. My knees weakened beneath me, and I leaned back against an old alder that was growing out of the stony soil beside the bridgehead. I felt I could not watch this battle, but of course I also could neither blink nor turn away.

Onça do Papa fought with his knees deeply bent, crouched low—a strange and awkward-looking posture, but I suppose one that gave his feet a better purchase upon the chaotically shifting boards. I saw his scimitar flash out suddenly toward Armand's ankles, and as Armand jumped up and back, the blade cut through two of the suspender ropes that hung vertically from the big hemp cables that held up the bridge. Deck planks fell out from under Armand's feet like a trapdoor, and he kicked spasmodically at the air below him with his injured leg, barely managing to avoid falling through.

"Oh God, please don't let Armand die," I prayed. It was at that moment, as he was once again fighting for his life—and mine—that I realized it was Armand I truly loved. That I had loved him from the first time we met. And the thought that he might die was unbearable.

Onça do Papa was devilishly nimble, and he leapt in to strike a vicious blow while Armand was struggling to get his legs under him. Armand fell back, barely dodging the blade and slashing at the air with his dirk to hold off the attack, his feet still scrabbling upon the slippery boards. "Please, please let him live." I was beside myself in terror and tears were being whipped from my eyes by the vicious wind.

Onça do Papa jumped gracefully over the gap that he had made and sank again into that strange, low crouch. Now he began to press his attack with rapid slashes of his weapon. Armand managed to find his footing just in time to strike a defensive blow, and I think this might even have connected; if so, the wound did little to deter the assassin's onslaught. Onça do Papa's scimitar flashed and darted in the moonlight, and Armand was forced steadily backward, warding off one slicing blow after another. It was evident that within a few seconds Armand would be forced off the bridge and the assassin would come within range of his real objective: the copper tube that I held in my hands. I realized with a sudden and absolute clarity that, if Onça do Papa managed to slip around Armand's protective guard, I would have to throw the painting into the abyss at my feet. The next thought followed automatically: if that should occur, then I had better throw myself in after, for my life would be forfeit from that moment.

At just this desperate juncture, the sky seemed to come crashing down: the rain fell upon us, starting abruptly and torrentially, driving down as dense as a waterfall, and it seemed as if the storm intended to crush us beneath its very weight. A mighty gust bent the old tree at my back until I heard its wood shriek with the strain. One of the heavy branches cracked like a cannon shot and gave way. The great old bough, big as a hay cart, tumbled obliquely out over the gorge, careening off the taut cables of the bridge. In complete silence, it simply swept the two combatants away, flicking them from the bridge's deck as helplessly as beetles whisked by a broom.

Chapter Thirty-Four

I screamed in horror, and moved closer to the bridge, my feet stepping of their own accord. Lightning flickered and ignited a nightmarish view, far below me. I saw in a single glimpse, as if frozen in a photograph, the mighty branch still tumbling down through the void, and silhouetted above it the black shape of a falling man. If Onça do Papa screamed as he plummeted to his awful fate, the sound didn't reach my ears.

Completely overwhelmed with emotion, I took two more steps, searching desperately for Armand. Tears were streaming down my face and I could hardly see where to place my feet. It was still pouring with rain and the wind howled around me. I nervously peered over the edge and suddenly Armand came into view. He had fallen against the retaining wall of the bridge's abutment, and was clinging to the stonework with both hands and one leg, with his other leg dangling over the abyss. I raced around to the other side of the tree, trying to find a path to reach him, but by the time I had found a way over the treacherously inclined stonework, Armand was out of danger and already climbing up to meet me.

I helped him to his feet, and we fell into each other's arms, clinging together like storm-wracked sailors holding to a mast, while the gale howled around us. His arms were wrapped around me tightly and he whispered into my ear, "Leaozinha."

I was nearly senseless, so stunned was I at our sudden reprieve from certain death. As I came to myself, I found that I was weeping and kissing Armand all over his face. I threw my arms around his neck and those beautiful, sensuous lips answered my kisses—tender at first, then hungry for more. He held me in his arms and he felt strong and warm, even as the rain continued unabated and the wind screamed around us.

We got ourselves away from that horrible place and made a camp among a copse of trees, which afforded us some shelter from the wind. I bandaged Armand's slashed arm tightly, to stop the bleeding, and he managed to find enough dry wood to start a fire. We sat before it, leaning against each other until I stopped shivering, and then I lay down and was immediately asleep.

I awakened late the next morning, if only briefly, to find that it was a beautiful, clear day. Armand was bustling about, stacking food and firewood close to where I lay.

"What are you doing? And where did you find this?" I asked, noticing that I had a thick woolen blanket over me.

"I have bought some simple rations from a farm nearby. They will suffice for a couple of days. You should stay here and rest," he told me. "You shall be safe here, but there is also a barn at the farm if you prefer to sleep there tonight."

I sat up, trying to clear my head. "What? Are you going somewhere?"

Armand knelt beside me and kissed my forehead. "I purchased a horse for our journey, but first I'm going to ride back and bury Paulo," he told me.

"Oh. Then, I want to come, too."

"No. You must rest."

I put up no more than a token argument, since I knew I was physically and emotionally spent. He was right: I desperately needed rest. He warmed some fresh milk over the fire and I drank it eagerly. Then he handed me some bread, but I couldn't eat it. I lay back down, exhausted. He arranged an oilcloth shelter over me, stoked up the fire and then knelt beside me. I could see the pain on his face when he put pressure on his leg. But he smiled and kissed me tenderly, "I shall be back very soon. Just rest now Leaozinha."

As soon as he rode away, I fell asleep without even eating a bite. When I next awakened, night was falling. I found the energy to build up the fire and eat a meal. A couple of hours later, I was asleep again.

Armand returned the next day, having buried his fallen comrade. He had also retrieved the horse that we abandoned at the site of the ambush, so once again we had two horses. He was sad and exhausted, and didn't want to talk. We rested for another day, and I cared for him: keeping him warm and fed, and changing the bandages on his leg and wrist several times. He slept on and off for twenty-four hours. The next day found him somewhat recovered. We rode to the closest village and found the doctor, who promptly placed half a dozen stitches in Armand's leg and hand. That night we took rooms at the inn and I soaked in a long and luxurious bath, before joining Armand for a wonderful fireside meal. Sleeping between sheets that night on a soft bed felt heavenly. The next morning we rose early and had breakfast. The doctor checked Armand's wounds and said they were looking better. So we collected our horses and rode south again.

Several days later, we passed into Portugal along a rural cart track in the dead of night. We spent the next day moving west until we came to a small village on the train line, where we gave up the horses and bought tickets to a village just north of Lisbon. Thus, we covered nearly two hundred miles of our journey in a single day.

Chapter Thirty-Five

I had only the vaguest notion of how we might begin to ferret out the leaders of the resistance movement, and if I had been left to my own devices I might have naively gone straight into Lisbon and simply walked up to Teófilo Braga. He was, after all, living quite openly in the city, as a free man. Armand laughed when I suggested this to him. "That would certainly be an effective way to place yourself in the company of partisans!" he teased me. "I'm sure that within hours you would be completely surrounded by important revolutionaries, down there in the royal dungeon."

Fortunately, Armand proved to have some vague information about which regions of the countryside around the city were hotbeds of discontent. We therefore disembarked from the train in an unprepossessing village that he had heard was rife with anti-royalist sentiment, and there we wandered the streets, visiting several inns and taverns. I was quite impressed when Armand managed to fall in with a little band of partisans within two hours of our arrival.

These three men looked so much like Souris Trempés that they almost made me homesick for Paris. Armand sat drinking Trappist beer with them at a candlelit table in the back of a tavern, far from the smoky beams of sunlight that pried through the shutters up front. I served as translator as they exchanged news, since Armand spoke hardly a word of Portuguese. I thought the exchange went quite poorly at first; our new acquaintances seemed remarkably ill-informed about what was happening in their own country, and their stories often conflicted with one another. Still, one of them, an old man, told us that he had a son named Singelo, whom he assured us could serve as a guide and take us to a camp of the partisan militia, hidden in the Estrela Mountains. He cheerfully described his son as "utterly useless," and seemed perfectly happy to dispense with the young fellow for a few days.

The old man took us home to a humble adobe hut, where his wife fed us dinner. The son, Singelo, proved to be a happy, scrawny youth, with a sort of bird's nest of coarse black hair sprouting out of his head. I'm not sure that he was mentally deficient, exactly, but he was the most scatterbrained person whom I have ever engaged in conversation. I soon learned that it was very important never to let the conversation wane when speaking with him, even for the space of a minute, because he had an almost superhuman capacity to forget what was going on. Still, Singelo was cheerful company, and it would turn out that he really did know the way to the hidden camp, exactly as his father had promised.

We left that evening and were in the montane wilds by midnight, and there we pitched a simple camp. For the next two days, we followed the Zêzere River and its tributaries as they split into wild gorges in the high country. Singelo had a maddening habit of dawdling behind us on the trail, though he was nominally our guide. He was very fond of talking to himself and occasionally became so engrossed in his soliloquies that he would simply stop upon the trail and stand there, expostulating to the trees and birds like Saint Francis, waving his hands about to emphasize his points. Two or three times we waited for him in vain, until Armand had to go back and retrieve him.

Thus it was that during our second evening, Armand and I were all alone upon the trail when we were confronted suddenly by two men in peasant clothes, holding guns with muzzles pointed at our bellies. They demanded to know who we were.

"We are friends!" I said hastily.

"Then why didn't you give the call?" the taller one demanded, sighting me along his barrel. "*Friends* give the call, when they come along this trail."

Sensing their continued disapproval, even though he didn't understand Portuguese, Armand placed himself bodily between me and the gunmen.

"We have a guide," I explained leaning out so they could see me and keeping my voice as steady as I was able. I had never had a gun pointed at me before. "I'm sure that he was going to give the call."

The gunman turned his attention to Armand and said, "Why didn't *you* give it? Eh, *friend*?"

"He doesn't speak Portuguese," I told him. "He's French."

The two gunmen exchanged a quick glance that seemed fraught with significance, as if Armand's nationality, in itself, might be sufficient damnation for the both of us. The shorter one said, "We're supposed to shoot them, you know."

"Shut up," the taller one snapped back. He turned his attention back to me and said, "Say the call word right now, senhorita, and we won't shoot you."

"Our guide knows it!" I repeated, more loudly. "He's just behind us, somewhere back there."

"They don't have a guide," the shorter man said, in a scoffing tone. "You know the protocol. We're supposed to shoot them."

"I told you to shut up! Who is this guide of yours, senhorita? Speak up quick, now!"

"His name is Singelo," I said. "*Please* wait just a moment! He'll be here shortly."

They both lowered their barrels, then looked at each other. "Singelo," the taller one repeated slowly, as if this one word explained everything.

"It figures," the shorter one replied. Then he looked at me and added, "I'm sorry that we were going to shoot you, senhorita."

I tried to come out from behind Armand, but he continue to try and shield me. "It's okay Armand, they realize it was a misunderstanding," I explained. He turned to me and smiled, obviously relieved.

The tall one shook his head and commented, "That boy is utterly useless."

Now that this little misunderstanding was cleared up, our two new companions escorted us back along the trail in the direction from which we had come, until we were reunited with Singelo. They treated him with patronizing friendliness, teasing him much the way one might tease a familiar child, even tousling his hair, and then the five of us proceeded up the trail together.

We turned some time later onto a well-hidden path among boulders and scrappy trees, and into a craggy valley where the rebel camp was hidden. The camp was rough, uncomfortably situated, and ill-equipped, but it was certainly well hidden—it would have been hard to spot, even by a passing aerialist in some sort of balloon. Although a dozen or so men would be sleeping at the camp that night, most of them were away at the time of our arrival, and only three people were there when we walked up. They were sitting together on the ground, chattering idly around a small fire built beside a fast-moving brook.

One of these men turned out to be the group's leader: a wiry, scarred little man named Pique, who affected a very hard demeanor. He didn't stand up as we approached, but casually indicated that we might sit by the fire across from him and explain who we were. As soon as I told him that I was the daughter of Hermes Tiago, he nodded once, staring at me with his unwavering brown eyes.

"Leaozinha," he said.

I was so startled that for a moment I almost felt that someone must be playing some sort of joke on me. I look at Armand, only to find him smiling with a great deal of satisfaction, maybe even smugness.

"You are surprised that I know your name?" Pique asked. "You shouldn't be. You are among friends here. I imagine that your name is known to every guerrilla cell in the nation." He nodded his head gravely, then graciously added, "We are at your disposal."

I certainly didn't feel at liberty to simply hand the painting over to Pique and his band, but I told him that Armand and I were carrying a parcel of great importance, which I must deliver to the leaders of the republican movement. He casually assured me that he could arrange safe escort. "But not before the morning," he added. "The evenings are short up here, and the nights are cold."

This matter settled, he lay back against a pile of logs and relaxed. He uncorked the leather bottle that he kept strapped to his shoulder, took a deep draft, and handed it our way. It proved to be filled with a local sort of extremely high-proof *aguardiente*— apparently the only provision with which the camp was fully stocked.

The men of the camp wandered home in pairs as darkness settled in. Some of them brought small game, others grain and other basic supplies that they had obtained from sympathists or perhaps through barter at the local farms. Two of these men proved to speak adequate French, and they quickly took Armand under their wings. I'm sure that guests were a rare diversion for these men; indeed, I suspect that their main business in such a remote location was simply to avoid detection, and to survive from day to day. A few drinks and everyone became quite merry, and so we feasted frugally but with great spirit, late into the night. At last, Armand accepted the loan of some extra blankets, and he and I slept under the brilliant stars, in the cold mountain air.

I awoke shivering in the middle of the night. Armand was asleep a couple of feet away, so I edged over to him. He woke briefly and seeing my teeth chattering drew me to himself, wrapping his arms around me and kissing my neck. He was deliciously warm and in a few minutes I was asleep again.

We set out just after dawn, leaving Singelo to find his way home to his father. Pique himself led us down from the mountains, along with two grim and silent men who seemed every bit as hard-spirited as their leader. Given the social conditions of Portugal at that time, I imagine that Pique and his men were all wanted on criminal charges, and probably hanging offenses at that. I'm certain that every one of them had lived a bitter life, and that each had lost much that was precious to him.

We came down from the mountains not far from the coast, and

we came in sight of the ocean not long after noon. For the next two days, we walked and camped along the footpaths and riding trails that hugged the rough coast. These were beautiful trails, but often steep enough to offer us hard going; I assume that Pique chose them because they were beyond the effective jurisdiction of royal authority. Armand strapped my bedroll together with his and carried them both, while I carried the scabbard holding our precious copper tube tied to my back.

I knew we were getting close to our destination when Pique and his men began giving a variety of piping little calls and whistles, presumably to discourage gunfire from hidden guards. We arrived abruptly at the edge of an immense camp, a sort of city of tents, that was spread out among the oaks of an open woodland beside a small and rushing river. The moment that we came around the bend, which brought us within the line of sight of the encampment, we were confronted by a band of six dour-looking men, all carrying carbine rifles. They were dressed in most unusual-looking garb: a mélange of worn-out soldier's uniforms and items of peasant clothing. They looked too ragged for the army, and yet quite a bit too military to mix with anybody else.

This alarming group offered perfunctory greetings to Pique and his men, evidently recognizing them well enough, and shook their hands and slapped their backs without actually smiling. Then everyone took out cigarettes and passed around sulfur matches in what appeared to be a sort of ritual. The six guerrillas barely glanced at Armand, even when offering him a cigarette, and not one of them made eye contact with me. Once all the cigarettes were lit, the apparent leader of the group produced a bottle and handed it to Pique, who immediately uncorked his leather flask of *aguardiente* and handed it over in return. Only after every man had taken a good, long drink did this leader ask Pique, with exaggerated casualness, what might be his business there.

At that point Pique introduced Armand and me, and described our mission in the somewhat vague terms that he understood it, saying that I was conveying a parcel which was apparently a matter of some urgency to the cause. He noted that I was the daughter of Hermes Tiago. Now at last, all six of the men turned and looked at me directly for the first time. The leader of the guards lifted his head slightly, as if comprehension were dawning upon him now.

"Ah! Leaozinha."

They led us along the riverbank and through the camp, where any number of men were working at various tasks: chopping wood, cleaning weapons, mending clothes, brushing horses. I was certainly not looking my best after two hard weeks on the road, but, predictably enough, my passage through the camp nonetheless drew a fair amount of attention and a few comments. Fortunately, none of these were so offensive that they couldn't be ignored.

We approached the largest tent and passed into it through a big flap between two standing guards. Then we paused inside, and I waited for my eyes to adjust to the dim light. When I could see, I found that there were four of us who had entered: Armand, Pique and myself, plus the leader of the sentry group. We were apparently waiting to be acknowledged by the other four men in the big tent, all of whom were uniformed as officers of the Portuguese army, though most of their crests and insignia had been removed.

One of the officers was a stocky, broad-shouldered man, wearing the uniform of a colonel. He was pacing around the large and tattered carpet that covered the ground under the tent, while dictating a lengthy set of instructions to an adjutant seated at a small scrivener's desk. The other two officers were young and wore captains' uniforms. They were sprawled lazily in chairs off to one side, smoking pipes and observing us with shrewd expressions.

The colonel came to the end of a paragraph, stopped his pacing and held up a peremptory finger at his adjutant. Then he turned upon us with a brusque expression, and examined Armand and me rapidly from head to toe with sharp black eyes that gleamed above a great shrub of black whiskers. He thrust his chest far out in front of him and pulled his shoulders back, then demanded of our escort, who was standing at full attention, "Well, what is it?"

"Colonel Falcão, sir! This woman claims to be the daughter of Hermes Tiago."

The colonel took a step toward me. "Is that so?"

"I was born Florbela Tiago, but since I was sent into exile I am known as Florbela Sarmentos," I confirmed. I was very nervous, and my voice caught in my throat.

The colonel snapped his fingers impatiently and called over his shoulder without looking, "Water."

One of the two captains jumped up from his chair and hastened to fetch me a glass. The colonel snapped the heels of his boots together and bowed to me, bending just a few degrees forward, rigidly from the waist. "I am Colonel Ricardo Machado, commander of the Western Division of the Republican Army of Portugal. My men call me Falcão, and I invite you to do likewise." It was evident by now, from the colonel's manner of speech, that he was an aristocrat by birth and that despite his abrupt manner and coarse circumstances, he was an educated and well-mannered man. He added, "I should like to consider myself a good friend of your father, and I hope that he would say the same of me. Regretfully, however, I believe that you and I have never met before?"

"I have lived abroad for several years, Colonel Falcão."

He gave a quick nod, and his eyes wandered briefly back to his adjutant, as if he hoped that this interview were about to come to an end. "Perfectly understandable," he allowed. "Well, Senhorita Sarmentos, you are quite welcome here at my humble camp. I shall have Captain Juanito escort you to the women's quarters. My wife is there, and she can help you to find suitable lodgings. Now, if you will excuse me, we are extremely busy today."

I slid the copper tube from the scabbard. "If you please, colonel," I said quickly. "I have not come here seeking asylum. I am a courier, and I bring you a painting and a message, which I obtained from Professor Almeida in Paris."

"Ah! From the professor! And how is the dear man?"

"He . . . he is dead, sir."

Colonel Falcão's smile vanished, and his eyes dropped to stare intently at the copper tube that I held before me. "I see. And you brought the thing here yourself, did you? That was most intrepid. I suppose that we shall have a look at this, then."

How to express the relief that I felt, as Colonel Falcão lifted that burdensome object from out of my hands? I prayed that I would never have to touch it again, and indeed, I made a point of never doing so.

The colonel strode across the carpet, imperiously swept a set of dominos off a card table, then extracted the contents of the copper tube and unrolled them over the tabletop. He picked up the sheet of foolscap and leaned over the table to examine the painting. His officers wandered over to circle the table, eyeing the canvas curiously. After a few moments, Falcão straightened up and pronounced to the group at large, "Disgusting." He beckoned to me, and I came closer. "What is this thing?"

I explained to him as succinctly as I could the import of the painting, its enciphered message to the Turkish emperor, the treachery of King Carlos against his own generals and the people of Portugal, and the economic ruin and turmoil that had befallen us when the plan had backfired. By the time I was done, he and his three officers were all standing around me in a semicircle, staring at me unblinkingly.

Colonel Falcão threw up his hand abruptly, to prevent anyone from speaking, then carefully read the foolscap sheet, which he was still holding in his hands. When he came to the bottom, he read it all again, this time more slowly. Then he looked at me.

I told him, "The translation was done by the Freemasons. I believe that the sheet you are holding includes an explanation of the cipher system so that you may check the translation yourself."

Falcão leaned over the painting again, stared at it for some time, then straightened and read the translation sheet yet one more time. When he was done, he panned his head around to look into the faces of his three officers. They only stared back at him wordlessly. He turned to face me again, frowning with every whisker on his face.

"Do you know what this means?" he demanded gruffly.

"Yes, sir. I think I do."

"Yes, but do you *know* what this *means?*"

He slapped the sheet of paper down on the painting, pointed at it and yelled into the face of his adjutant, "You! Roll that up, and don't let it out of your hands! Not on pain of death. Emílio, five mounted carabiniers and two scouts, ready in the square, on the double! Juanito, my horse!"

Chapter Thirty-Six

I remember the next three weeks through a haze of unreality, as if I had napped through all that time, whiling away some long and idle afternoon. I suppose that my memories of the time are infused with this strange, dreamlike sensibility as a result of the overwhelming relief I felt at no longer playing any crucial role in the fate of nations. Indeed, I apparently had no appreciable role of *any* kind, nor any responsibilities, and that was certainly very much to my liking. I felt that Armand and I had earned a bit of rest. For the first few days, Armand and I took advantage of our superfluity to sleep away an amazing number of hours each day. We stayed in the Sintro Mountains guerrilla camp, effectively as houseguests of Colonel Falcão's wife, Filipa. She was a sad and nervous creature, and gave every indication of being a displaced society dame who was bearing her rustic circumstances stoically, though probably not with much satisfaction. For one thing, she seemed to be effectively estranged from her husband; the colonel never once came home to her, as far as I could tell, but slept on a cot in his headquarters.

One of the officers, Captain Emilio, spoke excellent French, and he soon became close friends with Armand. I suppose that Armand had been longing for this sort of guerrilla life since his teenage years. Emilio certainly had a cheerful time passing along items of military wear that he thought would look well on Armand, but scoffed at Armand's suggestions that he might be trained with a rifle and put to some use in the coming times.

"You cannot become a conscript! You are a hero, and nobly

born," Emilio told him one evening, poking at the fire with a long stick and leaning back against a cask of wine. "You will become an officer, in due time. Leave the rifles to the carabiniers."

By the time we had been at the camp for a week or so, Armand had wrangled a sort of informal status as an "allied consultant."

During that second week, we began hearing occasional rumors told around the fires at night to the effect that symptoms of agitation were increasing in the nation. We heard that there had been a food riot in one of the village markets, brutally suppressed. There had been a series of arrests and show trials in the city, including two cases that involved nobility. Printing presses had been smashed, and one of the universities had been closed indefinitely. For the most part, we received these signs of the times with excitement and optimism.

I asked everyone who came to the camp if there was any word of my father, but I could find none. As September came to a close, life in the camp did not change in any substantial way—troops were not mobilized, rations were not altered—but the mood of excitement built to a crescendo. And then, on October 3, word came to camp just before dawn that the city of Lisbon was in a state of uprising. I awakened to a bugle call out under the stars, coming from the strip of gravel that served as the main square and point of muster for the camp. I emerged from my tent and watched, fascinated, as the camp's amorphous society of jovial and often flippant men polarized during a matter of minutes into an efficient rank-and-file system. Suddenly, every man was part of a group, and every group was neatly arranged under the control of a rigid chain of command. Armand proudly took his place of honor in the front row of Emilio's platoon, between a drummer and a flag-bearer.

The troops stood in readiness as the sun topped the ridge to the east of our valley. For once, the only people rushing about were the officers on horseback, exchanging messages and awaiting the order to either sally forth or stand down. I was obliged to stay well out of the way, watching from under the trees with the other women and children. No one came over to tell us what was going on.

In midmorning the colonel rode up, surrounded by his officers, and shouted out words of encouragement to the troops, though I don't imagine that any further encouragement was needed. I hung upon every word of his speech, hoping that he would hint at the state of affairs in the city, but he revealed nothing that I couldn't have guessed on my own. He certainly hinted that matters in town were chaotic and changing rapidly.

His short speech done, he raised his sword and shouted out the order to debouch. His small army formed into lines and tramped out of the valley along the narrow trails that led east toward Lisbon. The rest of us, the noncombatants, followed after.

There were few travelers on the roads, however, and those we encountered were almost all of them drunken peasant men wandering in small bands, carrying scythes and pitchforks and often howling with primal glee. These men stood by the road to cheer our passage, and no small number of them joined in our wake.

As we came to the suburban villages, the stragglers that we encountered upon the road came to also include bands of ragtag soldiers, deserters from the royal army who were wandering the roads in a state of open rebellion. Their uniforms were in disarray, and they swung bottles of Madeira wine and port like trophies of war. These men, too, often happily fell in to join our march, swelling our numbers considerably.

When we came to the customs gate at the city's edge, the army stopped its progress and broke formations. Colonel Falcão requisitioned an entire village and ordered rudimentary fortifications for its defense, in case we were attacked there. The villagers made a great show of welcoming our arrival, agreeing to billet the officers, troops and families with almost no protest. As soon as these preparations were well underway, the colonel gathered the main body of his troops, assigned half of them, including Armand, to the defense of our compound, and then marched with the other moiety straight into the city, heading for the palace.

Armand and I watched them go, marching along a boulevard lined on both sides with ecstatic celebrants, dancing and cheering. We held each other and marveled over the day's events. For one thing, we had come so far and as yet had encountered no resistance—not a single sign of Portugal's considerable standing army.

That evening seemed the longest of my life, and of course I would get no sleep that night. For hours, we continued to have no idea of what was really going on inside the city. Falcão had commandeered the home of the mayor, which contained the only telephone in the village, and had placed the building off limits to noncombatants. Filipa had a set of living room furniture carried out of a nearby house and set up on the mayor's lawn; there, she and I sat and waited to hear a report of any telephone calls that might arrive. One of the wealthy families, the Moutinhos, who lived three doors from the mayor's home, brought us a lavish picnic dinner that we ate on the lawn.

Somewhere around sundown, a deserter straggled into our compound, and he claimed that there were no troops in the city whatsoever. This man said that the king's army was bivouacked outside the city, much as we were, though several miles away. He told us that the officers had refused orders to march into the streets and subdue the rebellious populace, and that desertion was eroding away the army, hour by hour.

Sometime before midnight, an officer telephoned with the first full report of the situation in town. Colonel Falcão's division had exchanged only a few volleys of gunfire as they took control of the city center, and they were now camped openly in the Jardim de Belém, just beside the palace. Not only the army but also the navy was in a state of mutiny, and the warships anchored in the estuary of the Tagus River, facing the palace, were refusing the king's orders. Teófilo Braga was with Falcão, and the two of them were negotiating with the royal field marshals and fleet admirals, who had just formally requested the king's abdication.

Armand and several officers joined Filipa and me as we kept a vigil through the night, on the mayor's lawn. As dawn began to glow, the long and ominous stillness of the night was broken by the thud of distant explosions, and all of us leapt immediately to our feet. The deep, soft pounding came in an irregular series of percussions that sounded much like thunder, though far more punctuated.

"That's artillery," Emilio said.

Even I, with my negligible understanding of things military, could easily deduce the cause of his grave tone. Falcão's small army possessed no cannon, so it was certainly not *we* who were firing. We waited for the telephone to ring, and the wait seemed utterly interminable.

That dawn was a bad hour for me as I was sure some dreadful end would befall my father if Lisbon became the center of resistance, but it ended well. Colonel Falcão called personally, and an officer came to the door to request that Filipa enter the headquarters and speak with him. When she emerged, she was positively beaming with joy and relief.

"The King's troops have surrendered. Lisbon is ours!" she announced and we all cheered.

The shelling that we had heard had been several volleys fired by the warships in the harbor, pounding the royal palace and doing substantial damage, in order to force the abdication of the reluctant king.

The news spread in minutes through the entire village and led to great celebration, with corks popping before the sun had fairly cleared the horizon. Armand and I danced in the square, hugging our fellow revelers as if we were all one great family. Then, at last, our appetites returned, and we congregated in the Moutinhos' kitchen and ate ravenously.

The next news that we received came at noon, when we heard that Falcão's troops had stormed the palace, only to find it empty. No one is certain when the royal family absconded; it may even have happened during the night, before the shelling began. But King Manuel II and his family had fled to Britain, never to return to Portugal. A few hours after the taking of the palace, Colonel Falcão himself returned to our village, riding up the boulevard with a small group of officers and soldiers—little more than an honor guard. He immediately set to work to organize all of us, troops and hangers-on, into proper ranks so that we could march to the center of the city with dignity. I pestered Filipa relentlessly until she managed to bring me word from her husband's adjutant regarding the status of the dungeons in the city. But the only news she brought me was that there had been no word so far regarding the release of prisoners from the royal dungeons. This news fairly weakened my knees. It seemed to me that if my father had been released without harm, then he would by now have been reunited with Braga, Falcão and the other republican leaders. A terrible notion entered my head: that the besieged jailers might have committed an atrocity and massacred the prisoners in their charge.

By the time we were approaching the city center, it was perfectly obvious that I need not have worried myself unduly about the lack of news regarding my father. The city was in such chaos that no one who had seen it would have expected anything much to proceed in a rational fashion. We passed through throngs of people, a column of order penetrating scenes of madness, opposed by no impediment save the drunken mobs that wanted us to stop and dance with them.

The damage to the palace building was not nearly as bad as one might have imagined, given the great noise of the naval shells that had bombarded it. Only one wing had really been devastated; the rest was at least habitable, and was now swarming with guerilla soldiers, dissidents, and would-be populist leaders.

Filipa seemed greatly relieved to find herself back among finery. I allowed her to lead me through the palace halls and corridors, and noted a great change in her bearing. She carried herself with radiant confidence in these surroundings, really very much as if she owned the place. Through the fog of my own woes, I noticed her improved state well enough that I was happy for her, and even somewhat amused. She seemed to me like a duck that had been reintroduced to water after years penned up on dry land.

Exactly like the lady of a house playing hostess, Filipa gathered up two other women whom we encountered by chance in the hall, and they followed her orders as meekly as maids in waiting. The three of them installed me in a luxurious guest room, undressed and bathed me, and lay me down on a canopy bed with silk sheets and feather pillows. I maintained a continuous flow of objections to this treatment, but the truth was that I had slept only two hours in the past forty-eight, and so I suppose that I fell asleep, still ranting, the moment they blew out my candle.

* * *

I was quite literally dreaming of paradise when Filipa and one of her dragooned assistants shook me rudely awake. I pried my eyes open with difficulty and found that there was sunshine slanting in through the window.

"My father . . .?" I demanded groggily.

"I don't know," Filipa confessed. She was holding up a beautiful dress of white lace and blue velvet, draped over her arm. "I've only just awakened, myself. But if he is here, he will be at the ceremony. Do you think this will fit you?"

"Perhaps. Yes, I think so. What ceremony?"

"Teófilo Braga shall be president of the new republic," the other woman gushed with great excitement.

"There is no time to talk," Filipa said, with a cheerful sort of severity. "Teófilo shall be sworn in on the palace steps, and very soon. You only have time to dress. Please hurry!" She stopped at the door on her way out and added more mildly, "Isn't it exciting? It was all decided during the night." With that, she left me alone.

I have no idea whose dress I was borrowing, but it was so exquisitely constructed that I imagine it might have belonged to one of the absconded royalty. Filipa had a good eye, and the garment fit me perfectly. As soon as I was dressed, I ran out into the hall, found the palace completely empty, and dashed outside to find the ceremony already in progress.

When one is dressed in such a fashion, one receives a certain amount of deference from high and low alike. As soon as I began edging my way into the audience, which spilled out from the palace steps to vanish in the distance along the great avenues in all directions, I was ushered toward the front rows by one and all, as if by tacit consensus. Benches had been laid out there, and I soon spotted Armand and Captain Emilio. They quickly pried open a space between them, where I could sit. "You look so beautiful, Florbela," Armand whispered as he took my hand in his.

Speeches were being given, and gilded chairs from the palace's salons had been brought out and arranged into a semicircle around a makeshift podium, to allow the nation's new luminaries to face the crowds. There, for the first time in many years, I saw my father.

Father was sitting just beside Teófilo Braga and a few seats over from Colonel Falcão. He was dressed in an ill-fitting velour smoking jacket that was not really appropriate to the occasion. I could tell at a glance that it must have been hastily procured, which suggested that he had only just arrived. I squinted at him, studying him as minutely as I could at that distance, and suppressing a childish urge to leap to my feet and wave my arms over my head to get his attention. How gaunt were his cheeks, how much weight he had lost! But he was free, and we could fatten him up properly now. I noticed also that he had a lot of marks on his cheeks and neck, and at first I wondered if they were wounds sustained under torment. But then I realized that they were shaving cuts. I deduced that at some time in the past hour, he must have had his first shave in the past two years. His skin was as pale as that of a cavern fish, but he sat as erect and proud as a Grecian statue, his eyes sweeping slowly over the crowd.

Then he saw me, and our eyes locked together. I heard Armand make a muffled sound beside me, and I realized that my fingernails must be squeezing holes into his knee. I mumbled an apology and took my hand away without moving my eyes from the stage. My father's expression slowly broadened into a smile beneath sad, wan eyes.

Braga got to his feet soon after, and was sworn in as the first president of Portugal. During this momentous event, my father never took his eyes from me. An hour later, the ceremony adjourned under the tumultuous applause of the immense crowd. As everyone rose to their feet, I lost sight of my father for several minutes. Then suddenly, there he stood, just before me.

"Father!" I cried as I threw my arms about him and kissed his sunken, ill-shaved cheeks, weeping and laughing. Armand and Captain Emilio, as well as several others whom I hardly knew, formed a circle around us, admiring the spectacle of our reunion. The first words that my father said to me were, "Falcão tells me that you have been worried on my account, daughter. Please accept my apologies. No man would wish to be late to such an occasion."

"Where were you?" I chided, holding him as if he might try to escape.

"Alas, one of my comrades from the prison was most gravely ill. I fear that he might have perished, had I not attended to him until a physician could be found."

Of course. I should have known that he was being detained by something of the sort. For a moment I felt that I had been terribly selfish in my impatience to find him during the past day and night, but it was impossible at such a juncture to feel anything but happiness.

He held me at arm's length and looked me up and down. "You certainly are looking well," he remarked. "Bohemian life must suit you." He smiled. "I suppose that it runs in the family. And who is this? Some comrade?"

"Father, this is Armand Fontaine," I said. I'm sure that my father read anything else that he wanted to know, simply from a glance at my face. He had always had a poet's uncanny skill for perceiving the human heart.

"It is a great honor, sir," Armand said, as the two men shook hands.

"The honor is most certainly mine," Father replied. "Falcão has told me of your heroism—the two of you." He clasped me again by my shoulders. "How proud you make me, daughter! I wish that your mother could see the woman you have become."

I dropped my eyes briefly at this sad thought. When I looked up, I saw that my father was gazing about him, sharing his feeling of pride with the others around us. I hadn't realized how many were crowded there.

"Behold my daughter," my father called out, in that beautiful, rich voice that he used when he read his poetry to crowds. "A midwife of the republic! She has carried on the true work of our nation, while we who were its prisoners could not."

I cringed a bit with embarrassment at this high-flown praise. But my father was always given to dramatic gestures, so I smiled and endured it as best I could. I could begrudge him nothing at a moment like this. He placed his hand lightly upon my arm, as if offering me up to the crowd. "Behold the future!" he called out. "The new woman of Portugal."

For more information including
links to Facebook, Twitter, and Pinterest,
book club reading guide,
special offerings, giveaways and new releases,
character information (historical and fictional),
extra sections including an afterword,
or to open a discussion with Avery Hays
please visit

www.avery-hays.com